THE TALENT CONTINUUM, BOOK TWO:

THE CRYSTAL ISLAND

Phoenix McDonald

ISBNs: 9798991805933 (eBook), 9798991805940 (Paperback),
9798991805957 (Hardcover)

Cover Design by Dany Rivera
danyriverarts.com

Line editing and proofreading by Charlie Knight
cknightwritesediting.carrd.co

Typography and formatting by A.M. Weald
amweald.com

Published by Phoenix Rises Publishing, LLC
Portland, Oregon

For my children, Denny and Blake,
who are and always have been
everything to me

CHAPTERS & CONTENTS

PROLOGUE

PANDEMIC

Marcus

Taking his friends home through the portal, Marcus was awake and aware of traveling under his own control. Together, they had stepped into a dark doorway that sounded as if voices were screaming everywhere around them. They leaped out as the portal collapsed behind them. Landing in a heap in the damp grass of his backyard, Marcus was relieved to find himself on top of his friends and not crushed beneath their weight. He was also pleased to see they had arrived at the exact location he had been aiming for.

He lifted his head, and his nose crinkled as the rank odor of decay wafted on the light breeze. He barely noticed as Leopold pushed him gently aside and helped him to his feet.

He was staring in surprise at Deacon, who had lurched out of the back door and slumped heavily into a chair on the deck. He felt Sadie curl the fingers of her hand over his around the handle of his cane as he took a slow step toward the house.

"Stop!" Deacon cried out. His voice was hoarse, his haggard features pulling tight momentarily with obvious alarm. "Don't come any closer to me! Please, stay over there." He held out his hands, fingers stretched wide as if to hold them back. Marcus's father looked ill, with dark circles under his eyes and blistered red patches on his skin. After a moment, Deacon's arms dropped to his lap as if he no longer had the strength to hold them up, and he gasped weakly and coughed.

Leopold and Sadie stared at the big man who had been so vital and strong the last time they had seen him. "What's wrong with your dad, Marcus?" Sadie said quietly.

"Yeah, he doesn't look so good, bro," Leopold murmured.

Marcus shook his head. He didn't have any idea what could have happened since he sent his dad back to Earth.

"I've been waiting for you, son. I heard that portal scream, and it woke me up out of a dead sleep. I knew you were finally coming," Deacon said wearily. "The day you sent me back here, I found myself in a world of the dead. A virus broke out while we were gone, and it spread quickly. First here in the States, and then it spread rapidly around the world. It became a pandemic, and billions of people died."

"What?" Leopold said. "How long have we been gone?"

"A little over a month," Deacon said, coughing weakly. He rasped in another breath. "The house was empty when you sent me home, Marcus. Your mom wasn't home, and the cell service was down. I thought that was strange, so I tried checking the internet, but there was no wifi. Then I tried to check the news, but there wasn't anything on, not even a local channel. It wasn't until I found a physical newspaper that I had a clue as to what happened.

"I went next door after I couldn't find anything on the TV," he said in a heartsick voice. His eyes rolled until they met Sadie's where she stood to Marcus's left. "I checked on your family right away, Sadie," he said, shaking his head. "I'm sorry to have to tell you they're all gone."

"What?" Sadie screamed, jerking herself out of ashocked stupor. "*No!* I have to talk to my parents, my brother! They don't even know why I left!"

"Sadie," Deacon said softly. "They're all dead."

She scrambled for the gate, glaring back at Deacon with a look of anger on her face.

"Stop her, or she'll die." Deacon barked harshly. Leopold, looking bewildered, darted after Sadie as Marcus watched. He grabbed her by the arm just as she was reaching for the gate. Sadie screamed in protest, struggling to pull out of Leopold's firm grip. Marcus heard Leopold murmuring. She turned around and walked back toward him, wiping her face on her sleeve and nearly tripping with reluctance.

Marcus looked back at his father, dread rolling in his stomach. "What is this disease, Dad? What are you saying?"

"Marcus, this virus... It's got a mortality rate of over 90%. You have to take your friends back to Lysomnus, and you can never come back to Earth, or you'll all die. There's no way to know how long it will remain contagious, and even after that, there won't be anything left for you here.

"I'm already sick, so you can't come anywhere near me." He raised a shaking hand, indicating the blisters on his face.

Marcus started to move forward but stopped when Deacon barked at him to stop with a desperate expression on his face. Deacon snarled in frustration and weakly tossed a newspaper over the deck railing that landed on the ground between them. "Don't touch it, son. Just look." Marcus strained to read the headline that screamed of millions of deaths in the United States and other countries. As the others returned to his side, they saw the paper, too.

Sadie sniffled beside him, wiping at her cheeks with the heels of her hands.

"I checked on your family, too, Leopold. Your mother was still alive two days ago, but she was very sick. Your father and sister are already gone." Leopold grunted as if he'd been punched in the gut.

"Mom?" Marcus whispered, feeling tears fill his eyes as he stared at his father.

"She was a nurse, son. She...she... Hospital staff were among the first..." Deacon choked, unable to finish his sentence, and Marcus felt pain and loss tear through his chest. "Please, you all have to go back to Lysomnus. I'm so glad you have somewhere to go. Take your friends back, and see your sister when you can, Marcus. Tell her and Pelamis that I love them both. I love you, too, Marcus." Great, heaving sobs tore from his throat as he struggled out of the chair and stumbled back into the house.

"What about you, Dad?" Marcus called. "The Halfriez—I could take you back and heal you!"

Deacon stopped in the dimness of the hall and looked back, shaking his head. "I won't risk infecting you. This disease might also infect the people of Lysomnus. I won't take that chance. When you're thinking more clearly, you'll know I'm right."

Marcus closed his eyes, and the tears that had been standing in his eyes ran down his face. He nudged Leopold with his prosthesis and felt his best friend grasp his upper arm. Sadie cried out in protest as Marcus pulled her tightly against his body with his left arm. There was no time to t discuss it. They had to return to Lysomnus right now or they would all die. He opened a portal. Sadie cried out in angry denial as he stepped backward through the portal with his friends.

A heartbeat later, they arrived on Palaga's stone terrace. Sadie collapsed on the hard, dusty ground, sobbing. Marcus knelt clumsily and wrapped his arms around her. She clutched at him as desperately as if she were drowning. Leopold's arms wrapped around them both, and his sobs shook them all. The pain of their loss was too much to bear.

I apologize for the interruption, Tartarus said. *I could not help but overhear what happened. The Fyrtudo welcome you back, and we grieve with you for your loss. Come and stay in Palaga for as long as you need.* Colflur approached from beside her mate and held out her arms to them all to usher them inside.

Marcus blinked tear-filled eyes as Leopold clumsily helped him to his feet and then pulled Sadie up. They wrapped their arms around Marcus. The three friends staggered as they made their way inside. Colflur quietly showed them to the same room they'd been sharing here, so they could grieve in private.

They found themselves unable to eat, although food was brought directly to their room. The night that followed was the longest Marcus had ever suffered. This time, the pain he felt was deep within his chest—as if he had been stabbed through his heart. It was so much worse than anything he'd ever physically endured. Marcus removed his shirt and prosthetic and crawled into the closest bed, letting the tears come. Sadie sat down on the edge of the bed.

"Marcus, can I lie next to you?" He nodded wordlessly and pulled back the covers so she could curl up in front of him. He put his arm tightly around her and pulled her close as her body shook with sobs. Marcus's own tears flowed freely, dampening the pillow beneath his face. He could only watch helplessly as Leopold curled his body around a pillow in the next bed for comfort. Seeing his best friend's shoulders shake as he cried broke Marcus's heart all over again. He wished there were two of him so he could comfort them both.

Slowly, Sadie's body relaxed as her exhausted body eased into sleep. Marcus saw Leopold was finally sleeping as well. He closed his own eyes at last and sank into welcome oblivion.

When pain from lying in the same position for too long finally woke him up, Sadie was still asleep, breathing softly on his arm. As much as he'd started to care for her, these were not the circumstances under which Marcus had ever thought he would end up in a bed with Sadie. When he shifted slightly, she stirred and opened her eyes. She looked around. Tears welled up in her eyes.

"It's all real. We're still here, and my family is dead." she said dully. "I don't even know how to wrap my head around this." Marcus tried to move to where she sat on the edge of the bed, head in her hands, but it was difficult with his body so stiff and sore. "I feel like I should have died with them." She broke into violent sobs that shook the bed beneath her.

"We can't think that way, Sadie," Leopold said, climbing out of his bed and moving over to sit next to her. He put an arm around her shoulders. "This might be the hardest thing we ever live through, but we have to find a way to keep going."

"Leopold is right," Marcus said, finally getting himself up off the mattress and sitting on Sadie's other side. "All I can think about right now is my mom. I never got to say goodbye to her." His voice hitched as he pictured his mother reaching up to put a hand on his face. "I know disappearing so suddenly is tearing me up inside. It's my fault the two of you left your families. I wish I could go back to that moment and leave you behind. Instead, I brought you both here, and you lost the last time you had with them. I'm so sorry."

"That doesn't help," Sadie said angrily. "Nothing does. I can't believe they're just all *gone.* That they were *dying* while I was wandering about Lysomnus, hardly even thinking about them!" She burst into another spate of bitter sobs, slapping her hands onto her thighs.

"I know," Leopold said, his voice breaking. "I just keep thinking about my sister. She's—she *was*—only ten. She was probably asking where I was and I—I just never came back after I rode off on my bike to Marcus's house that day." Tears rolled down his face.

Marcus watched his friends breaking down, and it tore his heart apart again. If he'd never brought them here, they wouldn't be going through this pain. But then, he thought, if he hadn't brought them, they'd probably be dead. Every time he thought about his mom, he wanted to scream. All he wanted to do was to stop their pain.

"Hey—what if I *can* make you both feel better. Maybe I can take this terrible pain away from you. If I can fix physical pain, it's possible I could fix your emotional pain. You don't have to feel this way anymore." He looked at them hopefully.

Sadie raised her head from her hands to look at him. The aftermath of her stormy grief still clouded her puffy features. "*No*, Marcus. I know you just want to help. But this pain is all I have left of them. If you take away my grief, you take my memory of their love away. As much as this hurts"—she pounded a small fist against her chest—"and as angry as I feel, I would rather suffer this pain than have it taken away and feel nothing."

Leopold was nodding beside her. "I feel the same way. I don't want to lose how much I loved my mom, my dad, my little sister. They're gone, man, but I have to hold on to my love for them. And as much as this hurts, I don't want to feel nothing. I know it's going to keep hitting me, that they're gone, that I'll never kick my sister out of my room," Leopold swallowed hard as his voice thickened, "or talk with my mom about her projects, or practice driving with my dad, ever again. And I'll probably be a jerk sometimes. Please don't take that away from me."

Marcus thought again about his mom grasping his face in her strong hands, exclaiming over how tall he was getting. He saw her beautiful face with its scars, heard her laugh, thought of how she'd made him pancakes the morning before he came here for the first time. So many memories from his life. He felt as though his heart was breaking apart deep inside his chest. Then he thought about having that pain just wiped away and realized how wrong that would be. It really was a part of his love for her, and having it taken away would mean losing some part of that.

He knew his friends were right. They would all have to take the time to grieve, first for their families, and then, somehow, for their home—their entire world.

CHAPTER ONE

NEW DIRECTIONS

Marcus

On a late morning, several weeks after living in Palaga with the Fyrtudo, Marcus made his way to the library, curious to see what he could find out about the talismans he had received and what else like them might exist in Lysomnus.

There was a book pulled part of the way off the shelf where it was sitting. The vertical title on the side simply said TALISMANS. Sadie spent a lot of time here. Perhaps she had found it while studying and wanted to show it to him but had forgotten. He walked over and grabbed it.

There were tall tables in the library, and since the three of them had returned, a new, shorter table had been built and brought in for the humans to use while in the library.

Marcus paged through the book until he found a section on the Halfriez. The details were fairly simple. The cube *was* a healing stone, the book said, but it had also been known to amplify other powers for some users. Marcus remembered there had been a group discussion about whether it had amplified his own power at times. If it was also boosting his power, it might explain why he had been strong enough to do some of the things he had. Stopping the collapsing mountain, healing Anneberg from a long distance, reaching Awar's reanimated body. Not to mention defeating someone as powerful as Nun the Wiser. The Halfriez had always been with him, perhaps boosting his power enough to help him with those events. He wondered how much of his power was his own and how much was amplification from the Halfriez. He had healed Awar and Leopold without it, and his body had gotten warm while using his power. The Halfriez hadn't been a part of what he had been doing. He felt deep inside himself that he would continue to get stronger as he used his power, Halfriez or not. Especially since they were stuck here now, he thought as the memory of loss swiftly grew into pain deep inside his chest.

Apparently, there used to be more of the cubes, but they had been lost over time. At the bottom of the page, a sentence that was explaining something about a "Source" just ended abruptly, and the next page where the line would have continued was torn out, leaving a rough edge in the crease of the book. Marcus frowned as he rubbed his fingers over the ripped paper, wondering who would have damaged the book—and why.

Curious, Marcus looked through several sections about other talismans he hadn't heard of before. There was a small jug that would always pour fresh water and never run empty. A branch had existed that would protect the user from falling debris or water when held vertically. There was a collar that would translate the user's language into that of any other person to whom he was speaking. Marcus found this interesting since nearly everyone he had met in Lysomnus spoke English. He remembered Sadie mentioning other languages used by the people of Lysomnus she had discovered in several other books, so this talisman would have been useful back when the people of Lysomnus had each spoken their own language.

He eventually found the section about the Stikke. It was intended to help the user to stop traveling between their home planet and Lysomnus. A warning stated that if it was used for too long in the home world, the user would never return to Lysomnus. If it was used for too long in Lysomnus, the user would eventually never be able to return to the home planet. He wondered how close he had come to that limit, wearing it here in Lysomnus for so long. More than a month, anyway, or he wouldn't have been able to return to Earth at all. Part of him wished that he *had* worn it for too long and had failed to return home, rather than actually going back and learning that their families were dead.

Marcus realized what he had to do to ensure he would never return to Earth. He would continue to wear the Stikke forever, or as long as it took to be sure he would never return to Earth by accident in his sleep.

When he eased himself off the table and exited the library, Tartarus and Colflur were waiting for him just outside. Growan was bouncing with impatience between them.

"I'm so sorry. Were you waiting for me this entire time?" Marcus hurried to join them.

It is no trouble, Colflur said. *Growan can use the lesson in developing patience.*

"You could have gone ahead to the dining hall without me," Marcus said.

You will be a leader of this world, Tartarus said. *We wait for you, just as we would for any other leader. You must become accustomed to your rank, Marcus Talent.*

Marcus could feel his face flushing. "Of course."

They sat at the high table together. Leopold and Sadie were sitting at another table with several other Fyrtudo. As he took one of Leopold's favorite pastries at the end of the meal, Marcus asked, "Where do these yellow berries grow? I don't remember seeing them anywhere along my journey."

They are provided by the Scrybb. They require a very special soil and careful treatment. We trade for them, along with the other fruits and vegetables, by offering the emeristan and other tools and items we forge.

Marcus took the time to savor the pastry this time. It was truly delicious, with a flaky crust and a sweet, sticky substance coating the outside. "What is this stuff?" he asked as he pulled his sticky fingers apart and then licked the sweet substance from his skin.

That is loka, a sweet harvested by the Cativera. The insects who make it live in large mounds in the southern part of the Zabanara region. The Cativera help them maintain and protect their mounds, and in return, the insects allow the Cativera to take some of the food they produce.

"So much of what happens here in Lysomnus is symbiotic. Everyone is trading with each other, no hostilities between people—other than the recent exception—and it's so safe." Marcus marveled at the paradise Lysomnus seemed to be.

There are dangers here, Marcus. You three were extremely fortunate to travel all the way between Thicce Colpat and Palaga without any trouble.

"What?" Marcus exclaimed. "Cornus made it sound like we really had nothing to worry about."

Tartarus snorted. *The things a Scrybb has to fear are quite different from the things a human has to fear. Also, Scrybb children are taught very little about Lysomnus and then sent out into the world to learn about it alone firsthand, as you may have noticed from traveling with Cornus.*

Marcus thought about it. Cornus really hadn't known much about most of the things they'd experienced throughout Lysomnus other than some basic information. Even back when he had first met the young Scrybb, Cornus had been far away from the well-maintained Scrybb path and, after he had found Marcus, had taken him directly to a Brynar, the most dangerous place in Lysomnus for a human to go.

"I see your point. I need to learn more about Lysomnus while I also learn how to become a leader and make decisions. I'm not ready to do that second part on my own, power or no power. Being a part of meetings, having a voice, I'm happy to do that. But I need a teacher. Tartarus, what would you say if I asked to stay here at least part time in Palaga and learn from you? Plus, I'd like to have access to the library to learn more about Lysomnus."

I was hoping you would want to do something like that, Marcus. You can learn to become a leader while the people of Lysomnus become accustomed to seeing you as a leader. Tartarus put one large hand on Marcus's shoulder. *This is a very mature decision on your part, understanding that you are not ready for leadership and that you need to learn first rather than simply stepping into a position you are not ready for.*

Marcus felt good about his decision. He also wanted to take some time to visit the other people of Lysomnus and get to know them better, particularly to the Muirnati to spend time with his sister, Boehlkea. She was the only family he had left. With a jolt of surprise, he realized she didn't know about their father's impending death and he would need to tell her as soon as possible. Marcus knew both Boehlkea and Pelamis would be devastated by the news.

"Tartarus," Marcus said, "what about Sadie and Leopold? They had planned to return to visit Lysomnus occasionally, but what will they do now that they have to live here permanently?"

I have been thinking about that. I know that Sadie found some language books in our library she found interesting. She was also intrigued by the sign language of the Cativera. Cornus has already departed to visit them as he continues his travels, so perhaps Sadie would be interested in joining him there for a while and learning their language. With Cornus there, she will have the support of a familiar friend as she continues to grieve.

"That is a good idea," Marcus said, although he was heartbroken by the idea of being so far away from Sadie. "Maybe it will help her to have something to occupy her time."

Also, I wondered if Leopold would either want to try visiting the Scrybb or perhaps even the humans since both will need some help. The Scrybb are going to have to work on changing their prejudices against humans, and having Leopold around might help with that. The humans are going to have to consider moving closer to the other people of Lysomnus for trade, as well as learning how to develop a form of leadership and relate to the other people of this world. Leopold is very good at diplomacy and could help them, as well.

"I will talk to both of them," Marcus said. "I'm sure that together we can figure out what they'd be best at and also would make them happiest while settling in here." He grabbed his cane and stood up, making his way slowly down from the dais. He still felt uncomfortable just leaving his dishes on the table, but he knew it was something he'd have to get accustomed to doing now that he lived here.

Sadie and Leopold watched him leave the table and got up to follow. They had been talking quietly, and Marcus knew they had been waiting to leave after him. He waited for them by the door, and they all walked together out the front gates of Palaga to sit in the bright sunshine.

"So," Marcus said uncomfortably, rubbing one booted toe in the dust, "I was just talking to Tartarus about what you each might do here in Lysomnus since this is now our permanent home."

Sadie turned her head toward the tree covered path in the Grenewud that led to Thicce Colpat, swallowing hard. Leopold looked directly at Marcus, and Marcus could see his friend was doing his best to hold back tears.

"Sadie," Marcus continued, trying to keep his own voice steady, "we wondered how you would feel about going to visit the Cativera for a while. I know how interested you are in the languages of the people of Lysomnus and the sign language of the Cativera in particular. Cornus is already on his way there and would be good company for you since he's become a good friend to us all."

Sadiel sighed, and the breeze blew her long black hair across her face. She seemed oblivious both to the hair and the dust the breeze carried and threatened to blow in all their eyes. Finally, she pulled the strands out of the way and looked up at Marcus with tears standing in her eyes.

"I guess I do have to do something besides hide in the library and read all day," she said, brushing the tears away as they ran down her face. "I've thought about using the books in the library as a way of learning more about the older languages, but I can't do much without some frame of reference." She sniffed, looking toward the doors of Palaga.

"Perhaps Tartarus would let me take one with me, the one with the Cativeran figures in it, to see if I can match the languages in it up to their existing languages. It might be fun to figure out how they used to speak compared to how they speak now—they're the only people here who still have any of their original language left."

Marcus was glad to see a spark of interest in her dull eyes, even if it was only a small one, as she talked about the Cativera. It seemed the Fyrtudo King had thought of the right path for Sadie to help lead her out of her sadness and begin the journey toward healing.

"What about me, bro?" Leopold asked. "What have you thought of that I could do?"

"Well, that's kind of up to you, Leopold," Marcus said, smiling. "Do you think you'd rather try to help the Scrybb repair their preconceived notions about humans and restore their faith in us, or would you like to go and help the humans get organized and find a new bruwe closer to the other people of Lysomnus? They'll need to be closer in order to trade and figure out what to trade. They don't have any leadership right now or likely a clue how to organize."

Leopold stared down at his hands, folding his fingers together and squeezing until the skin over his knuckles turned white. "It's hard to decide. I mean, with the Scrybb... I like them, but after what they did, it's hard to think about going back there. I want to, but I'm still so angry about Awar." His voice broke as he mentioned the Stondefel who had given his life for Lysomnus. "Honestly, I think I could see myself going to the human bruwe and helping them get organized. I know they did some terrible things, but I think most of them were following Nun the Wiser, and there might be some good people there."

Marcus blew out his breath in relief. "I think you've both made good decisions. We'll have to talk about how you'll get to your destinations—the human bruwe, especially, is so far away—but we'll get you both started."

He wanted to get them both motivated to begin their journeys. Their pallid, somber faces made him feel sick inside. He was still grieving himself, but he had training with Tartarus to keep him occupied. His friends had been drifting through each day with nothing to distract them from their grief.

As Leopold and Sadie stood up beside him, a shadow darkened the stone terrace where they'd come to talk. They all looked up to see one of the Stondefel descending to land near them. Marcus automatically used his power as he had before to shelter them from the dust that blew around from the massive wings of the stone demon as he landed.

Anneberg's demonic face filled the space above them. "Tartarus tells me you are talking of journeys, my friends," he rumbled in his gravelly voice. "While it would be possible for Sadie to walk to Grasian, it is a long trip and would take many days if she began from here. To go alone the entire way would not be safe for a human. We would like to take her part of the way there, at least. And Leopold will certainly need help to travel to the humans since it is a very long distance to their bruwe."

Marcus couldn't help but laugh. "Tartarus always does have his hand in organizing things right from the start, doesn't he?"

Of course, the Fyrtudo King said, his heavy footsteps coming through the ground to them as he exited the Palaga doorway. Marcus was always startled by how quietly the Fyrtudo moved for their size. Marcus hadn't even had the opportunity to hear the enormous doors of Palaga opening. Since the human threat had ended, the doors had been left open during the day for easy passage in and out and to let more light into the bruwe.

One thing you will learn as a leader, Marcus, is to always be prepared ahead of time, to see ahead what will be needed and plan for all contingencies.

"Someday, I hope to be as good at those things as you are, Tartarus," Marcus said. Mentally, he marveled at the way Tartarus could see what would be needed and be prepared.

I do not do it all alone, Tartarus said, reading Marcus's thoughts, which he had not shielded, allowing the King to hear them. *My Queen is a useful partner when it comes to leadership, as well.*

"Yes, I have noticed that Colflur is very good at helping you organize," Marcus said.

"Agatho and I will be more than happy to help escort these two young ones to their destinations," Anneberg interrupted their conversation. "The Stondefel have been in mourning as well, and I welcome the opportunity to get out and spend some time with our friends."

Marcus looked at Leopold, knowing the presence of the other Stondefel made his friend more aware of the loss of Awar. The young Stondefel and the adventurous human had become quite close as they had gotten to know each other. The two of them had very similar personalities. It felt as though waves of grief just kept overwhelming them all. Marcus wondered how long it would be before it felt like they weren't drowning anymore and could finally catch their breath.

"I know I'm looking forward to meeting the Cativera and seeing Cornus again," Sadie said, "but I would like to be taken only part of the way to Grasian. I would like to have a few days to travel on my own before I get there. If Tartarus is willing to allow me to take that book with me..."

Of course, you are welcome to it. I know you would like to study it and learn more about the language of the Cativera while you visit, and I think it is a wonderful idea.

"Thank you," Sadie whispered.

"Little one, we will take you where you wish, but know we will be keeping an eye on you from above in case you need our help. It is our honor to protect all the people of Lysomnus, and that includes you." Anneberg put one taloned finger gently on Sadie's shoulder. She put a hand on it and looked up at him, eyes shining with tears.

With that settled, we will prepare you both for travel, the Fyrtudo

King said, turning back to the entrance to Palaga, and the others followed him inside. Anneberg waited on the stone terrace, ready to take a passenger on to the next stage in their lives. Agatho circled in the sky high above.

CHAPTER TWO

THE QUAKE

Sadie

Sadie walked out onto the terrace carrying a bulky pack on her back. She had packed a couple of changes of clothes, water, food, and the book she planned to study on the way to Grasian. She found Marcus and Leopold putting the harness on Anneberg for her flight.

"What are you putting on there?" she asked, pointing to what looked like a roll of thick padding on Anneberg's back behind where she'd be sitting in the harness.

"Oh, we added a bedroll and a small pillow for you. It's still late summer, and apparently, in the Zabanara region it stays pretty warm, but we thought you'd be more comfortable sleeping at night if you had something soft to lie on." Marcus said with a grin.

"Thank you, that's very thoughtful," Sadie said, smiling back. "But how will I carry it during the day?"

"It's remarkably light," Leopold said. "And check out how it's tied up before you unroll it. It should be easy to carry if you tie it back up the same way, with the pillow inside."

"Oh," she replied. "I'll do that." She swallowed nervously. Before coming to Lysomnus, Sadie had never been camping a day in her life, and she felt even more anxious thinking about trying to do it alone.

She mentally set her shoulders. She was determined to succeed at this. After everything that had happened, she needed a few days to herself. Everyone in Palaga, including Marcus and Leopold, had been incredibly kind and supportive, but there just wasn't any way to be alone here, and she felt as if she would explode with the need to be alone with her grief.

Marcus walked over to her, cane thumping on the stone. He reached out to her with his prosthesis, and she took it and followed him over to one shadowed side of the terrace, away from everyone else. She waited patiently to hear what he had to say, looking into the beautiful hazel eyes that had made it hard for her to breathe just a few days ago.

"I wanted to talk to you before you left," Marcus said nervously, the little vertical frown line appearing between his eyebrows as it always did when he was anxious. Sadie tried not to smile at the sight of it. "I know we've only known each other for a few weeks, but to me, it feels like so much longer. I don't know exactly how you feel, and I know things are awful right now, but I have to let you know how *I* feel before you leave.

"I still love you, despite what's happened. My feelings are still the same." His face flushed to the roots of his dark, curly hair. He let out a relieved breath. "It was hard for me to say that, but I had to tell you."

She looked up at him as he stood there, waiting. She felt the connection that had been growing since the day they had met—but it was buried, deep inside the pain of her grief.

"I...I love you too, Marcus." Sadie nibbled at some loose skin on her lip with her teeth. "It's just so hard right now; I feel so sad all the time. I need to take some time to get my head right. But I really do still love you." She stood up on her tiptoes and kissed him gently on the mouth. Then she walked away quickly to where Leopold was waiting next to Anneberg.

As she climbed up the Stondefel's leg, Sadie looked back at Marcus. He was still standing in the same place, the fingertips of his left hand on his lips where hers had been a moment before. Then he looked slowly up at her and smiled, his whole face lighting up. She smiled back as best as she could and climbed the rest of the way onto Anneberg's back, sliding her legs carefully into place in the harness.

Leopold looked up at her from the ground beside Anneberg. "Be careful, Sadie. I know these guys—" he slapped Anneberg's leg "—will be watching over you, but still, look out for yourself. I'll miss you."

"You too, Leopold. Please be careful while you're visiting with those humans. I know the really dangerous ones are supposed to be gone, but you never know about the ones who are left. I'll be thinking about you!" She called down to him.

With a final wave to her friends, she told Anneberg she was ready to go. The Stondefel took off with a mighty downstroke of his wings, and within seconds, they were high in the air. She looked down to see the Grenewud stretched out below them, with the lighter lines of the Scrybb trails showing up like a pattern traced through the trees.

She shivered and huddled against Anneberg's warm back. It was really cold! She had only flown once on the back of a Stondefel, and that had been with other people packed around her. It was fun to see so much of Lysomnus spread out below, though. A person didn't really get a grasp of the size of the continent while just walking around. She could see the blue-gray haze of the Diluvium as they flew south and the approach of the Zabanara grasslands. If Lysomnus was a planet, she wondered about the possibility of other continents. Was it possible this could be the only one? She would have to check it out in the library when she was back in Palaga. There must be *some* maps in there. Sadie had the feeling she could spend years in that library and not learn half of what she wanted to about this world that was now her home. She closed her eyes against the burn of fresh tears.

While she enjoyed the long flight, Sadie shivered with relief as Anneberg circled toward the ground and into warmer air. As they descended, Sadie saw a long, curvy road that wove through the dun-colored grasslands toward a wide, flattened area a long distance away. Sadie dismounted after untying the bedroll and tossing it down.

"Are you okay if I just leave the harness on?" she asked.

"Yes, thank you for asking," Anneberg replied. "I will be returning to Palaga, and I am sure Marcus will help me remove it there to be stored for later use."

"Thank you for the ride," Sadie said. "It certainly saves a lot of time, although we shouldn't presume you'll always give us rides everywhere."

"Oh, I certainly don't mind," Anneberg rumbled. "I rather enjoy the company on my flights around Lysomnus. We do our best to monitor this world, but it has been nice getting to know the people we protect and making new friends."

Sadie smiled at him. "Well, I agree with you. I never thought I'd have such friends, but I certainly appreciate all of you. I hope I will see you again soon." She stepped back far enough to give the massive Stondefel room to take off. He launched himself into the air and tipped his wings to her, waving as he flew higher.

She waved back, then bent to retrieve her bedroll. Leopold had been correct; it was surprisingly light for as puffy as it felt. She stepped onto the road and headed in the opposite direction from which they'd flown.

Sadie spent the next couple of days walking during the daylight hours. The quiet time with no intrusive thoughts or talking to interrupt her gave her plenty of time to think about her family. The worst of the agony, she had thought, was behind her in those first few days after returning from Earth. Yet there were still moments when the memory of her father telling a joke during a family game would drop her sobbing to her knees. The feel of her grandmother's hands guiding her own in the kitchen as she learned to cook her favorite family dishes. The smell of her mother's shampoo during a hug. Her brother's bright eyes asking her for a forbidden cookie while she was babysitting when he was just a little boy. Sadie began to wonder if a person could run out of tears, if her grief would break her heart and leave her emotionless, when she realized that she was walking a little farther between each storm of weeping.

She was spending more time wandering through memories now than they weren't just slamming unexpectedly into her mind. Walking for those couple of days definitely helped Sadie clear her mind. She spent the time thinking about her family, often still with tears streaming down her face. By the third day, she started thinking about everything *else* from her world she had lost—cars, cell phones, movies, even school. She had been a passionate student, enjoying her classes and learning about the world. Now, all that was gone. It was too much to take in all at once.

Every evening, she made camp and ate the food she'd brought. The Fyrtudo had thoughtfully provided her with cured meat and some prepared vegetables, along with some wrapped pastries. She also had fruit. Sometimes, she thought about the fact that she'd never have a Taco Bell burrito again or kimchi, and it got the tears flowing again. After dinner, she would pull out the book she'd brought from the Palaga library and study the images and strange words in it to try and decipher the language of the Cativera.

Sadie was fluent in two different sign languages back on Earth—both American Sign Language and South Korean Sign Language. As she studied the book, she noticed that the sign language of the Cativera, while different from both of them, was possible to decipher along with the pictures to accompany it. She was able to work out a few of the signs—or she thought she had them right, anyway. She'd find out for sure when she reached Grasian.

The verbal language in the book was much harder. She realized she was quite literally trying to decipher an alien language and cut herself some slack as she found herself getting frustrated.

On the third evening, she noticed in one of the pictures that the figure who was signing—one she'd already figured out meant "that, or this"—had a highly stylized word in the picture itself. It appeared to be *Sa.* She realized she might not need to work so hard on the writings in the book itself; if she could translate the signs, she would have the words to match them right in the pictures themselves!

She turned to another picture. Judging from the previous picture, this one might be 'there,' and the stylized word worked into it was *Set.* Hm. She wished she'd asked if there were any kind of writing tools used currently on Lysomnus. The only paper she'd seen was in the old books in the library, and she hadn't seen anyone writing anything at all. But the people here could read—or at least some could—if they used the library.

For now, she contented herself with marking the words she found in the book in the clay of the ground with a piece of broken stalk from the grassy fields around her. She had discovered when trying to slip into the grass to relieve herself that the wheat-colored plants weren't pliant grass like she'd thought they were but a heavy-stalked reed-like plant.

She practiced writing the words while making the signs they correlated with. Some signs had several words beneath them, which made it difficult to figure out what they might mean. Obviously, there were signs that stood for entire phrases, rather than taking the time to sign out everything word by word, which would be time-consuming. ASL and KSL did similar things. She would just have to learn. The Cativera had been willing to teach Cornus; hopefully, they'd be willing to teach her, too.

She was losing the light. The shattered moon had risen before the sun finally set, but it wasn't bright enough to read the book by. When she looked up at the moon, she was startled to see how large it looked. When she'd first seen it on their journey from Thicce Colpat to Palaga, it had seemed to be around the same size as Earth's moon, with the exception of the damage. Now, it looked much larger. As she gazed at it, she thought it actually looked as if it might be closer than it had been before—but that didn't make sense, did it?

With a sigh, she put the book aside and unpacked the bedroll and pillow. Bedtime was the hardest time of day. The act of closing her eyes and trying to fall asleep was real work; her brain wanted to keep her up thinking about a million things. She tried to let her mind drift, not thinking of anything at all. Thoughts kept trying to break in, but she just listened to the breeze blowing through the tall grass, soothed by the sound.

The next thing she knew, she was jolted awake by the ground rumbling beneath her. It was shaking so hard she was actually sliding away from the verge of the road and into the road itself. Over the loud rumbling, she could also hear hooting noises and what sounded like the thunder of many feet. A rustling in the grass grew louder, and she also heard the sound of stalks breaking as the pounding feet grew closer.

Sadie tried to get to her own feet, but the ever-increasing shaking of the ground threw her back down to her knees. Her possessions were bouncing madly about her. The precious book flipped open; the cover torn askew as the spine broke. Sadie cried out as she saw the damage.

Suddenly, a large figure darted out of the grass beside the road. "Git dina!" the Cativera yelled, pushing her to the ground and holding their body over hers. Their spear clanked to the ground next to them as they pulled her entirely beneath them.

As Sadie lay beneath the Cativera 's furry body, she could hear the thunder crest as feet broached the road and parted around them. She heard a grunt from her protector as they were struck by one of the animals running all around them. There was a sudden snap, followed by a screaming hoot. She heard the more solid thump of something heavy landing nearby.

Just as quickly as the thundering herd had approached, it was past, hooting and rattling into the reeds on the other side of the road. The Cativera remained above her, so Sadie didn't move, waiting as the rumbling of the ground beneath them stopped. The hooting cries from the injured animal nearby continued. Finally, the Cativera stood up slowly, with a grunt of pain. As Sadie rolled over, she saw him put one clawed hand to his side and wondered how badly he was injured from that kick.

The hooting sound nearby was coming from a large creature lying in the road. It had long, scaly legs, one of which was bent at a terrible angle. Those legs each ended in two large clawed forward toes and one wicked-looking claw curving down behind the leg. The body was very large and egg-shaped, draped with thick, leathery skin. It had a short neck with a blue crested head and a long, thin beak that looked razor sharp. This must be one of the Struthtaur.

The Cativera extended a paw to her. "Ma now," they said. Sadie took their paw, and they pulled her easily to her feet. They bent, grunting again, to recover their spear and then walked to the injured Struthtaur. As they looked down at it, they shook their head sorrowfully and then plunged the spear into its head. "Na kin liv now," they said, gesturing to the animal's obviously shattered leg. Then they waved her along, hoisting the dead beast over their shoulder by the legs, and began to walk down the road.

Sadie hastily gathered her things and ran after them. She noticed blood trickling through the fur on his back as she caught up. She touched the Cativera lightly on the shoulder to get their attention, then touched the blood and showed her bloody fingers to them. They shrugged and pointed down the road. She took this to mean they'd get it taken care of when they reached Grasian. The two of them must be fairly close if the Cativera wasn't worried about the walk, and she *had* thought she might have come far enough to be in the area where the Cativera watched over the Struthtaur herds in the grasslands.

It amazed her to see the strength of the Cativera as they hauled the huge Struthtaur along the road. The herd animal was as large as they were, if not larger, and yet they didn't seem to be straining, even though they were injured. After a couple of hours, Sadie stopped her companion by stepping in front of them and making the gesture she was pretty sure meant *rest*.

The Cativera 's small black eyes widened, and they dropped the Struthtaur in the middle of the road. They gestured to her slowly. She picked up *friend* and *visit,* but the rest was unknown to her. She stopped them with one hand held up, which she was pretty sure meant *wait.* They stopped, watching her hands intently.

Out loud, she said, “I’ve only learned a few of your signs,” while she made the sign for *slow.* She put her hand on her chest and said, “I’m Sadie, a friend of Cornus.”

The Cativera nodded to her and put a clawed paw on their own chest, saying, “Yati.”

“I’m glad to meet you, Yati,” Sadie said. She was pretty sure the Cativera understood more than they could speak since Cornus had reported that Suri had understood him when he first approached Grasian on his visit here. “Do you feel strong enough to continue?”

Yati nodded and picked up the Struthtaur, gesturing to her to continue with them. They seemed quite pleased by the exchange. She noticed that they were starting to slow down and seemed fatigued now as they continued on. She hoped it wasn’t too much farther to Grasian. Yati was still bleeding.

As they rounded a curve in the road, Sadie saw a stone structure rising high into the air. This must be what Cornus had told them about, where Suri had shown him the fields all around with the Struthtaur herds and the Cativera herders. Yati didn’t stop as they passed it. She realized that the herds must have stampeded when the quake happened; Cornus had said everything must be kept silent to keep from startling the herds. The herders must be trying to catch them and bring them back even now. She hoped more of them hadn’t gotten hurt. A surge of guilt ran through her when she realized Yati was only injured because they had saved her life from the stampede. She hadn’t even thanked them.

Finally, they approached a wide clearing in the grasses where a large number of Cativera were scrambling about in apparent disarray. As they neared, Yati put their paw to their mouth, putting two clawed fingers to the sides, and whistled loudly. The chaos stopped immediately as everyone froze. Yati gestured quickly. Another adult Cativera gestured back and pointed; a large group of small Cativera scrambled together off to the side of the wide, flattened area. The adults who had been running around gathered together. Yati gestured again, and one of the other adults entered one of the openings in the ground.

A moment later, Cornus emerged from the opening.

"Sadie? What are you doing here?" he asked, looking bewildered. "I thought you had returned home."

"That's a long story, Cornus. Right now might not be the time to tell you about it. Yati is injured, and it looks like things here are a bit crazy. I'll be glad to help after someone takes care of Yati. They were injured in the stampede."

Cornus turned to one of the Cativera. He made a few hesitant gestures and then pointed to Yati. The Cativera called to another, and they both rushed to Yati's side—just in time to catch the herder as they collapsed. Another Cativera came to retrieve the Struthtaur, presumably to do something with the meat before it spoiled.

As the Cativera carried Yati away, Sadie grasped Cornus's arm. "What happened? Do you know why the ground started shaking like that? Was it some kind of quake?"

"I do not know, Sadie. I have never experienced something like that before. It caused some damage in the tunnels of Grasian, and the Monarch is trapped in their rooms. Something is wrong with the doors; they will not open. Hopefully, those working to fix the problem will get them open soon; these people need their Monarch to get everything organized. I have been trying to do what I can, but I have not learned enough of their sign language to communicate clearly. They do understand our language fairly well, but I cannot understand what they say back to me!" Cornus was clearly frustrated.

"Okay, Cornus," Sadie said soothingly. "How bad is the damage to the tunnels? Do you think the Cativera can stay there safely?"

"Yes, they do seem structurally sound. There was some breaking of shelves and some things like that, and a few doors that are not working, like the one Cata is trapped behind. I think we just need to get everyone calmed down and organize a meal. They usually eat in individual family groups here unless there is a celebration," he said almost shyly, and Sadie knew he was thinking of the one they had thrown for him when he had first visited, "but I think we would be better off doing a large group meal tonight."

"Well, let's take care of that," she said, putting her hands on her hips. Her things were lying on the ground at her feet, and she gestured at them. "Do you know where I can put these?"

"Yes, I will show you. You can stay with me. I have a room with an extra bed, in a section of the bruwe that has been unused since the other humans have not been coming here." He led her toward the closest tunnel opening.

As she picked up her belongings, she noticed the damaged book. She felt terrible about the condition it was in. Perhaps there was some way to repair it, but that would have to wait. For now, she would wrap it up carefully when she wasn't using it. She was glad to have finally made it to Grasian, even under the circumstances they now found themselves in. Cornus would help her, and together they would help the Cativera, all while learning a new language.

CHAPTER THREE

MAKING NEW FRIENDS

Leopold

Leopold was eager to get away from Palaga and start working with the humans of Lysomnus. Even getting away from Marcus for a while would be good, as much as he loved his friend. Every moment around him was a constant reminder of home and his family, and everything he had lost and been forced to leave behind, and why.

As he waited for Agatho to land, he was also reminded of Awar, and tears stung his eyes. He'd never had the chance to say a real goodbye to his friend. The young Stondefel had been killed so suddenly, Leopold didn't know how to deal with the loss on top of everything else. Agatho and Anneberg were wonderful, but he just hadn't bonded with them in the same way he had with Awar.

Marcus was helping to attach the harness to Agatho's back and giving Leopold a strange look, most likely wondering why his friend was just standing there while he did all the work. "Sorry, Marcus," Leopold said, climbing up and helping Marcus finish the job. He worked himself into the harness and tightened everything down while Marcus lowered himself back down to the ground with his power.

"Are you ready, my young friend?" Agatho's voice grated as he turned his head toward Leopold.

"Yes, let's get going. It's a long flight."

Agatho launched himself into the air, and Marcus and the others on the terrace dwindled quickly into specks that disappeared as Leopold watched. Before he knew it, they were high in the air above the Beornan Rokk. As Leopold watched, he saw molten rock burst from one of the mountains farther down the chain.

"Whoa!" he exclaimed. "That's incredible!"

"Yes, it has been happening more often lately. While we are happy to have more food, it is worrisome. It doesn't usually happen so frequently or so violently," Agatho rumbled. He dipped suddenly to the right as he banked away from the mountains and over the Grenewud. Leopold gasped in delight, feeling his stomach drop at the quick change. He loved riding the Stondefel through the skies of Lysomnus.

"Sorry," Agatho said, hearing Leopold's gasp.

"Oh, please don't apologize! Do that as much as you want to!" Leopold called out delightedly. Agatho rumbled beneath him as the Stondefel laughed at his young friend's pleasure.

Leopold was glad he had chosen to visit the humans over the Scrybb just for the length of the ride. The Scrybb lived so close to Palaga that the ride was scarcely longer than half an hour, while the ride to the humans' bruwe was many hours long. While he definitely got cold, he could huddle up behind Agatho for the Stondefel's warmth. The flying demon was more than happy to drop into any air pockets he came across, making Leopold yell with excitement, forgetting his recent grief for a little while.

Leopold watched the Grenewud disappear slowly into the Zabanara grasslands, which spread out below him for quite a distance. Red paths that looked like pencil lines from this height crossed the land in seemingly random patterns. Eventually, the grass began to give way to the sandier ground that was typically seen closer to the Diluvium. He could see the ocean of this world in the distance as he felt Agatho begin to descend.

Once the Stondefel had landed, Leopold loosened the harness and pulled his legs free. He felt stiff as he descended the stony leg Agatho held out helpfully. It had been a long ride.

He looked up at the friend he would miss, even though he wasn't Awar. "Thank you for the ride, Agatho. I hope to see you again."

"Oh, have no worries about that, Leopold. I will fly over to check on you from time to time. You'll never be alone, even though you're far from everyone else." Agatho lowered his hand, and Leopold shook one taloned finger. He smiled and turned to walk toward the bruwe. A blast of sand struck his back as the Stondefel took off again.

Agatho had dropped Leopold off just a short walk from the humans' bruwe. As he approached, he was happy to see that they had been industrious, even though it hadn't been that long since he and his friends had been there. The garbage was gone, and some small repairs had been made to buildings that had been dilapidated.

He walked in cautiously. While Marcus had been on seemingly good terms with the humans when he'd left, Leopold wasn't so confident that they'd welcome just anyone back with open arms. They had been defeated, after all. No one who had lost a conflict would be happy about it. Plus, at least some of these people might still have powers. He didn't want to get blasted right off the bat.

"Hey!" someone shouted, and Leopold turned to see a man pointing at him from down one of the lanes. The man ran toward him, but not in a way Leopold interpreted as necessarily threatening, so he stood and waited.

"Who are you?" the man asked cautiously as he approached.

"My name is Leopold Larson. I'm friends with Marcus Talent, and I'm here to see if you need help." Leopold looked around, watching for anyone else who might be nearby. He saw several people looking at them, but no one coming any closer.

"I'm Sammael," the man said. He was pale with brown hair and eyes and was dressed in simple, loose, brown clothing. "We haven't done much yet other than clean up and try to repair some of our buildings. Marcus said we should do that."

"Yes, that was a good place to start," Leopold said. He wondered if

Sammael was in charge, or if anyone was really in charge here. Were the humans so used to being under the thumb of Nun the Wiser that they didn't know how to function without strong leadership? He would have to find out.

"Sammael, let's gather everyone together in one place to discuss what we need to do moving forward. Is there a gathering place here in your bruwe? A town square or meeting building or something?"

Sammael stood and stared at Leopold for a moment. He seemed almost lost. "You just want a place for everyone to fit? A big place?"

"Yes, that will work," Leopold answered.

"Okay," the man said. "Maybe we can go to the square by Nun the Wiser's house. She's gone now, and it's pretty big. Eris lived there too, but she's locked up." He turned and walked away.

Leopold's brow furrowed as he watched Sammael for a moment, then followed him down the lane. Sammael's responses seemed...off, somehow. He answered questions like a child would.

As Leopold followed Sammael, they came to the center of the bruwe. Leopold recognized it as the open area where the Stondefel had landed the day they'd come to rescue Marcus, where Abutilon and Buddleja had died. He swallowed hard. It was difficult being back here, although they'd won that day. It had been a day of loss, too. Leopold had come close to dying in this dusty place himself.

Sammael turned and pointed at a large house that stood on one side of the square at the center of the bruwe. It was immense! One of the Stondefel could have fit inside the building easily.

"*That's* where Nun the Wiser and Eris lived?" Leopold was surprised at first, but when he thought about it, he wasn't, not really. According to Marcus, Nun the Wiser had been one bad bitch, and seeing how they had treated all the people of Lysomnus, it wasn't surprising she would have housed herself so grandly here in her own bruwe. Leopold thought about all the different styles of leadership he had seen and heard of in Lysomnus. Monarchy, Councils, and here... fascism. The worst, of course, existing here in the heart of humanity. Leopold felt sick at the idea that even here, who knew how far away from Earth, such ugliness had still found itself a part of humanity.

He walked over to the house, noticing he was being watched closely by a gathering crowd of humans. The door wasn't locked as he pulled it open. Inside, he found grand furnishings, art that seemed out of place here in Lysomnus, and one room that was fully stocked with rich food that must have come from Earth.

He went back outside. "Sammael, do you know how many people there are in this bruwe?"

Sammael turned to look at the growing crowd. "Most are here. Not sure, really."

"Well, good thing everyone will fit right here in this square outside." Leopold waved a hand at the house where Nun the Wiser had lived. It had given him the creeps to be in there. "That house is full of junk, and there is not much room for people."

He addressed the milling, murmuring crowd. "My name is Leopold Larson. I'm a friend of Marcus Talent's. He asked me to come here to discuss and possibly help you move closer to the other bruwes if that's what you'd like to do so you can trade more easily with the other people of Lysomnus."

Most of the people in the square shuffled their feet and looked uneasily at each other. Some quiet talking could be heard, but no one spoke up. Finally, a tall, well-built boy in his teens pushed his way through the crowd. He had onyx skin, tightly curled black hair, and the darkest eyes Leopold had ever seen.

He gazed in Leopold's direction, not meeting his eyes but looking somewhere over his shoulder. "I'm Jarel. I'm sorry no one's really saying much to you yet. Everyone's been a little shaken up since Marcus showed up here and killed Nun the Wiser. It changed everything. It's been a lot for everyone to handle." The muscles in his square jaw clenched as he paused for breath. He had a very straight nose, Leopold noticed. His nostrils flared as he continued, "Things have been bad here for a long time, and your friend Marcus—he just showed up out of nowhere and killed Nun the Wiser and changed Eris and the others. Then he left, and everyone here has been kind of forgotten and lost." Jarel's voice was husky and sounded like music to Leopold's ears.

Leopold was suddenly very happy that he had decided to come here rather than the Scrybb village. It sounded like the humans really needed his help. He was very glad to have met Jarel, who seemed to have pulled himself together more than anyone else. Leopold definitely wanted to work with him and get to know him better. His good looks didn't hurt, either.

"Marcus didn't just show up; he was taken by force by the Stondefel who were working for Nun the Wiser. He killed her in self-defense when she tried to kill him. Eris and the others with power—he had to take their power away so they wouldn't hurt anyone else. I don't know if anyone here remembers, but Garrett nearly killed me with one of the spears he threw." Leopold saw several people nodding their heads.

"You haven't been forgotten. That's why I'm here," Leopold said. "I think we should talk more about what comes next for your bruwe and decide what we can do to help everyone get back on track. We need to plan for the future."

"I agree," said Jarel. "Let's go back to my house, and we can talk about all of this." He turned to the crowd. "I'll talk to Leopold, everyone. Then we can meet later and discuss our plans for the future."

The crowd slowly began to disperse. Leopold was again disturbed by how aimlessly the other humans acted, but he hoped he and Jarel could come up with a way to motivate them. He was interested to hear the other boy's story as he followed him from the center of the bruwe.

Jarel led Leopold to a small log house not far from the edge of the bruwe. It was well-kept compared to some of the other houses they passed.

Jarel's home was small, the door entering into a sitting area. To the left was a kitchen, and a bedroom and bathroom could be seen through open doors in the back of the sitting area. The taller boy waved Leopold toward a wooden chair as he eased his long frame into the one beside it.

"I'm going to tell you something that might surprise you," Jarel said. "I know you're from Earth—that's not the shocking part—and that you came here with Marcus," He leaned forward, forearms on his thighs, long-fingered hands dangling between his knees. "I'm from Earth too. I was stolen and brought to Lysomnus when I was five. Eris is the one who took me."

Leopold sat open-mouthed with surprise. "Eris kidnapped you from Earth? That's horrible!"

"Yes. Apparently, after Eris was born, she developed the power to travel to Earth. Nun the Wiser started sending her to take people as soon as she was old enough. The bruwe needed 'fresh stock,' as Nun the Wiser put it." Jarel cleared his throat and swallowed hard, staring out the window. "I guess I was easy enough to fool. I remember how Eris tricked me into following her with the simple promise of chocolates, something my real parents didn't give me often. She took my hand—and the next thing I knew, I was here, scared and alone with no way to get back home." He sucked in a deep breath and then blew it back out, lowering his eyes to the floor.

"After you were kidnapped as a child, who raised you? You obviously live alone in this house, but how old are you? You aren't an adult yet, are you?" Leopold asked nervously, rubbing sweaty palms on his pants as his emotions got the best of him.

"Nun the Wiser dropped me off with a couple who already lived here. I don't know if they wanted a child dumped in their laps or not, but they weren't given a choice. She just told them they had to take care of me. They did as they were told, but they didn't know very much about raising a child. They're decent people, I just don't know if they wanted a child. As soon as I was old enough to live alone, I moved out. Sixteen is considered old enough among our people."

"I can't imagine what it's been like for you," Leopold said. "You must have been so terrified as a child, to be taken from your parents and brought to another world. I can't imagine what that was like."

Jarel was still looking at the floor. "I've lived my whole life on Lysomnus, wondering about my parents. Did they look for me for a long time? Do they think I'm dead? I've always wished there was some way I could get back to Earth and see them again. Go back home. These people here—they aren't *all* bad people. Most of them have just been living in fear of Nun the Wiser and her loyal followers for so long, they don't know how to act on their own anymore. I can't say I ever did much, either. We've just always been too afraid."

Leopold looked down at his hands, which had clenched into fists as he listened to Jarel's story. "I don't know how to tell you this, so I'm just going to come out and say it," He took a deep breath. "Jarel, you can never go back to Earth to look for your parents. When Marcus tried to take us home—Sadie and I—we learned that a disease had wiped out most of the population of the planet, including our own families. Almost everyone on the planet is dead. If anyone goes back there, they'll probably die, and even if they don't, they won't be able to come back, or they would be at risk of bringing the disease back here and infecting the people of Lysomnus."

"Oh, man," Jarel said dejectedly. "I don't even know what to say. I'm so sorry. You must be devastated at the loss of your family." He stood and walked to the window, staring as if fascinated by the scenery outside.

Leopold was taken aback. He had expected Jarel to be upset for himself and the end of his dream of going home and finding his parents; he hadn't expected Jarel to extend sympathy to him for his loss and pain.

"I was—I mean, I am. We all are. It's something I think we're all going to be dealing with for a long time," Leopold said, blinking unexpected tears away. Jarel turned away from the window and was looking toward him. Leopold's heart sped up as he watched Jarel step toward him and reach out with long fingers, waiting. Leopold reached up and grasped his hand. The tears in his own eyes spilled over as he squeezed Jarel's fingers in his own.

"I don't remember my parents' faces anymore," Jarel said, "but I know how it hurt when I lost them. I want you to understand I know how you feel, losing your family forever and being forced to live in another world," Jarel said. They were both silent for a moment. Jarel finally met Leopold's eyes, and Leopold felt a moment of connection so real, it was almost a sound—like a *click!* in his head.

Leopold broke the silence first. "So, do you have power? I know the Talent family develops power, but do other humans?" Leopold asked. He chewed his inner cheek in disappointment when Jarel pulled his hand away.

"Only some of the people who were born here have them," Jarel said, looking away again. "I never got anything, and none of the other people Eris stole did either. Just descendants of the Originals. Several of them don't have their power anymore because Marcus took it away. They aren't very happy about it." His dark eyes scanned the room behind Leopold as he talked. Leopold resisted the urge to look over his shoulder. He had the feeling nothing was there—that this was just an idiosyncrasy of Jarel's. His behavior reminded Leopold of someone he had seen before.

"The Originals?" Leopold asked. "Who are they?"

"I was told that when Nun the Wiser first came to Lysomnus, generations ago, she could travel back and forth between Earth and this world like Eris. She brought people here. I think there was also a man who was special to her. The Originals who had power were descendants of theirs."

Leopold tried to imagine having a special ability and then suddenly losing it. Then again, he knew Marcus had only taken the powers from people who had used them during the battle. Leopold himself had nearly died when a spear made by one of those people had been thrown through his body by another. He couldn't find it within himself to feel much sympathy for them. Involuntarily, one of his hands rubbed his abdomen where the spear had pierced his skin. There was no scar, thanks to Marcus's healing power, but he would never forget what he had suffered that day. Blinking, he pulled his mind back to the topic at hand.

"Let me ask you, though," Leopold started slowly. "Marcus has developed his power since he came to Lysomnus, but he wasn't born here. Do your people believe that has to do with the Talent bloodline?"

Jarel focused on Leopold for a moment. "I'm certainly no expert when it comes to humans and their abilities. But I've heard people talking. Nun the Wiser wasn't born here either, but she and Eris were also Talents, and all the descendants of the Originals would be, as well. I don't know what makes the Talents so special," Leopold heard a cynical tone creep into the boy's voice, "but apparently, they're the only humans who weren't born here who start developing power after their *gift* for traveling brings them to Lysomnus."

Leopold sighed. He detected an undercurrent of dislike for Marcus in Jarel's tone. He wasn't sure what that was about, but he hoped that after Jarel got to know Marcus, the intriguing boy would come to like his best friend. He moved on to more important topics.

"What do you think of convincing everyone here to move?" Leopold asked Jarel. "I know you've all lived in this bruwe far away from everyone else in Lysomnus for a long time, but moving closer to the other people would be a good idea to help with trade and to get to know them. I think you'll find the other people of this world to be nicer than you expect, and I believe they will even be willing to forgive and work with your people." Leopold realized he was eager to convince Jarel and the other humans to become a part of the society of Lysomnus.

Jarel walked back to the window of his small house. As he looked out at the bruwe where he'd lived most of his life, he said, "It might be difficult to convince some people to move, but I think a change will do a lot of us some good. This place feels tainted to me, and I'm sure to many others as well. I think we should spend time talking to people individually. That way, you can get to know us on a personal level, and together, we can be more convincing."

"That's a great plan, Jarel. I'd really like to meet everyone, and one-on-one is more personal. Speaking in a crowd can make people feel put on the spot and too uncomfortable to speak up."

"So, let's do it," Jarel said. "Why don't we start with the people who raised me?"

Leopold followed Jarel out of the house. Jarel didn't live close to the people who had raised him here in Lysomnus, as it took some time to reach their house. Nor did he refer to them as his parents. He recalled that the other boy had said the couple hadn't particularly wanted a child. It was awful to think of a young boy stolen from his loving home and thrust into an uncaring environment here, on another world, frightened and unsure of what had happened and with no way to ever return.

The house they approached was so opposite of the neat little home Jarel kept, Leopold was startled. Then the tall boy slipped between the filthy abode they were approaching and another home, and Leopold followed him to the front door of a neat log home almost identical to Jarel's, only slightly larger.

The door was answered by a tall woman with a narrow, bony frame and long brown hair that hung limply to her waist.

"Jarel," she said in a quiet voice. "Come in." As she stepped back, Leopold followed Jarel inside, smiling at the woman, who looked at the floor rather than meeting his eyes.

"What can I do for you?" she asked as she led them to a long table in the kitchen. This home was as tidy as Jarel's small house, Leopold noticed, glancing around curiously.

"This is Leopold," Jarel said. Leopold smiled and nodded as the woman's eyes glanced across his face. "We came to talk. Is Janke around?"

"He is," a voice barked from the door behind them. Leopold jumped, turning to see a stocky, balding man with bright blue eyes closing the door. "I've just brought home dinner, and lucky for you, there's extra," he barked again. Leopold realized the man was laughing. His eyes twinkled with good humor as he brought a stringer of fish over to the woman.

"A right full stringer of fish today, Maril," he said, handing a chain with four good-sized fish hanging on it. "Enough to feed us and two strapping young lads too. You'll stay for lunch?"

Leopold looked at Jarel. With a sigh, Jarel nodded. "Why not?" he said. "We can talk while the fish is cooking just as easily."

"Good," Janke said as Maril took the fish from him. "They're all cleaned for ya, love," he said in a low voice as he brushed her cheek with his lips. Leopold looked at Jarel to see him looking away with his mouth pressed tightly closed.

"Can I help, Maril?" Leopold asked, hoping to break some of the tension he sensed in the room. A smile appeared on her narrow face as she pulled her hair back and tied it in place with a band that seemed to appear from nowhere. "That would be lovely."

Leopold made his way to the counter and took the knife Maril offered. He took one of the fish and watched her carefully. Imitating her, he slowly fileted his fish and cut it into pieces like she did. His were nowhere near as neat and smooth as hers, but he figured that his ragged edges could be forgiven, considering this was his first time.

He picked up and looked at one of the pieces of fish while Maril was preparing the rest for cooking. This was the first time he had seen the meat raw, and it was fascinating to see that, even in this state, it closely resembled chicken. There was a slightly different feel to it, not quite as firm or meaty, he thought, but it was definitely more like chicken than any fish from Earth.

He was pulled from his musing by the smell of smoke. The stove in this kitchen—he realized it was a wood-burning stove. Then he realized this just made sense since these humans would not be trading with the Fyrtudo. Although Nun the Wiser and the other humans with power were probably forcefully taking emeristan and other metalcraft from the people of Palaga when they "visited" there, the long-lasting burning metal would not be used here, and even if it were, Leopold doubted it would be shared among *all* the humans who lived here.

The fish was sizzling in a heavy iron pan now while Maril

chopped some wortang, tossed the vegetable in, and gave the mixture a stir with a wooden utensil. Leopold watched, interested, as she poured a small amount of water from a cup that looked suspiciously like plastic into the pan. He looked over his shoulder at Jarel, who was sitting near Janke at the table, staring silently out of the window. Janke also said nothing but sat looking at Jarel with an expression of affection. Leopold wondered if Jarel had been wrong when he'd said that this couple had not wanted a child.

"Maril," he started, waiting for her attention. He continued as she looked up at him with her dark brown eyes. "What is the water for? Just to steam the vegetables?"

She smiled at him. "This is diluted water from the Diluvium. As it cooks down, it leaves behind the flavor of the salt water and enhances the flavor of the food."

It was mere minutes until the food was ready. The kitchen was warm and filled with the delicious aroma of the food as Jarel stood up, grabbed plates and utensils, and brought them to the table. The next few minutes were full of nothing but the sound of utensils on dishes and chewing. Leopold enjoyed the food and thought how interesting it was that each of the communities of Lysomnus had its own way of cooking the same meat and other plants to accompany the protein, and because of this, it was always delicious. Part of him wondered if someday he would look back and remember that he once delighted in the food despite the fact that it was something he regularly consumed.

"...Leopold?" He jerked back to the present at the sound of Jarel's voice.

"I'm so sorry," he said, looking around at the others. "I was too distracted by this delicious food to pay attention." Maril gave him a startled look.

"It's just fish, for goodness' sake," Jarel said, rolling his eyes, but Leopold saw a small smile playing about Jarel's mouth that made him feel warm inside in a way that the food hadn't.

"I was telling Janke about your idea of moving the bruwe to a location closer to the other people of Lysomnus. You think it would be a good idea for us?"

Leopold nodded. "Yes," he said, meeting Janke's blue eyes with his own. "You'll be able to trade with everyone else once you decide what trade goods you want to create or contribute and get to know the other people of this world better. The building materials to get you started are already here. It will be hard work, but tearing down the existing houses to use in starting a new bruwe will provide you with a good beginning."

Maril was frowning at the food on her plate as she pushed it around without eating more. Janke reached across the table and grasped her small hand in his own, coarse with triangular scars on his thick fingers.

"I think it's a good idea, love."

Her hair fell away from her face as she looked up at him. Leopold saw the shining tracks of tears on her cheeks.

"But will you be happy moving so far away from the sea?"

Janke snorted. "I think I'd be glad never to toss another net into the water again. These people can work for themselves, for once. I've been feeding them long enough, Maril."

"Good," Jarel said. He stood abruptly and walked toward the door. Leopold stared after him, mouth hanging open. He reached across the table to grab Jarel's plate and then lifted his own. Maril put a hand on his arm. She spoke quietly as Janke went to speak with Jarel.

"It's just how he is. Don't worry about it. Since he was a little boy. He knows we care about him, but it's hard for him to acknowledge it or accept any affection from us. It took him years to begin talking again when Eris brought him here. Janke started taking him out fishing, and eventually, he responded. We can rarely touch him, though. I hope someday he'll find someone he's comfortable enough with that he accepts their love."

"Thank you," Leopold said. Maril nodded and released his arm. Leopold joined Jarel by the door in time to hear Janke mention a few names. Jarel grunted and nodded and led Leopold outside.

"We're going to talk to some people Janke thinks might listen to us 'young people,' and Janke will talk to others," Jarel said. Leopold watched with interest as the tension in Jarel's features eased, and they walked comfortably beside each other once more.

While it was nearly the same size as Janke and Maril's home, Leopold noticed the house Jarel brought him to next—the one they'd passed on the way—was unkempt, one of the few houses in the bruwe that still had garbage lying around, with few repairs to the damage the years had caused.

A few moments after Jarel knocked on the door, it was opened by a tall woman with graying red hair. She had faded blue eyes, a long nose, and a thin mouth that turned down at the corners. Her gray dress clung unbecomingly to her body, and she slumped over the broom she held in one hand.

"Eh? What's this?" She said as she saw Jarel. "What do *you* want?"

"Hello, Marta," Jarel said haltingly. "This is Leopold." He held out a hand, indicating the blond boy standing just behind him. "He's a friend of Marcus Talent's. He'd like to talk to you and Darin."

"Arright," she grunted, stepping back from the door. "Come on in, then."

The boys stepped into the house. Leopold struggled not to wrinkle his nose as the odor of old grease and unwashed bodies wafted into his face. He wondered why these were people Janke had selected as likely to listen to him and Jarel. These people were the very opposite of the clean, articulate boy who had brought him here.

Marta gestured half-heartedly at the chairs surrounding a table in the large cooking area. Leopold followed Jarel to sit down as Marta went to the bedroom. He could hear her talking to someone in a low voice.

"Darin sleeps a lot," Jarel explained. "He consumes a lot of the drink they call rusta, which makes them act ridiculous and then sleepy afterward. I don't like it, myself, although I've tasted it a few times. It makes me feel funny."

Leopold assumed rusta must be some kind of alcoholic beverage. They probably fermented it from some kind of fruit they either found or cultivated here on Lysomnus. Well, he wouldn't judge them for that, but it wasn't going to be a tradeable item and would cause problems if it was a regular activity for many of the humans. They needed to be clear-headed to be industrious enough to work at creating products to trade with the other people of Lysomnus.

Darin finally followed Marta out of the bedroom. He sat down heavily at the head of the table and looked blearily at Jarel and Leopold. "You, I know," he said, pointing at Jarel. Then he pointed at Leopold. "You, I don't. Who're you?"

"My name is Leopold, I'm friends with Marcus Talent. I came to your bruwe to talk about moving your people closer to the other bruwes on Lysomnus, so you could possibly start trading with the other people of this world. Start getting to know them, interacting with them."

"That sounds like a lot of work," Darin said. "Who's going to do that? Just load everything up and march down the road? Pick a spot and build all the new houses? And just hope that all these other people are going to accept us and start trading with us? What are we going to trade, by the way?"

"I know it sounds overwhelming," Leopold said, holding up a hand to Jarel, who was about to reply with an angry retort, "but I think if we all work together, we can do it. There are people in this bruwe with power who can do things that can help. We can scavenge materials from the houses to bring along to help build the new ones when we find the right spot for a new bruwe. We can build carts to haul those materials. Nun the Wiser's house is full of food stores. We can use that to feed everyone while we're preparing and to feed us while we're traveling."

Marta broke in. "You mean we've all been going hungry while there's been food right here in the bruwe this whole time?"

Jarel turned to Leopold. "No one who lives here ever dares enter that house. A lot of people were shocked to see you walk in there.

Nun the Wiser would punish anyone who came close. No one knew what was in there, and we already went through what we had stored. There's not a lot left in this area besides what the Diluvium has to offer—we've pretty much picked clean what was forageable."

Leopold was surprised. "Don't you know how to raise your own food? Plant the seeds of what you've eaten so more will grow?"

Jarel, Marta, and Darin all looked at each other. "Everyone just goes out and picks what's there," Jarel said. "Or goes fishing. In recent years, people have had to go farther and farther to find food."

"What do you do with the seeds, the husks, of the fruits and vegetables?"

"Well, a lot of the refuse goes into the sea. Some used to be burned by anyone with power that had to do with fire. Or Eris would send some through portals." Jarel explained, twisting his fingers and looking embarrassed.

Leopold recalled all the garbage lying around when he was here last and thought a lot of people had simply gotten lazy about doing even that much with their garbage. He couldn't believe how terribly these humans had treated this world.

"To be honest, it makes even more sense now to move," Leopold said. "Your people will have to learn how to farm, to *raise* food rather than just forage an area and damage it so there's nothing left. You'll need to learn to trade with the other people of Lysomnus for food as well, those who raise stock for meat or fish the Diluvium in sustainable ways. You'll need to learn how to return your plant and animal waste to the ground for regrowth and nourishment or to use parts of them. Leave this barren area behind so it can eventually regrow."

Darin rubbed his hands through disheveled brown hair. His weary face was lined with both age and the stress of the years of living under Nun the Wiser's rule. He and the others of this bruwe probably drank the rusta to forget about the seemingly insurmountable problems they were stuck with, living here by the Diluvium, facing dwindling food supplies, no contact with other people, and feeling they were hated by everyone else in this world. Leopold couldn't help but compare these two to Janke and Maril, who were so affectionate and clean and self-sustaining.

"I think, with help, we might be able to do it," Darin finally said. Marta reached over and placed a chapped, reddened hand on his. She smiled for the first time since Leopold had met her.

Jarel pushed himself back from the table. "Leopold and I will go and talk with others from the bruwe. We will need the agreement of everyone to accomplish this," he said.

Darin looked up at the boy, eyelashes crusty from drink-induced sleep. "You're right, Jarel. If you'd like me to come with you—"

"No," Jarel said abruptly. "We can do it ourselves." He walked out of the house.

Leopold hurried out after him, thanking Darin and Marta quickly on the way.

"Jarel," he began, following the other boy to the next house, "why don't you want to let Darin come with us? We can use the help to convince everyone to move."

Jarel was stony-faced. "I'm glad they're willing to do it," he said. "But I'd rather not have anything to do with them if I don't have to. We can convince others without them."

"Okay," Leopold said with a shrug. "I understand." He looked up at Jarel as they walked side-by-side and realized that Jarel was even taller than Marcus. Jarel glanced down at him with a slight frown.

"Why are you looking at me like that?'

"Sorry, bro," Leopold said, chagrined, " You're just so *tall.* I think even Marcus is shorter than you."

"*Bro?* What does that mean?" A look of amusement crossed Jarel's full lips.

"Um...it's just slang. Where we come from, we just call each other friendly names like that. Or other things, like 'man' or 'dude'." Leopold could feel his face growing very red. By now, he must've been glowing. "I'm sorry. I won't do it again if you don't like it."

For the first time, a full smile crossed Jarel's face, revealing white, even teeth. He laughed a little, too.

"You're a funny *dude,* Leopold," he chuckled. "And you're kind of cute, too. Even with such a red face."

Leopold groaned and buried his face in his hands. Then he sucked in a quick breath and grinned. "Cute? I'll take that." He said to himself. He hurried to catch up to Jarel, who was walking ahead without him.

They spent the next few days talking to all the people of the human bruwe, which, Leopold learned, had never had a name. Most people were willing to at least entertain the idea of moving, especially when Janke reminded them that their food resources in the area were severely lacking. It was no surprise to any of them that the people who still had power were the most resistant and wanted to assume leadership of the human community.

Finally, Leopold had Jarel call a meeting in the square in the center of the bruwe again. By this time, Janke, Jarel, and Leopold had met with at least one person in every household. The only exceptions were Eris, Ravenna, and Garrett. No one really knew what to do about them just yet.

"Consider this, everyone," Leopold said loudly once everyone had arrived. "I know it's tempting to use power to gain control and be in charge. But look what happened under Nun the Wiser and Eris. It's easy to let power go to your head and use it the wrong way. Marcus could have used his power to take over here, but he didn't. He has stronger power than any of you. He wants you to learn to work together, to operate as a collective. There's always the option of electing a group to make decisions for everyone—a democracy, if you will. But I really think a lot of things can wait until we get the bruwe set up in a new location."

He saw heads nodding throughout the crowd. Jarel stood beside Leopold but didn't speak up, so Leopold continued.

"We've spent a lot of time talking to each of you, and I think you've gotten to know me. I would like you to trust me to help you on this journey. I think Jarel and I have come up with a lot of good ideas, and I have come to know a lot about the rest of Lysomnus and the people of this world. While several of you have been among those other people, I don't think you've gotten to know them at all—just used their resources."

Leopold saw a few faces in the crowd flush, and several people looked down in shame. He knew most of them were people who had misused their power and guessed they were among the ones who had accompanied Nun the Wiser when they had visited the other bruwes of Lysomnus and forced them to allow the use of their facilities and give up their trade goods. Several had lost their power when Marcus took it away.

"Okay," Leopold continued. "Let's start talking about organization. We need to make carts and start taking the houses apart to see which materials can be reused. Someone will have to go through the food stores to see what can be taken along with us and what we should use up here first while we're working. I think we should break up into groups. Jarel, perhaps you could-"

Just as he was turning toward Jarel, the ground began to rumble beneath them. The shaking increased in intensity until people could no longer keep their footing, and they began to fall. Leopold saw several people begin to run away and yelled out a warning as a house collapsed on the edge of the square.

Logs tumbled down, falling onto them as they tried to run past. Suddenly, the entire house slid sideways and slumped into a pile of logs and thatch. Leopold heard screams, and from behind him, a louder crack and a sound like thunder boomed. From his position on the ground, he managed to roll over in time to see Nun the Wiser's house collapse in on itself, leaving an enormous dust cloud expanding into the air.

"Jarel!" Leopold cried out. "What's happening?"

"I don't know!" Jarel yelled back, reaching out with one hand toward Leopold. Leopold reached out and grasped Jarel's hand. They clung together in the middle of the square, the ground shaking beneath them, and watched as more houses collapsed around them.

People were screaming and crying, holding together tightly when they could reach each other.

Finally, the rumbling stopped. The two boys looked at each other, almost identical from under a coating of dirt and dust. Leopold's blue eyes and Jarel's black eyes were the only difference they could see in that moment as they stared; even their interlocked hands were the same color with a thick coating of the dust the ground had kicked up as it shook.

They looked around to see people slowly getting to their feet. A few houses were still standing, but many had collapsed. Leopold realized how fortunate it was that the majority of the population of the bruwe had been in the square for the meeting when the quake happened, or many people would have been killed. As it was, Leopold feared that most of the people who had tried to run were dead, buried beneath the houses that had collapsed.

"We'd better assess the damage," he said to Jarel as he got to his feet and dusted himself off, "starting with people. I'm afraid several people may have been injured or killed."

"I hate to say you're probably right," Jarel agreed. The boys grabbed a few people and started with the house at the edge of the square. As Leopold had feared, the people who had tried to run were buried beneath the logs that had cascaded down from the wall as it fell. There had been no chance for them.

The boys gathered a group together, asking them to move the logs and retrieve the bodies, and assigned other people to make their way down each street as best they could to check collapsed houses for people who may have been inside. They wanted to verify whether anyone else may have been caught inside their homes during the quake—Jarel was sure that not everyone had come to the meeting since there were a few people who had strongly opposed the idea of moving.

As Leopold and Jarel moved around the square, they had difficulty maneuvering around the logs and through the crowd of milling people. Jarel looked down as they reached one small house that had completely toppled to the ground and pointed with a cry that was audible even over the rumble of the crowd around them. Leopold looked down to see a pair of massive legs beneath some of the crisscrossed logs. Leopold covered his shocked face with his hands.

"This is the house where Eris and the others were locked up! Look, there are the bars from one of the windows!" Jarel pointed again and Leopold looked through his fingers at a set of twisted iron bars lying askew amidst more logs. As they watched, a person walking too close to the remnants of the house tripped over the bars and fell heavily to his knees.

"They didn't stand a chance," Leopold said, feeling guilt wash through him. The three people locked in the house were criminals, but death had never been part of the plan for them. They had only been held in this house because no one knew what to do with them. Now they were gone.

"Hey," Jarel said, reaching out hesitantly and putting a long-fingered hand on Leopold's shoulder, "it's not your fault. It's no one's fault. The quake just happened. No one locked them in this house with the intention of them dying in it. You can't blame yourself."

"I know," Leopold replied. Feeling unsure, he reached up and placed his hand over Jarel's. When the other boy didn't pull away, he left his hand there. "But I still feel bad. Despite all they did, we never would have decided this fate for them."

"It does make it easier for us, though," Jarel said rather bluntly.

Leopold looked up at him. "That's harsh."

"Sorry, I just think it's best to say what's on my mind," Jarel said. "That's honest. I didn't mean to offend. I'm sorry if it upsets you. People don't like it, sometimes."

"It's okay," Leopold said. "Let's just keep working on this."

It took most of the next two days to find and bury all the people who died in the quake. Afterward, everyone knew the move was happening; those who had been opposed were resigned to the fact that they needed to move. Most of their homes were destroyed already. They got to work building carts to haul the wood and other supplies for the long trip to find their new home.

CHAPTER FOUR

MENDING FENCES

Marcus

Marcus had been spending his days either in the library or working with Tartarus since they'd returned from their disastrous attempt to go home. After sending Sadie and Leopold off on their new ventures, he found himself lonely despite the company of the Fyrtudo. It was difficult to focus on the books, and even while working with Tartarus during lessons in leadership, he found himself distracted.

Finally, he decided to talk to Tartarus about it.

"I think I need a change of scenery myself," he said. "After giving Leopold the option of going to Thicce Colpat, I think it's important that one of us goes there. Since he went to the humans, I think I should at least visit for a few days just to see how they're doing."

Tartarus placed a large hand on Marcus's shoulder. *You are wise to come to this decision, Marcus. It is important to see the Scrybb and let them know you are thinking of them and want to support them. I think they will need some help as they learn to trust humans again.*

Marcus felt better about his decision. "I hate to impose upon the Stondefel again," he said, "but I know I am not up to the journey, even moving myself on a cart all the way to Thicce Colpat with my power. My body will not take that trip well, especially alone."

I do not think they will mind the imposition. Tartarus looked to the skies above. A large, winged shape circled above. *Anneberg comes already. Get some things together to take with you.*

Marcus went inside and gathered some clothes and the tools the Fyrtudo had made for him to help him put on his socks and boots, stuffing it all into a large pack. Next, he grabbed the harness they used when riding the Stondefel from the hook on the wall of their quarters. On the way out, he stopped to say goodbye to Colflur and Growan, who already knew he was leaving thanks to Tartarus. *We will miss you, Marcus, even though it is only for a short time. You are part of our family now,* Colflur said. *Please be safe.*

"I will," Marcus said with a smile, then made his way back outside, where Anneberg was waiting on the stone terrace next to Tartarus. He used his power to put the harness on the great stone demon before he said his goodbyes to the Fyrtudo King, then lifted himself to Anneberg's back for the short flight to Thicce Colpat.

With a quick leap and a downblast of his wings, the Stondefel was airborne.

"I really appreciate this," Marcus shouted above the wind.

"It is no trouble at all," Anneberg rumbled. "I enjoy every opportunity to see you, my young friend."

The flight between Palaga and Thicce Colpat seemed almost too short to really enjoy, as they were soon landing in Far Field. He hoped this time he'd be welcomed and not greeted with anger or find himself unwanted in the bruwe. Before the Stondefel took off, Marcus removed the harness so he could use it on the return flight when he was done visiting the Scrybb. He waved as Anneberg flew away.

The walk to the Scrybb bruwe seemed long to Marcus, although he knew it wasn't that far. He hadn't been walking that much lately, not since their long trek between Thicce Colpat and Palaga when they first came to Lysomnus. Now his back ached from walking, and he found himself leaning heavily on his cane as he approached the bruwe.

As usual during the day, the Scrybb were out and about, working busily. Many could be seen tending the plants, standing in rows on the far side of the bruwe from the entrance Marcus had used. He saw a new carving near the center of the bruwe, a likeness of Abutilon and Buddleja embracing one another. The sight brought tears to his eyes.

"Marcus!" a voice called out. He turned to see Davidia running toward him, white flowers fluttering in the breeze of her passage. She nearly hurled herself at him, holding herself back at the last second and hugging him carefully.

He threw his arms around her, cane dangling from his left hand. "Hello, Davidia," he said, a little breathless from the intensity of her hug. "I'm happy to see you."

She stepped back. "I thought you were going home for a while."

Marcus looked away, focusing on the children's dormitory to try to keep his composure. "It turns out we can't go home, Davidia," he finally managed, swallowing hard past a lump in his throat. "Apparently, while we were here, away from Earth, a disease ravaged our home planet. It was highly contagious and killed our families. We can never go back." Marcus looked back at Davidia's face, startled at the tears he saw tumbling from her eyes and down the leaves of her face.

"Oh, no, Marcus," she said softly. "I am so sorry. Are you okay? How are Leopold and Sadie? You must all be upset. I remember that humans are so close to your birth families."

"It has been *so* hard. We have all been grieving, each in our own way. It's been the hardest for Sadie, I think. None of us got to say goodbye to our families back home. We all feel like we abandoned our families."

"But if you had not come here to Lysomnus, *you* would have all died as well!" Davidia exclaimed. "I cannot help but feel grateful for that."

"I know, I keep thinking about that too. It makes me feel guilty."

"You should not. It was *not* your fault, Marcus. You did not plan any of it, and you could not have known what would happen on your home world while you were gone." Davidia had taken Marcus's arm and was leading him toward the school.

"Where are we going?"

"To see Cassiope, of course. She has been feeling guilty, too."

Marcus did think that Cassiope was the appropriate person to see first since she had originally been one of the most vocal Teachers in opposing the Stondefel. He wasn't surprised she was still feeling guilty—she had been pretty upset when he'd seen her last, and it hadn't been all that long ago.

As they entered the main hallway, he could hear the Teachers lecturing. Davidia peeked into the third door on the left. Marcus could hear Cassiope's voice from inside, and then she stopped speaking abruptly. The Teacher must have caught sight of Davidia.

"Yes? What is it?" Marcus cringed as he heard Cassiope's stern tone of voice.

Davidia gestured for the Teacher to approach her. Marcus could hear rustling footsteps, and then Cassiope was suddenly there in the hall. "Marcus!" she gasped. "What are you doing here?"

"I—I came to see if I could help as you try to work through your losses and try to change your views about humans and the Stondefel," Marcus said, squaring his shoulders and forcing himself to stand up as straight as possible.

"Hmph." Cassiope looked down her nose at him for a moment. "I suppose you may be needed. We could use a human to help us, particularly since we have a few Teachers who are still a bit obstinate about humans *and* Stondefel."

"I'm happy to help," Marcus said. "I can stay for a few days. I don't mind staying in the bunkhouse, and using the bathhouse will help my back while I'm here. I hope you don't mind that since it was the humans who forced you to create them for their use."

"You are welcome to them," Cassiope said. "In fact, that is something we need to work on with the other Teachers. We need to help them understand that it is possible to have human guests who are helpful and friendly, not just abusive and forceful."

She leaned back into the classroom and dismissed her class, who were all too happy to have an early day off. They rushed out with cheers and bolted down the hall despite the Teacher's admonishments, with Davidia laughing all the while. Cassiope tried to pin her down with a stern look. "That does not help," she said, as a small smile played about her mouth.

Cassiope led them down the hall out of the school. Davidia twined her left arm through Marcus's right arm so he could use his cane as they followed. Once they were out in the sunshine, Cassiope turned back to them. "It is early yet," she said. "Perhaps you would like to get settled first and visit with Davidia before the evening meal. Then we can meet with the other Teachers and start a discussion."

"That sounds like a great idea," Marcus said. Cassiope nodded and strode off toward the dormitory while Davidia led Marcus to the bunkhouse. He looked at the stairs and decided he wouldn't strain himself climbing them after his walk to the bruwe from Far Field. He used his power to move himself up to the sleeping area.

Davidia followed, looking thoughtful as she arrived at the top of the stairs.

"Marcus, are you not concerned about the physical toll using your abilities might be taking on your body? You told everyone what it did to Nun the Wiser."

Marcus sat on the bed he'd used the last time he had stayed with the Scrybb. "I've thought about that," he said. "I don't *feel* anything specifically physical when I use it, so I'm not really sure what kind of 'toll' it might be taking on my body. Nun the Wiser lived here and used her power for generations, and it took that long to get to the condition we saw her in. I think it's incremental, to be honest.

"Also, Nun the Wiser didn't have the power to heal. I do. Not only do I have the Halfriez, but I can also heal both others and myself. If using my power does cause me some damage or harm, I can just heal it the way my father did to Nun the Wiser."

Davidia looked disturbed. Marcus could read the thoughts on her face. Marcus knew everyone thought he should have more respect for his power and should restrict using it for important reasons only. His forehead creased with frustration as he considered the fact that he, the most powerful person in all Lysomnus, was basically being told what to do by everyone else who thought they knew what was better for him.

It was the same old song, he thought. Ever since he'd been disabled in that car accident, people had been treating him like a delicate piece of pottery that would shatter at the first touch. Well, now *he* was the one with the power. *He* knew what he could and couldn't do.

"Davidia, don't worry about me. I'm not going to use my power for evil purposes like Nun the Wiser did or for extreme things that sap me in huge ways like she did. Small things aren't going to have a large impact on me anyway."

"I hope not, Marcus. Just—keep in mind that there are risks, okay?"

"I will, Davidia, I promise."

Davidia smiled. "Now tell me what Sadie and Leopold are up to!"

Two days later, Marcus was feeling much better about the Teachers' initial reticence. Although they had been upset about the incidents with the Stondefel, their beliefs had been shaken, but they did begin plans to incorporate the flying stone demons into their Teachings in positive ways, as watchers and helpers of the people of Lysomnus. They were no longer to be portrayed as threats or beings to be feared. They were even discussing the installation of a signal flag like the Muirnati and the Cativera used to contact the Stondefel when they needed assistance. The Scrybb perception of humans was harder to shake.

The Scrybb had been sorely mistreated by Nun the Wiser and the empowered humans of Lysomnus. Of all the people of this world, the

Scrybb had been most often visited—and violated—by the humans. Their goods were stolen, both food and craft. The empowered humans had delighted in threatening to burn Thicce Colpat and the Scrybb themselves since fire was really the only thing that could really hurt them. The human with the power to make fireballs had apparently delighted in threatening to burn members of the Scrybb community whenever he was here. Just before Marcus and his friends had left Thicce Colpat, one of the Teachers had been badly burned by Nun the Wiser herself.

As the Scrybb interacted with Marcus and grew to know him better, just as they had Leopold and Sadie, they came to truly understand that there were humans who could be trusted and who cared for them. Davidia had told them of what Marcus had done for her when she was a prisoner of the humans and reminded them of how Abutilon and Buddleja had sacrificed themselves because they believed so strongly in Marcus and his love for Lysomnus.

On the last day of his visit, Marcus was sitting between Davidia and Malberis, facing all the Scrybb in the dining hall, telling them about his attempt to return to Earth with his friends. He told them about the disease that had killed their families and prevented them from ever returning.

"Do you not have *anything* to remind you of home?" asked one young Scrybb who sat at one of the beautiful long tables, listening to Marcus at the front of the room.

"No," Marcus said, "When we came here, we thought it would only be for a few days. We didn't bring anything with us. Just the clothes we were wearing, and we don't even have those anymore." A lump formed in Marcus's throat as he realized he didn't even have a picture of his mom. He rubbed his eyes with a finger and a thumb, trying to keep the tears at bay.

"Oh!" Cassiope suddenly exclaimed and ran out of the dining hall. Everyone stared at her unusual behavior. The strict Teacher was usually so self-contained. After a moment, they all turned back to Marcus.

"Anyway," he continued, "we can never go back, not even to get any of our things. The disease has killed almost everyone on our planet, and if we go back, it will kill us too," Marcus finished.

A flurry of activity at the door cleared to reveal Cassiope's return. She made her way to Marcus, carrying a bundle of folded material. She placed it carefully on the table beside him.

"Marcus, after you left before—to go to Palaga, Buddleja collected your soiled clothing from the bathhouse. All of it, yours, Sadie's, and Leopold's. She cleaned it and kept it in her home. I think she wanted to make sure it was here in case you ever returned and wanted it back."

Marcus reached out, lifting the sweet-smelling bundle of clothing, sorting the items. His Elden Ring T-shirt and blue jeans were on the bottom of the pile. Tears welled up in his eyes at the sight of them. When he'd taken them off in the bathhouse after arriving in Lysomnus, they'd been so soiled all he'd thought of was getting them away from his body. Now, they were all he had left of a world he'd never see again. He suddenly felt a wave of gratitude to Buddleja and wished he could thank her for this final gift.

"Thank you, Cassiope," he said, his voice husky with emotion. "I can't tell you what this means to me. I know Leopold and Sadie will be so grateful, too, for what Buddleja did and to you, for protecting them and returning them to us."

"Of course," the usually stern Teacher said, a kind look on her face. "They belong to you. I am glad Buddleja saved them, so you have something of your homeworld left.

"All right, everyone," she said, turning to the crowd of Scrybb. "It is time to say goodbye to Marcus. Our Trader made it to Palaga, for Berberis came from Far Field while I was outside to say that one of the Stondefel has landed there to take Marcus back."

She reached out to Marcus, taking his left hand to help him to his feet. Then she carefully embraced him, murmuring in his ear, "Thank you for visiting with us for these past days. I am glad to have restored our relations with you, and I know we all feel better about humans again."

As she released him, Marcus looked into her orange eyes and smiled. "I'm so glad I came. I wasn't sure how you would react to me, but I feel really great. I love being here with the Scrybb so much. Cornus was my first friend here, and you all were the first people to help me and my friends in Lysomnus. To be restored in friendship again feels wonderful."

Cassiope handed him his pack, to which she'd just added the pile of clothing. He put it over his shoulder, and they walked together out of the dining hall.

Outside, the crowd was still gathered. One young Scrybb stepped forward. "May we come with Marcus and see the Stondefel?" she asked shyly.

Cassiope looked at Marcus. "I think it would be good for all of the Scrybb, especially the children," he said. "You are teaching them about the Stondefel in a positive way, but meeting one of them will help more. They can see his appearance and experience what he is like in person and understand that he and his kind are not to be feared." He wanted their memories of the Stondefel to be happy ones and not the day that Anneberg had crashed into the bruwe and nearly dropped Cassiope to the ground.

She nodded. "Very well." Her eyes scanned the crowd, and she arranged her features to their very sternest. "But you will all behave with your very best manners."

All of them nodded, chattering excitedly. They followed Marcus as he made his way slowly down the path to Far Field. He felt like the Pied Piper, leading the children out of town, and laughed to himself.

Agatho was waiting in the field. He looked down with amused surprise at the throng of Scrybb as they surrounded him. He greeted them as they called out, smiling and rumbling with harsh laughter. Occasionally, he held out a carefully sheathed talon for one of them to shake or inspect. They babbled and rustled their leaves as they made their way around him, scrutinizing his stony legs, the sharp talons on his feet that dug into the soil, and the long, thick tail with its spikes that stuck out in every direction.

After carefully hugging Malberis and then Davidia, Marcus made his way through the children to Agatho and lifted himself to the Stondefel's back with his power, causing a chorus of *ooohs*, as most of them had not seen him use it openly before. He busied himself attaching the harness while Cassiope and the other Teachers who had accompanied the crowd got them rounded up and organized.

Finally, he was harnessed in place on Agatho's back and had his cane and pack tied down. He called out to Cassiope to say goodbye. The entire gathering called out nearly as one, "Goodbye!" Marcus laughed and felt Agatho rumble against him with mirth. Cassiope led the Scrybb back toward the path as Agatho launched himself into the air and banked around in a circle above Far Field. Marcus waved at all the Scrybb, who were waving vigorously up at them as they flew away.

"It looks like things went well there," Agatho called as they flew toward Palaga.

"Yes, it was definitely worth the visit," Marcus yelled back. "Relations are much improved with the Scrybb now."

"The Scrybb Traveler who came to Palaga seemed very friendly, as opposed to those who had been coming in recent times, Tartarus told me," Agatho said.

Soon, they circled to land on Palaga's stone terrace. Marcus realized this bruwe was starting to feel like home to him. Even as he had grieved for his home and family on Earth, he was embraced by the Fyrtudo and spent most of his time in Lysomnus here. He was comfortable in the caves and was close to the Stondefel, to whom he had also come to feel quite close.

Tartarus was standing in the open doors to Palaga, waiting for Marcus as he dismounted from Agatho's back. After Marcus had removed the harness, Agatho said his goodbyes and took off, flying up to return to his home in the caldera of the Beornan Rokk.

"Hello, Tartarus," Marcus said as he approached the King. "I can report that my visit to Thicce Colpat was a success. I think the Scrybb feel much better about humans, and they trust me again."

That is wonderful to hear, Marcus. I am glad you went there and had a good visit. Now, what do you plan to do next?

"Honestly, before we get back to my studies, I should travel to Fisc. It's important that I visit Boehlkea and Pelamis and let them know about my father. I probably should have done that first. They're both going to be devastated to hear about his—his death." Marcus found he still had a hard time even saying the words.

That sounds like the right thing to do. I know it will be difficult, but I'm sure they will be comforted to hear the news from you. They deserve the chance to grieve, too.

"Thank you, Tartarus. I will leave before too long, but before I go, there's a book I was reading in the library before I left that has a section on the Halfriez in it. There's a page missing. It looks like it was torn out. Do you know anything about it?" Marcus and Tartarus now began to make their way toward the library. The two of them had to pause occasionally to allow other Fyrtudo to pass by in the busy cavern.

I am not sure how that would have happened, Tartarus said. *I've never seen anyone damage any of the books we keep here. We can certainly look at it right now, if you'd like, before you leave for Fisc. Perhaps you should even wait until morning to leave.*

"Let's look at the book now, and we can discuss my trip after," Marcus said. They entered the great library of Palaga, and Marcus quickly found the book of Talismans again. He flipped through the pages until the book fell open naturally to the place where the page had been torn out. It had left a jagged ridge of torn paper close to the fold, with just a corner left at the top. He scanned quickly through the rest of the book, but no loose pages were to be found anywhere inside.

Perhaps it is somewhere else in this section, Tartarus said and reached for a couple of the other books beside the gap left by the book in Marcus's hand. Marcus set the book on a nearby table and grabbed another book as well.

They spent some time paging through nearly the entire shelf

where the book was kept, the shelf above, and the shelf below the spot where the book on Talismans had been found. None of them held the missing page or had any pages missing.

I do not know what to say, Tartarus said. *We could search the entire library, but that would take weeks. There are thousands of books here.*

"No, I can't imagine doing that," Marcus replied. "It seems unlikely that someone tore out that one page just to stuff it into another book. I think whoever took it left with it in their possession for some reason. We might never know what information was on that page."

They left the library together, stopping just outside the doors. Marcus turned to Tartarus. "I'd really like to leave tonight, to be honest. I'll pack up some things and head to Fisc if Agatho is still available. I really won't need much, because they have most of what I need to wear while I'm there. The nice thing is—"

Marcus! Colflur interrupted as she approached, another Fyrtudo by her side.

Tartarus looked irritated as they both turned to her. *Colflur, it is very rude to interrupt like that,* he admonished the Queen.

I apologize, but this is very important. She turned to the Fyrtudo who had come with her.

Hello, Marcus, he said. *I am Petromar. I have made something for you I hope you will find useful.* He held out his hands, a large object laid across them.

It was a new prosthetic arm! Made of forged steel, it would fit over Marcus's residual stump. It had an elbow joint, forearms, wrist, and full hand similar to the one that had been on his myoelectric prosthesis. It still had a harness like the one he wore now. The jointed fingers looked flexible, but he wondered how this one would work since there was no electricity here, and his other one had a rechargeable battery.

We have craftsmen who design complex machines, and they designed this for you based on yours when you stayed with us before while they were cleaning it, Colflur said. *Petromar has designed this arm for you, so you will have more use than you do now with your current one. We have used this technique before for Fyrtudo, who have been injured in mining accidents, who have dug too deep and been burned by molten rock.*

"This is amazing!" Marcus exclaimed. "I never dreamed this was possible."

Petromar and our other craftsmen have been working on this for you since you first came to us. They know how difficult it can be to try to function without the full use of your hand, Colflur said, indicating Petromar's left arm.

Marcus looked carefully at the Fyrtudo's hand, which was similarly forged to the prosthetic he had just received. It was darker, nearly matching Petromar's dark, armored skin. Petromar's fingers opened slightly when he moved his hand as well.

"How are you able to get the fingers to move?" Marcus asked.

Enough of my arm was left for this hand to pick up movement in the small muscles of my residual arm, Petromar explained. *I am honored to be able to provide this arm for you, Marcus Talent, but I apologize that it will not do all the things that my hand does for me without the harness.*

"No, I am the one who is honored," Marcus said, a twinge of disappointment in his belly. He told himself to appreciate the thoughtful gift even if it wouldn't do what his bebionic arm had done. It was still more than he had any right to expect. "Thank you so much. This means the world to me. I can't tell you in simple words how much I appreciate this."

Petromar nodded, bowing slightly, and turned, walking away. Colflur laid her hand on Marcus's left arm, nodding. *Please, prepare for your journey.*

Tartarus patted Marcus on the back. *I am happy that this gift was ready for you before your trip to Fisc.* He returned the book that he had so quickly handed off while removing his shirt to try on the new prosthesis to Marcus.

"Oh!" Marcus said. "What will happen to this in the Diluvium? Won't it be damaged?"

Never fear, Tartarus replied. *The metal is specially forged and treated to resist salt water as well, as are all the items we forge for the people who live in the ocean. It will last for your lifetime.*

Marcus smiled, reassured. "Will you contact the Stondefel while I change? I'd like that ride to Fisc and also to ask if they'd be willing to deliver some things to Leopold and Sadie."

Of course.

Marcus walked as quickly as possible to his quarters, eager to try the new prosthesis. He stripped off his shirt and his current prosthesis and removed the sock that fit over his residual arm. Using a bowl of water that was always kept fresh in his quarters, he carefully washed and dried the residual arm. He took a moment to look at the electrodes that were still left in his skin from the bebionic arm he had before. If only this new arm could somehow connect to them, he could use it like that prosthesis, giving him more use of his hand again...

Hm... he thought. *What if I could use my power to somehow connect the prosthesis to the electrodes?* Marcus slid the arm onto his own, watching as it slid into place. He saw where the electrode lined up on his arm. Sliding it off, he set his left index finger against the smooth metal inside and concentrated. A warm sensation increased rapidly beneath his finger until it nearly got too hot to maintain contact. Suddenly, the metal flared red for a second, and Marcus sucked in a breath through his teeth, expecting his finger to burn. When he pulled his finger away, it was unmarked, and he felt nothing. He wasn't burned, but there was a discolored mark on the metal. Feeling more confident, he repeated this process for the other electrodes on his arm. When all the marks were complete, he slid the harness over his body and replaced the arm over his own. It fit perfectly. There was no abrasive feel; it felt smooth and comfortable against his skin. Once it was firmly in place, he attempted to move his arm. The elbow moved smoothly, straightening and bending normally. Then he tried to flex the fingers. Nothing happened. Marcus felt his chest sink with disappointment. He had been so sure!

Then he stopped himself and took a deep breath, taking a moment to gather his wits and be patient. The bebionic arm needed a charge to work. Marcus gently grasped the prosthetic in his left hand and closed his eyes. He thought carefully about sending a small amount of energy into the arm. Power surged lightly down his arm and into the prosthetic. He could feel the energy taking hold and coming up the metal to meet his electrodes. When he released the prosthetic, he was able to open and close the fingers like it was his own hand. He made a fist. Then he stretched the fingers wide. He picked up his cane and waved it around.

If his back had allowed him, he'd have danced around the room. This new arm was even better than his myoelectric prosthesis had been! He felt great. He stopped for a moment to think. Marcus knew he had enough control over his power that he shouldn't need to touch the arm to charge it and move the fingers. There would be another learning curve for him here—to master powering the arm and using it without needing to concentrate. For a while, he would have to be careful and practice how he powered and used the arm so he didn't overcharge or damage it. The Fyrtudo had no idea just what a wonderful gift they had given him.

Finally, he grabbed his pack. He took out the clothes for Sadie and Leopold. He wanted to carry his own clothes with him because it just felt good to be able to look at them whenever he wanted to. He didn't think he would ever wear them again. They might wear out or become damaged. He wouldn't be able to live with that.

When he went back out into the cavern, Tartarus and Colflur were waiting for him.

The Stondefel have agreed to help with both of your requests, Marcus, Tartarus said.

If you will give me your gifts for Leopold and Sadie, I will wrap them for their travels to keep them safe, Colflur said. Marcus handed them to her, indicating which was which. She took them carefully and left to wrap them.

Tartarus walked him out to the terrace, where he found Agatho waiting for him once again. “I’m starting to think we should wear these harnesses permanently,” joked the Stondefel.

“I apologize for asking so much of you,” Marcus said. “I don’t want to treat you like our personal couriers.”

“And we keep telling you that we are happy to do it,” Agatho said. “Please don’t feel guilty. I only said those words in jest. We enjoy the company and the friendship. In fact, other Stondefel are jealous of us and want to start having a turn at sharing rides!”

Marcus felt better about asking the Stondefel for so many rides here and there. He lifted himself to Agatho’s back and attached the harness.

Safe travels, Marcus. We will see you when it is time for you to return.

“Thank you, Tartarus. I hope to return home before too long.” He waved at the Fyrtudo as Agatho launched himself into the air. A wave of affection followed him in Tartarus's thoughts.

CHAPTER FIVE

FOUND FAMILIES

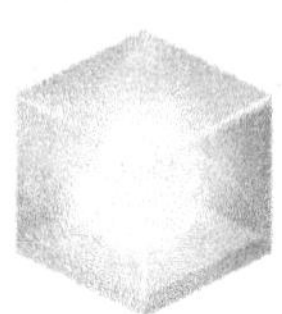

Marcus

As Agatho gained height, Marcus looked down at the Beornan Rokk. As they began to turn away, he saw molten rock begin to spew from multiple calderas along the entire chain of mountains.

"Agatho, what's happening?"

Agatho looked down at the mountains.

"I've never seen that happen before!" he called out. They were still flying at an angle, away from the mountains. Marcus saw the trees of the Grenewud were shaking wildly, and as he watched, several of them toppled over.

"Something bad is happening!" he yelled to Agatho. The Stondefel flew lower, and they heard rumbling as they approached a lower altitude. They saw more trees falling, and Agatho flew up higher to get a better view of the continent.

He was heading at a faster pace toward the Diluvium than they ever had before. The ocean became visible quickly. As they watched, a large wave became visible, rushing toward the shore. Marcus saw the water from the beach had been sucked back toward the main body of the ocean.

"That looks bad!"

"It is," Agatho called. "It will crash onto the shore and cause a lot of damage. Fortunately, the only bruwe close to the shore on this side of the continent is Fisc, and that's underwater. Hopefully, no one will be hurt."

"What is happening?"

"I'm not sure. The only time I've ever seen a wave like that was when an object from beyond the skies crashed into the Diluvium when the moon was broken. That was not all that long before you came, Marcus. Your father told Tartarus the damage to the moon might cause some problems for our world." Marcus pressed his lips together at more information that his father should have taken the time to share with him that first night he had traveled to Lysomnus. He shook his head as he realized it would do no good to spend his life blaming an imperfect man for petty mistakes.

As Agatho stayed high above the beach, the wave crashed onshore. From their height, Marcus and Agatho could see the water slamming into rocks and rolling them up the shore. Farther along the shoreline to their right, water surged into the Grenewud, and behind them, it knocked down the grasses of the Zabanara plains. Marcus gasped at the force of it. A few more waves followed the first, but surprisingly, the waves receded fairly quickly, leaving large areas of standing water behind.

Agatho landed when he could see that there were no more waves coming into shore from the ocean. He dropped Marcus off quickly as close as he could to the entrance to Fisc, explaining that he wanted to return to Palaga and ensure that both the Fyrtudo in their caves and the Stondefel near the eruptions were unharmed.

Marcus found himself on the sodden beach, quite alone. His cane sank into the sand with each step, so he stopped leaning on it and bore the pain of walking without its support. It felt as if forever passed with each step as his boots sank into the surface of the sand, and pain tore into his back as he pulled his foot out with each step. Finally, he held himself up against a tipped rock and pulled his boots and sodden socks off. It hurt, but Marcus had the feeling if he sat on the ground, he'd be crawling through the sand before he could get back to his feet. His steps were much lighter as he walked the rest of the way to the entrance to Fisc, carrying the boots with the socks tucked inside. He wondered if the Muirnati would even know he was coming since the turmoil caused by the massive waves had likely kept them from noticing Agatho in the skies.

Finally, he made it around the bend. The rocks that guarded the tunnel entrance were askew. Two were lying flat on the sand, and the others were leaning precariously on each other. He approached them cautiously, unsure as to whether they'd stay upright or collapse and crush him as he passed..

The rocks appeared stable when Marcus walked past them to approach the tunnel entrance where he'd first met Pelamis. This time the tunnel was empty. He looked out to sea. All he saw was turbulent water. He took a seat on the flat rock where his clean clothes had been when he'd left Fisc last time, hoping to see one of the Muirtani surfacing at some point. Waiting was all he could do for now.

Several hours later, a head broke water far out to sea. Then another followed, and a third. He painfully pushed himself to his feet. Sitting on a rock was not comfortable for his back. Hoping one of the Muirnati was looking his way, he waved his arms over his head. No response.

He stood watching the distant figures. Every couple of minutes, he waved or crossed his arms over his head. It took a long time and several efforts, but finally, one of them waved back. With a relieved sigh, Marcus sat back down and waited.

After a short wait, Pelamis surfaced in the water just offshore. She had Marcus's swimming mask in her hand.

"Hello, Marcus. I'm sorry you had to wait, but we weren't expecting you. Would you like to leave your things here? I didn't want to make you wait longer and go grab your suit. You'll have to walk in and then follow me in the water—that wave tore some of the tunnels apart pretty badly."

Marcus pulled off his shirt and laid it next to his pack, boots, and cane. He decided modesty was less important than the weight his pants were going to add and stripped them off too. He strode into the water in his drawers, took the mask from Pelamis, and slipped it over his head. Then he ducked under the water, gasping as it splashed his skin. It was unbelievably cold. He tried to focus on the relief of having the gritty sand washed out from between his toes.

Following Pelamis through the sea was challenging. The water was turbulent, pushing against him even here below the surface. He had expected smoother swimming underwater, as it had been on his previous visit when he had followed her to the Shoal. The waves must have really caused trouble even here beneath the sea.

Not only was the water turbulent, but Muirnati were frantically swimming everywhere. Some of the small arches that had protected entrances to their homes were damaged and shifted out of place.

Marcus slid his mask up when they surfaced briefly. "Was anyone hurt, Pelamis? Were your homes damaged?" Marcus's teeth chattered as he watched the Muirnati and asked his friend about the bruwe.

"A few of our people were bruised by the turbulence, but no one was badly hurt. Our homes are undamaged, other than what you see here, to the arches. I think we are more shaken up than anything else." Then she looked at him, and an expression of concern crossed her face.

"Marcus, we must get you inside and warm. This water is much too cold for you without a protective suit. You are freezing!" She seized his hand and led him to the home that had belonged to his father. Marcus slipped his mask back down just before she pulled him below the surface and into the tunnel.

Marcus found himself deeply affected by his return to the home of his father. The underwater suits his father would never wear again were stacked neatly on the shelf. He knew Pelamis and Boehlkea were expecting that Deacon would return to visit them now. Not only did he have to deal with his own grief, but now he had to share with them the news that Deacon was dead, ending that dream for all of them.

Pelamis was urging Marcus to leave the pool quickly. "You must get out of the cold ocean and into the hot shower. The sooner you get warmed up, the better," she said. "Take your suit with you. It will keep you warm when you come back. This water is from the deep ocean and is far too cold for you."

Marcus peeled off his face mask after he'd climbed out of the water. He grabbed the suit from its place on the shelf. The shifting blue-green color rippled in the light reflected by the pool. He eagerly stepped into the bathroom and closed the door.

He was shaking so violently with the cold that it was difficult to get the water going, even with his new arm and its working hand. The shower blasted warm water almost immediately after he turned it on, and he stepped into the stall carefully. The last thing Marcus wanted to do was fall.

With a sigh, he let the hot spray wash over his body, the chill gradually leaving his skin and the shakes stopping at last. His fingers and toes had been almost numb with the cold and tingled painfully.

Once Marcus had finally warmed up, he reached for the soap. As he brought it to his body and lathered up, the scent wafted up into his nostrils, and the nostalgic smell of his father came to him. With a sob, he let go and wept, allowing himself to grieve without feeling the need to show strength for anyone else. After he had cried himself out, he rinsed off and stepped out, grabbing a towel and sitting on the toilet to dry off.

It felt like it would never stop hitting him, losing his parents. The loss of his mother was simple, starkly painful and uncomplicated. He had left a world with her in it and returned to one where she was dead. That shattered his heart. But Marcus felt like losing his father was so complex, it was almost hard for him to comprehend all the layers. They had been at odds when he'd sent his father home, so terribly disappointed and angry at him. Then Marcus thought he'd been going home, sure he would have to deal with a freaked-out mother and a pissed-off father. His father had been standing right there, just a few simple yards away, and Deacon's only thought had been to save Marcus's life by sending him back to Lysomnus with his friends. Marcus *had* to leave him there, knowing he would die. The guilt was tearing him apart inside.

He stood up and finished drying off, putting on the suit. It was easier to get on than the first time, with the aid of the new prosthesis. He had some trouble getting the sleeve over the metal, but it was still nice to have the use of his right hand. He was hurrying because he felt like he'd kept Pelamis waiting for a long time.

When he emerged from the bathroom, Pelamis was waiting at the side of the pool. As he sat down on the edge, she smiled and asked, "Are you ready to go and see your sister, Marcus?"

Marcus tried to smile and managed what felt like a sickly curve of his lips and nodded. He pulled his mask back over his face and slid back into the water. It was a relief to have the protection of the suit between himself and the cold water of the Diluvium as he followed Pelamis back to the surface. Together, they swam to the stones that marked the home of Pelamis and her daughter. As he followed Pelamis down to where his sister would be, dread filled Marcus's stomach with roiling nausea.

When he surfaced in the pool, Marcus saw Boehlkea sitting cross-legged on the ledge beside the water, working with some kind of net. She looked up, a smile creasing her face as soon as she saw her brother remove his mask.

"Marcus!" she cried. As soon as he pulled himself up and sat on the edge, Boehlkea moved over and wrapped her arms around him. "I'm so glad to see you! But so soon... I thought you were going home for a while?"

"Um, well... I was... That is, we were going to, but... Well, hang on." Marcus gestured to Pelamis. "I think you should come closer."

A concerned expression crossed Pelamis's face as she pulled herself closer along the edge of the pool and looked up into Marcus's face with concern. "Is something wrong, Marcus?"

"I don't know how to tell you," Marcus said. His chest hitched, and he felt tears welling up in his eyes again. The pain was still so much, he didn't want to say the words. He knew he would inflict that same pain on both of them.

"I'm so sorry," he said, putting his hand over his face. He couldn't breathe, the lump in his throat was so big. He thought he might be choking. He gasped, the air whistling through his throat as he tried to suck some air in.

"Marcus, what is it?" Boehlkea asked in a frightened voice, pulling him closer.

"Our father, Boehlkea," he gasped, "Deacon," he said, meeting Pelamis's eyes, "He's dead."

Both of them shrieked. "How do you know?" Boehlkea said, pushing Marcus away. "What do you mean?" She shook him angrily when he didn't respond. "I thought you sent him home, Marcus. What happened?"

Pelamis was silent. Her yellow eyes searched Marcus's face as she waited to hear what had happened.

Tears ran down Marcus's face as he forced the words out. His breath hitched in his chest as he told them about the disease that had ravaged Earth, killing his mother and his friends' families before their return, and how his father had sent them all back to Lysomnus immediately when they had attempted to return home.

Pelamis sobbed in the water, hands over her face.

Boehlkea was angry. "So, you sentenced him to death when you sent him home? This is your fault, Marcus! You should never have done that!"

"I know, I feel awful, Boehlkea. I wish I hadn't. If only I had waited."

"You're right you should have waited! You stupid! You killed—my! You—you—killed—my—father!" Sobs punctuated her words until she burst into uncontrollable tears.

Pelamis raised her head. While she was clearly grieving, no tears stained her face. Deacon's humanity had given Boehlkea the ability to weep, but although she could shed no tears, Pelamis grieved no less for her inability to cry.

"Marcus, are you sure he's dead? You said he was alive when you returned, and maybe he wasn't *that* sick. Even the slimmest chance is a chance. Maybe he could be a survivor..."

"I don't think so, Pelamis. He said he'd already been exposed and that we had to leave and couldn't come back. I saw the rash on his face, too, from being infected, and we all heard him coughing. There isn't any way I can even go back and check because if I am exposed, I can't return, or I would risk bringing the disease here and exposing the people of Lysomnus to it, and I won't do that."

"You should be cursed to return to Earth and stay there! You deserve it for what you did to him," Boehlkea muttered as she glared at him through her tear-reddened eyes.

"Boehlkea!" Pelamis gasped. "I know you are hurting, but that is no excuse to say something like that to Marcus. He had no way of knowing about the disease on Earth when he sent Deacon back. He has lost his father, too—and his mother as well!"

Boehlkea looked away, cheeks reddened and a sullen look on her face. Marcus tried to quell his hurt and anger. He already felt guilty about sending Deacon back to die. He felt a little jealous, too, that Boehlkea still had her mother. He bit his lip to hold in the retort that came to mind—too often, he'd been guilty of saying the wrong thing, and he knew the pain she was feeling right now.

"Boehlkea, I'm sorry for causing you such pain. I'm hurting, too. I want to help you bear this pain; we both lost our father. We should grieve together."

Glaring at him, she dove into the pool and left.

Pelamis placed a webbed hand on Marcus's knee. "You have to understand, Marcus. She's been so hopeful about being able to see Deacon again. When she was taken last time you came here, she thought she'd see him. Instead, when she was held in that house in the human bruwe, she heard him say terrible things about her. She has been trying to work her way through that pain. I had thought that perhaps once you were able to bring Deacon back here, he might apologize and tell Boehlkea he didn't mean the things he said to her. And now..."

Marcus couldn't have felt worse. He had known he would bring pain to both of the Muirnati by telling them about Deacon's death, but now guilt was tearing him apart.

"Pelamis, when he told me to come back here, he did say to tell both Boehlkea and you that he loved you. He was thinking of you both. I think he regretted saying those things." Marcus couldn't be sure of that at all, but what could it hurt to give his sister and her mother some small comfort? Deacon *had* said to give them his love. "I hope it will help her to hear that, at least."

"Give her some time. Right now, we have to deal with the aftermath of this shaking and find out how widespread it was. We want to know if it affected more of Lysomnus than just us here in Fisc. We have only seen this happen once before. It was not nearly this bad then."

Marcus looked at her, wiping the tears from his face. He tried to push away the hurt feelings Boehlkea had brought up inside him and concentrate on the other problem that currently faced Lysomnus.

"Agatho said not too long ago, something came from space and hit your moon, then crashed into the ocean, causing a great wave like the one that just happened." He sniffled, trying to clear his nose.

"Yes, that did happen. The moon has been moving oddly through the sky ever since. Some of our people have said it appeared much larger on recent nights than before."

Marcus tried to think about the little bit of astronomy he'd learned about in school. He knew the moon of Earth affected tides and assumed the moon here would do the same. Would a collision with a meteor changing the orbit, making it come closer to the planet, cause earthquakes? Although, he thought, it probably wouldn't be called an "Earth" quake here on another planet. "Lysomnus" quake just sounded weird in his head.

"Pelamis," he said, still thinking, "do you have astronomers here?

By that, I mean people who study the stars and other things in the sky at night?"

Moving her legs and fins slowly through the water behind her, Pelamis pondered. "I don't know that I would call it a *study* of the stars, but our people use the stars to find their way when they travel farther out to sea in search of fish."

Marcus shook his head. "I don't think that helps. I just wondered if anyone here would know if the object that hit your moon might have altered its orbit and made it come closer to Lysomnus. If it's possible that could cause the quake that happened."

Pelamis now looked confused. "I don't understand what you're talking about, Marcus."

"I'm sorry, Pelamis. It's just an occurrence that might have made a difference. But there would have to be a way to move the moon to fix it, even if that were the cause..." Marcus trailed off as he pondered the problem in his head.

He looked down to see her staring at him, wide-eyed. "*Move the moon?* That is crazy! The moon! Just...move it!" She tossed her hands into the air, webbed fingers extended. Water splashed into the air around her as her body came down from her minor thrust away from the side of the pool.

Marcus laughed. "You're right. It does sound a little far-fetched, doesn't it?"

"A little! A little, you say?" She shook her head. "Move the *moon*."

Marcus was thinking of the day he pushed an entire mountainside back into place. Granted, a moon was a lot bigger than a mountain, but did that make it impossible? He wondered. If only there were someone to talk to about it!

"Hey, Pelamis, if you need the Stondefel for anything, is there a way you let them know? I know they fly overhead, keeping an eye on the people of Lysomnus."

"Yes, we have a signal cloth we raise on a pulley to the highest point of Fisc."

"Do you think we could do that? I'd like to go back to the beach and talk to one of them." He slid back into the water, holding his face mask in one hand.

"You want to leave already? I know Boehlkea is very angry, but I'd hoped you'd stay longer." Pelamis seemed upset at the idea of Marcus leaving so soon.

"No," he said softly. "I don't need to leave yet. I'd like to stay a while and hopefully work things out with Boehlkea, spend some time with you. I just need to talk to one of the Stondefel."

"Oh, good," she said, looking relieved. "All right. Let's go raise the signal cloth." She dove into the water. Pulling on his face mask, Marcus followed.

After they had completed that task, Pelamis escorted Marcus to the beach. His clothes must have again been cleaned for him, as they were neatly folded in his pack on the rock near the tunnel opening. He elected to keep his ocean suit on, however, as he intended to return to Fisc as soon as he'd concluded his discussion with whichever Stondefel responded to the signal.

He turned to Pelamis, waiting for him in the water. "I feel confident I can find my way back to the bruwe when I am done here," he said. "I don't want you to wait for me. I don't know how long I will be waiting for one of the Stondefel to see the signal or how long we will need to talk. I think Boehlkea needs you more than I do right now."

Pelamis nodded, turning and disappearing with a kick of her feet. Marcus walked slowly to the rock to retrieve his cane. He was relieved to feel that the sand beneath his feet was firmer now. It was easier for him to walk with the cane rather than try to move independently. Still, he moved farther up the beach toward the rocky area where the ground was more solid, but not so far as to get into the larger stones that would make it unstable for him to walk.

He returned to the area where Agatho had dropped him off and found a place to sit on a flat boulder. Hopefully, it would not take too long for one of the Stondefel to respond. The pulley and rope design for the signal flag was similar to what he had seen back on Earth and was impressively long enough to raise the cloth to the top of the highest of the bones surrounding the Shoal, which fortunately had been undamaged by the giant wave or the turbulence that followed. Pelamis had told him the giant bones sunk far below the surface into the ocean floor, which kept them very stable. Marcus was seriously impressed by the rope-making skills of the Scrybb and how the Muirtnati were able to continue to weave the long strands together to maintain its strength.

Marcus was nearly groaning in pain from sitting for so long on the hard rock by the time he saw a minuscule dot in the sky circling, gradually becoming larger and finally becoming recognizable as one of the stone demons of Lysomnus. As the beast flew lower, Marcus realized he didn't recognize this Stondefel and hadn't met him before.

With a blast of sand that Marcus blocked from flying into his face, the creature landed.

"Hello, young brother. I am Aldinoch. It is my pleasure to meet you and be at your service today." The Stondefel curved a taloned forearm before himself and bowed over it.

Marcus smiled crookedly, disconcerted by the display of honor by the Stondefel. He swallowed and then spoke, forcing his voice out of his tight throat. "Hello, Aldinoch. I am glad to meet you as well."

"What can I do for you today? Do you need to return to Palaga?"

"No, I don't require a ride right now. What I need are the answers to some questions that I have about Lysomnus and its moon." Marcus rubbed his left hand self-consciously over the metal of his prosthesis as his nerves got the best of him.

"I'd be happy to give them to you if I can," Aldinoch rumbled. "Please, tell me what it is that you would like to know." He settled himself to the sand, folding his wings to his back, looking interestedly at Marcus.

"Well, you know, this quake that just occurred. And the increase in molten rock that's been erupting along the Beornan Rokk lately—I think both are related, and they might have something to do with your moon."

"Hm." Aldinoch pressed his bony lips together pensively, looking out across the water. "This is an interesting thought. The rock from the stars that crashed into the Diluvium not that long ago damaged our moon as it approached. I take an interest in the objects in the night beyond our world, and I have noticed that since that incident, the moon has not been moving along the same course as it had before."

"So, the orbit *has* changed," Marcus said, standing and looking into the sky as if to see the moon right at that very moment. It wasn't visible, although sometimes, on Earth, he had been able to see the moon during the day.

"Orbit? I haven't heard that word before—*orbit*. Is that the word the people of your world use for the course of the moon through the sky?" Aldinoch peered at Marcus closely.

"Yes, on Earth, where I am from, we have a study called "astronomy". Our astronomers are the scientists who study the stars and planets, the moon, and other things in space, and orbit is the word they use for how each body in space travels around another. Like how the moon moves around Lysomnus."

"Hmmm. This is fascinating!" The Stondefel gazed at the sky. "I have always loved to look at the stars. Sometimes at night, I fly as high as I can to look as closely as possible. The moon is fascinating. It is lamentable to see it damaged so badly."

"Some of the Muirnati have said they thought it looked as though the moon has moved closer to Lysomnus since the meteor hit it. Does it appear that way to you during your flights?" Marcus asked.

"Meteor? Is that another word used by your... astronomers?" Aldinoch rumbled. "I should like to be an astronomer." he said wistfully.

"Yes, it is the word for a piece of rock or debris that comes from space and crashes on a planet. I can teach you what I know about astronomy. But what do you think of the moon's change in orbit?" Marcus hoped to bring Aldinoch back to the subject at hand.

"Oh, yes, you asked about that. I do have to say that over the last few weeks or so, as the moon traveled through the sky, it did look larger and was in a different location than I expected. I would agree that it seems likely the 'meteor' might have moved it as well as causing the damage."

Now Marcus took a deep breath. "Aldinoch, I'm sure you have heard about the power I developed. I used it to restore an entire mountainside that exploded above me. I've been thinking about that day and wondering if I could use that power to try to move the moon somehow?"

Aldinoch choked. A small globule of molten spittle flew from his mouth to lie sizzling on the sand. "I'm so sorry!" He gasped, putting a taloned hand to his mouth. "I'm just—it is just so—you want to *move the moon*?"

Marcus clenched his jaw. He felt so frustrated, what with Boehlkea's anger, and now his back ached miserably from sitting on the rock while waiting for so long for Aldinoch. These things were overwhelming, and he struggled to remain calm. Finally, he took a deep breath.

"Aldinoch, I know it sounds impossible. But there has to be something I can do to fix it, to save Lysomnus. I know there are limits to my power. I just thought that maybe there was a way, if you flew me very high into the sky, I could reach out with my power to try to push the moon back to its original orbit."

The massive Stondefel sighed, his warm breath blasting across Marcus in a gust of sulfur. "I apologize, Marcus. I do not mean to mock your idea. It's just that the moon is so large. It is very far away and bigger than the biggest mountains here on Lysomnus. I can't imagine how, even with your power, you could possibly attempt to do such a thing. We Stondefel can fly high, but there are limits. We must have air to breathe, and *you* need air too. It gets very cold when we fly high, and the air gets very thin up there, too thin to breathe and to stay up there, too. We cannot hold our own weight with our wings in that thin air."

Marcus sat back down dejectedly on the boulder. His head hung down in defeat. He wanted so badly to do *something*. While he was sitting there, the ground began rumbling beneath him. He looked around quickly, startled.

Aldinoch snatched Marcus up with sheathed talons, lifting him from the ground to protect him from the boulders that began to bounce around as the rumbling continued. After several minutes, it stopped.

“It wasn’t nearly as bad this time,” he said to Marcus. “Not here, anyway. It might have been stronger elsewhere. I will have to talk to my brothers to find out.”

Marcus gasped as Aldinoch gently placed him back on his feet. Pain lanced through his body as his legs bore his weight again. The demon pinched the boy’s cane between two talons from the ground where it had fallen and held it out to him. Marcus took it, thanking the Stondefel.

“Do you see why it is so important to try to solve this problem? These quakes will continue, or even get worse, as the moon moves through its changed orbit. It might even be on a deteriorating orbit that will eventually bring it down and crash into Lysomnus! That would kill everyone and everything on this planet. I *have* to figure something out!” Marcus was so frustrated, he found himself unable to keep from raising his voice.

“If only there was a way to help you reach out that far with your power, to make it stronger. Or someone else with power to help you,” Aldinoch said thoughtfully.

“That’s it!” Marcus shouted. “The Halfriez!” Then he stopped, his hand over the lump in the chest pocket of his suit. “But it’s so small. The one I have isn’t large enough to give me that kind of boost. It helped me heal Anneberg, but it isn’t strong enough for this.” If only there were more, Marcus thought. He realized he needed that missing page from the book of Talismans now more than ever.

“I guess I just need more time, as hard as that is right now with all this happening so fast. I’m going to stay here for a short while with

Pelamis and Boehlkea, but not as long as I'd hoped to. It's clear now that I will need to leave soon to try to find out more about the Halfriez and how to find more, if that's possible. Will the Stondefel be available if I need you quickly?"

Aldinoch placed a taloned finger on Marcus's shoulder. The weight of it hurt his back, but the warmth of it and the Stondefel's gesture of friendship made him feel good. "We will always be here to help you, Marcus," the demon rumbled. "Simply signal again, and whoever is flying in this area will be here as soon as they see it."

"Thank you, Aldinoch. I am happy to have met you. I hope we get to talk again soon and have the time to discuss astronomy in depth sometime in the future," Marcus said with a smile.

"I would like that also," Aldinoch said with a chuckle. He walked away from Marcus before launching himself into the sky.

Marcus sighed and carefully made his way back to the stones that marked the entrance to Fisc. He felt sweaty inside the suit he wore for swimming in Fisc. The sun was hot here on the beach, and the suit wasn't made for wearing outside the coolness of the Diluvium.

Leaning his cane against the rock once more, he grabbed the face mask. Once he walked a short way in, he lowered himself into the water and started swimming. Feeling the chill of the ocean through the suit was a relief.

He was moving more easily now that the ocean currents had calmed, and he soon surfaced in Fisc. He looked around, noting the home of Pelamis and Boehlkea and propelling himself in that direction. He hadn't been made aware of any way to announce himself or let them know he was there, so he hoped he wasn't going to upset them by just swimming down into their home.

When he surfaced in the pool, he saw only Pelamis, floating on the surface nearby. She appeared to be asleep. He carefully climbed out and sat on the ledge, trying to be as quiet as possible. With all that had happened, he knew she needed her rest. Marcus wondered where Boehlkea was; although she had been very upset after learning about Deacon's death, he didn't think she would stay away from her mother for too long. He had hoped to be able to talk to her again upon his return.

With a sigh, he made his way over to some pillows stacked nearby. Boehlkea must sleep on the ledge or lie on it since she didn't have to stay in the water all the time. Marcus realized he was exhausted. He crawled onto the pile of pillows and drifted off to sleep.

Someone was shaking Marcus. It hurt. His eyes snapped open to see Boehlkea looming over him, scowling with fury.

"You've made yourself quite at home here, haven't you?" she said, her blue eyes sparkling angrily. "Nice of you to appropriate my bed without asking."

"Uh—sorry," Marcus mumbled, trying to wipe the sleep from his eyes. He looked for Pelamis but didn't see her. "I came here looking for you and your mom, but you weren't here, and your mom was sleeping. I was so tired I just couldn't help it."

"Whatever." Boehlkea slipped into the water. "Put your facemask on and follow me. It's time to eat. Mom thinks you deserve our hospitality still, even after what you've done."

"Boehlkea—" Marcus began as he sat on the edge of the pool, reaching for his facemask.

She held up one blue-green hand. "I don't want to hear it, Marcus!"

With a sigh, he put the mask on and lowered himself into the water, following his sister. She led him out of her home and, once they had surfaced, to another, larger circle of stones and down another tunnel.

This time, they came to the surface in a much larger interior pool where many Muirnati swam about. Several called out a greeting to Marcus, and he smiled and waved before following Boehlkea, who was leaving him behind and swimming toward the side of the pool.

There, he found Pelamis talking to a small creature standing on the ledge that wrapped around the edge of the pool. This was a new one he hadn't seen before. There were more legs than he'd ever seen on a small sea creature and a round body. The creature walked on what Marcus counted out to be six legs. There was a torso with four arms that extended out in front of the body, all of which ended in useful appendages. Two were pincers, and the others were two fingered hands with opposable thumbs. The entire thing was bright yellow, about the size of a small dog, and covered in a protective carapace. A small mouth appeared at the bottom of his round head as he talked. Four tall stalks extended from the top of his head, ending in globulous eyes that looked in all directions. One of these was trained attentively on Pelamis as she spoke to him. Another appeared to be watching him as he approached.

"Oh, Marcus, there you are," Pelamis said when she caught sight of him. "This is Paracles. He is an Aragani. They live near Fisc and come and work with us here, doing things we are unable to do out of the water. We trade things that they need in exchange for their help. Paracles, this is Marcus."

"Hello," Paracles said. He had a squeaky voice that nearly startled Marcus into laughter. It was a struggle, but Marcus managed to keep a straight face. He thought it was fortunate that Leopold wasn't there.

"Hello, Paracles. Are your people the ones who dried my clothes for me?"

"Yes," Paracles said. "We also cook when the Muirnati choose not to eat raw fish or want to eat the other food they trade for or harvest in the ocean in prepared dishes. They make baskets and nets for us to catch fish with and give us food from their trades and other goods we ask for."

"Marcus," Pelamis said after Peracles had finished. "I thought you might be hungry since it has been some time since you arrived. We like to eat communally here in Fisc occasionally, and I asked Boehlkea to bring you here to join us. Please let Paracles know what you would like to eat, and he and the other Aragani will bring it to you. Feel free to sit on the ledge to eat. We want you to be comfortable."

Marcus admitted, "You're right, I am hungry. I wondered how humans eating worked here since so much of your home is underwater. I haven't heard anything about the Aragani the entire time I've been here in Lysomnus. I'm glad to have this chance to meet you, Paracles!" He held out his left hand to the Aragani. Paracles held out his own small hand, and Marcus shook it.

"I'm glad to meet you too, Marcus. You were not here for long during your first visit, so none of us had the opportunity to meet you. Not many of the people of Lysomnus come into Fisc—other than the bad humans. We are able to go out of the Diluvium to meet others, but they are all so large, we find it intimidating without a way to meet them safely. No one wants to get stepped on! I fear they may have forgotten about us."

"I am glad that I have had this opportunity to meet you, Paracles. And I will tell as many people as I can all about you when I get the chance!" Marcus assured the Aragani. "I hope it isn't an imposition if I ask for some food?" he said wistfully.

"Absolutely not!" Paracles squeaked. "I would be happy to bring you whatever you'd like!"

After Marcus had asked Paracles to bring him a selection of Muirnati dishes, he turned back to Pelamis. "I had a long conversation with one of the Stondefel. I know I said I want to visit for a long time, and I do, but I think this problem with the quakes we're experiencing is going to rapidly become urgent."

"I agree," she nodded. "Of course, we felt the one that occurred right before you arrived, but what can anyone possibly do about them?"

Marcus ducked behind his raised arm as water splashed him from a passing Muirnati's sudden dive. "Erm," he said, wiping water out of his eyes with his fingers, "I think it has to do with the damage to the moon like we were talking about before. Aldinoch told me a little more about the meteor that damaged Lysomnus's moon and the change in the distance from Lysomnus, and I believe it might even be traveling in a different pattern around the planet. I know this all sounds confusing to you, Pelamis. But it is extremely likely the quakes are going to get worse. I believe the end result could be the destruction of the entire planet."

Pelamis's face went pale just as Paracles' approaching feet clicked on the ledge. "Excuse me for interrupting," he said, "but I have your food, Marcus."

"Oh, thank you, Paracles," Marcus said, somewhat glad of the interruption. Pelamis needed a moment to deal with the shock of what he had just told her, and he was very hungry and needed to eat. Paracles had brought him a full plate and was followed by two more Aragani, each carrying a plate with more food. They placed the plates next to Marcus, murmured a greeting, and hurried away, obviously busy during this dinner hour.

Marcus was eager to try more of the food here in Fisc. He'd had the fish before, as some had been left with his clothes when he'd left the bruwe the last time. This time, it was prepared differently, with a delicious white sauce. The other plates held plants he had never seen before, with beautiful colors and flavors. Some were sweet, and others savory, but each was distinct and like nothing he had ever tasted. Everything had a hint of salt. He thought the emeristan the Fyrtudo mined for must be one of the most highly sought items on all of Lysomnus since it was so versatile. It was obviously used here, under the sea, to cook with and was also used by the Scrybb, who dreaded fire and would not be able to cook without it. He wondered if the Cativera used it, as well.

Pelamis waited politely while he ate his fill. As he was eating, she turned and gestured to one of the Muirnati on the other side of the pool. The man swam over, and Pelamis asked him a question. He soon returned with a gelatinous pouch. Nodding to Marcus, he handed the pouch to Pelamis and swam away.

"I hope you don't think everyone is rude for not coming to talk to us, Marcus," Pelamis said. "I quietly told some friends about Deacon, and they spread the word. Our people give the grieving plenty of time and space. We will not be bothered unless we seek out company."

"That is a thoughtful thing for your people to do," Marcus said.

She held out the pouch the Muirnati man had brought to her. "This is some juice, Marcus. We don't need to drink since we take in our hydration as we swim in the water, but we enjoy some fruit juice from time to time. You *do* need to drink, however, so I had this brought for you."

Marcus thanked her and lifted the odd pouch, untying the cord that held the limp bag closed. It felt weird against his mouth, but when he drank, he tasted the familiar juice of the sartine.

"What is this made from?" he asked after he'd swallowed, indicating the pouch as he tied it closed again.

"It is a creature that lives in the Diluvium. Once its life cycle is over, we harvest them to use for purposes like this," Pelamis said.

Like a jellyfish, Marcus thought, looking at the pouch. *But not.* He had noticed there were a lot of similarities between the two worlds, but they were also incredibly different. The symbiosis of Lysomnus was something he wished Earth had—or *had* had, he thought, grief stabbing at his heart.

"So," he began, ready to get back to the subject. "When Aldinoch and I were talking, one of the things I thought of was how the Halfriez I use can boost my power. I'm assuming you've seen it—my father used it frequently when he was here to help with his healing?" He raised his eyebrows as he looked at Pelamis.

She nodded. "The crystal cube, yes. But it's so small, it couldn't possibly boost your power enough to help you do anything about the whole *moon*, Marcus."

"Right. But when I was in the library in Palaga, I found a book about the Talismans of this world. There was a whole section about the Halfriez in there. Unfortunately, there was a page torn out. I couldn't tell whether that page had information about where the Halfriez comes from or if there are more—but I have to find it.

"Pelamis, I really don't want to leave right now. I originally intended to stay and visit with you and Boehlkea for an extended period of time, but now I *have* to go. I need to search that whole library and all of Lysomnus if need be. It is imperative that I find that page." Marcus stopped and realized his heart was pounding in his chest. Just by talking to Pelamis about the urgency of finding the missing page, he had gotten flustered again. Marcus's body was shaking with the realization that the fate of this planet and every living thing on it depended on him.

Pelamis had stopped moving—even her legs were still in the water—and she was staring at him. Her yellow eyes were as wide as he'd ever seen them. "Marcus, we don't have 'books' here in Fisc. We don't have a lot of things that can be found in the rest of Lysomnus because we live underwater. But—these books—are they made of slim, fragile leaves that have markings on them?"

"*Yes*!" Marcus shouted. Muirnati all across the pool turned to stare at him as his voice echoed through the room. Every other voice fell silent. Embarrassed at his outburst, Marcus felt his face warming at all the attention. "Sorry..."

"It's all right," Pelamis said. She turned to the rest of the Muirnati. "Everything's fine, everyone! We're fine." Slowly, the rest of the people in the crowded room returned to their own discussions.

Pelamis grabbed Marcus's hand. "Marcus, I think that—that—*leaf*—you're looking for is here, in Fisc! I think it's in my home. Quickly, put your face mask back on and follow me." She waited for him to slip the mask on and dove down under the water. Marcus felt like he couldn't swim fast enough this time, pushing his body through the water to keep up with Pelamis.

When they surfaced in the pool in Pelamis's home, Boehlkea was sitting on the ledge, propped up against the pillows where Marcus had slept earlier. As she caught sight of Marcus taking his facemask off, she rolled her eyes.

"Oh, for—"

"Boehlkea, just stop it." Pelamis's tone was stern, and she held up a hand to silence her daughter. "We do not have time for your petulant behavior right now. I am sorry that you are upset, but you're just going to have to get over it."

Boehlkea gasped in disbelief and slumped back against the pillows, crossing her arms over her chest. Pelamis ignored her and crossed to the far wall, where the ledge was very narrow. She reached over the ledge to the wall and pushed against one of the ridges just above the ledge.

With a click, a small section of the wall slid in and then over, exposing a compact space behind it. Pelamis reached in and rustled around, pulling out what Marcus recognized as an actual Ziploc storage bag from Earth. Inside was a page with an unevenly torn edge that had to be the one he'd been looking for since finding a page was missing from the book of Talismans back in the library at Palaga.

"What—how do you have that here?" Marcus cried out.

Pelamis turned to him and held it out. "Deacon," she said. "He brought it here a long time ago when he was much younger. He told me it could be very important someday and that the information on this page was too important to be available for anyone who might be looking in the library to find. He put it into this strange bag and asked me to keep it in a secret place where no one would find it. I hid it for him in my hidden compartment that day, and it's been there ever since."

Marcus had to restrain himself from rudely snatching the page from Pelamis's hands. He took it carefully, then set it on a wider area and pulled himself out of the water.

Boehlkea, who had listened to this entire exchange with a feigned look of disinterest on her face, now inched closer to Marcus, trying to see the page as he stared at it on the ledge beside him.

"Come look, Boehlkea," Marcus said quietly. "This has to do with our father. Of course I want to share it with you."

She slid closer to him. Together, they looked at the page. Writing at the top continued from the line Marcus had read from the one in the book—he didn't really remember what it had said now—but it read *a westerly course to the island only as a last resort, and do not go further for any reason.*

The map showed the Diluvium, with a compass at the top and a tall mound rising out of the water to the west. Below the picture was more writing. When Marcus read the words, he was speechless with shock. The Halfriez cube he had was just one small piece of a massive structure of crystal far out in the Diluvium! There was so much of this material, he could probably reach the moon with his power right from the ground with it. Apparently, it was dangerous to have a large quantity of it anywhere within reach of humans. The amplification effect it had on human power would be so great, it would be incredibly dangerous. For that reason, it was far out to sea, where it would be impossible to reach.

Marcus ran his hand through his wet curls. How could he get to this island of Halfriez material so he could use it to amplify his power to save Lysomnus? Maybe the Stondefel... He felt the plastic bag whisper across his hand as Boehlkea picked it up.

"Marcus, this is frightening. What would using this much of that crystal stuff to amplify your power do to you? A lot of what's on this page is warning people to stay away from this island. It's that far away for a reason." Boehlkea sounded anything but angry for the first time since he'd told her about their father.

"I understand that, Boehlkea. I really do," Marcus said earnestly, "but this could mean saving everyone—all of Lysomnus."

Pelamis put a hand on his right shoulder. "Marcus, it isn't worth losing your life in the attempt."

He looked down at her and put his left hand over hers. "Isn't it? Isn't it worth one life to save an entire planet? And we don't even know if the risk is really that high. It's worth trying. I know it is. Now I have to talk to the Stondefel and see if they can fly that far."

Boehlkea held onto his other shoulder and didn't let go. "At least let me come with you to the beach to see what they say. I want to see if it's even possible to ask them to fly that far."

"It's all right with me," Marcus said, looking at Pelamis. The

Muirnati woman shook her head and sighed. “I guess so, Boehlkea. But only to the beach. You know it’s not safe for you to go too far away from the Diluvium.”

Boehlkea chuckled as she looked at her mother. She slid into the water and hugged Pelamis. “No, I’d never do that to you, Mom. I know how hard it was for you when I was taken before. I don’t ever want to make you feel that way again. Especially now that—” Her voice caught, and she put a hand over her mouth.

“Thank you, my daughter,” Pelamis said softly, hugging Boehlkea back, her voice thick. “We’d better go get that signal flag back up so you and Marcus can find out if he can even make such a flight.”

Marcus slipped on his mask and followed them out. Once the signal was raised, Boehlkea came to the beach, where Marcus was waiting for her. She stepped out of the water, and they walked side-by-side to wait for one of the Stondefel to arrive.

“I’m sorry about how I acted before,” Boehlkea said, bumping Marcus gently with her shoulder as she walked next to him.

“S’okay,” he said. “I get it. I feel like I’m going to have to live with the guilt for the rest of my life, knowing that I sent him back there to die. I could have done so many other things,” he said, balling his left hand into a frustrated fist, “made so many other choices.” He stared up into the sky, looking for the shape of a Stondefel, but saw nothing yet. They sat down together on the rock where Marcus had waited before.

“No, brother,” Boehlkea said. “I do understand. As mad as I feel about *how* it happened, I do understand *why* you did what you did. Remember, I was there in that house. I heard everything that he said. Not just about you, but about Lysomnus and about *me*, too. That really hurt. And you couldn’t know what was happening on Earth, that he would be exposed to that disease.” She looked down at her hands, sliding her fingertips across them while the iridescent scales reflected the sun.

“Yeah,” he sighed. “You’re right. I couldn’t know. If he hadn’t been there to warn my friends and me, we would all have been exposed when we went home, and probably all would have died, too. But it still hurts." The pressure was back in his chest, and he could feel tears filling his eyes again. He wondered if he would ever stop feeling this pain.

Boehlkea put her arms around him. "I feel horrible for treating you the way I did, especially since you lost your mother, too. I can't imagine how that must feel to lose them both. I know it isn't the same in any way, but I will share my mom with you, Marcus."

Marcus tried to smile. The movement spilled tears down his cheeks that dripped on his legs. For a second, he felt embarrassed, crying in front of her, but if he couldn't cry with his sister, who was left? She was all the family he had, and he realized he was grateful to his father that he had her. He leaned his head on her shoulder, smelling the salt in her hair. Clumsily, he wrapped his left arm around her back. They sat like that together until Agatho landed with a sand-shaking thump on the beach nearby.

"Hello, young ones," the massive Stondefel rumbled. "What can I do for you this beautiful evening? Aldinoch has been telling us funny stories about how you think you can 'move the moon,' Marcus," he said, chuckling deep in his stony throat.

"Actually, Agatho, that's what I wanted to talk to you about," Marcus said.

Agatho gave him a wary look.

"Marcus, Aldinoch explained to you that we cannot fly high enough to get close to the moon. And you are overestimating your power if you think you can affect something so large as the moon itself! It is much larger than the mountainside you repaired and even farther away than Anneberg was when you healed him during your abduction." Agatho's voice grew even more gravelly as he attempted to sound as stern as possible.

Marcus held up his hands. "Wait, Agatho. I understand it's too far away to fly *up* there. But what I need to talk to you about is something different. My father found a page in a book about the

Halfriez—you know, the cube I use to amplify my power? I used it when I healed Leopold after his leg was broken. It's just a small piece, but my father used it his entire life here, and it helped him do a lot of healing. It's helped me quite a bit already.

"I've discovered, from this page, that there is a much larger source for the Halfriez. With that amount of Halfriez material, it's very likely that I *could* actually use my power to push the moon back to its original orbit and stop the quakes from damaging Lysomnus. If its orbit is deteriorating, it *will* eventually crash into the planet and kill everything and everyone here."

Agatho was listening carefully, but he also looked wary. "There is something else, isn't there? This sounds too easy. What do you need from us, the Stondefel?"

Marcus looked up at the massive Stondefel, grabbing Boehlkea's hand with his own and holding it tight. "It's quite a distance out to sea, apparently. So far out that all the people of Lysomnus have forgotten about it. I need to know if you, the Stondefel, can fly that far with me. Then I can use it to try to fix the problem with the moon."

Agatho looked at Boehlkea. "Little sister, how far out to sea? It must be a long way if your people have not heard of this island of the Halfriez. Have you tried to determine just how far away this island is?"

Boehlkea released Marcus's hand and held her hand out to him. Marcus unzipped his suit, pulled the baggie out from inside the chest of the suit, and held it out to her.

"Oh, gross!" Boehlkea cried out as she took it, dropping the baggie into the sand. "It is all wet and smelly!"

"Sorry," Marcus said, his face flushing. "I didn't have any other way to carry it, so I just tucked it into my suit. It's kind of hot in here, especially the way things have been going today."

Agatho roared with laughter. "Oh, I am sorry, little brother," he said, "I do not mean to laugh at you. I cannot help it!"

Boehlkea giggled as she picked up the baggie with her fingertips. "It is kind of funny, Marcus," she said as she got up and walked to the water to rinse it off.

Marcus couldn't help but smile at his own discomfiture. It *was* funny, especially after the emotional roller coaster of the last few days. He thought again of Boehlkea's reaction when she touched the sweaty baggie and burst into laughter himself.

"Don't let any water get inside!" Marcus called out to her as she swished the bag back and forth through the incoming waves.

"Do not worry, brother," Boehlkea said, turning her head and smiling at him. "It is still sealed tightly. It was more likely to get wet from being soaked inside your suit than it is from being rinsed off in the Diluvium!"

When she had returned, she held it up so Agatho could take it. He pinched it carefully between two sheathed talons and peered at the old page closely through the plastic baggie.

"It is difficult to see clearly through the wet and wrinkled material of this wrapping," he said after a few moments. "Can you remove it?" He handed it back to them.

Marcus was nervous about removing the precious page from the protection of the baggie, but it was important to figure out just where the island of Halfriez material was. He unsealed the plastic and slid the paper from inside, then held it up to the Stondefel.

Agatho held the page flat in one great palm, pinning it down with one sheathed talon. He inspected it closely. "I can see where the shoreline of the continent lies, and there is a line on here with some numbers. I do not know what that means."

Marcus held his left hand up. "I think that might be a scale! On maps, there's usually a scale that indicates distance. We should be able to figure out how far away the island is from the shoreline if we can understand the scale."

Agatho handed the page back to Marcus, then peered down over his and Boehlkea's shoulders as they hunched over it. Marcus saw, as he looked over the whole page, that the map was partial—it didn't show the entire continent, only the western shoreline where the Diluvium met the land. He could see the Grenewud and the coast where he and Leopold and Sadie had been when they first came to

Lysomnus. The lines of the paths the Scrybb maintained through the Grenewud were marked as far as the map extended; Thicce Colpat could be seen not far from the ocean shore. The Zabanara region was shown as well, but the map didn't extend as far as Grasian. Fisc was clearly marked, along with the bones of the Shoal. A great expanse of sea showed very few landmarks; some small islands here and there looked insignificant compared to the vastness of the Diluvium.

Finally, the island where the Halfriez could be found was shown toward the outer edge of the map. At the very edge was a strange symbol that looked like two stacked diamonds with a line through them vertically.

Boehlkea pointed at the scale at the bottom of the map. Marcus looked around for anything they could use to help them interpret the scale. He saw what looked like an old fish bone and carefully squatted to pick it up. He grunted with the effort.

"Marcus!" Boehlkea scolded. "I would have gotten that. You don't need to hurt yourself."

Marcus shrugged, handing her the bone. "I'm sorry I didn't stop to think about it. I guess I felt like I had to do it myself since the people I'm used to having around aren't here."

Boehlkea's blue eyes filled with pain. "I hope that it will not take too long for you to think of me as one of the people you have around whom you can ask for help."

"I...I'm sorry Boehlkea," Marcus stammered. "I didn't mean it like that. You're my sister, and I know you will feel like family. Probably faster than you think." Boehlkea smiled at him, and tears slipped over her lower eyelids to run down her face and drop to the sand. Marcus brushed them from her cheek with a smile before turning back to the map in his prosthetic hand.

He brushed the crumbles of sand from the bone before settling it on the page and said, "It really looks like that island is a long way out there."

Boehlkea shook her head, eyes wide with wonder. "I had no idea the Diluvium was so big. My people live in it, but I think we are somewhat too used to being comfortable in our bruwe. We don't often travel very far from home or have much of an idea of just how big the Diluvium really is."

Agatho pointed at the map. "What does that bone tell you?" he rumbled impatiently.

Marcus flattened the bone to the scale. It was almost exactly the same length. He laid it between Fisc and Palaga. Using his prosthetic finger as a marker, he moved the bone to the other side.

"So, it's two lengths of this scale between Fisc and Palaga. How long of a flight is that, Agatho?"

Agatho thought for a moment. "Probably four hours, depending on the air patterns."

Marcus started looking at the distance on the map between Fisc and the island of Halfriez. As he started laying the bone, Boehlkea placed a finger for each time he needed to move it. They could all see before long that it would take many flips of the bone to reach the island—more fingers than they all had together, several times.

"Marcus, it will take *days* to fly to this island. We can fly for several hours, but not even the strongest among us can fly for a full day without stopping. This map shows only a few small land masses between Fisc and that island where we could stop for rest. How could we carry enough supplies to get there, much less to return? Carrying food for a human is one thing. Carrying food for a Stondefel is quite another." Agatho shook his head. "This task is impossible."

Marcus wanted to scream. Every time a possible solution presented itself, another obstacle appeared to block the way. He sat down on the boulder, hands over his face. Even in his frustration, he noticed the difference between his warm, fleshed hand and the cold, metallic prosthetic he now wore.

Boehlkea sat down next to him, wrapping her arms around him. "We'll think of something," she whispered. "There has to be a way." Marcus dejectedly placed the map back in its protective bag, which had now dried in the sun, and tucked it into his suit again. When he opened the suit to tuck the bag in, he got a good whiff of himself and had to cough to cover a gag. He reeked!

Agatho paced back and forth in front of them. His taloned feet sank into the beach, leaving prints deep in the sand. Marcus imagined what some archaeologist from Earth would have made of them, had they found them back home. The impressions of six feet with those long, sharp talons on them? Such an alien creature! Well, Marcus thought, on Earth, Agatho would be an alien. Here, *he* was an alien. But he was allowing himself to get distracted from the task at hand.

"I just can't think of what to do! If we can't fly there—I don't know how we'll do it. It's so far. I really thought we had the answer when we found that page," he said, kicking at the sand in frustration, even though it hurt.

Agatho said, "Perhaps I can go to the other people of Lysomnus and see if there are any among them with any ideas. Your friends may have some thoughts, as well. The Stondefel will fly across Lysomnus to visit everyone and find a solution to this problem! We will get you to that island, Marcus."

"I guess all I can do is wait, then," Marcus said, using his cane to get to his feet again. "I'll stay with Boehlkea and Pelamis and wait to hear from you. I just hope it doesn't take too long because I believe these quakes are going to get a lot worse."

Boehlkea stood up beside him. "I know how urgent it is that we find a way to get out there, Marcus. Until then, it will be difficult to wait. But I do have some selfish reasons to be glad you'll be here with us while you do. I'd like you to meet Melacara. She's my girlfriend. That's where I went when I left before when I was mad."

"Very well," Agatho said. "You will be in good company here. I go with haste to my brothers. We will find a solution. And return soon!" He launched himself from the beach, disappearing into the sky with surprising rapidity.

Marcus turned to Boehlkea. "So, a girlfriend, huh? You never mentioned that before."

"We've never really had that much time to talk about regular things before," Boehlkea smiled, taking him by the hand. "I can't wait for you to meet her. Let's get back to Fisc. I have the feeling we're going to be waiting for a few days, at least."

CHAPTER SIX

YOU'RE GOING TO NEED A BOAT

Sadie

Sadie was sitting cross-legged in the sun with Cornus, several of the Cativera children, and one of their instructors, following along with the day's lessons in sign language, when she saw Yati entering Grasian at a run. They looked around, spotted her, and walked directly to her, signaling quickly.

"Please, slow down, Yati," she begged out loud. "I'm still learning, and you are signing so fast."

"Sadie," they said. "Stondefel. Ye kim." They pointed down the road leading out of the bruwe. Then they looked at Cornus. "And ye, Cornus." The Scrybb boy looked startled but got to his feet.

Sadie also stood up, brushing the dust from her pants. "What could they want from us? I wonder if that quake caused something bad to happen somewhere else?"

Cornus looked at her, a worried expression crumpling the leaves on his face. "I hope not. But I think we would have heard something by now if that were the case. It has been several days."

"Well, let's go find out," Sadie said, signing her regret to the instructor, who nodded and spoke sharply to the Cativeran students. They immediately returned their attention to the teacher.

Yati signed, "I will escort you," to Sadie, who signed back that she and Cornus would walk with them to where the Stondefel was waiting. The Cativera preferred that their visitors were always accompanied by one of the herders whenever they left Grasian, to ensure both their safety and to keep the Struthtaur calm. The quake had greatly disturbed the nervous creatures, and they had been much more agitated since then. It had taken several days for the Cativera to find all the Struthtaur and bring them back to their own fields. Several had been injured and had to be put down. Sadie learned more about butchering and preserving meat than she had ever really wanted to know.

For instance, most of the people of Lysomnus ate reconstituted meat that had been carefully dried so that it could be rehydrated and still retain flavor and texture. Only the Cativera truly enjoyed the fresh meat of the Struthtaur. Now that all the people had befriended and could ask the Stondefel, perhaps the rest of the people of Lysomnus could also benefit from fresh meat and fish as well—Sadie assumed the fish from the Muirnati were most likely traded in a preserved state like the meat.

Sadie walked alone with her own thoughts along the red clay road. They couldn't talk out loud as any noise might set off the Struthtaur. She and Cornus hadn't learned enough of the Cativeran sign language to keep up with Yati, although now that she thought about it, they would learn faster if they did practice by talking to the adults and not just while learning with the children.

She wondered if they should have grabbed their belongings; but then, hopefully this was just a check-in, to see how they were or to bring them some information. Neither she nor Cornus were ready to leave Grasian yet. They were both enjoying their time with the friendly people of the Zabanara region. She'd gotten to know so many of them, not just the instructors who were helping her learn their sign language and verbal language, but also the herders, and those who cared for the very young children, and also the people who nurtured the loka mounds to the south. Here in Lysomnus, in every bruwe she had visited, people all had specific duties they performed.

Not for money, or because someone told them to, but because they knew it was necessary and because they enjoyed their labor. All of Lysomnus was extremely harmonious. The relationships between the people, the creatures, and the other forms of life here worked because they lived in cooperation, traded goods or services, and agreed to a shared life.

Her own grief had nearly swallowed her. She had been very close to her own family. Losing her parents felt cataclysmic, but nothing was as excruciating as the loss of her little brother. He had been three years younger than her, and she had felt as connected to him as if he were her twin. Her love for languages came from learning to communicate with him. In a way, learning the languages here on Lysomnus felt like a dedication to his memory. It kept him fresh in her heart, even though the pain of losing him was still there.

Cornus walked closer to her, bumping her with an elbow. The two of them had grown closer while living together among the Cativera. Cornus's small size and somewhat immature behavior reminded her of a younger brother, and she couldn't help but respond to that. Learning Cativeran sign language together was fun, and they'd made it a challenge to see who could learn faster. Cornus had the early advantage, having been there first and longer, but Sadie was faster at learning new languages and more familiar with sign languages. She had caught up quickly and Cornus had been challenged to keep up with her. They could both communicate quite well with the Cativera in sign language, but usually, the Cativera had to sign slowly so Sadie and Cornus could translate in their heads. Fast signing left them lost, but Sadie had the feeling that a little more time would find them much more fluent. If they didn't have to leave for whatever this was.

Yati kept them moving at a brisk pace, and it didn't take long to reach the field where they found Anneberg waiting for them. The Cativera bowed gravely to the Stondefel, who asked them a question in sign language. Yati nodded, signing back. Sadie was amused to see that Anneberg was asking after Yati's family, since the herder's sibling had recently added a new baby to their family. It seemed the Stondefel missed nothing, even from their high vantage point above Lysomnus.

"Anneberg," Cornus cried out as quietly as he could, "why have you come for us? We don't have to leave Grasian, do we?" The young Scrybb was upset by the idea of leaving the bruwe he'd come to find so comfortable already. Sadie knew Cornus planned to spend several months of his Travel year here in the Zabanara region.

"Be easy, Cornus," rumbled the Stondefel. "I am only here with questions. Marcus has a problem, and we seek help."

"Marcus?" Sadie exclaimed. "Is he okay?" Then she flushed as the others turned to her, smiling with amusement at her obvious concern. "I—I only meant—well, *is* he?"

"Marcus is fine. No one was injured in Fisc, which is where Marcus is right now, visiting his sister. However, he has determined that the shaking that affected us all was caused by the damage to Lysomnus's moon, and he may have discovered a way to fix it." Anneberg was rapidly signing to Yati as he spoke to Sadie and Cornus.

"Fix the *moon*?" Cornus asked incredulously. "How would that be possible?"

"That is partly why I am here," Anneberg said. "You are all so full of questions, I cannot get a word in to tell you."

"Sorry," Sadie said. Cornus closed his mouth tightly.

Yati, who had said nothing, simply watched Anneberg intently.

"Marcus says there is an island made of the same material as his Halfriez far out in the Diluvium. It is too far away for us, the Stondefel, to fly there. No one can come up with a solution for him to reach it. If he can get to this island, Marcus feels he can use the Halfriez material to boost his power enough to move the moon and save Lysomnus."

Yati looked at them all. They sank their spear into the ground point first and signed, "This is surely a joke?"

"I don't think it is, Yati," Sadie said. "It does sound preposterous, Anneberg."

"Marcus *has* done some impressive things with his power," Cornus pondered. "But *moving the moon*?"

"I know it is difficult to believe," Anneberg said. "But he has convinced Agatho and Aldinoch, and I believe them. Our only problem right now is getting him to that island, which is quite a distance out into the Dilivium. It is too far for any of us to fly."

"Well," Sadie said, "if that's the only problem, why not find him a boat?"

Anneberg tipped his great horned head quizzically. "A what?"

"A boat," Sadie said patiently. "A vessel for traveling on water? Has no one from this land ever left it on the water?"

"I don't think so," Cornus said. "I have never heard of this means of travel. We have our carts, or we walk. The Muirnati swim. And, of course, recently, we have flown on the backs of the Stondefel. But I have never heard of a 'boat' before. Or anyone traveling *on* the water."

"Oh, my," Sadie said. "Well, I think that's what Marcus needs. Where is Leopold? He'll know what a boat is, and perhaps know how to make one or at least design one for other crafters to make?"

"Hmmm. Leopold is with the other humans. I believe Aldinoch went to find him. Perhaps I can intercept him or catch up with them, and we can discuss this 'boat'."

"Anneberg—" Sadie said quickly before the Stondefel could take off. He turned back to look at her expectantly.

"If it's not too much trouble, could you ask Tartarus if he could look for a few more language books in the library and have one of you bring them down to me? I'd take great care of them." She winced internally as she thought of the broken cover on the book she'd brought with her already, although that wasn't really her fault.

"Of course, Sadie," Anneberg rumbled. "As soon as I am done with Leopold and Aldinoch, I will talk to Tartarus. And that reminds me... Marcus sent you a gift from the Scrybb." He plucked a small package from his back and handed it to her.

"Oh, thank you," Sadie said. "I will wait until we return to Grasian to open this."

Anneberg nodded, then launched himself skyward with a mighty flap of his wings. The three of them watched as he dwindled to a tiny dot in the sky.

“That was an unbelievable tale,” signed Yati.

“I know it is difficult to believe, but we have all felt the shaking, and if Marcus says he can do something to stop it, I believe him,” Sadie signed back slowly.

“Moving the moon?” Cornus signed. “I believe in Marcus, but that is hard to imagine.”

They all turned together and headed back down the road toward Grasian. It was interesting news they had to bring back to Cata. The Monarch would want to know what plan was in the works to stop the quakes. The hours after the first one had been terrifying for Cata, as they'd been trapped in their office for a long time until the doors could be forced open. The second incident of rumbling had sent them dashing to the surface in terror. Sadie hoped this plan made the Monarch feel less fear and at least some hope for the future.

They all found themselves looking at the skies where Anneberg had flown away as they walked home, as if they could watch him as he journeyed to find Leopold.

CHAPTER SEVEN

BUILDING 'SHIPS

Leopold

Leopold was pulling a cart at the front of a long column of humans, head down as he pulled his side of a cart handle. Jarel was on the other side. The cart behind them was loaded with logs. They'd used the design of the cart that Leopold and his friends had received as a gift from Abutilon and Buddleja. He knew it wasn't as good as the incredible craftsmanship of the Scrybb, but the humans had made several serviceable carts and were moving most of the materials they'd salvaged from their destroyed bruwe.

Suddenly Jarel cried out. "Look!" Yells and shouts from the line behind them echoed Jarel's first call, and as Leopold looked up, sweat ran into his right eye. He armed it away irritably.

A Stondefel winged down to the red clay road cutting through the tall grasses of the Zabanara region all around them. With the sweat in his eyes, Leopold couldn't make out *who* it was. He blinked and wiped at his eyes furiously. His hands and face were wet with sweat, so he couldn't clear his vision properly.

"I'm sorry, have we met before?" he said to the blurry demon standing on the road before him.

"No, I don't believe so. I am Aldinoch, and I am searching for Leopold, friend to Marcus Talent."

"Lucky for you, you found him," Leopold said, releasing his side of the cart handle. He heard a thump as Jarel also let his side go. The tall Black boy took the opportunity to step back and pull himself up on the end of the cart, groaning. Jarel flapped a hand at Leopold when he turned to look in his direction.

"Go talk to your giant stone friend, *bro*. I'll take a break here." Jarel panted, wiping sweat from his face. Leopold rolled his eyes. Jarel had taken to using Leopold's slang but in a sarcastic way that Leopold found incredibly annoying. Jarel pulled a water pouch from his side and untied it, chugging thirstily.

Leopold turned back to the Stondefel waiting patiently on the road in front of him.

"Al-Aldinoch? So, you've seen Marcus? Is he doing okay?"

"Yes, he is fine. He is staying with the Muirnati, but has asked the Stondefel to help seek out his friends for assistance." A concerned look crossed the demon's stony face as he peered more closely at Leopold. "Are you all right, young brother? You appear to be unwell."

"I—I don't feel so good," Leopold said, bending over with his hands on his knees. Nausea churned in his stomach, and the world seemed to swirl around him. He gasped for breath, his legs feeling like rubber beneath his hands.

The next thing he knew, he was lying on his back, with Jarel kneeling beside him. Aldinoch's cooling shadow blocked the sun's blinding glare from his face as the Stondefel leaned over him as well.

"What happened?" he mumbled.

Jarel wiped the sweat from his face and then laid another wet cloth on his forehead. "You passed out," he said, not quite meeting Leopold's eyes. "I think you've overdone it a bit today in this heat. We should probably let the whole group rest for a while, have some water and food and take a long break."

Aldinoch opened his wings and moved them gently, creating a breeze that felt wonderful to Leopold's overheated skin. "Sorry," he said, not sure who he was apologizing to, but feeling embarrassed for falling apart at such an inopportune time.

"It is quite all right, young one," Aldinoch said. "The matter is not so urgent you cannot rest for a while and regain your strength. I can wait."

Leopold closed his eyes and took a few breaths to let his body overcome the dizziness and nausea

"Here," Jarel said, and Leopold felt a water pouch at his lips. He drank without opening his eyes. After a few careful sips, he drifted off to sleep.

When he opened his eyes again, the sky was darkening, with a few rust-colored rays of sun reaching from the west, still providing enough light to see by. A short distance away, he could hear people talking, and he turned his head to see most of the humans congregating around a fire built in a flattened area clear of grass. The smell of cooking food filled the air.

He lifted himself to a sitting position. Jarel's jacket had been folded up beneath his head, which throbbed with a headache. Looking around, he saw two Stondefel and Jarel in the middle of the road, talking.

Feeling a bit wobbly, Leopold climbed to his feet and walked down the road to where Jarel and Aldinoch were, now joined by Anneberg.

"Hey," he said as he approached.

Jarel turned to look at him. "You're awake!" He stood up, dark eyes unreadable in the swiftly falling twilight. Holding out a hand, he waited for Leopold to take it, then pulled him closer and then urged him to sit on the ground beside him. A plate filled with food sat nearby, which Jarel grabbed and handed to Leopold.

"Eat. You need it."

Aldinoch rumbled a gruff chuckle and nodded. "Listen to this one," he said. "He is right. You could have hurt yourself today."

"How long was I out?" Leopold asked, around a mouth full of meat.

"Several hours," Jarel said. "And gross, don't talk with your mouth full."

Leopold laughed. "You sound like Marcus."

Jarel looked at him. "Marcus must be wise."

Leopold choked, nearly spitting out his food. Jarel pounded on his back, laughing.

"Got you."

"Boys," Aldinoch said. "Let us get back to what is important." They both straightened up and looked at the Stondefel.

"We have been discussing Marcus's problem with Jarel," Anneberg said. "I arrived while you were sleeping. I stopped to talk to Sadie earlier, and she says what is needed is a 'boat', a thing that can be used to travel on water."

"Yeah, I know what a boat is," Leopold said, waiting until after swallowing this time.

"As your friend Jarel has told us, these humans have made "boats" before, traveling out on the Diluvium to catch fish for food. He thinks it should be possible to design a boat for Marcus to travel on the Diluvium. He is unsure of the mechanism, however." Aldinoch looked at Jarel.

"Using a boat to fish on the Diluvium offshore is one thing," Jarel said to Leopold. "Traveling far out to sea is quite another. I don't know about the Diluvium on the west side of the continent, but we often have big storms on this side that come in from the ocean. A small boat will be thrown about and smashed by such weather. And we use oars and small sails to move our boats about, but that won't take a boat very far across the Diluvium."

"Why the heck would Marcus want to travel across the Diluvium?" Leopold asked, confused.

"Oh, yes. You were asleep for that part," Aldinoch said. "Marcus believes he can move the moon to stop all this shaking of the ground that is causing so much trouble."

Leopold gaped at him. "*Move the moon*? Has he lost his marbles?"

Aldinoch pulled his head back and tipped it curiously to one side. "What are marbles?"

"Oh, not this again. Never mind the marbles! How is Marcus going to move an entire moon, and why does he think that will fix anything?" Leopold could feel his face reddening with frustration.

"Calm, young one," Anneberg rumbled soothingly. Jarel patted Leopold's back, then started rubbing in small circles between his shoulder blades. "Just take it easy, and we'll figure this out, okay?" he said. Leopold felt calmer just with Jarel touching him.

Aldinoch spoke again. "Marcus says when a 'meteor' hit our moon, it hit it hard enough to move it out of—what was the word? Orbit. Yes, orbit. He says the change in the orbit of the moon is causing the shaking as it gets closer to Lysomnus. And that it could be getting worse and eventually crash into Lysomnus."

"That's terrible!" Leopold cried out. "But what does Marcus going out to sea have to do with him trying to move the moon?"

Anneberg broke in. "Apparently, he has found a page from a book about the Halfriez cube that showed him there is a large source of the same material far out in the Diluvium. He believes if he could get to it, he could use it to boost his power enough to affect the moon, helping him move it back to its original place and stopping the shaking we have experienced. But time is of the essence, as we must create this 'boat', and get Marcus on his way."

Leopold felt like his head was spinning with all the news. On top of the heat exhaustion he had suffered earlier, he was overwhelmed. He pressed his hands to the sides of his head, thinking.

"Okay," he began, holding his hands out to the sides. "We don't just need a boat; we need a *ship.* I don't know much about actual ship building except that my dad and I used to build miniature ships inside bottles, so I know the basic parts, and what it should look like.

"We need to take the people from here who know how to make *actual* boats to Thicce Colpat. Their Crafters might be able to build a working sailing ship, if I tell them the parts, and the humans give them the basics about boat-making. They may have the idea for how to move the boat in the best fashion—they're the ones who are the best at crafting, so give them the challenge. Marcus shouldn't go alone on this trip. He needs to have people who know the Diluvium with him."

Both Stondefel pulled themselves up straight, looking pleased. "Excellent!" rumbled Aldinoch. "Talk to these humans, and we will bring them to Thicce Colpat first thing in the morning!"

"Um..." Leopold started, "I *think* it might be a good idea if I came along. The Scrybb might be a bit unhappy if strange humans are just dropped off in their bruwe. And maybe Jarel could come?" He looked hopefully at Jarel.

"Who will continue the journey with our people to find and start the new bruwe?" Jarel asked.

Leopold's shoulders slumped. "Oh, I forgot."

Anneberg put a sheathed talon under Leopold's chin. "Never fear, young brother. Aldinoch can take all of you to Thicce Colpat, and I will help the rest of the humans. I have seen several likely spots for a bruwe for them while flying that I was going to mention anyway. I can guide them."

Jarel smiled at Leopold. "I will be glad to go with you."

Leopold's smile felt so wide his face hurt. "Let's go find some boat builders!"

By the time Aldinoch landed in Far Field, Leopold felt a bit abraded. Without the harnesses they usually used when riding the Stondefel, they had needed to improvise and use the ropes the humans had, and while flying with four people, Leopold had gotten rubbed raw in a couple of spots.

Once they dismounted, he hardly noticed the soreness, with the excitement of three humans who had just experienced their first flight, and preparing to face the Scrybb again for the first time since that terrible day on Awar's back. His emotions were high and all mixed up.

Anneberg had told him about Marcus's visit to Thicce Colpat and the Scrybb's changed views about humans and Stondefel, but Leopold couldn't help but still feel anger for the way the Scrybb had hurt Awar. He hadn't been back here since then. Awar had died not long after that day.

Jarel sensed the change in Leopold's demeanor and asked what was wrong. As they walked slowly down the shaded, tree-lined path toward Thicce Colpat, Leopold told Jarel about Awar. He began with the time he'd met the young Stondefel and continued talking until he had to talk about learning of his friend's death from Marcus. He told Jarel about their connection, their instant friendship and the camaraderie they had developed. Leopold liked almost everyone he had met in Lysomnus, but he had forged a special bond with Awar. He hadn't felt anything like it—at least, not until he met Jarel.

Jarel grabbed Leopold's hand, pulling him gently to a stop. Then he put his arms around him and just held him. Slowly, Leopold raised his arms and embraced Jarel. He laid his head on Jarel's shoulder and allowed himself to be held and comforted. When he felt the tears come, he let them flow.

For the first time since Awar's death, Leopold cried for his friend. The pain of the Stondefel's death had been tearing at him, and he hadn't grieved. Then the loss of his family had forced his attention away from it. Now, he could finally allow himself to feel it again.

As his sobs quieted, he realized he didn't feel embarrassed about releasing his emotions in front of Jarel. Jarel had made him feel so comfortable, just letting him know he was there, and he had felt safe to let go.

Acting on impulse, he put a hand on Jarel's cheek, feeling the smoothness of the other boy's face above the rough hair on his jaw. Then he tilted his own face and kissed Jarel.

After a moment that seemed to last forever to Leopold, Jarel kissed him back. They stood there for a moment, mouths moving together, Jarel's arms around Leopold, Leopold's hand on Jarel's face. Then the kiss broke and Jarel stepped back. He looked into Leopold's eyes for the first time and smiled.

Janke and Maril were standing on the side of the path, looking discreetly away from the boys. When Jarel called out to them, they smiled reassuringly at the boy they had raised and joined him and Leopold on the path. The four of them walked together the rest of the way to Thicce Colpat. Leopold held tightly to Jarel's hand the entire way. He felt almost as if he were in a dream, and was afraid to let go of Jarel because the dream might end if he did.

When they entered the bruwe, Leopold looked around to see if he recognized anyone nearby. He had spent time with several of the adult Scrybb while staying in Thicce Colpat when he and the others had first arrived in Lysomnus and hoped to see some of them among the many people who were out and about in the bruwe.

He caught sight of a man he remembered from his time observing the Crafters, a taller Scrybb named Copros. His thick, waxy round leaves were easily identifiable, and Leopold made himself release Jarel's hand to jog after him.

"Copros!" he called. The Scrybb stopped and turned with a startled look on his face.

"Leopold! I am glad to see you." Then his face fell, remorse evident in every drooping leaf. "I am so sorry for how we acted when you were here with your friend, the Stondefel, before. Many of us were swept up in the madness, and I regret what we did. There is no excuse for our actions."

"I believe that many of you didn't want to attack him," Leopold said. "But I think that discussion is better left for another time. There is an emergency, and we need your help." He gestured to Jarel and the others.

"What can the Scrybb do for humans?" Copros asked warily.

"We need to build a ship, a vessel for travel on the waters of the Diluvium. These two humans—" he indicated Janke and Maril "—know how to build small sailing boats but we need a very big one. We would like the expertise and skill of your Crafters on how to make a vessel that can travel far out on the Diluvium. The humans' current boats are only safe for a short distance from shore, and we need the means to propel the boat farther and more safely."

Copros frowned. "I think we will need to gather the Teachers and the Crafters together to discuss this. I know we have made peace between us, but it is another thing if I were to offer our services to build something for you on my own."

Leopold looked around the bustling bruwe, seeing Scrybb scattered around everywhere. "I hope it will not take long to get everyone together and hold this meeting. It is of some urgency. Marcus believes he can do something about the shaking that has been happening, but he needs this boat to do it."

Copros nodded. "I will find Cassiope, and ask her to gather the Teachers, and I will assemble the Crafters. We will meet in the dining hall. I will see you there soon." He bustled away.

Leopold turned to Jarel with his hands on his hips, raising his eyebrows and blowing out a breath. "I hope they're willing to do this," he said.

"If not, we will simply have to try to do it on our own," Jarel replied. "We have the basic knowledge to build a boat, we just have to think of a way to make it bigger and then sail it across the Diluvium."

Leopold rolled his eyes at the mental picture of Marcus sailing across the Diluvium in a small boat. It would take so long he'd never get there!

"Doesn't Marcus have the same abilities that Nun the Wiser had?" asked Maril, peering through her long, dark brown hair. She seemed shyer now that they were away from the humans.

"Yes, he does."

"Can't he just move the boat himself then?" she asked.

"Well, personally, I'm concerned about Marcus using his power for other things all the time. Nun the Wiser suffered a lot of physical damage by using her power so much and I don't want to see that happen to Marcus. There's no Deacon anymore to heal him from those effects, and if he uses a lot of power to travel to the island, he needs to reach to actually fix the moon—if he is able to. If he weakens his body during the voyage, he may not be able to do the job when he gets there."

Janke was nodding. "That makes sense. Nun the Wiser was physically weak and suffered from using her power." His light blue eyes darted from Leopold to Jarel as he spoke; the burly man was eager to be a part of the mission. The idea of the ship had excited him a great deal.

Leopold caught sight of Copros returning to their little group near the center of the bruwe.

"I have notified everyone who we will need at our meeting, Leopold." He nodded to the others. "We should hurry to the dining hall. The Teachers and Crafters should all be there soon."

The tall Scrybb turned to lead the way. Jarel moved quickly to Leopold's side and asked quietly, "Why do the Teachers need to be at this meeting?"

Leopold looked up at him. "The Teachers are the leaders of the Scrybb. I don't believe the Scrybb do anything without their approval. The Crafters might be willing to build our boat and agree to do it, but the Teachers will have to give their consent to the project."

"That's stupid," Jarel said brusquely.

Leopold looked at him, surprised. "I mean, it might not be what we're used to, but it's just their way. The humans here might decide on a different form of government in their own bruwe, but we can't really make it our business how other people handle their business in their own society."

"I guess so," Jarel replied. "It just doesn't make sense to me."

"Did Nun the Wiser telling everyone what to do all the time make sense to you?"

Jarel stopped abruptly and stared at the ground. "No, but it never really felt like we had a choice. Nun the Wiser had such immense power over all of us that we lived in fear most of the time. We didn't have a say in how we lived or what we did. Especially those of us who had no abilities."

"I'm sorry, Jarel, I shouldn't have said it like that," Leopold said guiltily. He didn't want to make Jarel feel uncomfortable just when they'd started to connect.

"It's okay," Jarel said. Their group started walking again, hurrying to catch up to Copros.

As they entered the dining hall, they saw Scrybb sitting at tables throughout the building. They were separated into two groups of Teachers and Crafters. He saw Cassiope looking at him gravely, and the angry man sitting with his needled arms crossed, an angry expression on his face. His burns were still quite visible. Leopold definitely felt there would not be much support coming from him.

Jarel, Janke, and Maril all took seats at a table near the door, leaving Leopold standing to talk.

"Okay," he started after taking a deep breath, "did you experience any of the ground shakes here in Thicce Colpat?"

The Scrybb all nodded and several exclaimed to the affirmative, looking around at each other as they did so.

"Marcus Talent believes that the moon was knocked out of its usual course in the sky when it was damaged by a meteor strike. It is slowly falling toward Lysomnus. The closer it comes, the worse the quakes will get, and eventually it will fall and crash, killing everything and everyone."

Gasps and cries from the Scrybb filled the room. Several people put their hands over their faces.

"Marcus believes he can repair the damage," Leopold continued loudly "His power is strong, but not strong enough for him to reach out and fix it as he is now, because the moon is far away and very large. His energy needs a boost, like he gets when he uses the Halfriez. The cube he has now is too small, but he has located the source of the material.

"Unfortunately, that source is very far out in the Diluvium, too far away for even one of the Stondefel to fly. It will take at least several days to get there. This is where we need *your* help. These humans," he indicated Janke and Maril, "know how to build small boats that can float on and travel across the Diluvium. But their boats are too small, and they only use small sails to move them about, which are too slow to travel far distances. We need your Crafters' knowledge and expertise to help them design and build a larger boat, a kind that I know about, and calculate the best way to make it travel faster and farther."

Leopold stopped talking and sat down. The Teachers huddled and talked amongst themselves, while the Crafters looked at each other. Several murmured and nodded. Their expressions had changed from fear and dismay to curiosity and intrigue. Leopold could see the excitement on the Crafter's faces as they pondered the challenge of creation and eagerly started discussing the challenge of working on the ship.

Raised voices drew his attention back to the Teachers. As the shouting intensified, he saw Jarel put his hands over his ears and close his eyes. When Leopold put a hand tentatively on Jarel's shoulder, Jarel twisted away. Maril caught Leopold's arm and shook her head. "Best leave him be, boy," Janke said from behind her.

The Scrybb man with the burn scars kept yelling and abruptly stood up and stormed out past Leopold and the other humans, not glancing in their direction. As the room quieted, Jarel sighed and uncovered his ears, sitting up and finally opening his eyes. He slid closer to Leopold until their bodies were touching lightly, shoulder to ankle. Leopold sighed in delight and relief, and saw Maril's eyes widen in surprise.

Cassiope stood up, looking at Leopold.

"We will be happy to help." She turned to the Crafters. "Copros, if you and your fellow Crafters would work with these humans to design what is needed, that would be wonderful."

Copros nodded. "Of course, Cassiope. We will begin immediately." He and his fellow Crafters stood and walked up to Janke and Maril and began to introduce themselves, and the humans did the same. Copros shook his head and smiled at Leopold, who had started to stand up. "I will come and get more details from you later." Then they all left together, taking the older humans with them. Jarel and Leopold looked at each other, feeling a bit extraneous.

Suddenly Leopold felt arms embrace him from behind.

Leopold turned his head to see Davidia smiling at him. She giggled and pressed her leaf covered cheek against his.

"Come visit with me!" she exclaimed. "And who is this?"

Leopold looked tentatively at Jarel. The other boy nodded, his black eyes still on the table.

"I'm all right, Leopold."

Leopold looked at Davidia. "This is my friend Jarel. He's been living with the humans, but kind of against his will. Apparently, Eris was taking humans from my world and Jarel was one of them, when he was just a little boy."

"What? How horrible!" Davidia cried. "I am so sorry. But I hope that Lysomnus is home to you now, and we will certainly do our best to show you how wonderful it can be.

Leopold and Jarel stood up, following Davidia from the dining hall. The sun was shining brightly on the bruwe, making the pebbles along the paths sparkle. The buildings were all standing firm, showing no damage from the quakes that had occurred.

"Perhaps we should rethink our building methods," Jarel said, eyeing the structures of stone and wood. "These appear much sounder than our log homes were."

"How strong were the quakes here, Davidia?" Leopold asked the Scrybb girl as she danced along the path. He marveled at her constant joy; she had been the most positive person he had met here in Lysomnus.

"Oh, it was very frightening, but I do not think they were too bad. There was a lot of noise and rumbling of the ground beneath our feet. It was difficult to stand, and things fell off shelves. But not much more than that."

Leopold looked at Jarel. "I think the quake was centered much closer to where we were on the other side of the continent. While the log homes might not be as strong as these buildings, it's possible these would have sustained damage if the quake had been stronger here. Still, it can't hurt to find out more about their structure and the materials."

Jarel nodded. Leopold knew he was thinking about the people who'd been crushed by falling logs and collapsed houses during the quakes. They were people Jarel had known all his life here in Lysomnus, even if some of them had treated him and the others of his bruwe badly.

Davidia skipped back to them, holding out her hands. "Let us go and enjoy some fruit!"

Leopold reached eagerly for her hand, but Jarel didn't. "I'm sorry," he said. "I'm not comfortable doing that."

Davidia barely hesitated. "It is fine, Jarel." She dropped her hand. "Come follow me!" Leopold grinned at Jarel helplessly as Davidia pulled him along the path, stones scattering beneath his boots. Jarel laughed as he followed, a pleasant sound Leopold was glad to hear after the discomfort Jarel had been displaying at the meeting.

Together, the threesome found the fruit trees on the other side of the standing plant rows that took up one side of the bruwe. Pellod filled the branches of several of the trees, a bounty weighing them down heavily so they sagged halfway to the ground.

"How do you know when they're ready to be picked?" Jarel asked.

"When they have the pink color on one side, they are ready," Davidia answered. "The solid purple fruits are still unripe and will taste bitter."

Leopold reached for a nearby fruit, looking at Davidia. She nodded and he picked it, handing it to Jarel.

"Have you had a pellod before?" Leopold asked.

Jarel shook his head. "There aren't many fruit trees near our bruwe," he said brusquely. "Only some pryberry that were made into pies for special occasions. I've never seen one of these before. I think I've heard some of our people talking about them, but only the ones who have abilities, the ones who would travel to these other places and take them. They laughed about how they forced these people to give them their food and would use their living spaces as their own. I was jealous of them for what they had that we didn't. I also despised them when I heard what they did to people I would never get the chance to meet—people who would hate me for what those other people did to them."

Davidia and Leopold looked at each other.

"We do not blame you, Jarel, for things you did not do. Or for what they did," Davidia said softly.

"You may not," Jarel said, holding the pellod in his hand, "but don't tell me all the other Scrybb don't. I know why that man was so angry today. He's missing needles and has scars. He's the one who was burned by Nun the Wiser, isn't he?"

Davidia looked away, rubbing her hands along the leaves on her arms. "Yes," she said. "Grevil was scarred when she burned him to punish him. Cassiope said they weren't sure if they were going to be able to put the fire out in time to save him. He will never forgive humans, it seems, no matter how many good people we meet and what Marcus does to save Lysomnus."

Jarel frowned and bit into the pellod. His expression changed abruptly. "Oh, this is so good," he mumbled around his mouthful of fruit. Leopold laughed.

Davidia smiled tentatively. "I am confused by you," she said, "but I like you, Jarel. You say what you are thinking, all the time."

Leopold just shook his head. He really liked Jarel but was still struggling to understand him. He hadn't had a special person in his life before or gone through the process of getting to know someone intimately, their private self. In Jarel's case, he was happy to do it. He hoped Jarel was as eager to continue to get to know him.

"Would you like to try a different fruit?" Davidia was asking Jarel. "It is fun to open and tastes wonderful."

"Okay," Jarel said, handing his half-eaten pellod to Leopold. Leopold rolled his eyes as he gingerly held the mushy remains of

Jarel's fruit and waited to see his reaction to the next one. Jarel was following Davidia to a row of vines nearby. Leopold tagged along, interested in seeing how the sartine grew.

Vines snaked along the ground, thickly green with bluish streaks running along them. Broad green leaves with blue veins spread over the plants. Davidia pulled a leaf aside to expose a large, round blue sartine the size of her head hidden beneath. Grabbing it, she carefully twisted.

"Not ready," she said, setting it back down in the dirt. "It will release easily from the vine when the fruit is ready to be harvested."

Seizing another, she gently twisted the fruit, and the vine dropped away, leaving the sartine in her hands. She straightened up and held it out to Jarel. As Jarel took it from her, Leopold noticed he was careful not to let his fingers make contact with Davidia's.

"Now," Davidia began. "Hold your palms on each side of the fruit and slowly roll it between them, gradually squeezing it harder."

Jarel did as instructed. He stared at the fruit, then jumped as the sartine suddenly split into multiple sections between his fingers. Davidia pulled a leaf from the vine and laid it on the ground.

"Set the fruit here, on this leaf," she instructed Jarel. As he did so, it spread open, revealing the bright blue flesh inside. She picked up a section and handed it to him, then gave one to Leopold and took one for herself. Leopold put the remains of Jarel's pellod next to the sartine.

"It's so sweet!" Jarel exclaimed after he swallowed his first juicy bite. "I've never tasted anything like it!"

Davidia smiled. "It is delicious to eat just like this," she said, "but we particularly like to make juice out of the sartine to drink. There are so many other wonderful fruits and vegetables, but the sartine is a particularly good fruit for making juice."

"What are the yellow berries that the Fyrtudo make pastries out of?" Leopold asked her.

"Oh, those are gorling berries. They are over here," she led them to a row of standing bushes. The yellow berries stood out brightly against the darker green leaves. "These are ripe," and she plucked a handful and gave them each some.

She laughed at their expressions as they both scrunched up their faces at the tartness of the berries. "Eogh!" exclaimed Leopold, spitting out the mouthful of berries. "They didn't taste like that when I had them before!"

Davidia giggled. "They are very tart. Usually, they are sweetened and baked within a pastry crust or shell. They are not typically eaten raw."

"That was a mean trick," Jarel said when he'd finally cleared his mouth of the berries.

"I am sorry," Davidia said. "I should have warned you. But Leopold asked..."

Jarel walked back to the sartine and ate another section to wash the taste of the gorling berries out of his mouth.

"I promise, Jarel, when we visit Palaga, you'll like them much better," Leopold said. "The pastries I had there were delicious."

"We'll see. I don't know if I'll want to try them now," Jarel said, eating more of the sartine with his back to them.

"Oh, forgive me, Jarel, I am very sorry. Please, accept my apology. I will not do that again," Davidia was obviously very contrite.

Jarel sighed. "It is hard for me to trust people, Davidia. I will give you another chance because you are Leopold's friend."

"Oh, thank you," Davidia smiled. "Please, let us go back and I can show you my home. I no longer sleep in the children's dormitory. Since I have completed my Travels, I am now training to be a Grower. We have our own homes over here." She waved her hand toward the end of the rows of plants, where smaller buildings stood near the edge of the Grenewud.

The boys followed her as she danced along the rows of plants, touching a leaf here, a flower there. It was obvious how much she loved the gardens and why she was chosen to become a Grower.

Leopold thought about Jarel's reaction to Davidia's offer to take his hand, earlier when she wanted to lead them to the gardens. She was a person who loved to touch and hug, and it was natural for her to reach out to everyone. Jarel did not like to be touched, as he had demonstrated by refusing to take her hand and even avoiding touching her fingers when taking fruit. Leopold thought about how Jarel had spontaneously hugged him when he had been overwhelmed with grief about Awar, and how Jarel had both accepted Leopold's kiss and held his hand while walking to Thicce Colpat. Suddenly, he felt very special.

CHAPTER EIGHT

THE LANGUAGE OF THE PHANTASMS

Sadie

Suri found Sadie and Cornus in their quarters just after they had returned from the evening meal. They were carrying a pack in one clawed paw.

As they set it down on a table, they signed, "A Stondefel returned to the field today. He asked that we bring this to you."

"Oh!" Sadie cried out. "It must be the books that I asked for!" She signed her words at the same time, aware of wanting to communicate with the Cativera in their way at the same time. Eagerly, she reached for the package, opened it, and found several books stacked inside.

"Sadie," Suri said out loud. She looked up. They started signing. "Anneberg also said to tell you that the humans have heard of this watercraft and are now in Thicce Colpat working with the Scrybb to design one for your friend."

"Thank you, Suri," she signed. "That is wonderful news. Please, go get supper and rest."

The Cativera nodded to each of them and left.

"They must be so tired after a day in the fields," Cornus said.

"I'm sure the herds are still very agitated after all the quakes," Sadie agreed. Her attention wasn't fully on her friend, though, as she brought each book out and put it on the bed. She was happy to see they were all books from the languages section, as she'd hoped.

"It is good news about the boat though, right?" Cornus said.

"Hmmm?" Sadie murmured, paging through one of the books.

Cornus sighed. "I know you are very interested in those books, Sadie, but I do not understand why they are so important right *now*. You have all the time in the world to decipher the languages within them—at least, if Marcus is able to accomplish his goal."

"I know, Cornus. But I can't help but feel it's important to keep looking at and learning the languages in these books. Just look at what good it's done so far with the Cativera. I'm glad to hear that Marcus is going to get his boat and move further on his journey to stop these quakes. But *we're* not able to do anything to help him. I miss him so much, and I want to feel useful in some way." She flipped to another page, looking at the pictures beside the indecipherable writing.

"I do understand. I also want to help Marcus. Before, we were able to at least do *something* to assist him, but now all we can do is sit and wait. It is frustrating. Our friends are in Thicce Colpat right now, anyway, and I cannot go there even if I wanted to."

Sadie looked up at him. Evening light slanted in through the opening in the ceiling, highlighting the sadness on the drooping leaves of his face. "Why not? Even if they needed you?"

"No, it is forbidden during my Travel year," Cornus said morosely. "I was almost severely punished when I returned after meeting Marcus the first time. After I left with the three of you, my Travel year began again, and I cannot return until I have completed it. Adulthood is not reached, and adult assignments are not allowed until I return from a completed Travel year."

Sadie was taken aback. "I had no idea it was so serious. I understand why you have been so adamant about your Travels now," she said. "I am curious—you have been to Palaga, and the bruwe of the humans, and now Grasian. Will you leave here at some point and make your way to Fisc? Do you need to visit all the people of Lysomnus?"

"Not every Scrybb does," Cornus replied, lying back on his bed and staring up at the ceiling. "In fact, in recent years, I think most have simply Traveled about the Grenewud paths, perhaps stopping by Palaga and staying away from any other bruwes. I was originally advised to do something similar, which is why I was on the other side of Thicce Colpat when I met Marcus the first time. I did not know the paths that well in that direction, and I got lost." He smiled. "In a way, it was the best thing I have ever done. If I had not, I would not have met Marcus!"

Sadie smiled. "I'm glad you did. From how Marcus tells it, you saved his life that day. You warned him against going out into the Brynar and then tried to shield him from the phantasm when it showed up. It might have killed him instead of just hurting his arm if you hadn't been there."

"Possibly," the Scrybb boy said with a shy smile. "It is still funny to me to hear what you three call the <<null>>."

"It is still bizarre to me to hear Lysomnians say a word that I can't even fully hear or understand," Sadie said, laughing. "It doesn't make any sense! Why can't I hear it?"

"I do not know," Cornus said. "It must be something about you coming from a different world. Although the strangest thing to me is that you come to this world the same way the <<null>> do and yet cannot hear their name!"

"That is odd," Sadie pondered, her chin on her hand. Her feet were tucked under the edge of the bed she was sitting on, the books in disarray around her where she'd laid them as she pulled them from the pack on the table. Her eyes fell on the small pile of clothing beside her that she'd found when she opened the package from the Scrybb, and she felt tears sting her eyes. The clothes were an amazing gift. She'd never wear them again, wanting to preserve the last items she would ever possess from her life on Earth.

Sadie picked up one of the books again, opening it to see the pictures of the Fyrtudo. She set it aside and opened another, which showed the Muirnati. The examples in the book looked different from Marcus's description of Boehlkea. Then she remembered that Boehlkea was half-human. So her hair, eyes, and freckles came from Deacon. Even having a nose was somewhat different from the Muirnati pictured in the book.

Another book revealed strange images. On the first pages, there were swirling vortexes, followed by a depiction of the open nothingness she remembered seeing when Marcus had opened the portal back to Earth. She turned the pages rapidly to find terrifying illustrations of things that looked straight out of a horror movie. Multiple mouths and eyes were surrounded by sharp spikes. She cried out in fear.

Cornus leapt off the bed, looking around to see what had frightened her. When he saw her looking down at the book, he stepped over and glanced down at the picture.

"That," he said gravely, "is a <<null>>."

Sadie covered her mouth with one trembling hand and looked up at Cornus. Her eyes were filled with fear.

"That—that is what attacked Marcus? The thing that took his arm?"

"Yes."

She swallowed hard. Her hand returned to her side, mostly because she felt like she needed both of them pushing against the bed to prop herself up.

"I can't believe Marcus faced that thing and stayed sane," she said, feeling like there wasn't enough air in the room.

"Honestly, I cannot believe he survived the encounter," Cornus said. "I was there and I thought that he died."

Sadie forced herself to look at the book again, this time avoiding the picture and trying to look at the words. They didn't look like words to her; it was almost as if she couldn't see them.

"Cornus, take a look at this, will you?" she asked, pointing at the page with a slightly shaky finger.

He sat down beside her, and she slid the book into his lap.

"What is it?" he asked.

"Can you see the words here?" she pointed at them, the blur where she thought the words should be.

"Yes, I see them. I do not know what they say, but I can see them."

"That's so odd. I can't even see them. I wonder if this is the language of the phantasms! If we could find a way between us to figure this out, maybe we could communicate with them!"

Cornus looked at her sharply. "Sadie, what are you saying? *We* could communicate with them? The second a <<null>> appeared, it would kill you!"

Sadie persisted. "But maybe if we could find a way to stop them from trying to kill me for a second and listen, we could communicate and find out *why* they want to kill humans! Maybe we could fix the breach and find out what is wrong!"

"I do not know about this, Sadie. But let me try to figure out this language first. I will have to find a way for you to know what these words look like so we can decipher them."

Sadie sighed. "It's worth trying, Cornus. If we can make the Brynar safe for humans, Lysomnus will be a better place for us since we have to live here forever. I want to know that my children won't have to live in fear here. Let's get to work."

CHAPTER NINE

SHIFTING RELATIONSHIPS

Marcus

Marcus was sitting on the ledge in his father's home. Boehlkea sat next to him, dangling her legs in the water, while another Muirnati floated at her feet, one webbed hand on Boehlkea's knee. She had bright green scales that blended to a lovely rose shade on her abdomen and chest.

"Melacara," Marcus said, "you really are the fastest swimmer I've ever seen, even here among the Muirnati!"

"Melacara wins the races every summer, ever since she became old enough to compete. I think the adults are nervous about her once she comes of age!" Boehlkea laughed, curling her fingers around her girlfriend's hand. "She won't tell you, but she has a shelf full of awards for the races she's won."

"You have summer races?" Marcus asked.

"Yes," Melacara said. Her voice was deeper than Boehkea's, a rich tone that was very pleasant to listen to. "For several days, we stop all work and do nothing but have fun! The Aragani prepare special treats ahead of time and participate in the games along with us. We feast and have competitions and play music."

"Music?" Marcus was surprised. "How do you play music?"

Boehlkea laughed. "We have instruments made from the shells

and reeds we find in the Diluvium. Pipes, horns, drums, and there are some wonderful singers among us. My mother sings beautifully. You will have to join us this summer to enjoy all the festivities."

"Absolutely," Marcus said with a grin. "Only I won't compete in any swimming races. I can't swim fast physically, and it wouldn't be fair if I used my power."

"There are other games you can play," Melacara laughed. "We have many entertaining activities going on all day and into the night." Her yellow eyes glowed with anticipation.

Their conversation was interrupted by Pelamis's entrance. The flaps of her nose and ears opened, and her translucent eyelids slid back, revealing her eyes clearly. She focused on Marcus.

"There is a Stondefel on the beach, Marcus. We can only assume he is here for you, as you have been waiting to hear about your mission to travel across the Diluvium," she said as water streamed from her shoulders.

"Oh, finally! I hope it is good news," Marcus said as he made his way carefully to his feet. He reached up to the shelf above and grabbed his mask. The Muirnati had kindly had more suits made for him to wear while he stayed among them, and he had put on a clean one just that morning, so he immediately sat down and slipped into the pool, getting ready to put his face mask on.

"I'll come with you," Boehlkea said. "I'd like to hear what has been discovered." She kissed Melacara and dove under the water. Melacara kissed her back fiercely and whispered in her ear before releasing her. Boehlkea nodded and followed Marcus, who was waiting for her.

It didn't take long to emerge from the surface of the sea above; Boehlkea had broken through first and was waiting for Marcus. She led him across the bruwe to the beach.

Marcus's cane was waiting for him on the flat rock inside the circle of stones that sheltered the tunnel entrance to Fisc. He kept it and a pack holding his regular clothes there for when he left the bruwe of the Muirnati. Marcus grabbed his cane and placed the map, still in its bag, carefully in the pack. He would change later, hopefully after returning to say goodbye to Pelamis if the Stondefel had good news for him.

The sun was shining high in the sky, and the sandy shore was firm beneath his feet. Boehlkea walked slowly beside him as they headed toward the place the Stondefel typically landed to meet with Marcus.

"I hope they have answers for you, Marcus," Boehlkea said. "I've been so worried about these quakes and what you said about the moon crashing into Lysomnus. That's such a terrifying thought!"

"I know. I don't even know if I'm right about that part, but I'd hate to do nothing, and then it happened."

The Stondefel waiting for them was Aldinoch. He turned his horned head as they approached, red eyes blazing. His spiked tail was lashing impatiently.

"Finally! I thought you'd never come." His voice boomed across the beach at them. "I have news for you, Marcus."

"We came as quickly as possible, as soon as Pelamis let us know you were here, Aldinoch," Marcus said as he did his best to hurry to the demon's side.

"It is all right. You are here now. Your friend Sadie mentioned a type of transport called a 'boat'."

Marcus slapped himself in the forehead. "Now why didn't I think of that?"

"We have found humans who know how to design small boats and have used them on the Diluvium before. They have been working with the Scrybb Crafters to make a larger version—called a "ship"—that you can use to travel across the sea, and a way for it to move quickly and safely.'

"Where is this ship? When will we launch it? Is it in the Scrybb bruwe?" Marcus was stumbling over his own words in his excitement.

"Now, hold on, Marcus," Boehlkea said. "What do you know of the ocean on your own world, much less here on Lysomnus? You cannot make this journey alone. I am going with you."

Aldinoch was nodding. "You certainly cannot undertake such a venture alone, Marcus. While we Stondefel cannot accompany you, you must take others who know about the Diluvium and can help you in case of trouble.

"The ship is on its way here, as are your friends. In fact, here come your friends now!" He gestured at the sky, where a speck was rapidly growing larger into the shape of another Stondefel circling to land on the beach nearby. Marcus automatically reached out mentally and blocked the flying sand. Boehlkea smiled at him in appreciation.

The Stondefel was Agatho. On his back was Leopold with another boy Marcus had never seen before. The way Leopold had his arms wrapped around the boy's waist seemed unnecessarily tight since they were wearing the flight harness and had already landed. Marcus felt a flare of jealousy that surprised him.

They were climbing down now, anyway. Marcus found himself reluctant to move, unsure of himself for some reason. He hadn't seen Leopold in a while and had missed his best friend. He wondered who this new boy was and why they seemed so familiar with each other.

"Hey, bro!" Leopold called out as he approached, shifting into his usual boxing stance. "Man, it's good to see you!"

"Hey!" Marcus said, slapping Leopold's hands out of the way and wrapping him into a hug. "I've missed your face, buddy. How's it been going?" He looked at the new boy, but his brown eyes were looking off down the beach.

"Let me introduce you to Jarel. He's been living with the other humans. Man, I gotta tell you, things are so complicated there. Nun the Wiser and Eris really treated those people like shit."

Marcus swallowed, then smiled. "Hey, man," he said to Jarel. "Nice to meet you."

"Hey," said Jarel. "Nice to finally meet the legend in person." Marcus frowned, detecting a note of sarcasm in Jarel's voice.

Boehlkea stepped past Marcus and opened her arms. "Nice to

meet you, Leopold. I've heard so much about you. I'm Marcus's sister, Boehlkea."

Leopold threw his arms wide and embraced her, lifting her off the ground until she squealed. "Thanks, Boehlkea. It's great to meet you, too. I'm glad Marcus has some family left after everything that happened."

"So where is this ship?" Marcus asked as Boehlkea and Leopold stepped away from each other.

"It's coming by sea!" Leopold exclaimed. "You're going to love this thing. We're going to be pirates, mate! The Crafters at Thicce Colpat are amazing—they built the entire thing in just a few weeks! With the help of Janke and Maril, of course. I may have given them some schematics from my days building ships in a bottle." He raised his nose and his tone loftily.

"Janke and Maril?" Marcus was confused.

"They're two of the humans from Jarel's bruwe. Kind of like his foster parents. They're boat builders and fishermen, but they usually only build smaller boats that they propel with oars or small sails when they fish in the Diluvium. We brought 'em to Thicce Colpat to work with the Scrybb to come up with a *real* ship to take us where *you* need to go!"

"That's—amazing," Marcus gulped. "You've really been busy. I feel like I've just been sitting around on my butt while everyone else does all the hard work."

"Nah," Leopold brushed off his words. "The hard work starts now and really happens when we get to this 'Halfriez island', doesn't it? For you, anyway. Janke and Maril are bringing the boat—well, ship, here, and then we'll get you to where you need to go."

"*We?* Who's we? How many people are going on this trip, Leopold?"

Leopold grinned at Marcus. "Well, Janke and Maril, because they're kind of the most knowledgeable people when it comes to boats, even though no one here has ever actually sailed a full-sized ship before. And me and Jarel, because Jarel knows Janke and Maril, and I know Jarel. Everyone will be more comfortable that way."

"And me," said Boehlkea. "No one knows the Diluvium better than I do who can go with you." The stubborn set to her shoulders and face let everyone know that she would brook no arguments.

Aldinoch and Agatho roared with laughter. "Well, Marcus, it looks like your crew is set," Agatho said.

"All we need now is the ship!" Leopold yelled, kicking up sand as he turned to look as if to see the vessel approaching at that very minute.

Marcus noticed the small smile playing about Jarel's mouth as he watched Leopold's antics. He frowned at the apparent closeness between the two when they could have only known each other for a short time.

Aldinoch cleared his throat to get their attention. "We must leave. Anneberg stayed with the humans to help them with their journey to find a new place for their bruwe and to start building it. We want to check on them, and Agatho here will return with a small boat for you to use to reach the ship when it arrives. *We* will be flying over the Diluvium for the first days of your trip to keep an eye on you."

He and Agatho spread their wings and launched themselves from the beach. They waved as they gained altitude. Marcus waved back, and the others followed suit, dropping their hands as the Stondefel rose too high to see them anymore.

Marcus and Leopold looked at each other. Marcus knew the others were looking at them, too, but he wanted to reaffirm his connection with his best friend. It felt like it had been much longer than only a few weeks that they had been separated; so much had happened that a feeling of disconnect had come between them.

Leopold had the same look of affection for Marcus that was always on his face when he saw his best friend. Marcus felt better at the sight of it. He had to trust his friend and get to know Jarel; Leopold was good at seeing the best in people, so this boy must be a trustworthy person.

Boehlkea walked over to Jarel.

"Hello," she said a bit shyly. "I'm Boehlkea. I'm half-Muirnati and also Marcus's half-sister."

Jarel was standing with his hands in his pockets. "I've heard of the Muirnati. Some of the people who traveled with Nun the Wiser and Eris talked about you. I'm sorry about how they treated your people."

"I get the feeling from what Leopold said that you didn't have anything to do with that," Boehlkea said. "I can't blame you for it. I'm sorry you were treated so badly by them, too. And that you've lived on Lysomnus and never gotten to know any of the rest of our people.

Jarel looked down, smiling nervously. "Thank you. I'm glad to meet you, my first Muirnati. But you said you're only half? And Marcus's half-sister?"

Boehlkea smiled at Marcus and then looked back at Jarel. "Yes, his father, Deacon, who you might have seen when he was a prisoner in your bruwe, was my father too. He traveled here, to Lysomnus, for many years, and he and my mother were together."

Jarel looked at Marcus. "So, did you know about her?" He slid a hand out of his pocket and gestured at Boehlkea.

Marcus was startled by the blunt question. "Um, no, actually, I didn't. I found out about Boehlkea when I came here myself and met her. That was after my father was kidnapped by Eris."

"That must have been quite a shock, finding out you had a sister you didn't even know about. Your father had two families your whole life, and you didn't even know it? Like, he was living a lie?"

"Yeah, I was pretty mad about it at first. I never got the chance to talk to him about it, not really. One thing I regret is that I got angry and sent him home, and then he died before we had a chance to talk about it." Tears stung Marcus's eyes as he said the words.

Boehlkea slipped an arm around him. "It's been hard on both of us, Marcus. I never got to talk to him about the horrible things he said about me," she said, her voice breaking. "It's going to hurt forever, but we have to find a way to go on."

Leopold broke into the uncomfortable silence that followed her words. "Jarel was stolen by Eris from his parents on Earth when he was just a little kid."

Jarel nodded, his dark eyes darting to Marcus's and Boehlkea's faces and then away again.

"But that's terrible!" Boehlkea cried out. "How did you ever manage to deal with such pain?"

Jarel shrugged. "I cried all the time at first. I don't think I even understood that I was actually in a different world. I was just in a strange place with people I didn't know. I never saw any other people than the humans who lived in our bruwe—they said a lot of strange words," he laughed, "like *bruwe,* and I saw the people with power doing crazy things I'd never seen anyone do before. I was just handed over to Janke and Maril, who raised me. They weren't parents; they were just the people I lived with."

Marcus saw Leopold give Jarel a funny look.

"We've all been through some crazy things on our way to life here on Lysomnus," Marcus said. "None of us planned on being here or making this our home. But now we'll just have to make the best of it —if I can save it." He looked out at the Diluvium, where the setting sun reflected off the waves, a red glow filling the horizon.

"Do they know how long it will take to sail the ship here?" he asked, turning back to Leopold and Jarel.

"Since they haven't sailed a ship before, they're learning as they go. The Scrybb designed the whole system after I drew up a model like the ones my dad and I used to build. The basic boat building they designed off what Janke and Maril said the boat builders in the human bruwe did. They said they would teach Janke and Maril before they left. I don't know if it's even the same system as the way things work on sailing ships back on Earth," Leopold said. "Janke said he thought it would take a few days to get here, based on the distance between the shore off of Thicce Colpat and Fisc, and they wanted to take some time to practice while getting to know the ship."

"Why did Aldinoch say we would need a small boat to reach this —this—ship?" Boehlkea asked.

"Because of the size of the ship," Jarel broke in. "It's too big to come in close to shore. It would get stuck in the sea floor, and we'd never get it back out to sea. We'll use the boat to paddle out to the ship and then climb on board."

"Oh, I see," Boehlkea said, and she and Marcus looked at each other, nodding in feigned understanding. Marcus saw the same baffled look on Boehlkea's face that he felt on his own.

"Boehlkea, you should go back into Fisc," Marcus said to his sister. "You need to hydrate, and you should talk to Pelamis if you're going to come on this journey. I'm sure you'd also like to say goodbye to Melacara ." He turned to Leopold and Jarel.

"Did anyone discuss stocking up for this journey? We'll need a lot of food for this many people, clothing, and what will we do for drinking water?"

Leopold raised his hands, smiled, and shook his head. "Don't worry, Marcus. You'll be very happy to see what the Scrybb have done for us. They've provided us with a good supply of fruit and vegetables and dried meat, and they made these watertight casks that they filled with water and loaded on the ship for us. It has a large storage area that is fully loaded! Plus, another storage area where we put several changes of clothing for each of us from the supplies in the bathhouse."

"I will see if we can get some salted fish to add to the supply," Boehlkea said. "I know Mother will want to say goodbye to you as well, Marcus, so you should come with me. *We* will go in to say *our* goodbyes."

"All right," he said. Leopold said he and Jarel would wait on the beach for them to return.

As they walked, Boehlkea looped her arm through Marcus's. "I like Leopold. He is a good friend to you. I have the feeling he would do almost anything for you, the way strong heart friends do for each other. That is the way Melacara and I started out—as heart friends, and then we just fell in love."

"Leopold has always been my best friend—I guess what you would call a heart friend. We aren't in love, though," he laughed a little, "since he likes guys, and I like girls."

"I wondered if that was true for a bit," Boehlkea said. "Seeing how jealous you are of his new friend, Jarel."

"I'm not jealous—at least, not like that," Marcus said, irritated. "It's just strange, seeing him so focused on someone else. "I guess I always knew a time would come when he would make other friends and our friendship would change, but he's only known that—Jarel—for a few weeks! How do I even know if he's a decent guy?"

Boehlkea smiled. "You can only get to know him and find out. And—maybe, trust your friend to know what he likes and what is best for him?"

Marcus sighed. He winced as his sore body struggled with loosening up from the morning.

When they reached the stones that marked the entrance to Fisc, Marcus slipped his mask on, following Boehlkea into the waters of the Diluvium.

When they reached her home, Pelamis wasn't there. Marcus and Boehlkea settled in to wait. Before long, she darted into the pool with Melacara behind her.

Marcus told them both about the ship and the journey ahead. Boehlkea told them of her intention to join him on the ship.

"So, you are both really intent on undertaking this journey?" Pelamis said, looking worried. "I will be so worried with both of you gone."

"I understand, Pelamis. But honestly, I will feel safer having Boehlkea along. She knows the Diluvium, and she can also safely be out of the water for periods of time. We will need her knowledge. If it weren't so absolutely crucial to do this, none of us would be going."

Pelamis pressed a blue-green hand to her forehead. "I do understand. But I will be worried the entire time you are gone. I wish I could go with you."

Melacara, arms wrapped around Boehlkea, groaned as if in pain. "I wish I had spoken with you earlier, Boehlkea. I thought we had more time."

Boehlkea looked bewildered. "I *am* coming back, my love."

"But—but I need to tell you something," Melacara looked at Marcus and Pelamis.

Pelamis put a hand on Marcus's arm. "Perhaps we should give them some time alone."

"No," Melacara said, looking over at them, "I want to say this in front of all of you. You are Boehlkea's family." With a deep breath, Melacara grasped Boehlkea's hands and looked earnestly into her eyes. "I have known for some time that I am not what I thought I was."

Boehlkea looked confused. "Melacara—what? I do not understand,"

"I am not the 'lovely girl' you believed that I am. I have been terrified to talk to you about this, Boehlkea. I haven't been honest with you because I didn't know what you would think or how you would react. The truth is that I am *not* a *girl*, Boehlkea. I am a *boy*. The changes are coming, and I can feel them. And I want them to happen. I don't feel like a girl. I am not the 'pretty girl' you have loved all these years."

Boehlkea stared at Melaraca's nervous face for a moment. She looked surprised, then slowly she smiled and wrapped her arms around her partner. "What shall I call you then, my love?"

"Uh—Melacar. I will be Melacar. You are not upset?" He pulled away and looked back at her. "I have been so terrified you would not want to be with me anymore."

Boehlkea smiled and smacked kisses all over his surprised face. "But I love *you*, Melacar! That does not change whether you are a girl or a boy. You are *you*! It is who you are *here*—" she put a hand gently over the center of his chest "—that matters to me. All our lives together, you have been my dearest heart friend. That is all I care about. As long as I have you, I am happy."

"You do not care about—about—" Melacar glanced uncomfortably at Marcus and Pelamis. They both glanced away, trying to give the young couple as much privacy as possible. "You don't care about my body changing?" He whispered. "You know that it is something I cannot control."

Boehlkea giggled. "No," she whispered. "I am attracted to *any* parts, I have realized. I was going to talk to *you* about that soon to see if it was a problem for you."

"Oh—*oh*," Melacar whispered. "Uh, no, Boehlkea, that will not be a problem for me." He let out a muffled laugh that set off more of Boehlkea's giggles. Marcus tried desperately to control himself so they wouldn't think he had been listening, but he couldn't help it. He lost control and burst out laughing. Almost immediately, Pelamis did, too.

"I am so sorry, Melacar," she said, pulling herself together. "You deserve more respect than that from me. I didn't mean to laugh."

"I'm sorry too, bro," said Marcus. "So uncalled for. Really happy for you both."

Melacar looked uncertain. "Then you are both... accepting me? You are not upset by this?"

Pelamis beamed and glided through the water and embraced Melacar. "You are part of the family to me, my son. My daughter loves you, and that is enough for me. You have always had a kind heart and have treated her with love. I am happy as long as you are both happy, Melacar."

Marcus grinned. "I'm glad for you, bro. It's not easy to tell people who you are when it's something that other people think might be outside of the normal spectrum. My friend Leopold came out to me—he told me he was gay—before he even told his family because he was scared. Thank you for trusting me today."

Melacar smiled. "Thank you all for being so supportive."

Boehlkea suddenly gasped and looked at Melacar, a worried look on her face. "Do you still like me? You still like girls?"

He laughed. "Yes, Boehlkea. I still love *you* more than anything, and I still like girls."

"Hm." She snorted. "I know. When I really think about it, I just love *you*." Then she cried out and covered her face with her hands.

"What is it?" Melacar asked, pulling her hands away with his and lifting her face with a gentle finger under her chin.

"We are leaving! You tell me this now, and I have to go!"

"It's all right. My body will be going through the changes while you are gone—I can feel them starting already—but I will be okay, Boehlkea. Marcus needs you more than I do right now."

"Have you told your family?" Pelamis asked.

"I tried," Melacar said, his face clouding with sadness and inner eyelids blinking rapidly. "I tried talking to my mother, but she got quite upset. She told me not to say anything to my father, and then she told me I have to try to stop my body from going through the changes." Pelamis and Boehlkea gasped aloud. "I am afraid to go home."

Pelamis took his hand in her own. "Melacar, you will stay here with me while your body is going through the changes, and I will help you through them as comfortably as possible. I will go and get our meals and bring them here. When you feel like going to a community meal, we will go together. If there is any trouble, we will return to my home. If your parents cause trouble, we will bring you before the Shoal. This issue is an old one, and their sort of behavior isn't tolerated anymore. The Shoal will protect you from them."

Marcus was confused, but Boehlkea caught his eye and shook her head before he could say anything.

Melacar hugged Pelamis and thanked her profusely. Marcus could see the relief on his face. Then the young Muirnati turned to Boelhkea and embraced her, squeezing her so tightly she squeaked.

"I love you," he said when he released her.

She gasped a little and put a hand on his face. "I can tell," she said with a little laugh. "I love you, too. Melacar. I'm so sorry I won't be here for your change."

Marcus reached out a hand. "I'm happy for you, brother," he said. Then he cried out in surprise as Melacar seized him and gently hugged him. "Take good care of Boehlkea," the Muirnati said as he let Marcus go. "Now go save the world!"

He turned to Pelamis, who was saying goodbye to her daughter.

"You will be careful?" she asked Marcus. "I don't want to lose my daughter, or you either, my son." Tears pricked his eyes at her words.

"I know. I can only promise you that I will be as careful as I possibly can while doing whatever is necessary to save Lysomnus."

She sighed. "That is all I can ask for." She raised her arms, legs and tails waving behind her in the water. Marcus embraced her one last time.

As they swam away, Marcus saw Boehlkea staring back at Melacar until the last second, when she had to follow the curve of the tunnel out of her home.

Trying not to sigh audibly with relief when he had finally changed back into his clothes on the beach, Marcus straightened his body and pushed himself to his feet after he changed. His shirt was damp from the evening dew, but he knew it would dry quickly in the warm evening breeze.

When Marcus and Boehlkea walked back down the beach toward where Leopold and Jarel were waiting, they saw the glow of a fire as soon as they rounded the bend.

"How did they start a fire?" Boehlkea asked Marcus in wonder. They had been picking their way carefully by the light of the immense moon in the sky, with Boehlkea's luminescent skin lighting up a small area around her.

"Hey, Leopold!" Marcus shouted, unable to wait until they were closer.

"Marcus?" Leopold called back, sounding startled.

"How did you manage to light a fire out here?"

"Oh, Jarel has flint," Leopold said, closer now, as they approached. Marcus could see his dark outline between them and the fire. The brightness had obscured his vision momentarily.

"Flint?" Boehlkea asked. "What is flint?"

"It's a type of stone. When you strike it just right against another rock, it makes a spark," Jarel said, overhearing her question as they approached. "While there was a person in our bruwe who could start a fire just by using power, the rest of us had to do it by hand. I think there are other people on Lysomnus who use flint; at least, I heard some of the other humans talking about forcefully taking it from them when we had trouble finding enough in our area."

Marcus and Leopold looked uneasily at each other when Marcus and Boehlkea arrived at the fire. "Maybe the Cativera?" Marcus said. "Cornus said they had a big fire while he was there. I know the Scrybb would never make fire—they use the emeristan, and the Muirnati obviously don't, if Boehlkea doesn't know about it. I never saw fire at Palaga, and they'd just use the emeristan or the forges for most things, I believe."

"Makes sense," Leopold said. He leaned companionably against Jarel. Marcus eyed Jarel warily, wondering just who this strange new person that Leopold was so comfortable with already.

Boehlkea sat down and opened the large, gelatinous bag that had been waiting for them, along with Marcus's clothes. "Are you hungry? Most of this is to add to the stock on the ship when it gets here, but we should certainly eat something tonight." She handed salted fish to Marcus, Jarel, and Leopold. All three boys thanked her and ate hungrily. Marcus didn't realize how hungry he was until he started eating.

As the fire burned down, the four of them stared into the flames as if mesmerized. Jarel told them about the people in his bruwe and how alone he had felt, even though he'd been surrounded by people all his life. He explained about the people who were descendants of the original kidnapping victims of Nun the Wiser and how they were the ones who had sometimes developed power. The three of them looked at him in awe, wide-eyed, as he described his own kidnapping in the middle of the day as a young child. He told them he wasn't the only human in the bruwe who had been taken as a child; there were others who were a few years older than him, and there were even a couple who were younger. Most of the humans, however, were adults. Nun the Wiser and Eris wanted people who could work. The children were experiments, Jarel told them, to see if any could develop power since they were so young when they were brought to Lysomnus.

"But none of us did," Jarel concluded. "Eris stopped taking children a few years ago. Nun the Wiser decided she was willing to wait for the children of those who were born here to develop their own power."

Leopold was looking at Jarel, his eyes filled with tears. "Is it okay if I hug you?" he asked. Jarel nodded, and Leopold wrapped his arms around him. Jarel put his cheek against the top of Leopold's head.

Marcus wondered why Leopold had asked first. Leopold was usually spontaneous with his physical affection. He himself had been the victim of hundreds of Leopold's impulsive hugs, arm punches, and other affectionate gestures. And he wasn't usually so emotional about other people's life stories. Marcus shook his head.

Boehlkea was still looking at Jarel. "I am so sorry for what you suffered under the rule of Nun the Wiser. We, the people of Lysomnus, have always felt ourselves to be the only victims of her power, but I do not think any of us ever thought that there were other humans who were suffering under her rule. I am glad you are free of her and the others who followed her."

"Thank you," Jarel said. "It is a relief to know they are gone. It feels even better to be able to find new friends and see something good and beautiful in this world that I have hated for most of my life."

None of the rest of them knew what to say after that. They tried to find comfortable spots to lie on the beach and sleep, hoping the ship would arrive soon. Boehlkea made her way to the water, lying in the sand where the tide was lapping on the shore.

While the others seemed to drop off to sleep easily, Marcus could not find any position that didn't hurt miserably. Finally, he made his way to a boulder not far from the fire and propped himself up against it. He found himself dozing off and on, waking up when his neck began to hurt from his head tipping into awkward positions. He eventually got tired enough to curl up on his side and sleep for a while until the pain in his back spreading to his hips woke him up again. The sun was just beginning to rise.

A ship rocked gently in the water of the Diluvium a short distance from shore. It was larger than Marcus had expected; it reminded him of pirate ships he'd read of or seen in movies. Tall masts rose above the beautiful wooden ship with sails unfurled, and an anchor line dropped from the bow, holding it in place.

Painfully, Marcus pushed himself to his knees. His back was a misery after spending the night on the ground. Breathing hard, he tried to use his cane to get to his feet, but he couldn't do it. As he slipped back to his knees, he cried out involuntarily.

Leopold was on his feet in a flash, looking around. When he saw Marcus kneeling in the sand, he ran over.

"Marcus? What can I do?"

"Can you pull me up? I can't get to my feet. I don't think sleeping on the ground was such a good idea." He tried to smile but felt it slipping into a grimace.

"Okay, buddy, I gotcha." Leopold started to grasp Marcus's upper arms.

"Wait," Jarel said from behind them. Leopold jumped. "Jeez! Don't sneak up on a guy like that."

"Sorry." Jarel walked around behind Marcus. "Let me help." He held Marcus under his armpits while Leopold grabbed him from the front, and together, they lifted him to his feet, holding him in place while he got his bearings.

"Are you alright like this?" Jarel asked from behind him.

"Yeah, I think so," Marcus said, tightening his grip on his cane. "I just gotta walk a little bit to get the kinks out."

Jarel immediately let go and walked away.

"Thanks!" Marcus called after him. Jarel turned his head and nodded.

"What's *with* that guy?" Marcus asked Leopold in a low voice.

"He's just different," Leopold said. "Nothing's 'with' him. He's not a big fan of being touched, and he doesn't like eye contact. So, don't judge."

"I'm not—"

"You kind of were."

"What's with *you?*" Marcus asked, pushing his fist against his lower back. "You're awfully defensive about someone you haven't known that long."

"Damn, you can be pretty stupid sometimes, Marcus," Leopold said and walked away down the beach, breaking into a jog and calling Jarel's name.

Boehlkea was sitting cross-legged by the remains of the fire, looking at Marcus.

"What did I do?" Marcus said as he limped toward her. She shook her head. "What?" he asked.

Boehlkea got smoothly to her feet with a grace Marcus envied. She looked down the beach to where Leopold and Jarel were walking side by side, talking quietly. With one hand, she gestured after them.

"Do you not see it, brother? They are clearly together."

"Togeth—oh. Oh, I'm stupid. How didn't I see that?" He pressed a hand over his eyes, groaning. "I'm such a jerk."

"I am not sure what you mean by a 'jerk', but if it is the same thing as being mean to your friend, then yes, you are a jerk." Boehlkea laughed. "You have some apologizing to do."

Marcus sighed. "I'll never catch them. I'm just going to have to wait until they come back." Then he brightened. "Oh hey, did you see the ship is here?" He pointed out to the vessel floating on the waves behind her.

Boehlkea turned, and she started in surprise. "It's lovely! How did I not see that great thing floating out there while I was waiting for you to wake up," she said. "I think it will be such fun to travel on the sea."

"Hopefully," Marcus said. "I only hope none of us gets seasick."

"Seasick?" Boehlkea asked quizzically. "Why would anyone get sick of the sea?"

Marcus scrunched his face as he tried not to laugh. "Oh, no," he said as he lost control and snorted instead. Boehlkea giggled at the sound. "Sometimes people get nauseated when they travel on board a ship." He explained. "The rocking motion of the boat on the waves can make people feel nauseated."

"Ah, I understand. I hope that will not happen. It sounds unpleasant."

They both looked up as a shadow crossed the sand. They saw Agatho circling above, a boat clutched in the talons of his six legs. He flew low over the edge of the water, setting the boat down carefully where the waves washed up on the shore.

"I see your ship has arrived!" He called down. "Your boat is ready, and the 'oars' are inside. I will not stop and delay you further. Good journey!"

"Wait!" Marcus called out. Agatho looked down at him, a bemused expression on his face. He circled, waiting.

"Can...can you bring Sadie and Cornus here so we can say goodbye? I know it's only supposed to be a short trip, but who knows if things will work out perfectly, or-or if more quakes will happen while we're gone." Marcus missed Sadie badly, and even Cornus's steady presence was something he sorely needed right now.

"Of course!" Agatho called down and rose quickly, disappearing in the direction of the Zabanara region.

Jarel and Leopold were jogging back up the beach toward them. He began to walk in their direction. They slowed to a stop as they drew near him.

"Leopold, I owe you an apology," Marcus began. "I'm sorry for being so blind."

"It's okay, Marcus," Leopold said. "I understand. You were just jealous!"

"I'm trying to be serious, Leopold," Marcus said.

"I know, man. I accept your apology. And if I'm honest, too, I think you *were* a little jealous. It's been just you and me for so long, I think you were a bit threatened by another guy around me. But you know I'll always be your best friend, right?"

Marcus sighed. He could feel Jarel's eyes on him. "I owe you an apology, too, Jarel. I never should have made any assumptions about you or your intentions toward my friend. Maybe he's right, and I was jealous. You seem like a nice guy, and I do want to get to know you better. It seems like we'll have quite a bit of time now since we're going to be traveling together on that ship." he gestured toward the waiting vessel.

Jarel's full lips curved slightly. "I accept your apology. Leopold has told me about your accident. You've been through a lot. I admit I was wary of you because you have power similar to that of Nun the Wiser. I look forward to getting to know you, too."

Leopold clapped his hands together. "Great! Now let's get in that boat, head to that beautiful sailing ship, and go save the world!" He started for the boat.

"No, not yet!" Marcus said. "Agatho is bringing Sadie and Cornus here. I want to say goodbye before we just...sail away. They deserve to know where we're going—and why. Besides, what if this doesn't work and I never see her again?" Tears stood in Marcus's eyes as he stared at his best friend. Leopold looked at Marcus and sighed. He walked over and wrapped a supportive arm around Marcus's waist.

"At least sit down while we wait, Marcus. No sense hurting yourself like this." He took Marcus's arms and eased him to the sand. "Hey, what is this?" he asked, knocking his knuckles against the metal of the new prosthesis. "I didn't even notice it before."

"I guess you've been too distracted to notice," Marcus laughed, then filled Leopold in on the details, showing off the moving parts and grip strength of his new prosthetic.

CHAPTER TEN

ARGUMENTS AND GOODBYES

Sadie

Sadie could hear Cornus yelling her name, excitement evident in his voice. She stopped grinding grain with the pestle in her hand, looking with some satisfaction at the mound of flour in her mortar. She dumped it into the half-full sack on the floor at her feet and rose, arming sweat from her forehead.

"I'm coming!" she called, apologizing and then signing to the startled Cativera around her that she needed to leave and would return soon. They nodded, returning to their work as she left.

Trotting through the shafts of the bruwe, she looked for Cornus. At last, she found him all the way back in their room.

"What is it? I thought you were going out to work with the Lokin mounds with Suri today since he doesn't have herd duty."

"Yes, I was going to do that. However, I was looking through this book one more time, and I have started to make sense of some of the words in it," Cornus said, looking up at her, his orange eyes bright with eagerness. "I think I might be starting to understand the language of the <<null>>."

"*Really?*" Sadie exclaimed. She plopped down on the bed next to Cornus, looking at the book in his lap as if she'd suddenly be able to read it, too. Of course, it still looked as indecipherable as it had before.

"Do you think you could learn to speak it?" Sadie asked, trying to control her own excitement. She didn't want to get her hopes up.

"I am not sure. It does seem that if I could make sense of the words, I could say them. It is more a matter of figuring out what they mean and learning how to communicate them to the <<null>>," he said.

Sadie sighed. "You're right, of course. It doesn't make much sense for you to be able to read them or say them if you don't know what they mean," she said.

"It is, however, a step in the right direction," Cornus said shyly, looking up at her out of the corner of his eye. She grinned back as she recognized one of her own phrases coming from the Scrybb boy's mouth.

"I'd help you study if I could," Sadie said, "but I know there's not much I can do. I'm going to go back and help finish grinding grain. If you figure something else out, that's where I'll be. I don't think you should just holler my name next time, though, Cornus. It startles everyone. The Cativera don't speak out loud that much as it is, much less holler throughout the bruwe at the top of their lungs."

Cornus smiled sheepishly at her. "I was just so excited," he said. "I will be more circumspect in the future."

As Sadie returned to the grain room and resumed her task, she thought about what it could mean if Cornus really did learn how to translate the language of the phantasms. If they could travel to a Brynar and communicate with one, could they find out why the phantasms wanted to kill humans? Could they find a way to make peace?

Sadie rolled her eyes with mild annoyance when Cornus came rustling into the grain room just a few minutes later. He looked around anxiously but didn't call out.

"I'm over here, Cornus," she sighed. She hadn't even been grinding long enough to work up a new sweat yet. "What's going on now?"

"Yati came down looking for us. Apparently, something is

happening with Marcus and the—'ship'"? Yes, the ship they were making, and Agatho has come to bring us to go and see Marcus and the others."

Sadie got to her feet in a hurry, nearly dumping the flour from her pestle as she set it aside. Several of the Cativera nearby watched her curiously. She signed to them quickly that she had to leave. Malu, the person closest to her, signed that they would take care of her flour and remaining grain. Sadie thanked them and made her way carefully out of the room full of busy Cativera.

Leaving the sounds of grinding behind, Sadie followed Cornus down the round red tunnel that led to the entrance of Grasian. She brushed miserably at herself as she walked.

"Couldn't we have gotten a little notice? I'm a mess!" She exclaimed. Flour puffed from her clothes as she slapped her hands against them. Cornus turned to look back at her.

"Sadie, you do not look half as bad as you think. It is only a little bit of flour dust." He chuckled as a small white cloud filled the air around her head when she shook it, making her long hair fly about. She sneezed as she inadvertently breathed in some of it.

"Oh, why now?" Sadie complained. She was hot and felt sticky and gross. "A little warning would have been nice. Then I could have had a bath, at least."

"Are you not at least excited to see Marcus?" Cornus asked. He sounded puzzled. "I know how much you like each other. I would have thought you would be happier. I know if I was going to be able to see Davidia..." He trailed off, a melancholy tone in his voice.

Sadie took his arm, squeezing it tightly. "Oh, I am. I think about Marcus all the time," she said. "I would just like to look my best now that I'm finally going to see him again."

Cornus cleared his throat. "I am not claiming to be an expert on Marcus," he said, "but I am pretty sure he will not be concerned about how you are dressed or whether you have flour on your shirt."

"Oh, Cornus," Sadie laughed. "Maybe being a Scrybb makes it difficult for you to understand since you're always dressed in your best leaves, clean and smelling fresh. But for humans, we do like to wash and smell good and dress nicely."

"I do remember from our first trip together how you all liked to be clean and change your clothes. I am sorry you cannot change clothes this time."

By now, they were out of the underground bruwe and rounding the curve. It was time to stop talking and walk slowly and quietly. Sadie liked to take the time to practice signing whenever she had the chance. She and Cornus were both getting better at speaking in the Cativeran sign language. When they were alone, they practiced together, and both of them understood more signs and were able to sign faster. Sadie no longer felt like one of the children in Grasian.

"Do you really think Marcus will be able to actually do something about the moon?" Cornus signed to her.

"I don't know," she signed back with a sigh. "It's hard to believe that he could actually do something so—so—big." Sadie couldn't think of the sign for the word she wanted to use. She hoped the plan Marcus had wasn't *too* dangerous.

Finally, they reached the landing area where they found Agatho waiting patiently for them. He greeted them with a Cativeran sign.

After returning his greeting, they both rushed to his side. The two-person harness was already in place behind Agatho's torso, and Cornus gave Sadie a hand as she climbed up his leg to sidle into place in the harness. She turned and reached down to pull Cornus up behind her. Once they were secure, Agatho vaulted into the air.

"Cornus," she called back, "you could just create vines on your own and pull yourself up, couldn't you?"

"Hm, yes," he said against her back, "I could do that. I had not thought about it before."

"Then you probably don't *really* need this harness, either," she called again. "You could just create your own and hold yourself in place."

"I—I really do not want to talk about that right now, Sadie," Cornus said from behind her. He sounded scared. Perhaps he was unsure of the strength of his own vines and ability to hold on? Maybe Cornus was afraid of heights. She shook her head. Of all the things she had learned about Cornus, she knew that he was far stronger than he gave himself credit for.

The flight to the shore of the Diluvium was about a two-hour journey. Sadie gasped in awe as she saw the beautiful ship at anchor in the sea just offshore. Why hadn't she thought of that? As many books as she had read back on Earth, the thought of a sailing ship hadn't even crossed her mind.

As Agatho circled and landed on the beach, she saw Marcus waiting, and she forgot all about reading and sailing ships.

Cornus had to get down first, and Sadie had to stop herself from snapping at him impatiently. When he was finally out from behind her, she was able to maneuver herself out of the vines that had held her safely in place and climb down Agatho's leg. When her feet thumped to the sand, she looked up to see Marcus walking toward her. Part of Sadie wanted to run to him and grab him, squeezing him tightly in her arms. But she held herself back. This was *Marcus*. She would not hurt him.

Instead, she stepped toward him as he approached her. They came together in what felt like their own special bubble of space. Sadie slid her arms around Marcus and felt his arms wrap around her, his hand sliding into her hair to cup the back of her head, and their lips came together for a kiss.

Sadie was still breathing, but at the same time, she felt breathless. Marcus's lips were full and soft against her own. His fingers tightened against the back of her head, and he grabbed a handful of her hair and pulled lightly, then let go and slid his hand down her back to her waist. Her body tingled everywhere Marcus touched.

"Uh, guys?" Sadie heard Cornus say from below her. Sadie opened her eyes to see that she and Marcus were floating three feet off the ground.

"Marcus!" she cried against his mouth. His hazel eyes opened wide in surprise.

"Oops," he muttered and eased them down until the sand was back beneath their feet.

"Kinky," said Leopold. Marcus glared at him. Leopold shrugged. "Hey, just think of all the implications." A Black boy she had never seen before smacked Leopold in the arm with an affectionate smile. "Ow, Jarel."

"You look beautiful," Marcus said, holding her at arm's length and staring into her eyes. Cornus signed to her from behind Marcus, "I told you!" and she smiled, feeling a flush climbing her neck to warm her face. "Thank you, Marcus. You look good, too." She looked at his metal right hand on her left arm. "What is this?"

He let go of her and told her about the new prosthesis the Fyrtudo had made for him. Cornus moved closer to look at it and was immediately pulled into a bear hug. After that, introductions were made all around. Sadie was thrilled to meet Boehlkea, who was gorgeous, making Sadie feel painfully self-conscious about her own dirty appearance again.

She was delighted to meet Jarel, so happy that Leopold had found someone who obviously cared for him. Jarel's face didn't reveal his emotions, but in the way he stood so protectively close and placed one arm affectionately around Leopold's shoulders, Sadie could see it. Sadie saw a frown crease Marcus's brow as he looked over at them. She wondered what that was about as she walked over to give Leopold a hug.

"Sadie!" Leopold exclaimed, throwing his arms around her and lifting her off her feet. Sadie squealed a little as Leopold squeezed her so hard that her back cracked between her shoulder blades.

"Put me down!" she insisted, kicking at him a little while trying not to hurt him.

"Sorry, Sadie, it's just been so long since I've seen you! I missed your cute face!" Leopold said. He started to reach for her cheeks, and she grabbed his wrists.

"If you touch my face, I will break your hands," she growled. Jarel appeared behind Leopold and wrapped long arms around him, pinning his arms to his sides.

"I think this girl has asked you to stop touching her, and you should respect that, shouldn't you, Leopold?" he said quietly. Leopold relaxed and smiled at her, saying, "You're right, I was just excited. I haven't seen Sadie in weeks!" He turned slightly, sliding an arm around Jarel's waist. "I'm sorry."

"It's okay, Leopold. I know how ebullient you are. So you were living with the humans?" She raised her eyebrows as she looked up at Jarel, who was gazing at the ship.

"Yes," Leopold said. "He lived with—in the human bruwe. He's coming with us on the ship. His, uh...I guess they're kind of like foster parents? They are coming with too. They're basically the experts on sailing the ship, or will kind of be now since they sailed it here from Thicce Colpat. They were boat builders and fisher people in their bruwe." Sadie giggled a little as Leopold realized he was babbling and stopped talking. He blushed, and Jarel began to murmur quietly in his ear.

Cornus joined them, having finished a conversation with Marcus. Sadie watched as Leopold held himself back from an overly enthusiastic embrace that the more somber Scrybb boy would not appreciate. Cornus allowed himself to be hugged and seemed quite happy to meet Jarel. Hesitantly, he held out one leafy hand and looked quite pleased when Jarel grasped it and shook it in return.

Sadie smiled as Marcus stood beside her, shifting his cane to his right hand and putting his left arm around her shoulders. She reached up and held his hand with her own while sliding her right arm around his waist. It felt very natural to stand here with him, even after the weeks apart. Boehlkea came and stood with them to watch Cornus, Leopold, and Jarel in an intense conversation. From what Sadie could overhear, the human boys were talking about Davidia—a subject she knew Cornus would gladly talk about for hours. She smiled to herself at the joy on her friend's face. Cornus burst into laughter as Leopold made a face and spit into the sand.

"So, Sadie," Boehlkea broke into her thoughts, "what is it like, living with the Cativera? Since I have been restricted to living here in Fisc, I have only heard stories about them."

"Grasian is a wonderful place, and the Cativera are friendly and hospitable people," Sadie said. "Although, that does seem to be true of all the people of Lysomnus, honestly. Cornus and I are thoroughly enjoying learning their sign language and joining them in all their different tasks. All except herding, of course. Neither of us is capable of doing that!"

"What are the Struthtaur like?" Marcus asked. Sadie leaned against him carefully, enjoying the physical contact after so much time apart. She was glad Agatho had brought her and Cornus to see Marcus and the others before they left.

"They're tall, strong creatures," she started and then proceeded to tell him and Boehlkea about her first time seeing one on the day of the quake when Yati had saved her from the stampede.

"How terrifying!" Boehlkea exclaimed, hearing of Sadie's near miss and the death of the injured Struthtaur. "I really must find a way to visit the other people of Lysomnus. The Cativera sound so fascinating, and they are such an important part of our lives, providing meat and flour and the loka. I would also like to learn this sign language of theirs."

"I wish I could come with you," Sadie said wistfully, looking up at Marcus. "I could start to teach you some of the Cativeran sign language..." She trailed off as an expression of fear crossed Marcus's face.

"I...I don't want you risking yourself, Sadie. It's not safe." Pain slammed into her chest as if Marcus had struck her, and she gasped at the force of it, pressing her hands to her sternum.

The pain of feeling unwanted made Sadie want to cry. She swallowed hard against the restriction in her throat, but it wouldn't loosen up. When she sucked in a deep breath, air whistled down her throat past the stricture.

"Marcus, if you don't want me to come along, just say so," she said thickly, hearing the tears in her own voice, forcing it past the obstruction. Out of the corner of her eye, she saw Cornus look at her.

"Are you okay?" Cornus signed. "What's wrong?"

"I want to go home, back to Grasian," Sadie signed back. She twisted out of Marcus's one-armed embrace and stepped away, swiping angrily at tears she couldn't stop. Dismay was visible on Boehlkea's face for a moment before more tears blurred her vision.

"Sadie!" Marcus exclaimed, sounding surprised. "I just want you to be safe. We have no idea what this journey is going to be like. None of us—including Janke and Maril—are experienced sailors. The only people going are people who *have* to go."

Sadie looked at Leopold. "Are you going?"

He flushed and nodded.

Sadie looked bitterly at Marcus. "And what expertise does your *bro* offer for this expedition that you need him so badly? This—*person*, I understand," she tossed a hand in Jarel's direction. "He has experience in boats on the ocean, right? And your sister, too," Sadie gestured at Boehlkea. "For her experience in the Diluvium. But what is *Leopold* possibly going to do for you that *I* couldn't do?"

Somewhere inside her mind, Sadie was shocked at how quickly the pleasant gathering had turned into an unhappy argument. She was screaming at herself inside to stop, to wrap her arms around Marcus again, and enjoy the time that remained before he and the others left. After all, Cornus wasn't going with them either. But she couldn't do it. Every time she saw the guilty look on Marcus's face and the unsure expression on Leopold's, her anger exploded back so hard her heart was nearly pounding out of her chest.

Jarel cleared his throat and looked at Marcus, eyebrows raised. Leopold looked away, embarrassed. When Marcus reached for her hand, she pulled away from him. She walked stiffly over to Cornus and grabbed his hand instead. Tears were still running down her face, and her throat was tight, making it difficult to get the words out.

"Cornus, I think we should go. I feel like we were just brought here to say goodbye so they could feel better before they left." Sadie choked as she tried to draw a breath because thick mucus clogged her throat. She tried to pull Cornus along with her to head down the beach to the place where Agatho rested patiently.

Cornus, however, was not ready to leave. He pulled his leafy hand out of hers and stood resolutely on the sand, crossing his arms. "I am sorry that you are upset, Sadie, but I am not ready to leave yet. Our friends are going on a dangerous journey, and I want to visit with them and see them off. We do not know what could happen, and I for one am not wasting this opportunity. Of course, I would like to join them, but if I cannot be of use on their journey, our friends back in Cativera expect us to return."

Sadie's shoulders slumped. She looked up at Marcus, tear-streaked, her tousled hair blowing in the wind, and slowly stepped back to his side.

"Marcus," Sadie whispered, "I am so sorry." Her face was hot with embarrassment. With just a few words, Cornus had chastised her in front of everyone and made her feel like a child throwing a temper tantrum. Marcus looked at her, jaw clenched tightly, hazel eyes blazing, and she could see that, for the first time since she had met him, he was furious with her.

"I'm not the one you should apologize to, Sadie," he said angrily. She turned her head to see Leopold staring at his feet, a hurt expression on his face. Jarel's arms were wrapped tightly around Leopold. At first, she wanted to scoff and badger Leopold for pouting. As she took a couple of deep breaths and replayed the things she had said, she realized she really had hurt her friend's feelings.

"Oh," she said and took a few quick steps to face him. "Leopold, I am so, so, sorry. I was feeling so left out, I didn't think about what I was saying. I didn't mean any of the things I said." She could almost feel the waves of cold anger coming from Jarel as he stared down at her.

"Leopold, please, I'm sorry. Won't you forgive me? I spoke thoughtlessly." A long moment that seemed to last forever stretched out after she stopped speaking. Then Leopold looked up at her, his bright blue eyes meeting hers through tousled blond hair that had grown long since they had first met. Then he slowly smiled.

"Sadie, I can't stay mad at you. I know you didn't mean it." He stepped forward and threw his arms around Sadie, pinning her own arms to her sides. "We'll always be friends, goof, no matter what," he whispered in her ear while he squeezed her tightly.

"Oof!" Sadie grunted as the air was forced out of her body. She could hear Boehlkea and Cornus laughing at her discomfiture and wriggled, drawing in a breath. "Leopold, could you please put me down?"

He laughed, giving her an affectionate smack on the cheek through her hair as he set her back on her feet. Jarel's lips were curved in a smile when Sadie looked up at him. She was most concerned about Marcus, and it made her feel a rush of relief when she saw he was relaxed and had a grin on his face when she caught sight of him. When she was free of Leopold's hug, she returned to Marcus's side and slid her arms around him.

"Hey," she said quietly, "I don't want to fight. But can you tell me why you're taking Leopold along and not me?"

Marcus sighed and gestured at a nearby rock. She let go of him so he could walk with his cane to sit down. When they were settled side-by-side, he took her hand and brought it to his lips. After a gentle kiss, he lowered their interlocked hands to his lap.

"Sadie, I honestly don't want you to risk your life. We have no idea what we'll be facing out there on the Diluvium. Even Boehlkea doesn't know much about what there could be once we get farther out than her people have traveled from Fisc. Janke, Maril, Jarel, they've all taken boats out to sea to fish, but only *smaller* boats. They've experienced storms out to sea and seen people from their bruwe die when caught in them. This large ship should be safer. Leopold *does* bring some knowledge of sailing ships since he and his father used to research and build model ships together. He helped the Scrybb figure out what the ship should look like, the sails, and that stuff. Jarel and his foster parents, Leopold, and the Scrybb crafters all worked together to design and build the ship. Janke and Maril sailed it here." He took a deep breath and continued.

"Basically, we decided who was going to go on this journey that way. As hard as it is for me to leave you behind, I can't bring you along. Everything inside me is telling me that what lies ahead is going to take everything I have. If I have to focus on that, I can't be distracted. And you," Marcus lifted Sadie's hand to his mouth to kiss it again, "*you* distract me, Sadie. You have no idea how much. All I want to do right now is tell you yes, that of course you can come, but I can't. I have to say no. I'm just glad you'll have Cornus with you." Marcus was still holding Sadie's hand against his mouth as he talked. The movement of his lips and the feeling of his breath raised the hair on her skin. She put her other hand against the side of his face and pulled him closer. Their mouths met in a gentle kiss that slowly grew hungry and passionate.

"Gross!" Leopold yelled from nearby. "Get a room!"

They broke apart, and Sadie felt her cheeks flush. When she looked at Marcus, his face was relaxed, showing no discomfort. His hazel eyes burned as if he could see into her soul. "I am not embarrassed by my feelings for you, Sadie," he said. "Leopold can make his jokes. There's nothing funny about this, not to me." He pulled her close again. She could see the others turning back to their conversation, and she eagerly kissed Marcus back.

Sadie's lips were puffy from Marcus's kisses when they rejoined the others later, who were standing around a small fire Jarel had built at nightfall. Agatho was talking to Cornus; she could hear his rumbling, harsh voice in small bursts. It was so sweet to spend the afternoon hours just talking to Marcus, kissing Marcus, talking and kissing, and kissing-and-talking. Marcus wiped her tears away when she cried at the thought of never being able to tell her family about finding love. "At least they met me before we came here," he said to comfort her and then kissed her on the nose.

"Don't patronize me," Sadie retorted, and Marcus laughed.

"Keep flirting with that big vocabulary," he said. "I'm sapiosexual, you know." Sadie giggled.

Now, she gasped at the sight of several odd-looking yellow

creatures approaching them. Each carried dishes laden with food. Marcus looked to see what had startled her, then relaxed. "Sadie, come meet the Aragani," he said, tugging her by the hand.

"Hey, Paracles!" he called and turned to wave the others over. Boehlkea brightened when she saw them. "Freshly cooked dinner!" she said. "Paracles, thank you all so much!" She turned and introduced Sadie, Cornus, Jarel, and Leopold to Paracles and his companions.

"The Aragani help us in the Diluvium, doing things like handling the emeristan, drying clothes, crafting things that we cannot," she explained.

Jarel seemed interested at first in meeting the Aragani, but as he squatted and they came up close to him, a strange expression crossed his face, and he stood up quickly, nearly falling over, and walked rapidly away down the beach. Sadie watched as Leopold ran after him, calling his name. She was distracted as Agatho lifted one of the yellow creatures in his talons, and shrill screams filled the air.

"Agatho!" Boehlkea scolded the immense Stondefel. "Put Paguru down! You're scaring her!" The Stondefel, looking contrite, set the dainty Aragani back on her feet.

"Apologies, little one," Agatho rumbled. "I just wanted to see you up close. I have never seen your kind before." Boehlkea was comforting a shaking Paguru, murmuring to her and explaining why the giant had picked her up. Sadie wanted to help but wasn't sure what she could possibly say since she didn't know the creatures. She took a plate one of the Aragani was holding out to her.

"Agatho," Marcus said, "It's not polite to just pick people up without their consent. You could at least *ask* first." He laughed before taking a mouthful of fish stew from a steaming bowl Paracles had set down in the sand.

Before too long, Leopold and Jarel appeared in the firelight. Leopold came over alone, looked over the food, and picked up a plate. "Jarel and I are going to eat on the other side of the fire, okay?" Sadie wondered why the boys didn't want to join them for the delicious meal and meet the Aragani, but she kept eating and didn't say anything. She had put her foot in her mouth enough for one day.

She was delighted to be personally introduced to each of the Aragani as she ate. They were interesting, and their voices were funny. She made sure not to laugh as they spoke to her. The delicious food she was eating had been prepared by these people, and they had carried it all the way down the beach. For people the size of the Aragani, the distance must have seemed like miles.

"Magistera," Sadie said to the Aragani closest to her, "I have to tell you just how much I appreciate the Aragani for making this food and bringing it to us! It's so delicious, and I don't know if we had plans for anything else to eat out here."

"No," Boehlkea confirmed. "I was just telling Paguru the same thing. They didn't have to come all the way out here for us!"

"We insisted!" Paracles declared from beside Marcus. "If you are going to risk yourselves to try to save Lysomnus, then bringing you a meal is the very least the Aragani could do." Seeing that the food had been consumed and the plates and bowls were empty, Paracles began to order the others around, gathering things together for their return to Fisc. Leopold quickly brought the dishes he and Jarel had used back to the Aragani before they left.

Once the Aragani were gone, Jarel and Leopold returned to sit with the others.

"So," Marcus began, a cautious look on his face, "what was that all about? I thought you wanted to meet the other people of Lysomnus?" he directed this last at Jarel.

The tall boy winced. His dark skin was ashen in the firelight. "I...I couldn't talk to them. Or rather hear them talk. I didn't know they were...That they were—" His chest hitched, his voice caught, and he swallowed, dropping his head to Leopold's shoulder.

Leopold put an arm around Jarel, pulling him tightly against his own body. "Apparently," he explained, "those creatures—those people—have been caught and eaten by the humans in Jarel's bruwe."

Boehlkea let out a small scream, then covered her mouth and started crying. Sadie wrapped her arms around the Muirnati girl. "How could you?" Boehlkea cried out, glaring at Jarel.

"I didn't know," he said, staring at the crackling flames. "I've never seen one alive before. Janke and I have caught fish, but there are different fishing grounds where people go to catch food in the Diluvium. Other people in our bruwe brought those...those creatures in when they caught them. It's been several years since I've seen any. I just didn't know, Boehlkea. I'm sorry."

Boehlkea was crying harder, and Sadie thought of how Paguru had screamed when Agatho picked her up. Wouldn't the human people who caught them hear those screams or the words the Aragani were speaking? Then she thought of humans on Earth, hunting whales, and dolphins dying in nets when tuna fishermen caught them, and she realized that those humans probably didn't care any more than humans on Earth had.

Boehlkea shoved Sadie away, bolted to her feet, and stumbled off toward the incoming waves. A few moments later, Sadie heard the sound of Boehlkea throwing up. Jarel got up and walked off in the opposite direction, telling Leopold not to follow him in a harsh tone of voice. Marcus, Sadie, Leopold, and Cornus were left sitting by the fire with Agatho looming over them.

"What a terrible misunderstanding," Agatho rumbled. "I feel badly for both of them. I hope this does not cause problems for your journey."

Marcus looked up at his friend's terrifying features. "I'm going whether they can get over their issues or not." Sadie reached up and grabbed his hand, squeezing it to let him know she was there for him. "I can understand why Boehlkea is upset. It shook me up too, thinking about people like Paracles or Paguru being captured in nets and then killed and eaten. But she has to understand that not everyone on Lysomnus has lived the same life."

Leopold stood up. "That's true. Jarel's people were close to starving a lot of the time. Nun the Wiser and the other humans with power might have been eating well while visiting and abusing the other bruwe of Lysomnus, but the rest of the humans were left to their own devices. That doesn't mean eating other sentient creatures is acceptable, but Jarel didn't even know the Aragani were actually people who are aware and can speak. He was devastated when he realized what they were."

"I understand," came Boehlkea's voice out of the dark, the crash of the surf behind her. The green-blue glow of her body lit up the darkness as she approached them. "It is not Jarel's fault. Many of my people might not understand such a thing, but we can sit and think rationally of just how many ways there are that Nun the Wiser's rule devastated the people of Lysomnus. At first, it might seem as though it was just the brute force she and the other empowered humans used to manipulate the people of each bruwe, taking advantage of the resources available and making the people feel as if they were mere slaves to the humans. But now we are learning that there were others who fell victim to Nun the Wiser and her followers, as well. Her own people, living in her bruwe, were starved and treated cruelly. They lived in fear. And because of that, they had to find ways to feed themselves in a world they knew little to nothing about. Fish are food—we all eat them—but the Aragani are people. How would a human, blindly catching creatures from the sea, know the difference?"

"Janke would have," Jarel's voice came from the dark beyond the fire. "He knew every species he brought in. He studied them. Janke would have realized the Aragani were sentient and trying to communicate if one ever came up in *his* nets." Jarel's dark features slowly materialized in the light of the fire as he walked to Leopold's side and sat down. "But they were only ever dead when brought in with the day's catch from the people who fished to the south."

Sadie watched sleepily as Leopold looked up at Jarel and took his hand. He wove his fingers through Jarel's tightly and squeezed. Jarel looked at him gratefully. She realized just how happy she was that the two of them—who could have both been stuck in this world, alone and miserable—had found each other.

Sadie found herself lulled by the soft sound of murmuring voices as the others continued to talk. Her eyes drifted shut as she watched Boehlkea gracefully lower herself to sit beside Jarel. Marcus's warmth beside her lured her deeper into sleep as she snuggled herself against him and slipped away.

Early gray dawn came all too soon, and Sadie and Cornus had to say goodbye. Tears trickled down Sadie's face as she hugged each of her friends in the chill fog that had drifted in from the sea. She saved Marcus for last and found herself crying even as he kissed her. She didn't allow herself to admit until she and Cornus were harnessed on Agatho's back that she was terrified this might be the last time she would ever see Marcus. If that ship sank in the Diluvium or the moon caused more quakes or if it actually crashed onto Lysomnus before Marcus could use his power to stop it or if he couldn't stop it! Sadie had to fight to make herself stop thinking about it before she said anything to Cornus or let it drive her crazy. Instead, she told Agatho to take off, wrapping her arms tightly around his stony torso and smiling as cheerfully as she could as they flew away, watching as Marcus and the others dwindled to tiny specks blurred by her unstoppable tears.

CHAPTER ELEVEN

SETTING SAIL

Marcus

After Sadie and Cornus were out of sight, Marcus sighed and looked around at the others. "I guess this is it," he said. "It's time to get to the ship and start this venture. Let's get ourselves into that boat and over to the ship. Do you two feel like rowing?" He looked at Leopold and Jarel, who glanced at each other and nodded. As a group, they walked slowly with Marcus, who was regretting another night of sleeping on the hard ground. Although he couldn't regret that he'd been holding Sadie close as he lay on the sand—never that.

The small wooden boat rocked back and forth on the sand as waves slid up the shore and crashed against its hull. Jarel and Leopold removed their boots and tossed them inside, then held the boat steady while Marcus braced himself with his cane and held Boehlkea's proffered hand, stepping carefully over the side to sit on one of the boards that served as seats. Boehlkea followed him. Once Marcus and Boehlkea were seated in the boat, Jarel joined Leopold, and together, they pushed it out into the ocean. They jumped in enthusiastically, splashing water everywhere with their feet as they lifted them over the side.

"Hey!" Marcus shouted, wiping water from his face. "You did that on purpose."

Jarel and Leopold looked at each other, laughing. "We had to get the boat out deep enough to keep it from grounding," Leopold said as he reached for his boots.

"I'd swear I saw you splash water at Marcus with your hand as you jumped in," Boehlkea said.

"Who, me?" Leopold pressed a damp hand against his chest, wide-eyed.

Marcus rolled his eyes as Jarel took up the oars and began to row them toward the ship. He noticed Jarel had well-developed muscles that rippled beneath his shirt as he rowed. Clearly, this boy who'd grown up in Lysomnus had worked hard—hard enough to develop a strong body that Marcus, with his slender body, envied.

It was only a few minutes before they arrived at the much larger vessel that floated at anchor. A man and woman leaned over the side rail above them, dropping a rope ladder that clattered and unrolled as it fell, just reaching the water. They also dropped rope lines that Jarel and Leopold grabbed and tied to the front and back of the boat.

"You first," Jarel said to Boehlkea and then waved to Marcus to follow her after she'd started up the ladder. Climbing the rope ladder was difficult for Marcus. He found himself struggling as he neared the top. The new arm was working well, and he was able to hold some of his weight with it, but the pain shooting down his legs and the ache in his back made it hard for him to continue. He closed his eyes and pushed through it. Leopold went next with Marcus's cane. Jarel came up last.

Once they were all aboard the ship, Jarel turned to help get the rowboat on board. Leopold quickly jumped to the slender woman's end to help her pull the heavy boat.

"Hey, I can help with that," Marcus said. "You guys don't have to do so much hard work."

"No," Leopold replied quickly, breathing heavily as he pulled on the rope. "You need to save your power for this planned moon venture of yours. No sense wearing yourself down along the way."

Sweat had dampened the clothing of all four of them by the time they'd gotten the boat up to the side of the ship. Once it was onboard, they moved the boat farther up the deck where it would be out of the way and lashed it down.

Once this was done, everyone sat down where they could find a comfortable place. Leopold and Jarel introduced Janke and Maril to Marcus and Boehlkea, and greetings were voiced all around.

As Marcus looked around, he admired the workmanship that had gone into building such a beautiful ship in a very short time. Gleaming wood formed the deck, and at each end, steps led to a small upper deck. At the rear, a large standing wheel with spokes and handles stood in the center of a raised platform. A thick mast soared into the sky from the middle of the ship's deck, and two smaller poles stood front and back of the mast. Each held sails that were currently furled. Next to the stairs of each upper deck, walls stood with doors that obviously led to the decks below.

Maril was saying something.

"I'm sorry?" Marcus said, returning his attention to the conversation.

"We have stores of food, water, juice, and clothing beneath us and at this end of the ship, or *stern,* as Leopold says it is called, along with a kitchen for us to cook and eat," she indicated the rear of the ship, "and rooms for each of us in the *bow.*" A wave of her hand indicated the door in the front wall. "Now we need to haul the anchor and get underway. Janke and I have practiced with the sails on the way here and feel like we have a good grasp of the basics. We will teach all of you, as well."

Janke nodded to them all and stood up with Maril. He told them all to follow, and they climbed the steps to the upper deck on the bow. There, they saw a massive chain that had to have been forged by the Fyrtudo while the Scrybb had been building the ship. Marcus wondered how all the Crafters had created this ship in such a short time. He didn't think shipbuilders could build a full sailing ship on Earth in a matter of a few weeks. A crank stood nearby, with a chain wrapped around it.

"We are lucky here, so close to the shore," Janke said. "The bottom is sandy, so there are no rocks or other obstacles for the anchor to catch on. Otherwise, we would have to raise the sails and move the ship over the anchor to lift it out once it was up and down. We had to do that on the way here. Right now, we can just crank it up since it is sitting in soft sand." He and Maril demonstrated, each taking one side of the crank's handles and turning them. The chain wound around the crank, a loud clanking sound shattering the morning quiet. Marcus realized that even Maril must be very strong —deceptively so, for her narrow frame.

Finally, they all heard a booming *clonk!* as the anchor struck the side of the ship. Quickly, Maril moved to the side of the ship as Janke locked the crank into place with a lever on the side. He joined Maril, and together, they leaned over the railing to secure the anchor as the others watched from farther back along the railing. "That way, it won't smash against the side of the ship and damage it," Janke explained to the others after the job was done.

Next, they all trooped back down to the lower deck to watch Janke and Maril open the sails. The breeze was freshening, and the heavy material filled quickly. The ship began to move. Janke jogged to the back of the ship, climbing the stairs to the raised deck of the stern and grabbing the handles of the wheel while Maril manipulated the ropes attached to the sails.

"It's complicated," she said to them. "There's definitely a knack to it. You have to use a combination of turning the sails to use the wind while the wheel turns the 'rudder'—a piece below the water in the back of the ship to move it left or right. And it all depends on the wind. If we lose the wind, we won't go anywhere."

The ship was turning and moving out to sea as she spoke. The sails moved above their heads as Marcus watched.

"You see, we thought at first that we would always have to have the wind at our backs," Maril continued. "But it turns out that at times, we can have the ship turned so that we are nearly facing the wind, depending on how we use the sails. It seems to change how the air pressure affects the sail. They might not appear full, but the ship still moves."

"Fascinating," Jarel murmured, watching her move the ropes and the way the sails moved. "This large ship isn't all that different from the smaller sailboats we used on our side of the world."

Boehlkea appeared to have no interest at all as she was moving around and inspecting the details of the ship. Jarel, Marcus, and Leopold stayed by Maril, recognizing they'd need to take their turn on the sails in order to reach their destination as fast as possible.

Boehlkea turned back to them from the side of the ship.

"How did you and the Scrybb build this marvelous ship so quickly? It seems impossible!"

Janke nodded at her from his position at the wheel. "I never thought it could be done. It takes us much longer to build our small boats. The Scrybb Crafters have skills such as I've never seen before. They used steam to bend the wood, but still—they cut trees and had keel timbers and planking ready so fast. They had the framing in place in a few days. They set the deck timbers in so tightly and well joined that nothing could slip into those joints. They made tar from peat and sealed the ship, and these ropes as well," he indicated the rigging for the sails, "and their Weavers! They have looms that made this canvas for the sails with waxed thread by the time the ship was built. I think the Fier...Fyrtudo?" He looked at Leopold for confirmation, who nodded. "The Fyrtudo were hard-pressed to forge the anchor chain, winch, and anchor in time. I don't even know what they concocted to seal the deck." He shook his head in disbelief.

Boehlkea and Marcus looked at each other in wonder at the accomplishments of the Scrybb. Marcus had witnessed their craftsmanship before, but nothing like this amazing ship.

An hour or so after their departure, Leopold and Jarel stood watching Maril run the sails. Marcus was just getting ready to lie down on a deck chair Janke had hauled up from the hold that had been designed especially for him when they all heard a splash.

Leopold and Jarel ran to the railing, with Marcus making his way behind them as quickly as he could with his cane. Maril tied down the sail ropes and joined them.

They all leaned over the railing to see Boehlkea swimming alongside. She waved up at them.

"I thought this was a fast-sailing ship!" she called up to them. "Most Muirnati can swim much faster than this!"

"But not for several days and nights!" Maril called back. "You children." She shook her head. "When she gets tired of swimming, lower the ladder down to her. I am not stopping this ship every time she wants to jump overboard."

Marcus was laughing with the others at his sister's antics as she cavorted in the deep blue waters of the Diluvium but sobered quickly. Boehlkea would need to spend time in the water every day to survive. He hoped it wouldn't create problems as they sailed farther out to sea, and the ship gained speed.

It was amazing how quickly the shore dropped out of sight behind them. The blue of the sea deepened, and the sun rose quickly to blaze down from the sky above them. Marcus had moved his chair from beneath the sails and was enjoying the sun's heat, finally removing his shirt.

"Marcus," Leopold's voice jerked him from a near doze. "Wake up."

"I'm not sleeping," Marcus said irritably.

"Sure looked like it from here," Leopold laughed. "Or are you just checking the back of your eyelids?"

Marcus peered at him, cracking one eye open. "What do you want, Leopold?"

"Well, you're the one who knows where we need to go. We need to plot a course before we get too far out to sea."

Marcus groaned. He'd just gotten comfortable. Whoever had designed this chair had definitely done a good job—it was long enough for him to stretch his legs out, and he could adjust the back so he was laying at an angle. His back was almost quiet, for once.

Which was probably why he'd nearly fallen asleep. Of course there was a reason he had to get up again.

Leopold reached out a hand, automatically knowing his friend would need help getting up. Marcus grabbed it, letting Leopold do a lot of the work of pulling him to his feet. Catching his cane on the way up, he found his footing and put a hand to his forehead.

"Now where did I put that map?" He thought hard and pictured himself changing outside the tunnel. Envisioning the bag the map was in, he remembered taking it out of his suit and putting it into his pack.

Looking wildly around, Marcus was panicking. What if he'd left the pack behind?

"Calm down, Marcus. Did you have the map in your pack?"

Marcus nodded.

"Well, you had the pack on your back when you were climbing the ladder ahead of me to get onto the ship. It has to be here somewhere," Leopold reassured him. "What did you do when you got on board? We haven't gone too many places since we got here."

"Other than the sails, we haven't gone to see anything except—ah!" Marcus exclaimed. "We watched Janke and Maril pull the anchor up. I think I put the pack down when we were up there." He pointed up toward the bow of the ship. They walked toward the steps leading to the upper deck where the anchor crank was.

"I can't believe I'd be so stupid as to let that map out of my sight," Marcus shook his head. "It's literally the most important part of this whole mission." He grimaced as he climbed the steps slowly. "There isn't much point in going if we haven't got the map."

"We're all a little distracted right now," Leopold comforted him. As they reached the top of the steps together, Marcus spied the pack lying on the deck near the anchor winch where he'd been standing earlier. Not wanting to wait, he reached out a hand and used his power to pull the pack to himself.

Leopold frowned. "You shouldn't do that too often. I'm literally right here and can go pick it up for you. I know you love being able to do things you couldn't before, but we're all depending on you right now. You need to conserve that energy for this plan."

Marcus could feel his face getting hot. "You're right," he said, taking a deep breath to try and calm himself. "I do need to keep that in mind. Even if we *can* find an entire island made of Halfriez material, I don't know if that will be enough to help me push the moon away from Lysomnus. I saw how draining it was on my dad to heal generations of damage to Nun the Wiser all at once."

"Exactly," Leopold said. "And that was just a *person.* You're planning to try to repair and move an entire celestial body."

Marcus nodded. "I will be more careful. Guess I'll be asking for more help from now on and letting you guys do more of the work."

"Don't worry, bro," Leopold said. "No one will mind helping you. Not when you're going to be saving the world again."

Marcus laughed, and Leopold carefully threw an arm around his shoulders as they made their way back down the stairs.

CHAPTER TWELVE

A CLOSE CALL

Sadie

Sadie was back in the grain room when the work leader called a halt for the day. It was time for the evening meal, and delicious smells had been tempting them all from concentrating on their work for the last hour or so. Everyone quickly picked up their materials and put their tools away, signing busily as paws and hands were freed.

As everyone hurried down the crowded corridor, the ground started shaking around them. Shrieks filled the air, and Sadie found herself struggling to stifle her own screams as she squatted down, hands over her head. There was nowhere to go with so many bodies crushed together in the tunnel.

Dust sifted down from the ceiling and through the opening to the sky above, A large crack fractured the wall to Sadie's left. Squeals erupted behind her, and she was suddenly shoved violently forward into the Cativera ahead of her, who grunted with the impact.

The shaking grew stronger, knocking Sadie off her feet. Her head slammed against the cracked wall. As soon as her head hit the surface, the unstable wall shifted, and she heard a crunch behind her. Sadie tried to get up but couldn't move her head. She grabbed at the curved wall behind herself and realized her hair was trapped inside the crack. The Cativera, who had also been thrown off their feet with the violence of the shaking, were climbing to their feet, and several had already run away.

Sadie screamed for help, and one of them turned and tried to help her up.

"I can't—I can't move!" Sadie cried out, jerking her head as panic set in. She had never felt so afraid. The Cativera signed, "I will find a way to help you," and hurried off in the same direction the others had gone. The rumbling grew quieter and then stopped abruptly. The sudden silence was deafening.

"Hello?" Sadie cried out. She was terrified of being stuck alone in the tunnel.

"Sadie?" she heard Cornus's voice answer.

"Cornus! I'm down here!" she yelled. Out of the corner of her eye, she saw movement that swelled to become a green blur that became Cornus, followed by the Cativera who had promised to help her. They had a knife in their hand. Sadie's eyes widened in fear.

"Oh, Sadie," Cornus said as he knelt down to get a better view of her predicament. "You are trapped! It is fortunate it was only your hair and not your head that slipped into the wall! Another inch or two and you would have died." He grabbed her hand and pulled it to his face, and she felt the warmth of tears against her skin.

Sadie hadn't thought of that possibility. She shuddered at the thought of losing her life by being crushed in the wall. She realized with an internal jolt of fear just how close she had come to dying.

The Cativera squatted down beside her, placed the knife on the floor, and signed to her. *I will have to cut the long fur on your head to get you free.*

Sadie closed her eyes. "I understand," she said. She hoped it wasn't too much of her hair that was caught. She couldn't move her head very much; she was dreadfully afraid it was a lot. Then she felt stupidly shallow for worrying about how much hair she might lose when she had just come so close to losing her life.

She kept her eyes closed as she felt the Cativera cutting gently.

Slowly, she felt the pulling on her hair ease, and her head was released from the wall. The relief to her neck was immediate, and she climbed to her feet. Then she put a hand to her head.

"Oh!" she cried out. Long strands of hair still hung around her face, but in the back, her hair had been cut off close to her head. It hung at different lengths due to how it had been caught in the wall.

"I must look ridiculous!" Tears trickled down Sadie's cheeks. She had never considered herself a vain person, but she had always loved her long black hair. It had felt like part of her identity. Now most of it was gone.

"No, Sadie," Cornus said, and embraced her tightly. "Not to us. None of us have hair anyway, and we are not used to seeing humans. We might be used to seeing you with your long hair, but this is just a small change. You are still you, and *I* am just grateful you are still here." Cornus did his best to reassure his distressed friend.

Sadie tucked the long hair back from around her face behind her ears. "I guess I'm going to need a pair of scissors," she said. "I'll have to cut it all short now. Guess I'll just have a new look!" She laughed half-heartedly, trying to stop the tears.

"Oh," she said, looking up at the Cativera, whose name she didn't know yet. She signed, "Is everyone all right? Was anyone hurt in the quake?"

"One person," the Cativera signed back. "From the back of the tunnel, a room collapsed, and their leg was broken," they pointed back the way everyone had come. "They were carried past, but you might not have been able to see with your head caught in that position."

"I'm so sorry," Sadie signed back. "I feel terrible, worrying about my hair when someone was actually hurt.".

The Cativera shook their head. "You shouldn't," they signed, "you could easily have been killed." They held out a paw, helping Sadie to her feet so the three of them could all leave the tunnel and make their way to the surface.

"Sadie! Cornus! Leta!" Cata came out of the crowd that was

gathered together when they emerged from the entrance to Grasian. "I am so relieved to see you all safe! Now everyone is accounted for, and only one person was injured." They stopped and looked at Sadie. "But what happened to your head?"

Sadie put a hand to her hair self-consciously. "My hair was caught in a crack in the wall, and Leta had to cut it off so I could get out."

"I'm so sorry. Does it hurt?"

"No, cut hair doesn't hurt any more than your...fur does," Sadie explained.

"Oh, I understand," Cata said. Cornus was smiling wickedly at Sadie from behind Cata, and Sadie almost wished the young Scrybb had not learned so much about humor.

"Well, come over here with us. The cooks are carrying dinner outside tonight, and we have had the seating logs brought out for a nice communal dinner under the evening skies," Cata said, trying for a jovial tone. "We will make the best of this."

They soon found themselves seated with bowls of hearty stew filled with rich gravy, thick chunks of meat, and plenty of vegetables to fill them up. As Sadie was wiping the bottom of her bowl with the last of her bread, some of the children she and Cornus had shared lessons with ran up to them and held out their paws, claw-tipped fingers curled tightly shut. Sadie and Cornus held their hands open with palms up. The children dropped round yellowish objects in them.

Sadie grasped one of them between two fingers and looked at it. "It's sticky," she said. She stuck out her tongue and tasted it. "It's loka!"

"Oh," Cornus remarked. "This must be the candy Suri was telling me about when we were discussing the Lokin mounds. Sometimes, they make this for the children." He popped one in his mouth and sucked on it. "It is good," he mumbled around the piece of candy.

Sadie tried one of the candies she'd been given. Loka was sweet, reminding her somewhat of honey, but had a smoky flavor and a citrus undertone. She knew the creatures that made it were insects of some sort, living in dirt mounds they built. The Cativera helped them maintain the structures and defended them from predators that would break into their mounds to steal the loka. In exchange, the insects allowed the Cativera to take some of their loka harvest.

"What are they called again?" she asked Cornus once her mouth was empty.

"What are who called?" Cornus asked.

"The insects that make loka," she snapped, somewhat disgruntled that he hadn't immediately known what she was talking about.

"Oh, they are the Lokin. Hence, loka is the product they make."

"That makes sense, I guess. More sense than bees making honey."

"What?" Cornus looked at her, puzzled.

"Never mind. Hey, did you get any further on that book at all?"

"Actually, I think I might have figured out a couple of words. If I'm right, I might be able to get the rest of it." He looked at her hopefully.

"Cornus, that's amazing!" Sadie squeezed the remaining candy in her hand absently, regretting it immediately as it turned her fingers into a sticky mess. She could only laugh at herself as she pulled at the candy that stuck firmly to her skin. Finally she gave up and got to her feet. "I'm going to look for some water to wash this off with. We're going to work on that book tomorrow!"

When Sadie opened her eyes the next morning, she knew immediately there was something to be excited about, but she couldn't remember what it was. As soon as she rolled over and saw the book on the table between her bed and Cornus's, she knew.

"Cornus!" she shouted, sitting up.

"Wh-what is wrong?" the Scrybb boy cried, leaves rustling as he leaped out of bed, looking wildly about the room in alarm.

"I'm sorry, I just got excited thinking about translating the book today." Sadie tried to look remorseful as she looked at him.

Cornus sighed and sat back down on the bed, rubbing his eyes tiredly. It had been very late by the time all the Cativera had calmed down from the quake, and once again, all the herders had been absent, searching for the Struthtaur, which had all stampeded in fear at the shaking of the ground. Everyone had gotten to bed late, and Sadie was sure many herders were going to be working double shifts.

"Okay," Cornus said, picking up the book. He flipped through the pages, searching. "Okay, here are the words I found yesterday just before the quake occurred. These two words look clear to me, and I think they are *human* and *kill.*"

Sadie covered her mouth. "Oh, my gosh," she mumbled through her fingers. "That's awful."

"Well," Cornus said. "I do not think that means anything in particular just yet. We do not know the context of these words. I do not think we can assume their use here. I would rather use them to determine the other words in the book since I can use the letters from these words to match letters in other words. Then I can figure out what those other words are."

"That makes a lot of sense, Cornus," Sadie said. "It is a better idea to do that than just assume because those two words happen to be the first ones you can understand. I hope the other words are less sinister, though."

Cornus looked at her anxiously. "Me, too."

Because she didn't want to just sit and watch Cornus trying to figure out the book, Sadie went to find something else to do. She happened to come across a mirror in the washroom and shuddered at the appearance of her hair. She sought out one of the Cativera in the kitchens, asking if they had a very sharp knife she could borrow to fix her hair.

"Would scissors work better?" They signed to her.

"You have scissors?" Sadie signed back, surprised. Steam rose between them from a pot as the Cativera lifted the lid off of it and dropped in a pawful of seasonings, then gave the contents a stir.

"Yes," they signed after they had emptied their paws again. "We use them to cut leather we make from the skin of the Struthtaur. When you need more clothing, we can help you make some out of our leather. It will last longer than that worn rag you have on now," they looked pointedly at her worn shirt. "We trade for them with the Fyrtudo. Go to the west end of the bruwe, and you will find the leather workers."

"Thank you," Sadie signed, deciding to ignore the comment about her shirt. They nodded and turned back to their cooking.

She wasn't sure which way was west but asked a Cativera she met in the tunnels which way the leather workers were as she made her way through Grasian. She realized that although she and Cornus had been here a few weeks, she certainly hadn't learned all that much about it. She only knew a limited number of people personally so far and knew just a few kinds of the work that was done here. In her head, she made a determined vow to learn more about Grasian and get to know more of its people from now on.

The leather makers were very friendly and eager to help her, quickly offering her a pair of scissors when she asked. As Sadie turned to leave, one Cativera put a furry paw on her arm. They pressed a paw on their own chest. "Mari," they said out loud.

Then they signed, "What are you going to do with the scissors?"

Sadie pointed to her head. "I need to fix the mess being caught in that wall made of my hair. It isn't supposed to look like this."

"How do you want it to look?" Mari asked, head tilted to one side, their ears perked forward with curiosity.

Sadie signed back, "I would like it all one length, the same length as it is in the back where it was cut off."

"May I?" Mari reached out hesitantly. Sadie nodded. Mari gently grasped Sadie's shoulders, turning her around to look at the back of her head. Then the Cativera reached up and ruffled Sadie's hair, seeing the different lengths. They turned Sadie around again, teasing the long hair that remained around her face and ears.

"I can fix this if you will allow me."

Sadie thought for a moment. She didn't have a clue how to cut her own hair and make it look right. Mari might not have experience with hair, but at least they had experience with scissors. It was worth a shot. Sadie nodded.

Mari led Sadie to a nearby seat. Then they walked all around Sadie, looking thoughtfully at her hair. Occasionally, they reached out and pulled a length straight out. Finally, they began to cut slowly and carefully.

It seemed to Sadie like it took a very long time for Mari to complete the haircut. It felt nice, feeling Mari's paws in her hair and their gentle touch on Sadie's head. Sadie only hoped the end result would look good. She couldn't ever remember having short hair; even as a young child, her parents had let her hair grow out long.

At last, Mari stood in front of her and nodded. The other leather workers had all stopped their work and had been standing as still as statues, watching the whole time since they had never seen a haircut before. They whistled and stamped their feet, some clapping their paws together and others slapping a paw on a thigh. Mari smiled, so Sadie thought they must all approve.

"Thank you very much," Sadie signed.

"It was my pleasure," Mari signed back. "Come back sometime, and we will show you how to make some clothing for yourself. That top you have on is nearly worn out."

Sadie smiled at Mari and sighed to herself as she left the room. Apparently, her clothes weren't holding up to being washed and worn every other day or two. She only had three changes of clothing, and she wasn't going to wear the clothes from Earth Buddleja had saved for her. Perhaps she should have asked for more to be sent from Palaga or Thicce Colpat, but if she could learn to make more here, that would certainly be convenient, and judging by the comments of the Cativera, they'd respect her more for it.

She stopped by the washroom to inspect her haircut in the mirror. The highly polished metal they used here reflected her image back nearly as well as any glass mirror she'd used back on Earth. The image in the mirror was startling.

The remaining strands around her face had maintained the illusion of her long tresses before, but now even that was gone.

Sadie had to admit, as she ran her fingers over her short hair, it wasn't a bad look on her. Mari had certainly done a nice job, particularly considering they had never cut human hair before. Sadie's remaining hair was just barely an inch long, now lying in a pixie cut that lay forward to frame her face. In the back, it felt nearly shaved. She giggled at the sight of her ears sticking out from her head; she was unaccustomed to seeing them so clearly when they were usually hidden under her hair.

Suddenly, she found herself scratching at the irritation around her neck. When she looked down and pulled out her shirt, she noticed all the tiny bits of black hair that had fallen down inside and were stuck to her skin. With a sigh, she headed to her room to grab fresh clothes so she could take a bath. There was no way she was going to live with this itching all day!

When Sadie arrived in their quarters, Cornus was sitting on his bed, staring down at the book. He was flipping back and forth between several pages. As Sadie crossed the room to retrieve her clean clothes from a shelf, he didn't even look up.

"Are you figuring that out?" Sadie asked.

Cornus jumped, crying out. He looked up at her, leaves standing out all over his body. The book slid from his lap to the floor.

"Do not scare me like that!"

"Sorry," Sadie said with a shrug and a grin. "I didn't know you didn't see or hear me come in. I walked all the way across the room before I said something," she continued.

"Oh," he replied, relaxing, his leaves subsiding from their extended positions.

"I've never seen you do that with your leaves," Sadie remarked.

"It is an instinctual reaction. We make ourselves look larger, to intimidate potential predators," Cornus said.

"That's interesting. Animals do that on Earth with their fur," Sadie told him. "How's it going with the translations?"

"Oh, very good," he replied. "I have deciphered several more words, and now it is just a matter of using those letters to discern the rest of the words since I figured out the alphabet."

"That's amazing news, Cornus!" Sadie exclaimed. "You could have us communicating with the phantasms so soon!"

"It is indeed possible. We will have to carefully plan how we will do such a thing, though. It will be a terrible risk, particularly to you." He looked at her gravely.

"I understand. But it's so important. I know we can do it. We've got to find a way to talk to them, find out why they attack humans. Anyway, while you finish that, I'm going to take a bath."

"All right. And you should consider perhaps a way to acquire more clothing—what you have is becoming quite worn."

"Not you too!" Sadie said, exasperated. "Fine, I'll figure out a way to make some more. Now leave me alone about it!" She stormed out in a huff.

Once she was soaking in a hot tub, Sadie felt guilty about the way she had talked to Cornus. He couldn't have known that several of the Cativera had already mentioned the state of her clothing to her, and he was a fastidious little person. Of course, he would let her know she needed to attend to her clothing. But it was embarrassing to think that she was walking around in clothing that everyone noticed was falling apart. At least the items she would be putting on after her bath were in slightly better condition than what she'd been wearing before.

After she climbed out of the water, she was drying herself off and realized that having short hair was pretty convenient. All she had to do was towel it off for a couple of minutes, and it was nearly dry.

Sadie wondered what Marcus would think of her hair. She missed him. It had been such a whirlwind over the first few weeks as they had gotten to know each other, but she really had fallen for him. She thought of their last day together, all that kissing. She touched the back of her head and remembered how he had grabbed a handful of her hair and pulled it while they were making out. She hoped he wouldn't mind the feel of her newly short hair, but honestly, she knew how much he loved her and that he wouldn't care. She had felt it in the burning gaze of his eyes on her face. He was such an amazing guy. She would worry the whole time he was gone and hope he was safe. Sadie rubbed her bottom lip and remembered how it had swollen from the force of their kisses. Her body heated with the memory. She shook her head and dressed quickly. There was no use getting herself all worked up thinking about Marcus when she knew she wouldn't see him for weeks!

She left the washroom as she straightened her shirt. Realizing she was hungry, she headed for the dining area. Hopefully, there was still some food about—there was usually something to be found to munch on throughout the day.

Just as she was about to turn into the tunnel that led to the dining hall, she heard running feet behind her.

"Sadie!" Cornus gasped, his leaves rustling as he caught up to her. "I have done it! I can talk to the <<<null>>>!"

CHAPTER THIRTEEN

CHANGING RELATIONSHIPS

Marcus

Boehlkea climbed back up to the deck and was drying her hair on a piece of fabric when Marcus and Leopold joined the others. Janke came down from the wheel so he could find out where they were headed along with everyone else. He eyed Boehlkea with a look of discomfort. Marcus was pretty sure it was because she wasn't wearing clothing, despite the fact that her scales hardly left her indecently exposed. Marcus knew there were still many bridges to be crossed when it came to the humans who had been isolated from the rest of Lysomnus by Nun the Wiser.

After pulling the map from his pack, he carefully removed it from the bag. Smoothing the paper flat on a raised wood surface where the mast connected to the deck, he moved to the side so everyone could see the page, holding it down along one side with his left hand.

Maril eyed the map carefully.

"Mostly a westerly course, with perhaps a southwest tack toward the end. Easy enough to navigate since we'll just keep the sun at our backs in the morning and our bow in the evening," she said, looking at Janke for confirmation. He nodded, pointing with one coarse finger at one of the few islands marked on the map.

"There's no information about these indicated on here. No way to tell if there's food or fresh water, or maybe danger on any of 'em. This one's close to our course," he said, tapping a larger island. "Might anchor off this one and check it out with the rowboat. It's not far off course, so 'twon't cost a lot of time to stop, and we might need to restock at least water by then. Juice won't last more'n a few days."

Marcus felt all eyes on him.

"Uh, I guess so..."

Boehlkea winked at him. "You're part of these decisions, Marcus. Leadership has its challenges, doesn't it?"

Marcus sighed. "It certainly does. Janke, I think you're right. It's worth taking the time to stop at this large island to look for water, at least. We'll check it out from the ship before we row to shore."

"It's not like we have to worry about it for a while, anyway," Leopold said. Jarel watched the blond boy, smiling a little. Marcus wondered what Jarel was thinking. "It's going to be a little while before we get there."

"All right," Maril said firmly. "We know where we're going. It will be easy during the day, as we'll have the sun to guide us. At night, we'll use the stars. I'm guessing you two," she indicated Marcus and Leopold with the fingers of one hand, "don't know our stars yet. So, you won't have night duty. How about you two?" She looked at Jarel and Boehlkea.

"You know I do," Jarel said. "I've been out with Janke on overnight fishing trips more than once."

"Yes, of course," Boehlkea said. "All Muirnati know the stars. We often fish far away from Fisc. We know the Diluvium well, but it's always helpful to be able to navigate by the stars also. Mava Prime guides us when we are far from home."

"Good, then you'll both take turns with a night shift, swapping with one of us. We'll make much better time if we keep sailing at night without stopping to anchor. Hopefully, we will have fair winds and weather for most of the time."

"I'd better get some sleep, then," Jarel said. "Let's go find the sleeping area." He headed for the door in the bow end. Leopold dashed after him. Marcus started to follow, but Boehlkea grabbed his hand.

"Let them have some time alone, brother," she said softly. "I know you want to visit with your friend, but there will be plenty of time as we travel across the sea. Leopold and Jarel want some time to continue to get to know one another."

Marcus knew she was right, but there was still a core of jealousy inside of him. He'd known Leopold was gay for a long time, but the blond boy had never had any serious relationships before. Marcus had never had a girlfriend. He and Sadie had developed strong feelings for each other, but they had been separated by their grief, and now this necessary trip. He was very glad he had taken the privilege of that single day to spend with her before they left. He wondered if Leopold was jealous of Sadie but knew that, if anything, his supportive friend was thrilled for him.

Somehow, he had to come to terms with the idea of sharing Leopold with Jarel. Every time he thought about it, he felt angry and jealous. He wanted to go and tell Jarel that Leopold was *his,* Marcus's, friend! But Marcus could never be to Leopold what Jarel was. Was that it? He leaned over the railing of the ship, feeling the wind in his face. He closed his eyes. Was he jealous because Jarel could be more to Leopold than Marcus could?

Thinking about the terrible loss they had all suffered, he realized he wanted to cling to Leopold. Marcus had fallen in love with Sadie, and had found himself attracted to her humor, her strength, and her intelligence over the past weeks. Leopold had been Marcus's friend for most of his life and was all he had left of the life he'd lived before discovering he could travel to Lysomnus. His parents were gone. His entire *world* was gone. And Leopold was the one thing he had left of it.

With these thoughts churning about in his mind, he opened his eyes and looked around. He saw Boehlkea leaning on the railing beside him. She smiled at him.

As he looked at her, he noticed she was looking back at him with their father's blue eyes. Her wavy red hair had come from their father. She had freckles all over her scales that were a mark of her paternity.

Leopold wasn't the only thing Marcus had left of the world he'd lost. His sister was a precious reminder of the father who'd been taken from him. She carried within her the same genes that Marcus himself did, was another half of their father. He might not have known Boehlkea his entire life, but he had the rest of his life to get to know her well. Her mother had been a life partner of his father's and would also share precious memories of their lives together here in Lysomnus.

He had family here. He was lucky. Sadie and Leopold would only have the connections they could make here, and he was wrong to be jealous of anyone they found and came to love. But as he looked around and realized that it had been some time since they had gone below and Leopold had still not returned, that burning core of jealousy flared up again, and Marcus knew he still had some work to do.

"Marcus," Boehlkea's voice broke into his thoughts, "look there." He looked and saw her pointing down at the water. "I saw them when I was swimming earlier."

He leaned back over the railing and stared down at the water. Several sea creatures were leaping joyfully alongside the ship. They were long and black, skin shining under the sun when the water ran from their backs with each jump. Rather than having a solid body with one tail, their bodies split three-quarters of the way back, with a red caudal fin on each side. Several tall silver spikes stood in a row along their backs, and their teeth jutted from both sides of their heads. Marcus tilted his head as strange sounds came up over the rush of the water.

"They sound like they're screaming!"

Boehlkea laughed. "Yes, it startled me when I heard it. You should hear it down there!" She pointed at the waves where the creatures were leaping and darting alongside the ship. "I nearly screamed myself. But they're very friendly, despite their appearance. I don't think they've ever seen anyone out this far before, so they wanted to say hello."

Marcus straightened up, the pain in his back making it difficult to keep leaning over to watch the sea creatures as much as he wanted to.

"On Earth, there are these mammals that live in the oceans called dolphins. They come and swim alongside boats and ships, just like these." He swung a hand over the railing, indicating the creatures below. "I suppose there's no name for them?"

"Not that I know of since I've never seen or heard of them before." She frowned, then brightened. "Maybe that means we get to name them!"

Marcus laughed. "I wouldn't begin to know what to call them!"

A voice from behind them made them both jump.

"What are you looking at?"

They turned to see Leopold standing there, his lips puffy and his blond hair tousled. Marcus felt something ugly flare inside him and tried to ignore it.

"There are some fish or sea creatures or something swimming beside the ship," he said and turned, holding his arm out so Leopold would come and look. The other boy stepped to the railing and leaned out, looking at the water.

"Oh!" he exclaimed. "Those are kind of freaky, aren't they? Like sea darts or something!"

Boehlkea's blue eyes met Marcus's hazel ones, and they both laughed.

"I think Leopold has just given us a name for them," Boehlkea said, putting her hands back on the rail and looking down at the black sea creatures.

"Huh?" Leopold looked around at them. "What do you mean?"

"No one has seen these before, as far as we know," Marcus said. "Not even the Muirnati, and they *live* in the Diluvium. We figured we needed a name for them, and you just gave them one. Sea darts! Sounds perfect to me."

"Hey, who am I to say you're wrong if you think I gave you the right name," Leopold said, grinning widely. Marcus was happy to see the expression on his friend's face—it was one he'd missed.

"I waited until Jarel was asleep," Leopold said, and Marcus's good mood vanished. "We were just talking," the blond boy said hastily, but Marcus was put off by the blush that reddened his friend's face.

Boehlkea stepped up to Leopold and looped her arm through his. "It's none of our business, anyway," she said, looking pointedly at Marcus. "Let's go find out what they have for dinner on this ship, shall we?"

Marcus followed, letting them walk ahead while he took his time with his cane. He had to do something about this possessive resentment he was feeling toward Jarel about Leopold. No matter how much he logically worked through it in his mind, it was eating him up emotionally. He'd already offended both Leopold and Jarel once. He didn't want to do it again but felt jealousy rising inside him every time he was around one of them, or their relationship was either visible or mentioned.

Boehlkea and Leopold had reached the door in the stern wall and were waiting, holding it open for him. Leopold went first to ensure he could support Marcus in case he slipped or fell.

"I'm not helpless, you know," Marcus snapped, still feeling the restless anger from his emotional upheaval.

"Fine," Leopold said, raising his hands and moving quickly down the stairs. There was light at the bottom of the stairs, and Marcus saw that there were openings high in the sides of the ship that allowed light to enter the hold.

When they were all together, they inspected the large storage area. There was a table and chairs for dining and a small iron stove that was warm to the touch.

"How would this get hot enough to cook on?" Boehlkea asked.

Leopold showed them the back of the stove, where a handle extended a few inches. He pulled it farther out. Then he lifted a small cover on top of the stove, and Marcus and Boehlkea looked down inside to see one of the emeristan exposed by an iron plate that had slid back when Leopold pulled the handle. Its heat was rapidly warming the small stove. Leopold pulled a heavy iron pan and cooking utensils from a wooden cupboard.

Marcus looked into some nearby boxes that were built into the floor, finding fruit, root vegetables, and cured meat in each one successively.

"I suppose everything had to be built in to keep things from sliding around as the ship moves," he said.

Leopold tapped the side of his head with one finger, nodding wisely at his friend.

"Hand me some of those root vegetables. They're delicious sauteed." Leopold stood at the table and started slicing the white round vegetables Marcus handed him. "Hand me some wortang? They're a little spicy, but with some allsop to cool them down a bit, they'll be tasty."

Marcus lifted the lid again and grabbed a couple of the yellow plants Leopold was asking for. Boehlkea was pulling out some of the meat, which she tasted.

"Smoked Struthtaur," she said, chewing. "I left the bag of salted fish up on the deck. I'll bring it down later. It will be nice to have a variety. And when I swim, I will see if there are any fish that appear edible along the way. It will be nice to have fresh to mix in with the dried meat."

Leopold was scraping the vegetables onto plates he had grabbed from another cupboard while cooking and asked Marcus to grab forks from a drawer he pointed at. Then they all sat down together.

"This is really good, Leopold," Marcus said after swallowing the first bite. "I didn't know you could cook."

"Hey, I'm a man of many talents," Leopold said, tossing his hair out of his eyes. "Speaking of which, one of us is going to have to discover a talent for cutting hair or something. My hair is getting long enough to be a hassle."

Boehlkea laughed. "What if you just let it get long and start tying it back? It might be easier for you."

"Yeah, Leopold," Marcus said. "You could be a pirate, sailing ship and all. Maybe a long-haired look could be your thing now."

Leopold rolled his eyes. "I think it will take a while for it to get *that* long, and it's just going to be a pain in the butt until then. I dunno, we'll see."

Boehlkea swallowed her last mouthful of food, then said, "Maybe see what Jarel thinks? Who knows, maybe he likes long hair on guys. It can't hurt to get his opinion."

Marcus slammed his fork down on the table, making all their plates jump. As much as he wanted to run out of the room, he couldn't do it. All he could do was grab his cane and walk at his frustratingly slow pace, fuming the whole way.

"Marcus?" He could hear Leopold following after him, sounding uncertain. The stairs were killing him, making him want to just use his mental energy to lift himself to the deck above. He knew he shouldn't since everyone kept harping about him saving his power up for the important job at the end of this journey, but he couldn't resist. He was in so much pain, and he didn't want to get into an argument with Leopold in the middle of the stairs.

He reached into his pocket and gripped the Halfriez. Maybe it wouldn't be too much of a drain if he let the Halfriez amplify his power. The cold cube heated up in his grip as he concentrated, and he felt his feet leave the stairs. He moved through the air to the deck above, settling himself down carefully to the gleaming wood.

As he made his way to the deck chair, he could hear Leopold running up behind him.

"Marcus! What is going *on* with you?" Leopold panted as he reached the chair. He stood with his hands on his hips, glaring at his friend. "I'm getting a little sick of you getting mad every time Jarel's name is mentioned. I thought we had this worked out back on the beach!"

Marcus stared toward the horizon, where the sun was starting to slowly descend. The froth on the waves turned pink in the light the oncoming sunset.

"Marcus, we have to talk about this. You can't just ignore me and stay angry."

Marcus finally looked up at Leopold, looming over him in his chair.

"I know. I've tried working through this in my head a hundred times, and I just can't get past it. It's just... After everything that's happened, I can't bear the thought of losing you, too."

Leopold dropped to his knees beside Marcus's chair. "Man, I can't believe you think I'd do that to you. We're friends to the end. That's the truth. No one can ever change that."

Marcus looked at Leopold's earnest face. "But it sure feels like that's what's happening. It's always been you and me, together against the world. No matter what came along. And now—now it's you and Jarel. I'm the third wheel, looking in from the outside."

"Come on, Marcus! You aren't that person anymore. After everything that's happened to you, you can't let yourself think like that. Yes, you used to be an outcast, depending on me, feeling alone. But *you* changed that. Here. You've become someone I've always known you could be." He shook his head. "And I don't mean this power you have. You're strong, bro. You've made connections with so many people. You'll never be alone again."

Marcus found himself rubbing the fingers of his left hand along the metal of his new prosthesis. He felt ashamed of his behavior. He'd been so wrapped up in his jealousy of Leopold's new relationship, he hadn't even thought about how much he himself had changed.

Leopold went on. "And what about you and Sadie? You don't see me getting upset about *your* new relationship. This is what happens when people grow up, man. Yes, we're young, but we will grow up and have adult relationships. And we'll *still* be friends. Even back on Earth, this would have happened. I'd find someone, you'd find someone. Maybe even get married someday or have kids. I need to know that you're going to still be there for me, Marcus." Now Marcus could hear Leopold's voice thicken and catch when he spoke. "I need to know you'll be there to talk to when things aren't going so great in my life, when I need a friend to hang out with. Don't bail on me now just because you're jealous of the first real relationship I've ever had."

Marcus looked at Leopold and saw tears standing in his friend's eyes. He reached out with his left hand, and Leopold reached out and took it. Then he pulled Marcus forward and wrapped his arms around him.

"You're my best friend, man, and you always will be." Leopold's voice was muffled against Marcus's shirt. "I shouldn't have to tell you that. Please trust me, and don't ever make me have to say this again."

"I won't," Marcus said, his own voice thick with emotion. He swallowed to try to clear the lump in his throat. "I promise." Tears stung his own eyes when he sat back in his chair again.

"Now," Leopold said, wiping his arm across his eyes and sniffing. "We have some learning to do from Janke and Maril. Let's concentrate on that so we can take our turn running this ship. I guess we really are pirates now!"

"Except we won't be stealing from other ships on the high seas," Marcus laughed, wiping his own eyes.

"Only because there aren't any. You don't know what I'm capable of now that I've got this mighty ship in my hands!" Leopold said, standing and posing with one foot propped on Marcus's chair. Marcus slapped it off with his prosthetic hand.

"Ow, Marcus! That really hurt," Leopold complained. "No cyborg attacks allowed."

Boehlkea was approaching.

"Thanks for leaving me to clean up," she said, looking disgruntled.

"Sorry," both boys said together.

"Jinx!" they yelled, pointing at each other.

Boehlkea looked from one to the other. "What is wrong with you? Are you making up these words?"

"No," said Marcus. "It's just a silly game from Earth. I'm sorry we left you to clean up. Next time, Leopold will take care of it."

"Hey!" Leopold said while Marcus laughed. He felt better now that he had talked through his jealousy. It didn't feel like such a big deal anymore.

Marcus saw Leopold's eyes focus on something behind him, and he turned his head to see Jarel approaching, scrubbing one hand over his coarse hair. Muscles rippled in his arm at the movement. Boehlkea said quietly, "You have to admit, it's not hard to see why Leopold likes this guy."

Marcus turned back to her and rolled his eyes. "Seriously?"

"Hey, I have a boyfriend," she said with a smile. "That doesn't mean I can't appreciate the beauty of another person, even if he is a human."

"Who's a human?" Jarel asked, catching the end of her comment as he approached. He reached out and wrapped an arm around Leopold's waist as he came past Marcus's chair. Marcus could see the happiness on his friend's face and felt bad that he'd been jealous of Leopold's relationship. Anything that made his friend so happy should make Marcus thrilled for him.

"You, man," Leopold said, putting an arm around his boyfriend. "You're a human."

"And you're a bunch of weirdos," Jarel said, grinning. "I got as much sleep as I could, but it's not easy to sleep on a rocking ship, especially during the day. Just wait until you all get to try it."

"I am not looking forward to it," Marcus grimaced. "I don't know how much my back is going to like all that rocking."

"Oh, hey, if you're hungry, I'd be happy to cook you some dinner," Leopold said.

Jarel didn't look at Marcus or Boehlkea but somewhere over the railing of the ship. Marcus wondered why the other boy had such trouble making eye contact but was afraid to ask because he had committed so many gaffes already.

"Sure, that sounds great."

"Hey, I've got to bring the salted fish down anyway," Boehlkea said, dashing to the railing and grabbing the bag she'd put there earlier. "I'll join you on your walk down there. I wanted to grab some fruit. Marcus, would you like any?"

"I wouldn't mind a pellod."

He watched the trio walk down the deck together, each staggering occasionally as the ship tilted with the motion of the waves. Marcus had read about sailors getting their "sea legs" and imagined it must have something to do with being able to walk around on a rocking ship without feeling like you were going to fall down all the time. He imagined it was going to be even harder for him. It was certainly much more painful, as he was constantly fighting to maintain his balance. He was glad of this chair, where he could sit and rest without overworking his body while on deck.

Janke was approaching. "Marcus, I wanted to give you some lessons on operating the sails while Maril is on the wheel," he said. "Are you ready for that?"

"Absolutely," Marcus said, trying to push himself up from the chair. Janke extended a hand, pulling Marcus to his feet with ease. Marcus marveled at the casual strength of the man.

Once he was standing, Marcus followed Janke to the mast. While he was listening to the stocky man explain how the ropes worked to control the sail, Boehlkea walked up beside him. She held out a pellod, and Marcus took it, eating the purple fruit absently while Janke taught them both how to manipulate the sail. Janke explained how the sail worked, using air pressure to keep the ship moving, able to head in any direction except directly into the wind. Marcus and Boehlkea exchanged glances, amazed at the technical marvel the Scrybb and humans had created together.

Janke also explained how the wheel worked, moving the rudder beneath the water at the back of the ship to steer it. He told them that they had to turn the wheel to the left to turn the ship to the left and to the right to turn right. Using the sails and the wheel together, they would keep the ship on course to reach their destination. Of course, they were dependent on the wind to get there.

Together, Marcus and Boehlkea spent the rest of the evening with

Janke, literally learning the ropes. They had been joined by Jarel and Leopold after the boys had emerged from the hold. Everyone began to feel fairly comfortable with the sails by the time full dark had fallen and the moon had risen over the Diluvium.

With the light of the huge moon illuminating the ship from above and its reflection off the water, they could see nearly as well as they had been able to in the late evening sunlight. Maril emerged from the sleeping quarters where she had gone earlier to nap in preparation for a night shift of sailing with Jarel.

The others were eager to head down to bed. Marcus was curious to see what the sleeping area looked like. When they reached the bow of the ship, he carefully descended the stairs behind the others. He disliked going first since it took him so long to descend; he felt like he was holding everyone up who could move so much more quickly than he could.

Several doors opened off the hall that led forward from the bottom of the stairs. Looking into each room, Marcus saw a bed platform attached to the wall, a chest of drawers, a basin for water, and an opening high in the wall that allowed the glimmering light of the moon in.

"Toilet room is at the end of the hall," Leopold told him. "I found it when I was down here earlier. This first room on the left is Janke and Maril's," he pointed to the older couples' quarters, "and this one is yours," he pointed to the right. "Right by the stairs. We really debated whether to put you closer to the stairs or the bathroom, but we thought it would be easier for you to be right by the stairs since they're hard for you, and you'd probably want to be able to get right into your room when you get down here."

"Thanks, man," Marcus said. "I do appreciate that. He peered in, then turned and looked into the room across the hall. All the rooms looked like they were the same size if these two were examples.

Marcus entered his room, feeling the bed as he sat down. Similar to all the beds he'd slept in so far in Lysomnus, it was soft yet firm and felt like it was filled with some kind of grass. The fragrance that arose from the bed as he lay down on it filled his thoughts with nostalgia. It reminded him of lying in his backyard as a child, smelling fresh-cut grass in the summer. He wondered where such grass was found here; did the Scrybb harvest it somewhere? He should ask... as he wondered, he drifted off to sleep.

Marcus felt pain everywhere as he was violently thrown out of bed. He slid across the floor and slammed against the wall.

“What the... Hello? Hey!” He yelled. He heard a muffled thump and a cry from the next room.

He grabbed at his cane as it flew by. When he missed, he scrambled after it, trying to ignore the flare of pain in his back that sent electric bursts down his legs. He caught it as it bounced off the far wall. His prosthetic hit the wall beside him as if it had been thrown at him; he seized it and put it on quickly. Then he used the wall and the cane to push himself to his feet.

The ship was rocking so violently, he had to lean against the wall to stay upright. He carefully made his way to the door and pulled it open, sticking his head out into the hall.

“Hello?” he called again.

“Marcus?” he heard from the adjoining room. Leopold came staggering into the hallway, where he was immediately slammed against the far wall. Barely managing to stay on his feet, the stocky blond boy made his way to where Marcus was clinging to the door frame to keep from being thrown to the floor again. “What's going on?”

“I have no idea,” Marcus said. “I just woke up when I was literally thrown out of my bed!”

“Holy cow, are you okay, man?” Leopold asked, wide-eyed. “I can't believe you're standing. You've got to be in so much pain.”

“Yeah, but I want to find out what's going on. We'd better get up on deck.”

"All right. I'll go first, but stay right behind me and *hang on*." Leopold worked his way around Marcus and grabbed the railing, pulling himself up the stairs as the ship continued to rock violently back and forth. Occasionally, it surged forward, disorienting both boys as they struggled to keep their balance.

Marcus held his cane in his prosthetic hand, using his left hand to pull himself up the stairs with the sturdy railing. The stairway seemed interminable, the doorway at the top the distant end of an extensive tunnel.

At long last, they made it to the top. Leopold tried to open the door and found himself pushing with all his might to open it. As soon as he did, it was torn from his grasp and thrown violently back against the wall.

Driving rain lashed both boys, soaking them instantly. Wind blasted into their faces, and Marcus was nearly pushed back down the stairs, catching himself and clinging to the doorframe. They both gaped with astonishment at the storm that raged around them. The ship was being tossed across the Diluvium like a bath toy.

Leopold pointed. Through the driving rain, they could see a figure under the mast. He grabbed Marcus's arm firmly, and together, they tried to make their way toward the person. After a few steps, they fell and began to slide across the slippery deck.

Marcus felt Leopold's arm wrap around him tightly and heard his shout.

"We have to try to catch the mast!"

Marcus shouted back an affirmative, hoping Leopold could hear him over the raging storm. He did his best to cling to his cane, squinting against the water pouring into his face to try to see where they were going. As they began to slide past the mast, Marcus saw Leopold reach out and grab at it, but he missed. Marcus reached out and snatched at Maril's leg, catching the material of her pants. She was standing behind the mast, looking up. As Leopold and Maril helped Marcus to his feet, they all looked up to see Jarel climbing around in the rigging. Marcus heard Leopold's cry of fear over the roaring of the storm.

"What is he doing up there?" Leopold yelled as he guided Marcus's arm to the ropes on the mast.

"We've been stowing most of the sails," Maril shouted back. "I just got back down—it takes a team to get the higher ones. We just needed to get this last lower sail stowed, and the ship should be a lot safer."

"What about those two sails up there?" Marcus asked, raising his voice to be heard above the storm as he pointed high above the ship.

"We need those to keep the ship pointed into the storm, along with the rudder," Maril answered. She pointed toward the wheel where Janke stood, barely visible under the driving rain and the waves that smashed against the ship and splashed across the deck.

"You two shouldn't be up here!" she shouted as if just realizing they were there now that she had answered their questions. As they all watched, Jarel carefully unhooked a safety line from a belt around his waist and climbed down to the deck, jumping the last few feet.

"Jarel, take these fools back below deck. Go to the food storage and try to eat," Maril directed when the boy had joined them.

"What about you?" he asked. "You've been up all night!"

"I'll be fine," she said gruffly, squeezing his hands in her own. "Just get to safety. I have to manage the upper sails through the storm. When this is over, Janke and I can rest, and you can come up and relieve us. Now *go!*"

Her tone assured them all she would brook no further argument, so the boys joined arms, with Marcus in the middle. Fighting the heaving of the deck, they carefully worked their way toward the bow wall, slipping and sliding, until they reached the door that led to the kitchen.

Marcus was very aware that if the other boys hadn't been there, he would have been washed off the deck of the ship and into the turbulent water of the ocean. The boards were slippery underfoot, and waves kept sweeping over the railing, washing water across their legs with a force he couldn't withstand. The wind gusted at their bodies every few seconds, pushing them back. By the time they reached the rear of the ship, Jarel and Leopold were carrying Marcus between them, and all three boys were exhausted.

Welcoming the relative quiet of the hold, the boys panted heavily as they descended the stairs and dropped into chairs that were secured to the floor. Now Marcus truly understood why all the furniture and storage were secured to the body of the ship itself. He was glad there were arms on his chair because if they weren't there, he would already be on the floor from the continued heaving of the ship. Despite the noise of the wind through the openings on the ship's walls, it was much quieter in the hold. The rain made its way in but wasn't enough to do much more than occasionally spit water at them where they sat in the middle of the room. They were already soaked, so no one cared.

Nausea roiled in his stomach as the odors of various kinds of food filled his nose.

"There's no way I'm going to be able to eat," he said. "I already feel like I'm going to throw up."

"Seasickness finally caught up to you?" Jarel said, grinning.

"Ha, ha," Marcus replied sourly. "And where is my sister? Did we leave her in the sleeping area? I can't believe she'd have slept through this and not come to find us."

"Oh, she went overboard," Jarel said.

"*What?*" Marcus shot to his feet despite the pain. He staggered, almost falling down. Leopold jumped up and grabbed him, forcing him back into the chair, glaring at Jarel.

"How can you be so callous, Jarel? She went overboard? When?" Leopold's face was red with fury.

Jarel rolled his eyes. "Seriously, you two? I just learned about her people, and I already know you guys are overreacting. She *chose* to go. Said she'd be safer in the Diluvium than trying to stay on the ship and getting hurt."

Marcus groaned and dropped his face into his hand.

"I'm an idiot. Of course she'd be fine in the water. It's just, in our world, someone going overboard in the middle of the ocean in a storm is certain death, and I just thought—"

"I get it," Jarel said. He was looking vaguely at the wall, obviously uncomfortable with Marcus's apology.

Leopold lurched his way over to Jarel and reached out with one arm while keeping a tight grip on a chair. After a pause, Jarel pulled Leopold onto his lap and held him.

"I'm so sorry," Leopold said. "I shouldn't have snapped at you like that. I should have known better, that you'd never have been so cold about Marcus's sister if something bad had happened to her."

Jarel looked down at Leopold, a hurt look flickering across his face and disappearing.

"Yes, you should have. I know that I speak without tact sometimes, but I'm not cruel. I have emotions and empathy. As much as we've come to care for each other, Leopold, I hope you can learn to give me the benefit of the doubt before thinking badly of me."

"I will, I promise," Leopold said, putting a hand to Jarel's cheek. They stared into each other's eyes as if no one else existed.

Marcus tried to look anywhere but at the two boys, not wanting to interrupt their intimate moment. Unfortunately, the ship took a forceful pitch right at that second, knocking Marcus to the floor. Both Jarel and Leopold jumped to lift Marcus back into the chair. Marcus was groaning loudly in pain from the force of the impact against his body. He was helpless to stop because he was in so much pain.

"I think we need to tie you to that chair for your own safety," Leopold said as Jarel released him from the firm hold that had kept him in place as the ship moved. Jarel looked for something to tie Marcus down with, while Leopold found some padding that had been used to protect the fruit from being bruised or crushed.

"Better some smashed fruit than a smashed best friend," he said as he tucked the padding beneath and around Marcus. Jarel had found some of the vine ropes the Scrybb made tucked away in one of the many cupboards. He used it to tie Marcus to the chair, winding it around Marcus's upper chest.

"Maybe we should tie ourselves down too," Leopold said as he was thrown into the table, banging his hip hard against a sharp corner. He rubbed the sore spot as he sat down in his chair, watching as Jarel finished with Marcus. Jarel managed to make his way back to the food stores and grabbed some fruit and salted fish.

"I'm starving," Jarel said with his mouth full, tucking some fish back in as it nearly fell out.

"Gross," Leopold commented.

Marcus chuckled. "You should be happy," he said. "He's just like you." Then he clamped his lips together again as another wave of queasiness rolled through his midsection. He was glad he hadn't eaten since the previous night; seeing Jarel eating made the nausea worse. When Jarel bit into his piece of fruit, the rich, juicy odor of the flesh filled the air and made Marcus gag. He could only lean over helplessly and retch.

"Sorry," Jarel said. "I didn't realize it would affect you so much."

"Ugh," Marcus groaned, trying to spit. "At least I don't have anything in my stomach to throw up. It hurts just to gag. If only this awful rolling would stop." He wiped his mouth on the shoulder of his own shirt.

"I have to admit, I'm not really hungry either," agreed Leopold. "I haven't eaten since last night, but this is a ride I'd rather not be on. It's not exactly stimulating for the appetite. I don't know how you can eat, Jarel."

"I've never been in a storm quite like this, but I've been out fishing on pretty rough seas before," Jarel replied. "After the first few times, you get used to the motion. And learn to eat when you get the chance."

The storm lasted for hours. Despite the padding, being thrown back and forth in the chair and the violence of the ship's movement made Maarcus's pain worse than he could remember since his initial accident. It felt like torture that would never end.

At last, the noise of the wind and the rain died down, and the ship stopped rocking so violently. A ray of sun shone through the nearest slit in the wall.

"I think the storm might finally actually be over," Leopold said. Marcus sighed in relief.

"Finally," he said. "Please get over here and untie me."

Footsteps sounded on the stairs. They all looked up as Boehlkea appeared in the doorway. She gasped at the sight of them, one hand on her chest, then ran to Marcus's side and hugged him tightly in the chair he was still tied to. Then she looked around at them all grimly.

"You'd all better come up on deck," she said.

CHAPTER FOURTEEN

MAKING PEACE

Sadie

Sadie turned to Cornus, feeling her breath catch in her throat. "Really, Cornus? You can understand the language of the phantasms?"

"I can, I can read their language!" He stopped to catch his breath, more from his excitement than exertion. "As I translated the words, it got easier and easier to figure them out. And it just clicked! I realized I was reading them easily. I know I can speak to them, and I believe I will be able to understand them! I believe I can now talk to the <<null>> if we are able to figure out a way to meet with them!"

Sadie reached out and hugged him, feeling his leaves crunching a bit against her. She knew by now how difficult it was to damage a Scrybb and didn't worry about hurting him as she embraced him tightly. He squeezed her back in joy.

"I'm so excited, Cornus! I feel like we can really do this! Let's go find Cata and see what we need to do to contact the Stondefel. I think they may be able to help us too." She couldn't stop smiling, even as she released Cornus from her embrace. He was grinning too. Together, they ran through the halls until they reached the doors of the Monarch's official rooms.

As they both knocked excitedly, Sadie heard Cata exclaim from within.

"What on—hold up there!" After a moment Cata opened the door and looked down at them. "Oh, hello. Is there an emergency?"

"No—no, I'm sorry," Sadie said. "It's just—Cornus has been able to translate a book of the language of the phantasms."

Cata looked at Cornus, a look of wonder on their face.

Cornus smiled and nodded. "Yes, the <<null>>. I believe I can speak to them if we are able to go to a Brynar and get one to come out. Perhaps we can finally do something about them killing humans here!"

"Oh, my," Cata said. "This is quite the proposal. There is certainly an inherent amount of danger involved, particularly for any human. Do you have a plan?" They gestured for Sadie and Cornus to enter their office and closed the door behind them.

"Well," began Cornus as he sat down facing Cata's desk, "we thought we might begin by asking you how you contact the Stondefel. They would seem to be the first choice in aiding us in our approach to the <<null>>."

"Hmm," mulled Cata. "It is easy enough to contact the Stondefel. We simply post a signal cloth on the stone steps you saw on your way here and meet them in the field where you landed when the herders notify us that they have arrived. I am concerned about your safety, however. I assume, Sadie, that you want to go to a Brynar with Cornus to be a part of this?"

"Yes," Sadie said. "A human has to be present, or the phantasms won't come out at all. It's my hope once one emerges Cornus can talk to it and find out why the phantasms are so determined to kill humans. I'd like to try to talk to them, with Cornus interpreting, and find a way to make peace."

"The most difficult part of that plan is keeping you alive to negotiate, Sadie," Cata said seriously. "The last thing we want is for you to come to harm in this endeavor. It isn't worth your life, when humans can just avoid Bryars and the <<null>> altogether."

"But I know we can do this, now that Cornus can talk to them," Sadie insisted. "That's why I want to include the Stondefel. If they can help keep me safe long enough for Cornus to get the phantasms talking, maybe we can solve this once and for all. I don't want to have to worry that any human, especially one day one of my own friends or children, might stumble into a Brynar and be killed when we could solve this now."

Cata rubbed one ear with their paw. "All right," they relented. "We will post the signal flag and bring you and the Stondefel together. They had better keep you safe, though. They will have me to deal with if anything happens to either of you!"

Sadie relaxed, relieved. "Thank you so much, Cata! This means so much to me."

Cata cocked their head to one side, small black eyes on Sadie. "Did you do something new to your head again?"

"Yes, I had to cut the rest of my hair off because it just looked silly with all those different lengths," Sadie said. "I should say, I'm so grateful I was rescued when one of the people cut some of it for me to set me free, and then Mari cut the rest of it to make it look better."

"It looks much more natural," Cata said. "Much more like a regular head, without all that extra-long fur swinging around!"

Cornus laughed beside Sadie. "I had not noticed right away, Sadie, with all we have been doing," he continued to chuckle, "but it does look very nice. I—I did also like it before," he added as she gave him the side eye.

"Thank you, Cata," Sadie said, standing up and taking Cornus by the hand. "We'll be going now. We've just got to grab something to eat and work on our plans while we wait for our meeting with the Stondefel."

As they were leaving the room, Cata said from behind them, "Sadie, you might want to consider talking to the leather workers about making some new clothing. Yours are looking a bit worn."

"Not you, too!" Sadie groaned as Cornus pulled her out into the tunnel.

While they sat in the dining hall and ate lunch, Sadie asked Cornus to tell her some of the things he'd figured out how to say in the language of the phantasms. When he opened his mouth and started talking, it was like he was talking from the other side of a solid barrier. <<null.........null>>. Sadie felt like she was trying to make sense of static.

"Stop!" she cried out. "I can't even hear you!"

"Really?" he said, astonished. "It is a complete and complex language."

"Really." Sadie replied. "I can see your mouth moving, but it's like no sound comes out. Kind of. It almost hurts my brain to try to make sense of the words. Just like when you say the name of the phantasms, I can't hear it."

"How odd," Cornus said. "I wonder if it is because you are not from this world. But you can say the words in the older language of the Cativera and use their sign language. It is all very confusing."

Sadie shivered. "I can't imagine why I can't hear it. I guess I'm just going to have to get used to it, though, since I will have to be there when you talk to the phantasms, and you'll have to tell me what they're saying so we can decide how to negotiate with them."

"This is true. I wonder if the Cativera will hear it?"

"Let's find out," Sadie said as she finished her food. "I want to go back to the leather workers and ask them to help me make some new clothes. You can come with me and see how they react to the language."

"All right," Cornus said affably. "I do not have any other plans right now anyway."

Together they walked down one of the corridors, and Cornus continued a recitation of the language. Sadie shuddered occasionally, as it was so disturbing to hear the strange—unsounds? —coming from his mouth but did her best to try to get used to the feeling inside her head.

When they reached the large room where the leather workers completed their labor, Sadie peeked in and waved as Mari looked up at her. The Cativera gestured for Sadie to enter. She walked in shyly, pulling Cornus behind her.

Abruptly the two of them stopped, staring in astonishment at the other people in the room.

Apparently, giving Sadie a haircut had awakened the artist in Mari, or the others had felt like making a change in their own appearances. Every Cativera except Mari had gotten a “haircut”. One tall Cativera had gotten just the fur between their ears on top of their head clipped short, leaving a tall strip down the middle. Several others had different geometric patterns cut into their fur throughout their entire body. Sadie guessed not much leather work had gotten done today.

“Oh, you all look so nice,” she signed, nudging Cornus.

He jerked, distracted from staring. “Yes, you have wonderful patterns in your fur! Sadie must have inspired you all,” he signed, obviously trying to appear supportive.

“We thought you looked so nice, everyone wanted to try something new,” Mari signed back.” Is there something else we can do for you?”

“Yes, I would like to learn how to make myself some clothes,” Sadie signed. Everyone clapped, and Sadie felt her face warm. She was determined no one would have the opportunity to remark on the worn condition of her clothing ever again.

“And I would like to try a new language I have learned and see how it sounds to you,” Cornus signed.

“We would be happy to help with both,” Mari signed, ushering them deeper into the room. A burly person with narrow lines cut diagonally into the fur on their face stepped forward. “I will help you cut patterns for your clothing,” they signed. Sadie followed them to their workstation.

Cornus sat on the same seat where Sadie had gotten her hair cut earlier. He began to talk in the language of the phantasms. The Cativera perked up their ears, but did not appear to experience any discomfort the way that Sadie did.

After a brief period of talking, Cornus stopped and asked Mari, "What did you hear?"

"I hear you speaking words, but they aren't words that I know or understand, except the word<<null>>. It just sounds like a different kind of talking."

Cornus looked at Sadie with a wry smile on his face that reminded her of Leopold.

"It appears that I'm the only one—or at least we humans from Earth are the only ones—that can't hear it. Hopefully, this means we will have success when we are trying to communicate with the phantasms."

Cornus slipped off the seat and stood beside Mari, asking if he could help them with their work. They began to show him what they were working on, and soon the room was quiet, except for the industrious sounds of labor.

Several hours later Suri found them back in their room. Cornus was sitting on his bed, admiring Sadie's new leather shorts and sleeveless shirt. She had also made a pattern for pants and a long-sleeved shirt but planned to return to make those more difficult pieces later. Her hands kept rubbing over the soft, pliant leather. It was amazing how comfortable the material was, given its thickness and promised durability. Both pieces were made from leather that had been tanned to a golden hue that nearly matched her skin.

"Suri!" Sadie cried out when she saw the herder in the doorway. "Do you have good news for us?"

"Yes, Anneberg is waiting for you in the meeting field," the Cativera signed. "I came as soon as I saw him land. Another herder went to ask him to wait for you."

"Oh, we must hurry, Cornus!"

"Yes, but stay calm, my friend." Cornus collected his book and took her arm, pulling slightly to try to calm her down. "I know this is important, but we must keep our minds on the task at hand."

They followed Suri back to the surface. It was late; the sun had set, and the moon was high in the sky above. It was so large it appeared to be looming over them. Sadie eyed it nervously as she followed Suri and Cornus down the road that would take them to Anneberg. The celestial body had gotten so close it looked as if it would crash into Lysomnus at any moment.

Even though they'd worked all day, she wasn't tired at all. It must be the excitement, she thought. She was glad they'd had the distraction of the leatherwork to keep their minds off waiting for Anneberg to arrive, or she might have gone crazy thinking about all of this. Cornus probably wouldn't have. The patient Scrybb was always so calm. Sadie wished she could emulate him more often.

The light of the moon was bright enough, they could have chatted via sign along the way, but Suri had a tendency to be taciturn near the herds, though they were friendly enough when they were in the bruwe. Cornus would have a hard time signing while carrying the book. Sadie tried to be patient as the three of them walked along the red clay road as quietly as possible. She knew the Struthtaur were still very nervous, with all the recent quakes. The herders had their hands full, keeping them calm, and came home exhausted every morning and night. Sadie felt bad for them; out of all the workers in Grasian, they definitely had the hardest job.

Finally, they reached the last bend in the road and Anneberg came into view. He sat quietly in the field on his six stony legs, watching them with his glowing red eyes. Sadie marveled at the warmth that rose in her chest at the sight of him—a feeling of friendship and love. This demonic creature would have been considered a nightmare from a horror movie back on Earth, but here he was one of her best friends. Knowing they were a safe distance from the Struthtaur fields for a little noise, she ran to meet him, throwing her arms around one of his massive legs.

Anneberg rumbled with quiet laughter. He patted her on the back with one finger. She pulled back and looked up at him. "I am happy to see you too, little sister," he signed. "I will be happier still when we go where we can speak aloud."

Sadie turned to Suri. "Thank you so much," she signed. "We will be back as soon as we can. Please tell Cata we are very grateful." Suri nodded and bowed to her solemnly. Cornus, who had been talking in sign to Suri while Sadie spoke with Anneberg, picked his book up from the ground and walked to the Stondefel's side. They watched Suri walk back to the road and waved when the Cativera looked back before disappearing from sight behind the tall grass.

Without talking, they climbed up and arranged the harness Anneberg had brought around themselves on his broad back. With a heave, he launched himself skyward. After only a few weeks, flying had become a novelty again. Sadie looked down at the dwindling dots of the Struthtaur and the Cativera herders in the grasses of the Zabanera region.

As they flew, Anneberg took them on a flight path that led over the Diluvium. As Sadie looked across the deep blue of the great ocean of Lysomnus, she wondered where Marcus was at that moment. Was he close to his destination? Was he safe? She knew there was no way for her to know, but she wondered just the same. She closed her eyes and pictured Marcus's face, his hazel eyes, his warm, light brown skin, his curly black hair. His smile always made her feel warm inside. She hoped she would see him again soon.

Cornus sighed behind her. Sadie opened her eyes to see the Grenewud spreading out below them. She knew how much he must have been missing the immense forests where he had grown up before beginning his Travels.

As they approached the Beornan Rokk, both the riders gasped. Several of the peaks had collapsed into the caldera below, leaving gaping cavities along the mountain range.

"Anneberg!" Sadie shouted. "Did that happen in the last quake?"

The Stondefel rumbled assent.

"Was anyone hurt? Any Stondefel? And what about Palaga?"

"We felt the shaking early enough that we all took to the air immediately, and fortunately, none of us were injured," Anneberg called back to them. "Several Stondefel lost their homes, so we have been sharing caldera. Palaga suffered some minor damage, and I believe several Fyrtudo were injured when rock fell in their tunnels."

Sadie put a trembling hand to her mouth. "Oh no!" She hoped desperately that none of the injuries were serious. None of them could be healed with Marcus far out to sea.

Anneberg was circling for landing on Palaga's stone terrace below. Everything looked peaceful as he dropped to the surface and Sadie and Leopold dismounted.

"I have called Tartarus," Anneberg told them. "He should be joining us shortly."

It took only moments for the great doors of Palaga to begin opening, grating loudly. Clearly the quakes had done their damage in more ways than one. Tartarus approached them, with Colflur by his side.

It is good to see you both again, he said to them for all to hear. *We are glad to see the quakes have left you safe and unharmed.*

Sadie put a hand to her head with a laugh. "Well, almost," she said.

Oh, your head does look different, Colfur said. *What happened, were you injured?*

"My hair was trapped in a crack in the wall during that last quake and it had to be cut to free me," Sadie told them. "The rest had to be cut off to make it look right."

It looks nice, Colflur said.

"Thanks."

Now tell us what you need so urgently, Tartarus said.

"Well," Sadie began nervously, swallowing. "Cornus here has deciphered the language of the phantasms." She turned to him, holding out one hand.

"Yes, the <<null>>," the small Scrybb said. "Much of their language is contained in this book—enough that I was able to figure out how to speak to them." He held out the book he'd brought with him.

How astonishing! Colflur exclaimed.

What do you intend to do with this knowledge? Tartarus asked.

"We hope to go to a Brynar and talk to the phantasms, to discover why they want to kill humans and try to make peace," Sadie announced.

There was uproar as Anneberg rumbled out loud and the Fyrtudo mentally exclaimed their disapproval of the idea.

"Please, hear me out. I know we all are afraid of the phantasms and their danger to humans. But this is important. We have made peace with the humans of Lysomnus. They will be moving more freely about this world, increasing the risk of crossing a Brynar, particularly if they are unaware of the danger. Marcus, Leopold, and I will be living here from now on, and some of us may have children eventually. I don't want to fear those children being lost to a phantasm if they run across a Brynar. If we can end that danger by making peace with the phantasms now, why not try?" Sadie was emphatic in her effort to convince them all.

How would we accomplish this? We would have to have you risk your own life by being present on the Brynar just to draw a <<null>> out so Cornus could talk to it, and how would you be kept safe? Tartarus looked at her, concerned evident on his usually placid face.

"I-I haven't figured that out yet," Sadie said, dejected.

"I may be able to help," Anneberg said. Sadie looked up at him hopefully.

"You can? How?"

"Well," he growled, "if you were sitting on my back, you'd be out of reach. I don't know how fast the <<null>> move, but I can always take off if it comes after you before Cornus is able to talk to it. You step out with Cornus, and I'll grab you and hold you out of the <<null's>> reach while Cornus speaks with it. If it looks as if it will be able to get to you, I will take off into the sky with you."

Sadie's eyes lit up. Her hands curled into fists that she pumped into the air in jubilation. "Yes! That's a great idea, Anneberg!"

"This *is* a wonderful idea," Cornus added. "I can shield you from the <<null>> if it comes after you too quickly—when I was on the Brynar with Marcus, I do recall that it moved very fast."

You are very determined to do this, Tartarus said. *I certainly understand why. If you are all sure of your plan and want to attempt it, you have my blessing to try. Please be safe and come back to us in one piece,* Tartarus said. Colflur added her agreement to her mate's.

"I promise, Tartarus, I have no desire to die, but this *is* very important to me. We will do everything possible to stay safe. But we have to try!" Sadie said. Then she grasped Cornus by the hand and pulled him to Anneberg's side. "Let's go!"

"I only hope we are not rushing into this without considering every possibility," Cornus expressed his doubt as he climbed onto Anneberg's back behind her.

"We must pursue the most important task as quickly as possible, when we know we have the knowledge and tools necessary," Anneberg rumbled as he gathered his legs beneath them. Tartarus and Colflur had withdrawn to the doors of Palaga to watch them take off.

With a powerful thrust, Anneberg launched them skyward. Sadie was surprised when he passed over the Brynar that they'd found in the Grenewud on their way to Palaga on their journey with Marcus on foot, that seemed so long ago.

"Why aren't we stopping here?" she shouted to the Stondefel.

"While we are doing this with limited planning, I do want to take some precautions," Anneberg called back to her. "We will go to the Brynar on the other side of Thicce Colpat. It is between the Grenewud and the shore of the Diluvium. I can land beyond the edge of the Brynar and we can walk in prepared rather than just landing directly on top of it and immediately confronting a <<null>>."

Sadie realized that this was a very good idea. She hadn't thought about the fact that Anneberg, being so large, had no way of landing anywhere in the Grenewud surrounding the Brynar where Davidia had been taken. It would certainly be a rushed and much more dangerous attempt if they landed directly on the Brynar, without being prepared for an immediate attack by the phantasm.

The next Brynar was about an hour's flight beyond Thicce Colpat. Sadie found herself dreading the upcoming challenge. Although it had been her idea, now that it was actually happening her belly churned with fear. She remembered Marcus telling Leopold and herself about his terrifying encounter with the phantasm when he'd first come to Lysomnus. Would Anneberg really be able to keep her safe from the phantasm?

Her attention was abruptly brought back to their surroundings as Anneberg began circling to land on the beach near the Brynar she could see below them. It looked as harmless as the one she'd seen in the Grenewud. Plain brown dirt lay listlessly in a rough square, small rocks and gravel casually strewn across the surface.

"It's hard to believe it's so dangerous," Sadie found herself whispering as Cornus dismounted, landing in the rough sand. She carefully climbed down after him.

"They do look harmless. To most of us, they are. We walk across them without concern. It is only to humans that they are so perilous," Cornus said from beneath her, also keeping his voice low.

"It is not necessary to be so quiet, young ones," Anneberg rumbled, humor threading through his voice. "Sadie will not face danger until she actually sets foot onto the Brynar itself. Let me know when you are prepared to do so."

Cornus opened the book he'd been clutching under his arm. He paged through it, mumbling to himself, occasionally running his fingers underneath a word. Then he sighed and closed the book.

"If I do not know enough by now, I will not ever be ready," he said. "I say let us go for it."

"Sadie?" Anneberg rumbled. She could feel the vibration of his deep voice throughout her body as he spoke, because she was clutching his leg tightly. She released the harness and nodded, then realized he couldn't see the movement. "Yes, I'm ready," she said, stepping from beneath his body and clutching Cornus's hand.

"All right, here we go," Cornus said, taking a step with Sadie at his side. Anneberg stepped slowly forward above them, and together they moved onto the Brynar, nerves screamingly taut.

With a high-pitched scream, the air in front of them spun into nothingness. A hole twisted open; Sadie expected to be able to see into it or through it, but it was as if nothing was there at all. It was just an absence of the physical space that had been there a moment ago, just as when Marcus opened the portal to take them home.

Out of the void rolled a black nightmare. The void popped out of existence behind it and the screaming stopped abruptly. The awful entity unrolled, exposing the multitude of eyes, tentacles, and tooth-filled mouths, just as Marcus had described them. He could never have adequately depicted the horror of reality, Sadie realized.

As soon as the phantasm became aware of Sadie's location, it swept rapidly in her direction. Her heart nearly stopped in her chest at the speed with which it moved. Sadie was suddenly high in the air above Cornus and the phantasm, looking down at them. She realized that Anneberg had picked her up. For a moment, the disorientation and swinging movement made her feel nauseated.

Then Cornus called out in the language he had learned from the book. Sadie couldn't hear his words, any more than she had before, but the phantasm stopped abruptly. She couldn't tell if it was looking in any particular direction with its many eyes, but it spoke in the same language with all of its mouths.

The *unsound* of it was awful. Sadie was tempted to cover her ears; she could barely control the impulse. The discomfort was lodged in the center of her brain, However, she had to be able to hear Cornus when he told her what the phantasm was saying.

Cornus spoke again, and the phantasm answered. Cornus looked surprised. He looked up at Sadie.

"This <<null>> says humans are being targeted because of the violations humans are committing against the <<null>>," he said.

"What?" Sadie exclaimed. "What could *we* possibly be doing to *them*?"

"Hold on," Cornus said, putting his hands up to quell any further indignant responses from Sadie. He turned back to the phantasm.

Sadie winced, waiting for the awful sounds of its language to begin.

When the phantasm answered Cornus's inquiry, it seemed to last forever. The unsound came from every mouth in its constantly moving and shifting form, blasting her ears and mind with discomfort that bordered on pain despite her attempts to block it out with her shaking hands.

Finally, it stopped, and Cornus looked up to her, a deeply concerned expression on his leafy face. He looked almost sick.

"Sadie, the <<null>> says that when they kill humans, they are defending their people. Every time one of the humans opens a portal between your world and Lysomnus, they tear apart the fabric of the dimension between the worlds where the <<null>> live. Entire generations of the <<null>> have been killed when this happens. The <<null>> have been killing humans out of desperation to try to stop them, hoping to kill anyone who has been destroying their people. They don't know which human is the one who can do it—as far as they know, any or all humans can. They only get a glimpse of a human tearing through their dimension. The Brynar, for some reason, are thin spots that they use for access points out of their dimension because they can see into Lysomnus through them. This <<null>> is one of several sentinels, who volunteered to spend their entire life watching for a human to come into view by crossing the Brynar. The sentinel will come out and kill the human in the hope that it is the one who has been destroying their people. So far, they have never been successful in finding the one."

"That—that's horrible!" Sadie cried. "I can't believe it!" Tears filled her eyes at the terrible idea that Marcus had been killing this creature's people simply by traveling back and forth, that *she* had been part of killing them when she had traveled with Marcus. The tears spilled over and ran down her cheeks when she grimaced at the thought.

"This is indeed terrible news," Anneberg said. "These creatures we believed to be so evil have only been trying to defend themselves and protect their children." Beneath them, the phantasm roiled and shifted, but to Sadie's eyes, it no longer looked so terrifying. It appeared almost sad, and somehow noble, now that she knew it was giving up its life and any chance at a family to defend its people.

"Can you explain to them, Cornus, that Marcus didn't know?"

"I have, Sadie. But think of all the times that Nun the Wiser traveled back and forth to take people from Earth. And then Eris, after she discovered her power. Also consider the lifetime of trips made by each generation of Marcus's family, night after night, as they traveled here to visit this world. Millions of the <<null>> must have died over that time—whether the Talents were aware of them or not." Cornus looked grim.

"We have to *try*, Cornus." Sadie was having trouble forcing the words through her tears, but she pressed on. "At the very least, we have to explain to them—the phantasms—that Earth is no longer an option for Marcus anymore so there can't be any more trips through their dimension by humans. Nun the Wiser is dead, and Eris's power is gone, so even she can't hurt them anymore."

"Actually, Eris is also dead," Anneberg rumbled. "She was killed in the first quake."

"Oh, that—that's awful!" Sadie said, pressing her hand to her mouth.

"Well, it is one problem solved," Cornus said indifferently. He turned back to the phantasm and began speaking to it again in the unintelligible language that hurt Sadie's brain.

The phantasm replied abruptly. Then Cornus spoke some more, and the phantasm responded for a longer time. Sadie gripped her head and thought the torture of the terrible unsound would never end. Finally, the screaming vortex appeared, and the phantasm disappeared into it. Blessed silence descended.

Cornus looked up at Sadie. "I think we have done the best we can. The <<null>> do not seem to be a vindictive people, which is fortunate for Marcus and the rest of all humans in Lysomnus. It understood when I explained that Marcus and the other Talents had no knowledge of the damage they were doing or ever knew that the

<<null>> lived in the dimension through which they crossed when traveling to Lysomnus. However, it was still very angry, and I do not think they will ever feel very forgiving about the many generations of <<null>> who have lost their lives, especially the children, to those many travels through their dimension. It has agreed that the <<null>> will stop any further attacks, with the understanding that there will be no more breaches by any humans, ever again. Returning to Earth is truly now forever out of your reach, even if the disease there were to somehow end. You and the others will never know if that happens."

Sadie pressed her hands against her face as Anneberg gently lowered her back to the ground. In her heart, she knew she had held some glimmer of hope that someday she might be able to return to Earth, that she might have *some* family left alive there. Now that hope was gone forever. Sobs wracked her body as she wept at the loss.

Then Sadie thought of the phantasms, trying desperately for so long to stop the deaths of millions of their people, their children. It was selfish of her to be upset about a world she had already lost, when the phantasms were still fighting to protect themselves and faced the danger of losing more. What if Marcus tried to use his power to go back, just to see? He would kill many more phantasms. She couldn't be a part of that, not now that she knew the truth. It was time to truly say goodbye to Earth and ensure the safety of the phantasms. She realized just how much she'd let their appearance affect her. They might be terrifying to look at from a human's perspective, but they were really just people trying to live peacefully and protect their own.

"Thank you, Cornus. And thank you, Anneberg, for your assistance." Sadie said. "We couldn't have done this without you. I feel we've accomplished something truly great today here, Cornus. Saving lives is always a wonderful thing. We will make sure Marcus knows the truth when he returns, and that he never uses his power to travel across the phantasms' dimension again."

CHAPTER FIFTEEN
LOSSES AND GAINS

Marcus

Jarel and Leopold struggled to loosen the knots in the rope holding Marcus to the chair. The lurching of the ship had tightened them to the point that they were now impossible to untie. Jarel pulled a knife from a sheath on his belt and cut the ropes, freeing him.

Marcus cried out in agony as the boys pulled him to his feet. Every time he did something that overtaxed his body, the effects were cumulative. It would take several days to recover from this experience, just to return to his normal level of pain and discomfort. He had several days of rest ahead. Taking his cane from Leopold, he set his shoulders and turned to follow the others up the stairs. Every step was agonizing.

When they had all reached the top, they gathered around Boehlkea, looking around. The seas were calm, the sun shining from the west. Dark clouds could be seen drifting away to the east, and the air smelled fresh and clean, with the strong smell of salt they'd become accustomed to over the last few days.

At first, they couldn't understand what Boehlkea was so concerned about. All was quiet, the deck empty. The ship appeared undamaged, although none of them could tell if they were still on course or not.

Marcus wondered if Maril would be able to tell them if they had been blown off course. He looked around but didn't see her. He looked at Boehlkea.

"Where are Maril and Janke? Did they head down to their sleeping quarters already? I thought they were going to stay on deck to steer the ship through the storm?"

"I can't find them anywhere," she said nervously. "I was relieved to see the three of you in the hold—for a minute I thought everyone had been lost in the storm. I couldn't find anyone in the sleeping quarters." Boehlkea bit nervously at her fingernails; Marcus realized at this odd moment that he hadn't noticed such a human trait in her before, or even that she had fingernails.

Then the importance of the empty ship struck him, and Marcus gasped and clapped his hand over his mouth. Leopold looked at him, startled, and then up at Jarel with a horrified expression. Jarel stood rigid and stone-faced. His hands slowly curled into tight fists.

"They got washed overboard? *Both* of them?" Leopold exclaimed, unbelieving.

"I don't believe you!" Jarel yelled, running for the bow. He dashed up the steps, running to the wheel as if Janke would suddenly appear, gripping the handles with his feet spread in his usual stance. Then he ran back down and disappeared down the stairs where the sleeping quarters were. He returned a moment later, wild-eyed.

"They aren't here!"

"I *told* you already," Boehlkea said.

Marcus frowned at her.

"I'm sorry, Marcus," Boehlkea said, arms spread to her sides, "but I checked everywhere before I came down to the hold and found you guys. They aren't here. And I was in the water before I climbed onto the ship. Lucky thing the rope ladder held through the storm, or I wouldn't have been able to get back onboard." She looked at Jarel as he rejoined them. "Jarel, I know they were like parents to you. But we are going to need you now, more than ever. You and I are going to have to keep us on course, especially at night. And you're the only one who really knows how to manage the sails—we all had a lesson, but you were up there with Maril all night, and you learned more than we did."

Jarel shook his head, looking distraught. "I can't handle this. I'm not a leader, I don't know how to do this by myself." He dug his fingers into his tightly curled hair.

"You aren't alone," Leopold said, putting his arms around Jarel and pulling him in tight. "I'll be right beside you, doing everything I can to help. And we'll all do our part to learn as fast as we can, so you don't have to do it all by yourself."

"I know the stars," Boehlkea said. "We'll chart together and keep track of our course.'

"I can't climb the rigging, but I can run the wheel," Marcus said. "I understand how the rudder works, at least."

Jarel looked less anxious. He blew out his breath. "Okay. If we do it together, I think I can try to handle my part if you all help me with the rest. I just get overwhelmed when I feel like it's all on my shoulders."

"Believe me, I know the feeling," Marcus said, shaking his head. "I've been in that place, bro, when it was all riding on me. It was the scariest thing—"

"Excuse me, but you don't know," Jarel said. Marcus stopped and stared at him. "Sorry, *bro,* but my whole life I've been like this. I can't deal with things when everything comes at me at once, or when people want me to do things differently than what I'm used to or touch me without asking. I say what I'm thinking and sometimes people don't like me for it. Sometimes people say things that upset me and then they say they were joking, but to me it doesn't feel so funny. The world is confusing to me, and I struggle with it every day. So don't try to tell me you know the feeling when you don't." He walked away, shoulders slumped.

Marcus looked at Leopold.

"What did I do?"

Leopold shrugged. "Jarel's just different, that's all. I think—remember the stuff that everyone was talking about before we left about autism and stuff? I think that might be what Jarel has going on. You weren't very into social media, and you've also been pretty wrapped up in what you have going on and not aware of what is happening in the world around you. Just—be patient and try to be understanding, dude. It's going to take some time to figure it all out, but *I* have all the time in the world. I hope so, anyway." He winked at Marcus and followed Jarel, trotting to catch up.

Boehlkea looked at Marcus. "Everyone has something they need to work on, Marcus. Yours may be to try to understand people for who they are, not to try to relate to them by making your story the validation of their experiences, as well."

"What do you mean?"

"Well, when something has happened to someone, you have a tendency to tell them about something similar that has happened to you. I think this is your way of trying to show them how you know how they feel. To some people, it feels like you're making it all about you, instead, and taking away from their own feelings. Instead, learn to listen and just take in what they're saying." Boehlkea smiled as if to take the sting out of her words.

Marcus pondered what she was saying. When he heard someone telling him how they felt, he wanted to let them know he understood how they felt, but his way of relating had always been to share his own experiences. Sharing his story felt like the right thing to do, but now he could see how it could sound like he was making it about himself and not understanding their point of view.

"Hey, brother," Boehlkea said. "We cannot always dwell on sad things. It is a serious problem that we have lost Janke and Maril. I liked them both very much. It's also going to be devastating for Jarel, who has just lost his parents. We can all help him with that grief, since we have recently experienced a similar loss. But we must focus on the rest of our journey now. Let me show you something that will make you feel a little better." She led him to the railing.

Leaning over, she pointed toward the bow. His eyes followed her finger to a net full of wriggling fish that hung just above the water,

"I kept busy while I waited for the storm to end!" Her laugh was infectious, and he found himself laughing along with her.

"What kind of fish are they? Are they the same ones you catch back near Fisc?"

"No, these are different. I've never seen them before. I guess we will find out how good they taste—I have tested them to be sure they are not poisonous."

"What? How did you do that?" Marcus was mystified.

"I caught one first and ate just a little bit, to test it on myself. I suffered no ill effects, then ate a bit more. Eventually I consumed an entire fish. I had plenty of time, waiting for that storm to blow over. Now I know the fish are not poisonous." Boehlkea smiled, her teeth glinting in the light of the setting sun.

"That sounds so dangerous! Why would you risk yourself that way, Boehlkea? And raw fish?" Marcus was both frightened for her and grossed out.

She laughed out loud, throwing her head back. "Oh, brother. You know so little about the Muirnati yet. We eat raw fish all the time. Cooked food is a luxury, for group meals and festivals. And testing new varieties of fish and plant life is something we learn how to do from a young age. I may be traveling farther from home than any Muirnati ever has, but that does not mean we do not ever leave our home waters."

"Oh," Marcus felt foolish for making assumptions again. "You're right, I really do have a lot to learn. What do we do about the fish you have down there?"

"First, we have to get them on board."

Marcus followed her to the rope that hung down to the net holding her catch. As he helped her haul the full net up onto the ship with his power, he had to admit it would be nice to have fresh fish instead of rehydrating the dried meat and salted fish they already had in the hold.

The silvery fish inside the net didn't look all that much different from fish Marcus had seen back on Earth, except they had small spikes standing up along their backs instead of fins, and their gelatinous eyes stood out from their heads on stalks, rather than the flat eyes he was used to. Like fish on Earth, they were still slimy and covered with scales.

As they removed them from the net, Boehlkea showed Marcus how to take each fish and rap its head sharply against the deck rail to kill it.

"It's much more humane than allowing them to die of suffocation," she said. "They die very easily when struck on the head."

As they were completing their task, Leopold and Jarel approached. Marcus had looked behind them earlier when he heard a loud flapping noise, seeing that the boys had released the sails and had them all back in place, belled out with the evening breeze. The ship was heading toward the sunset.

"What are you two up to?" Leopold asked. "Oh! Looks like we'll be having fish for dinner. Who gets to clean them?"

Marcus felt like Jarel was watching him in particular, but every time he glanced at the other boy, his dark eyes were looking somewhere else. Marcus wondered if he was being insecure about the way he had acted earlier.

Boehlkea was saying something. Marcus tried to pay better attention.

"-got to get them all gutted so they don't go bad."

"Ugh," Marcus said. "I don't know how to clean fish!"

"Time you learned, brother," Boehlkea said with a smile, getting to her feet. "There are good sharp knives in the hold. We can clean them right here. Gutting them over the side is best. That way we can just let the entrails fall into the water and feed other sea creatures."

Marcus felt his nausea returning. He watched his sister as she went to retrieve the knives for them. Leopold carried Marcus's chair to his side so he could rest while they waited, sitting on the deck beside him. Jarel stayed on his feet, one hand toying with the handle of the knife on his belt.

"I could start cleaning these fish and show you how to clean them," he said quietly. "I know how to do it as well as Boehlkea will."

"Sure," Marcus said. "Help me up, Leopold."

After they were on their feet, they watched Jarel grasp one of the dead fish with his thumb pressed firmly inside the lower jaw, which was smooth.

"It will be easier to clean these fish than some other varieties, since they don't have teeth," he said. Then he held the fish over the railing and sliced its belly open from behind the gills to just before the tail, putting one finger inside and pulling the entrails out, letting them fall into the water below. "See? Easy. Once we have them all gutted, I'll show you how to fillet them."

"Looks like you have some skills, Jarel," Boehlkea said from behind them. "Between you and me, we can have these fish cleaned in no time. We'll let these two do their best to keep up." She grinned as she handed long, thin knives to Marcus and Leopold.

Boehlkea and Jarel soon made it apparent they were competing with each other as the piles of fish at their feet grew rapidly and they raced to see who could clean the most fish the fastest. Leopold and Marcus stood back, happy to let them go about it and escape the dirty work.

Laughing, Jarel pulled the last fish out of Boehlkea's hand by the lip and quickly gutted it over the side of the ship. He triumphantly added it to his pile.

"I know I have you!" he exclaimed.

"We will just have to count," Boehlkea said, "since I am not just going to capitulate to your claim of victory." She began to count her pile. Jarel knelt beside her and started sorting his own fish.

"Twenty-three!" he chortled, looking over his shoulder at Leopold with a grin.

"Twenty-one," said Boehlkea with a rueful twist of her lips. "You are the victor. Your knife skills are impressive. Now, let's show these two how to filet the fish and they can do them all, since we did all the gutting!"

Marcus and Leopold recoiled. They exchanged horrified glances at the idea of all that work, knowing they were unprepared and clueless.

"Are you kidding?" Jarel exclaimed. "They'll butcher these filets! I'd rather do them all myself than let these two hack them into pieces. Why don't we take care of them, and they can do the cooking and wash up while we relax!"

Boehlkea laughed. "Excellent idea! I'm liking this boyfriend of yours more and more, Leopold."

Marcus watched as Leopold froze and looked fearfully at Jarel. Marcus wondered how Jarel would react to the title of "boyfriend" when they clearly hadn't defined their relationship yet.

Jarel looked over at Leopold, meeting his eyes squarely. "Your friend's sister likes me, boyfriend," he said. Marcus watched delightedly as Leopold relaxed and his face lit up. He knew he couldn't be jealous of the happiness he saw on his friend's face. Anyone who could make his best friend feel that way was worth making room for in his life. He could share his friend's time with Jarel. He would just make sure to get used to it.

While Jarel and Boehlkea fileted the fish, Leopold and Marcus cleaned up behind them, tossing the remains overboard, and then cleaning up the deck after the filets were carried down into the hold. Leopold insisted Marcus accompany him to the hold so they could prepare a long-overdue dinner for the four of them while Jarel and Boehlkea rested, after being up the entire night before.

Since it was long past dark, Leopold showed Marcus how to use the emeristan to light twisted vines mounted along the walls. Leopold had to use tongs to hold the small piece of emeristan he took from the stove, but Marcus found he was able to hold the hot piece in his specially forged prosthesis.

"That's handy," Leopold remarked as they finished.

Then Leopold started cutting the filets into chunks, while

directing Marcus to dice up some of the different root vegetables as he sat at the table. The stove was hot when Leopold had the fish ready, and he seared it in a deep, heavy iron pan. Then he added water and had Marcus toss in his vegetables.

After the vegetables and fish had simmered for a while, Leopold stirred together a small cup of seawater and some flour-like powder.

"The Scrybb get this from the Cativera," he explained. "They make bread with it too. They harvest their own grain, but not in large quantities, not when they can trade for it with the Cativera."

He slowly added the mixture to the pot, both boys watching as it thickened the cloudy water into a gravy-like consistency. They each tasted it, blowing on their spoons and nibbling carefully to avoid burning their mouths.

"Not bad," Marcus said. The wortang had added a spicy flavor to the stew, complemented by the salt of the water. Marcus had also chopped up some allsop, which he'd remembered from their travels on the road to Palaga. It added a slightly sweet flavor and thickened the stew as well.

"Not bad! I'd say pretty darned good, for someone who's never cooked fish before, thank you very much!" exclaimed Leopold. He reached back and closed down the cover over the emeristan, ensuring the stove would cool down and not overcook the stew.

Once they'd awakened the others and everyone had eaten their fill, they all returned to the deck so Jarel and Boehlkea could find Mava Prime. Marcus had the map and Jarel showed them the bright star, nearly directly in front of them, above the horizon.

"She'll keep rising until she's directly above us in the middle of the night," Jarel said. "As long as we keep her directly in front of, above, and behind us, we're on the right course."

Marcus and Leopold exchanged glances. "That's odd behavior, for a star, isn't it?" Leopold asked.

"Maybe it's a more distant moon?" Marcus replied. "In an orbit that stays in place all the time? I don't know that much about astronomy."

Leopold shrugged. “Beats me,” he said. “As long as it helps us with navigation, I’m happy.”

Jarel was waiting for them to finish talking, looking impatient. “*Anyway,* I don’t know how far off course we are, but if we follow this for a few days, and then start heading southwest, I’m hopeful we’ll still catch the Halfriez island we’re looking for. We could miss it easily if it isn’t big enough to see from a distance, or we pass it at night.”

Marcus felt uneasy at the idea of missing the island or not finding it at all.

“We just *have* to find it,” he insisted.

“We’ll do all we can,” Jarel said. “But I have to get some more sleep. I was up all last night during that storm with—with Maril and Janke.” He cleared his throat as his voice caught, swallowing hard. “That short nap wasn’t enough to get me through another night.”

“I’ll stay up if one of you will stay up with me,” Boehlkea volunteered.

“I’ll do it,” Marcus said. “I need to learn all this stuff anyway, the sails, the stars, and everything.” He also knew Leopold would want to keep Jarel company. His thoughts were confirmed when he saw Leopold look at him gratefully.

Jarel took Leopold by the hand and the two boys headed off to the sleeping quarters for the night.

“Well, brother,” Boehlkea sighed, “it looks like we’re in for a long journey. I hope you’re up for all of this.”

“I have to be,” Marcus said. “Now you’d better start by teaching me what you learned about these sails.” Boehlkea grabbed the closest ropes and placed them in Marcus’s hands while he sat in his deck chair and looked up.

CHAPTER SIXTEEN

THE BEAUTY OF LYSOMNUS

Marcus

Marcus was sleeping soundly when Leopold burst through the door into his room. With a yell, the stout blond boy leapt to the bed, landing beside his friend.

"Wake up, Marcus! You aren't going to believe it! Wake up!"

Marcus rolled slowly onto his back, scrubbing at his face with his left hand.

"What the heck, Leopold—what's going on?" he mumbled. He had been having a dream about eating a big roast beef dinner. Lately he'd been finding himself dreading dinnertime. Despite Boehlkea's offerings of frequent fresh catch to supplement the salted stores, Marcus was tired of fish.

"That storm blew us a little off course, but not the way we thought. We're actually closer than we thought we were—remember that island where Janke wanted to stop? We can see it! Jarel says we can drop anchor there by this afternoon and check it out."

Marcus rolled to his right side and sat up, dangling his legs off the side of the bed. He was wearing shorts, cut from one of the pairs of pants that had been packed for him. The temperatures had risen slowly as they sailed west over the last several days, and the boys had found their warmer clothes uncomfortable. Boehlkea, of course, didn't wear clothes.

He slid a sleeveless shirt over his bare torso, then put on the prosthesis he had gotten from the Fyrtudo. Having once hit himself in his face while wearing it, he made sure to take it off before dropping into his bed each time. His face still bore the faint traces of the scrapes.

"Hurry up, Marcus!" Leopold was nearly dancing with impatience by the door. Marcus laughed.

"I'm coming," he said, grabbing his cane. "You look like a little kid on Christmas morning." After he slid his feet into his boots, he followed Leopold out of his room and up the stairs, wincing when he hooked one foot halfway up and nearly tripped. Leopold turned and looked at him, concerned.

"You all right?"

Marcus nodded. "Caught myself before it was too bad." He waved at Leopold to continue, and they went the rest of the way to the deck.

As they walked along the deck, Marcus saw Jarel and Boehlkea standing on the upper deck. They were looking and pointing at something off the bow of the ship, talking intently to each other. As Marcus and Leopold climbed the steps to join them, Jarel pointed off to the southwest.

"Hey, guys, I got him!"

The others turned as they approached.

"I was just telling Boehlkea where we should drop anchor," Jarel said, looking off over Marcus's shoulder.

"There's a good-sized cove on this end that I believe will be deep enough to avoid grounding the ship. Then we can lower the boat and row in and check the place out. We need to restock fresh water and see if there's any fruit or other food there."

"You think we'll be there by this afternoon?" Marcus asked, stepping to the railing, looking in the direction Jarel had been pointing. He could see the island in the distance. It was long, perhaps a mile, rising abruptly from the water on the end opposite the cove where Jarel wanted to anchor. He frowned.

"Doesn't it look like white rock?"

"I thought so, as well," Jarel said. "No way to tell for sure until we get there."

The day seemed to pass interminably for all four of them, although Jarel and Leopold napped for a while, having been up during the night managing the sails and the rudder. Boehlkea harassed Marcus to eat.

"I know you are tired of fish, brother, but you need to eat to keep your body healthy. The root vegetables will help make it easier. I'll even cook for you."

Marcus grimaced. "Don't use the salted fish, okay? I'm just so sick of the taste of salt. Use that spicy vegetable -that wortang, it kind of drowns out the taste of everything else."

"I'll see what we have left," Boehlkea sighed and descended to the hold. After a short time, she reappeared and called to Marcus, who was leaning on the railing, staring at the island. He was certain he'd seen something moving along the white background of the high end of it.

As they ate, Marcus asked Boehlkea how she and Jarel were certain they were still close to being on course.

"This island appears to be the one that Janke talked about when we were looking at the map, plotting our course originally. There aren't many islands in the Diluvium, according to that map, and most of them are quite small. Only one, besides the Halfriez island, looked to be of any size, and this is a fairly large island. Last night we passed a small one, and the placement of this one lines up with a small island on the map as well. We're pretty sure this is the large island on the map. So, it looks like we are right on target. We make this stop, get back underway, and Jarel thinks only a day or two until we reach the source of the Halfriez after that."

Marcus felt a combination of anticipation and dread at the idea of reaching their final destination. He wanted to hurry up and get there to accomplish his goal, but he was suddenly terribly afraid he wouldn't be able to do what he had actually set out to do: move

Lysomnus's moon back into a safe orbit and stop the quakes that were threatening the planet. Would he let everyone down? While they were traveling each day, it was easy to just concentrate on sailing and visiting with the others, but now that they were getting close, the actual act was becoming all too real.

Boehlkea swallowed her last bite of food and collected their dishes. "You have plenty of time before we get there to worry, brother," she said, reading the fear on Marcus's face. "Let's concentrate on *this* island first and hope we can find fresh water there. The three of you are going to be in some trouble if we can't find any. We're nearly out, and we need enough for the return trip, once we reach your Halfriez source and do what you've come to do."

Marcus groaned, leaning his face into his hand so the skin pulled taut. "I didn't even think of that," he said. "So many more days of eating fish!"

Boehlkea laughed as she washed their dishes and put them away.

"Now, brother, let's go see how close we are and see if it's time to wake Jarel and Leopold," she said, brushing one hand lightly across Marcus's shoulder. He realized just how quickly he had come to care for Boehlkea as his sister, to embrace the idea that he had family right here in Lysomnus. He smiled to himself as he followed her out of the hold.

Leopold and Jarel were still sleeping when Marcus and Boehlkea knocked on their doors.

Marcus snuck in, grabbed the spare pillow from beside Leopold's head, and thumped him with it.

"Hey!" his friend yelled. "What the hell, man?"

"You weren't any nicer when you woke me up earlier," Marcus laughed. "Quid pro quo, dude."

Leopold threw his own pillow in Marcus's direction. Marcus batted at it with his prosthetic hand, but the material caught in the flexible metal. Leopold snorted laughter while Marcus pulled the pillow loose with his left hand.

"C'mon, get up. We're almost to the island. We can drop anchor and go check it out." He slipped out the door, Leopold right on his heels. Boehlkea was stepping out of Jarel's room. She turned to Marcus and Leopold, putting her hands on her hips.

"He's very rude when he wakes up," she said, an annoyed look on her face.

"He's rude all the time," Marcus muttered.

"What was that?" Leopold asked, grabbing Marcus's shoulder and stepping around to face him.

"Um—nothing. Just clearing my throat." Marcus coughed a little and continued down the hall toward his sister, shining blue-green with her hands still on her hips. Leopold followed, head cocked to one side, a suspicious look on his face.

Jarel emerged from his room, wide-eyed to see all of them standing around right outside his door.

"What is this, some kind of welcoming committee? Why are you all crowding me?" He backed up until he was in his doorway, gesturing for them all to move down the hall.

Marcus and Boehlkea rolled their eyes at each other, making their way to the stairs. Leopold hung back, reaching out one hand to Jarel, who shook his head.

"Not now, I'm sorry. I just can't. I feel like my skin is crawling."

"It's okay." Leopold let his hand drop back to his side. He followed the others and Jarel came along behind him, closing his door as he stepped out into the hallway.

When everyone was back on the deck, Marcus made his way up to the bow. He stood and stared at the island. It was much closer, close enough to see that it was a white rock rising from the sea at one end. It gleamed under the sun's bright rays, almost blinding as they stared at it. Jarel yelled up to them.

"I'm going to maneuver the sails! Leopold, run back and turn the rudder. We want to bank the ship to the left, so turn the wheel to the left. We need to sail straight into that cove!"

Leopold dashed down the stairs from the upper deck, nearly falling in his haste. He pelted down the long deck and ran up to the wheel, grasping the handles and turning the wheel as Jarel had instructed. Meanwhile, Jarel was manipulating the sails, using the steady breeze to aid them in turning the ship.

Marcus and Boehlkea were watching the island fill their vision as they sailed into the cove. The water remained a deep, twilight blue, assuring that the cove was quite deep.

Marcus heard Jarel coming up the bow stairs.

"Time to drop anchor," he said, white teeth flashing against his dark skin as he grinned at Marcus. Leopold followed close on his heels. "Boehlkea," he called. "We'll need your help with this. That anchor is heavy, and we don't want to just drop it." Leopold smiled apologetically at Marcus, knowing it would rankle his friend not to be able to help them. They'd been over and over why he couldn't use his power for anything before they got to the Halfriez island.

Marcus could do nothing but watch as the other three struggled with releasing the catch on the huge crank that held the anchor chain, then slowly let the anchor down. All three sighed heavily with relief when it reached depth and rested on the bottom. Jarel went back to the sails, moving the ship until he felt the anchor drag, then furled the sails with Leopold's help, who had joined him.

Boehlkea looked at Marcus. "I'd put an arm around you, my brother, but honestly, they both feel limp right now," she said, shaking her arms loosely. "I think my muscles will hurt tonight!"

"You still have to lower the rowboat," Marcus said, smiling at her. He ducked as she swatted at him, grimacing at the pain in his back with the sudden movement.

"Ha!" she barked as he groaned. "I don't even feel bad about that! You deserved it. After all, what work are *you* doing?" She smiled to show she was just playing.

"Hey, I've been doing my share of the cooking and washing up," Marcus said. "And I'd drop that boat into the sea in a heartbeat if you'd all let me. I don't think it would drain my power to use it here and there like you all think."

"We are not taking chances, Marcus! So just stop talking about it.

You'll be doing enough when we get to the Halfriez island. Ugh, I'm just getting tired of saying this to you." She walked away, taking the stairs with a skipping motion Marcus envied. Not that he'd ever change himself even a little.

Leopold was lying spread eagle on his back on the deck when they reached the mast where the sails had been neatly furled.

"What are you doing?" Marcus asked, poking the blond boy with the tip of his cane.

"I'm done, Marcus. I feel like a noodle. It's all over." He rolled his head to the side, poking his tongue out of the side of his mouth. Marcus rolled his eyes and laughed, used to Leopold's behavior.

Boehlkea knelt beside Leopold, laying one hand along his face. "Are you all right, Leopold? You don't feel warm. Have you injured yourself?"

Jarel laughed. "He's fine. Just a weakling, for all that he *looks* like he should be strong."

Leopold rolled to his knees, a hurt look on his face. His pale face turned red, but he didn't say anything. Marcus knew Jarel had hurt Leopold's feelings. For all Leopold's cheerful and gregarious exterior, he had a sensitive side that could be easily hurt when he opened himself up to other people.

"Leopold isn't weak, Jarel," Marcus said, feeling the need to defend his friend. "He just isn't used to a lot of hard physical labor. In our world, we didn't have to do that. Our lives were different there, and we're still trying to adapt here."

Jarel looked at Leopold carefully at Marcus's words. He walked over to Leopold and reached out one hand, waiting patiently. Leopold looked at it for a moment, then took it. Together they walked away and sat down on the steps to the bow deck, talking quietly.

"I admire the way you defend your friend, Marcus," Boehlkea said. "He is like a brother to you, isn't he?"

Marcus sat down in his deck chair and looked at her, seeing the shadow of his father in her blue eyes, freckles, and the shape of her nose. It made him able to visualize their actual family connection.

"He is, although not in the same way that you are my sister. I've known Leopold my whole life. He's been pretty much my only friend since I was a little kid, to be honest."

"A little kid…?"

"A child."

Boehlkea's eyes widened. "Why? I don't understand why you would have no other friends among the humans of your world. Weren't there very many of them where you lived? I had the impression from our father that you went to a place of learning with many other children."

Marcus rubbed the back of his neck uncomfortably. "People on Earth, or at least in the country where I lived, aren't—or weren't—like the people of Lysomnus. Most of them weren't very understanding of people who are different, or who they thought weren't good enough."

"Really? Not good enough? That's terrible. Why would people think someone was not good enough or too different?" Boehlkea looked very confused.

Marcus lifted his prosthesis and pointed to his cane. "My disabilities made people feel uncomfortable around me or look down on me."

"But why?" Boehlkea lifted her arms, beginning to sound angry. "Those things aren't your fault! Our father told my mother and me about the terrible accident that hurt you, that you and your mother could have been killed! Why would people look badly on you for that?"

"It's difficult to explain. It's not even just that. Lysomnus is a wonderful place, Boehlkea. People here don't judge each other based on how they look, or because they're a different kind of person. Like the Muirnati or the Scrybb. You work together and care about each other."

"Why would we judge each other?"

"On Earth, people were often judged by the color of their skin, or where they came from, or the language they spoke. Sometimes it was used as a reason to hate each other."

Boehlkea looked from Marcus over to where Jarel and Leopold were sitting. "Color of—do you mean how Jarel is darker in color and Leopold is very light? Like our father was also light?"

"Yes, like that." Marcus nodded.

"But that's ridiculous," she said with a helpless laugh. "You are a different color than Jarel *or* Leopold. Sadie is also. This makes no sense," she continued. "The Muirnati are all different colors. We could never hate each other because of that. It is what makes us each beautiful and special."

Marcus closed his eyes, feeling the breeze caress his skin. "Yeah," he said, nodding. "Yeah. That's why Lysomnus is wonderful. And just one reason I have to save it."

CHAPTER SEVENTEEN

THE ISLAND OF BEASTS

Marcus

"One, two, three!" Jarel counted off as they heaved the rowboat over the side of the ship. Grabbing the rope at his end, he looked to make sure Boehlkea and Leopold had the rope at the other end before signaling to begin lowering the boat to the water. Marcus tossed the ladder over the side when the boat was floating on the surface.

"Well, let's get going," Leopold said. He took Marcus's cane in one hand and grasped his friend's left arm in the other, holding him firmly as Marcus climbed carefully over the side of the ship and onto the ladder. Jarel had clambered over quickly as soon as the ladder was in place, and was directly below Marcus in case of an accident.

Everyone made it to the boat without incident. There was some grumbling and maneuvering as they found comfortable positions that still worked for Jarel to row with the empty water casks. Leopold and Boehlkea untied the lowering ropes, and Jarel got them underway.

"You'll have to jump out and pull us up onto that beach when we get there, Leopold," Jarel panted, nodding toward the shore.

"Okay," Leopold replied, reaching for his boots.

"No, keep them on," Jarel said quickly. "You never know what kind of plant or animal life could be lying around there. You could step on a thorn or a stinger that could poison you or infect you."

Leopold sighed. "Great. Well, it's going to be fun to walk around in wet boots."

Jarel was strong, and with his steady rowing, it didn't take long to reach shore. Leopold jumped out and pulled the boat onto the sand. Small rocks grated against the wood underneath them. As soon as the boat was somewhat stable, Leopold reached out and took Marcus's left hand to help him step carefully out of the boat. Marcus had been clutching his cane the whole trip from the ship and held it carefully in his prosthetic hand as he stepped onto the sand.

The beach extended along the entire length of this end of the island, the sand a bright, shining white. As Boehlkea stepped out behind Marcus, he heard her take a deep breath.

"This is beautiful! So very different from any beaches along the Diluvium I've ever seen before," she said in a voice filled with wonder.

"Me, too," Jarel agreed. "The sand along the shores I've seen is gray or brown, and the rocks, too."

"Anyone want to help me with this?" Leopold grunted. They all turned to see him pulling on the rowboat, trying to bring it further up onto the beach to keep it from being pulled back out into the sea. "I'm sure a higher tide will come in at some point."

Jarel and Boehlkea immediately jumped to his assistance. When the boat was in a more secure location, Jarel pulled a rope out and tied it to the front of the boat. He grabbed one of the empty casks and tied the rope to the cask.

They grabbed the rest of the casks while Marcus stood and looked at the island. The beach extended back about fifty yards, he estimated, before the sand gave way to trees. He had been so focused on the white rocks as they approached that he hadn't noticed the blue cast to the foliage. The long, narrow leaves were decidedly more blue than green. He thought Boehlkea could climb into one of the trees and be camouflaged well enough to nearly disappear.

"All right," he heard Leopold say behind him. "Let's go do some exploring." Marcus turned to see the casks lined up neatly next to the boat. "When we find water, we'll come back for these." Leopold indicated the casks. "I'm certainly not carrying them along with us while we wander around."

"Should we split up?" Boehlkea asked. "Cover more ground that way?"

"It couldn't hurt," Jarel said. "Leopold and I will head to the south side of the island. You two can take the north." He reached for Leopold's hand, and they headed toward the tree line at an angle.

Marcus grinned at his sister. "I guess that's decided then." He laughed. "No diplomacy in this group."

"Not with Jarel around," she smiled back. "He tends to say what he wants and forgets to wait for anyone else's input, doesn't he?"

"Yeah," Marcus agreed. "It's alright though. I think it's a good idea anyway." He and Boehlkea started in the opposite direction.

When they reached the tree line, Marcus saw it would be no easy trek through these woods. The trees grew close together, with thick turquoise vines hanging down between them in loops and tangles.

"Wish I had a machete," he remarked as he and Boehlkea took turns pulling the vines out of their path.

"What's a machete?" Boehlkea asked.

"It's a long, wide knife that people use to chop their way through thick foliage like this," Marcus told her.

"Oh, that sounds useful."

Together, they forced their way through the brush, pushing vines aside that Marcus inspected carefully to ensure that they weren't some type of snake.

Just as Marcus was beginning to feel like he wouldn't be able to take another step, they stumbled across a path that meandered through the trees. As they stepped onto it, Marcus turned to Boehlkea.

"I'm just going to lie down on the ground for a minute. I need to rest my back," he panted.

"I understand," she said sympathetically. "I will help you stand up when you feel like you can continue."

Marcus lowered himself carefully to the path, which was worn into the dirt from regular use.

"I wonder what made this path?" he pondered. "Clearly, there's some type of living creatures on this island. Do you see any tracks?"

Boehlkea inspected the dirt, stepping carefully around Marcus's prone body. "I don't see anything—the dirt is firmly packed—wait. Here's something. Huh! I don't know what this is; it's an odd footprint. Maybe like a Cativera's, but much, much larger?"

Marcus rolled onto his left elbow, trying to see what she was looking at. "Do you mean a pawprint? Don't the Cativera kind of have paws?" He was trying to remember how Cornus had described the grassland herders.

"Yes. Like one large, oblong impression in the center, with several round impressions around it across the top. It's big!" She said, opening her hand and holding it above the print she was inspecting. "Bigger than my hand is."

Marcus pushed himself to his knees and crawled over to look. Boehlkea had very long fingers, so he really had to see this pawprint now. "Holy shit!" he cried, seeing the impression. "It looks like some kind of cat print. Or maybe a bear? We may be in real danger here!"

"Now I really wish you had that match-that machete." Boehlkea wrapped her arms around herself and shivered. She reached down and helped Marcus to his feet, then picked up his cane and handed it to him. "I know you are in pain, brother, but I think we should keep moving, and quickly."

"I agree—and keep our eyes open! I hope that Leopold and Jarel don't run into whatever made these tracks."

Together, they moved as quickly as Marcus could go along the worn path. It continued through the trees, which were dense enough to make it nearly impossible to see anything more than a few feet off the path. They found themselves jumping at every little noise. Marcus finally saw the source of one of the noises they were hearing;

a small bird with teal feathers that blended into the trees, legs as grey as the tree trunks, and a long, sharp blue beak. He only saw it because it flew right in front of him. When it stopped moving, it virtually disappeared.

Marcus had lost track of time and had no idea how long they had been walking when they finally sighted the end of the jungle. Sunlight glistened on the sparkling white rock that rose at the far end of the island they'd seen from the ship. Both of them were relieved to hear the splash of water as they walked out of the gloom.

"Look there!" Boehlkea pointed, and Marcus followed the direction of her arm to see a waterfall pouring over the highest edge of the rocks to splash into a wide pool of the clearest water he had ever seen.

"Well, at least we found water. Too bad the casks will have to be brought all the way here to fill them," Marcus said.

"Perhaps it will be possible to carry them down in the boat and find a place to bring them from shore at this end of the island."

"We can certainly check," said Marcus, "The path continues here. Let's keep following it and find out if it goes to the water. Maybe it goes to the top, and we'll be able to see if there's a beach along this end."

Boehlkea looked at him doubtfully, and he knew it was because the rocks rose so steeply above them. "I'll be fine," he grumbled. She turned and continued along the path, which was quickly turning to stone as they left the woods behind.

While the rock did soar above them, the path itself cut deeply into the rock, allowing for a more gradual rise that Marcus was relieved to be able to traverse. Walking up an incline was always incredibly taxing. He pondered the paw print they had seen in the jungle as they walked. There had only been the one, and no sign of any large animals as they walked. Perhaps it was a creature that had been here a long time ago and was now dead.

They reached the summit, and Marcus watched Boehlkea turn toward the ocean. She held one long-fingered hand over her eyes to block out the brightness of the sun. They walked the short distance to the edge, and together they looked over an abrupt drop that led straight down to the sea. White-capped waves crashed against white stone straight below them at a dizzying height.

"Well, there goes that idea," Boehlkea sighed.

Marcus heard a scratch on the rock behind them. He turned to see a formidable white creature that blended almost completely into the rocks rushing straight toward them.

"Boehlkea!" he yelled, knowing there was no time or room to run. He reached out and shoved her over the edge, hoping as he heard her scream that the water below was deep enough for her to survive the fall. Then he jumped the other way, crying out at the impact of his body hitting the ground.

The creature whirled when it saw its remaining prey had changed locations. As it moved, it stood out against the blue sky. In his terror, all Marcus could think of was a tiger, but this six-legged predator was no cat. It leapt toward Marcus, jaw open wide. He was plunged into shadow as it came between his body and the sun, and his vision was filled with two long, curved, dagger-like teeth pointing toward him side-by-side from the center of its upper jaw. He raised his arms over his head involuntarily in fear. Then its mouth clamped down on his prosthetic arm with a *CLANG!*

Marcus opened his eyes to see those fangs curling over his arm, with the mouth of the cat closely tightly around his prosthesis. Two glistening drops hung from the ends of the teeth, and as he fought to push the creature away, one dripped onto his cheek. Instantly, his face began to burn.

Marcus suddenly didn't care about any of the things the others had said about not using his power; he wasn't about to lie here and let this thing kill him. He *pushed* with his mind and forced the thing's jaws open. He pushed again and sent it flying backward. It landed on its back, sharp-clawed paws waving frantically. Then he lifted himself to his feet, cane in his left hand to steady himself.

Snarls filled the air around him. Marcus looked to his right to see three more of the creatures stalking toward him. Six short legs kept their bellies low to the ground, but they moved fast. Long bodies rippled with muscles as they approached. Narrow faces stretched toward him with eyes that were slivers of blue-green. Round, blunt noses hid the fangs beneath. Their sleek fur perfectly matched the white rock they crouched on. They were nearly invisible until they moved.

Marcus created a barrier with his power, and the creatures stopped, confused. The one he had tossed flipped back onto its feet and slunk along the barrier, watching him with its narrow eyes. As he watched, its long tail arched over its back, and it rapped a sharp stinger at the end of the tail against the barrier between them as if testing it. "Oh, hell, no," Marcus breathed. "What in the—" His cheek stung where the venom had dripped on it, and he touched it lightly, pulling his fingers away to see blood on the tips.

"Looks like we have a standoff here, guys," he called out to the creatures. They growled and sat down, blinking at him. Round white ears swiveled to catch his words. "Um," Marcus said. This could be a problem. Heat built in his chest as he held up the barrier and he knew he would have to let go eventually. Then these weird snake-cat-lizard-things would attack him. He didn't really want to hurt them, either, though. They were just doing what they did naturally, and he had invaded their home territory.

A figure covered with leaves and mud came running up behind the cats, screaming and waving its arms, holding long vines streaming with more leaves.

Startled, the creatures took off in all directions, bounding down and across the rocks and disappearing. Marcus kept the barrier up, watching the figure warily, not sure what to expect next.

"Marcus, it's me, you fool!" Leopold's voice came from behind the mud and leaves. "I need your help. Jarel is hurt. He got bitten by one of those things!"

Marcus dropped the barrier and took a deep breath, pressing one hand to his chest. "You scared the hell out of me, dude! Although you also saved me, scaring those things away like that. Hold on a sec." He stepped to the edge of the rocks and looked down, terrified of what he might see.

All he saw below was the sea, battering the base of the white cliffs. There was no sign of Boehlkea, alive or dead. Marcus hoped she had made it safely and had been able to swim around the island to find a way back to them. He also hoped she would forgive him for pushing her off the cliff.

"Marcus! Jarel *needs* you, man!" Leopold sounded desperate.

"I'm coming," Marcus said, turning and following his friend. He moved as fast as he could, wondering why in the world the other boy was covered in leaves and mud.

Leopold led Marcus to a path across the rocky summit from where he and Boehlkea had arrived. It led down to the pool Marcus and his sister had seen when they'd first emerged from the jungle. Jarel was lying on more of the smooth white sand beside the clear water. His eyes were closed, the movement of his chest barely discernible. His dark skin was ashen.

Leopold dashed to his side and called his name. Jarel didn't respond even when Leopold shook him.

Leopold looked up at Marcus. "He's much worse since he was bitten. He was still awake when I left to find you," he said, tears spilling from his eyes. "Please, man. I know we've been telling you to save your power, but please use it, please use it to save Jarel."

When Marcus knelt next to Jarel, he saw two large holes torn through the boy's pants. He had seen the fangs that had made those. He tore the fabric open and put his hand over the holes in Jarel's skin beneath. He closed his eyes and felt the heat build inside himself. Deep within Jarel's body, he could feel the poison working, shutting down organs and beginning to impact his brain. Marcus concentrated on *pulling* the poison back through the blood toward his hand. He could feel the toxin drawing back from the boy's organs, along his veins and arteries, and finally coming out of the holes in the boy's leg, soaking his pants. At last, Jarel's blood was clean, and

Marcus healed his leg and the acid burns on his own face.

Jarel slowly opened his eyes and looked around. "What happened? I thought I was dead."

Leopold, crying harder, pressed his muddy face to Jarel's. "I thought you were too, but Marcus got here in time. He saved you."

Jarel sat up, wrapping his arms loosely around Leopold. Then he looked Marcus directly in the eyes. "Thank you for my life, Marcus. I hope using your power on me doesn't cost us the world."

Marcus sighed. "I don't think it will. I feel fine."

"Where is Boehlkea?" Jarel asked, looking around for the Muirnati girl.

"Well..." Marcus began. "We were also attacked by the cat creatures. We were standing on the edge of the cliffs at the top of the island, and I pushed her off."

"What?" Both Leopold and Jarel exclaimed at once.

"Damn, Marcus," Leopold said, "how could you do that? You don't know if she could even survive that fall!"

"I know," Marcus said. "It was a split-second decision. *I* barely survived the attack. I wouldn't have without this," he said, holding up his prosthetic arm. "I had to use my power to save myself, and Leopold came along just in time to scare them away, or I don't know what I would have done. I could never have saved us both if I hadn't pushed her."

"How will we know if she made it?" Jarel asked. "Did you see her body?"

Leopold gave his boyfriend a sharp look. "Babe, you don't *always* have to be so blunt."

Marcus looked at Jarel coolly. "No, I didn't, and I looked. I'm hoping she swam away and found another way onto the island. She mentioned looking for a beach on this end, hoping we could row down here to fill the water casks without lugging them through that jungle."

"Yeah, wouldn't *that* be fun," Leopold said. "We saw those things when we were coming out of the trees, and that's when I decided to make the mud and leaf disguise to scare them off. It worked pretty well, except one of them ran into the jungle and right into Jarel. I dragged him to the water, hoping I could flush the poison somehow."

"So, we know at least one of them went into the jungle. Well, maybe if we return on the path Boehlkea and I took, we can avoid that one. We didn't see anything but a few birds."

"Yeah, except to get to your path, we have to go back up there," Leopold pointed to the summit, "and that's where the whole group that I just scared off is. Better to go our way and face one than all those up there."

"There may be other creatures in the jungle that we haven't encountered yet," Jarel said, folding his arms across his knees. "Those large beasts must be eating something. No telling if their prey is any less dangerous to us than they are."

"Now that's a pleasant thought," Leopold said, standing up and walking to the edge of the crystal-clear pool. He squatted down and scooped some water into his cupped palms, splashing it onto his face. It took several tries to get the caked mud off. Then he went to work on his arms. When he was acceptably clean, he turned back to the others.

"I guess we'd better get started and see if Boehlkea made her way down to the beach by the boat." He held out a hand to Marcus and helped him to his feet as Jarel stood up beside him.

They were making their way along the sand, looking carefully around them for the white beasts, when they heard a voice.

"Hello! Marcus? Leopold?"

"That's Boehlkea!" Marcus exclaimed, trying to hurry back to the path.

"Jarel?" Boehlkea called.

"Boehlkea!" Marcus yelled. "We're here!"

"Brother!" her voice sounded closer. The boys climbed higher, Jarel and Leopold watching above anxiously as Marcus looked below. On this side of the island, the rock sloped gently toward the water, but trees grew between the path and the shoreline, making it impossible to see what was there.

Boehlkea's voice came from just inside the trees. "I can see you! Can you wait there for me?"

The boys stopped.

"Yes, but try to be quick," Marcus said. "Did you see the cats before I pushed you?"

"Fortunately for you, yes," Boehlkea called back as she stepped out of the trees. The rippling blues and greens of her scales really did match the color of the leaves perfectly, Marcus noticed. "But please never do that again. I've never been so terrified in all my life."

He grimaced as she picked her way across the rocky slope to reach them. "I'm really sorry. I just didn't know what to do when those things attacked."

"Lucky for you *and* me, the water is very deep on that side of the island, and I had time to turn falling into diving," Boehlkea said dryly. "How did *you* survive the attack?"

Marcus told her about the creature's fangs and venom and how his arm had saved him from being bitten. He also admitted he'd had to use his power to save himself from the other ones and how Leopold had saved him with his camouflaged rush from behind. Boehlkea looked at the blond boy with a slightly awed look on her face.

"That was brave *and* dangerous," she said.

"I had to do it," Leopold said. "Jarel was actually bitten by one of them. I needed Marcus to come and heal him."

"Oh, no," she gasped. "But you are all right?" she asked, looking at Jarel.

He nodded. "I have gained some admiration for Marcus's skill. I must admit to having had some doubts about him and his motives, but now..."

Leopold turned and looked at Jarel. "Really? You didn't trust Marcus? Then why are you here?"

Jarel gestured at Leopold. "For you. You believe in him, and I wanted to be with you. I have simply been waiting to see whether

Marcus really had good intentions."

Boehlkea snorted. "Even after what he did to get rid of Nun the Wiser and help all of Lysomnus before?"

"I was under the impression he did that to save his father. Once we returned to our bruwe, I saw all of you come and save Marcus when that Stondefel went crazy, and then everyone left."

"Is *that* what you think happened?" Leopold asked incredulously. "I know it was crowded, and things were kind of crazy that day, but that isn't even close to the truth."

"Uh, guys?" Marcus broke in, eyeing the top of the rocks. "Can we maybe keep moving while we have this conversation? I really don't feel comfortable just standing here in the open like this."

"That's a good idea," Jarel said. "I don't want to get bitten again."

"Fine, but this conversation isn't over," Leopold said.

"I believe we should make our way back to the boat and then come back around to this side of the island," Boehlkea said as she followed them down the path toward the jungle trees. "There is a good beach landing down there, and the trees on that side are not as thick and difficult to walk through as these are, despite the lack of a path."

"Excellent," said Jarel, entering the shade of the trees. "Now we hope to avoid the cat that ran in here and attacked me."

"I wonder..." Boehlkea mused.

"What?" Marcus said, turning to look at her.

"There is a venomous fish that lives in the waters not far from Fisc. We are careful to avoid being bitten by it, but it is succulent eating, so we catch it when we can. However, one thing we have learned about it is that once it has ejected its venom into a victim, it takes some time to build up a new dose to attack with. I was just wondering if these creatures are the same way."

"Except Jarel was bitten by the creature's fangs, and when I was behind the barrier at the summit, I saw that they also had some kind of stinger on the end of their tails.

Jarel snorted as he pulled at a vine that hung down across the path. "That figures. It wouldn't matter anyway because even if we came across one of these creatures, we have no way of knowing if it's the same one that bit me or not. Marcus and Leopold did say the creatures ran in all directions when they scared them off. Who knows where they went."

"At least they should be fairly easy to see in here," Marcus peered into the shadows. "They're bright white enough to stand out in all this gray and blue."

"Hey, what's this?" Leopold bent and picked something up from the ground, just inside the edge of the trees. It was a long, twisting cylinder that tapered to a sharp point. The opposite end was flat and smooth. Narrow blue and green stripes wrapped around it horizontally. When he held it up against the long, thin leaves of the trees, it blended in with them perfectly, making it almost invisible.

Jarel reached out and felt it. "It's quite thick and heavy, for all it appears so delicate. Almost like a weapon."

"It doesn't look like someone created it, though," Leopold said. "It feels like a horn or something."

"Yeah, like an animal horn, right?" Marcus met Leopold's eyes. "From a nature show about Africa or something!"

Jarel and Boehlkea looked baffled, as they usually did when the other two started talking about something from Earth.

"Let's just keep going, shall we?" Boehlkea said. "And keep an eye out."

"Jarel," Leopold said, "you said you thought we all came and saved Marcus in your bruwe after he killed Nun the Wiser?"

"Yeah," Jarel said shortly, his dark eyes on the path in front of him. "I was upset by all the noise and everything. I don't handle that stuff well, so I went back to my house. Once everything quieted down, you had all left, and Eris and the others were locked up. A lot of people were mad at Marcus. Others seemed to think he was some kind of hero or something. I just didn't believe he could have done so much by himself, even though I had seen him do some pretty powerful things while I was still watching with the crowd in the beginning when he first came. It was hard to believe there was someone as powerful as Nun the Wiser who wouldn't be out to do things the same way. I decided maybe he wasn't as powerful as it first seemed, and he needed your help, and I also thought maybe he wasn't the nice guy he pretended to be."

"I promise you, dude, I'll never use my power to hurt people the way Nun the Wiser did," Marcus said earnestly. "All I want to do is help this world."

"I think I'm starting to believe that now," Jarel said. "Even though we're on this journey to try to save Lysomnus, you used your power to save my life. I would have died if you hadn't."

Boehlkea turned from where she stood on the edge of the path, looking grim. "I only hope that using your power here has not decreased your ability to accomplish what you set out to do in the first place."

Marcus sighed. "I honestly just don't think it works like that. I know my power is much stronger than most peoples' who have abilities and that Nun the Wiser suffered physical effects from the use of her mental energy. But none of those things diminished anyone's power. They stayed the same. Even if it affects me physically in some way the way it did Nun the Wiser, I'll still have my abilities. Also, after I first found out I had this power, it got *stronger* the more I used it and practiced controlling it. I should still be able to move the moon with the Halfriez island boost."

"I hope so," Jarel said. "Because as grateful as I am to still be standing here, I don't believe saving my life today is worth losing the lives of everyone in this world."

"Ugh, guys," Marcus said, pounding the tip of his cane into the dirt in frustration. "*Please* have some faith in me."

"I do, buddy," Leopold chuckled, carefully tossing an arm around Marcus's shoulders. "But I really think we need to get moving again. We can't keep stopping to gab every five minutes, especially not with those murder beasts lurking about."

Jarel snorted. "Murder beasts, that's a good one."

Boehlkea sauntered ahead of them along the path. Marcus noticed that if it weren't for her red hair, she would be almost invisible against the backdrop of the teal leaves. It was dim enough that even the movement of her legs wasn't that easy to pick up against the gray of the smooth tree trunks, with the turquoise vines looping between them.

As he watched her, he saw movement just beyond her in the trees.

"Boehlkea! Stop!" he called out as quietly as he could. She halted and turned her head to look back at him, body frozen in fear.

"What is it?" She whispered. "Is it a murder beast?" Her eyes darted back to the trees.

"No," Marcus murmured, trying not to smile. "I mean, I don't think so. I just saw something moving, but it wasn't white. I couldn't see it clearly."

Boehlkea moved quickly back to Marcus's side, clutching his arm with her cool fingers. Jarel and Leopold both stared into the trees, trying to see anything moving around. Something snapped directly in front of them. Everyone froze.

An animal stepped cautiously onto the path, turning its head toward them as it did. Six long legs moved gracefully beneath a deep-chested body with narrow hindquarters. It gazed at them with blue eyes that looked overlarge for its head, which tapered to a pointed muzzle. Two long, twisted horns stood out from between ears that looked as if they had been lined with velvet. Each foot had four widely spread toes and a sharp-looking hook on the back of both front legs. The entire creature was striped with the same green and blue colors as the leaves all around them.

"Oh," Boehlkea breathed, "how lovely!"

"Indeed," Jarel agreed. "I wouldn't want to find out what it can do with those talons, though."

"Now we know why we couldn't see it before," said Marcus. "It would be invisible inside the trees. I couldn't even see anything but some movement, and it was almost right in front of me."

As they talked, the animal stepped back as if in alarm and suddenly raised its tail. Long, feathery plumage extended in a half-circle behind it, white fringes standing out brilliantly around the turquoise at the center of each pinion.

Without warning, the creature looked back into the trees behind it and leapt across the path, tail streaming behind it, disappearing into the jungle almost immediately. Only seconds later, they heard crashing, and a white blur hurtled across the path where the animal had been standing just a moment before.

“Okay, I think that’s our cue to leave,” said Leopold, grabbing Jarel’s hand and heading down the path at a jog.

Marcus and Boehlkea hurried along behind them at the fastest pace Marcus could manage.

“I can’t believe that just happened,” Marcus panted.

“Now we know what the cats are eating,” Boehlkea said.

“That’s morbid.” Marcus looked at her sideways as he hurried along. “You sound like Jarel.”

“Sorry,” she said. “We knew the cats couldn't be surviving out here on nothing, or they’d be gone. And I’d say those jungle creatures have some good defenses between their camouflage and their horns and talons. They must be effective, or the cats would have eaten them all already and would have starved.”

“I see your point. Do we have to push through these trees soon?” Marcus dreaded the idea—it had been very painful for him the first time.

“I don’t think so—I think we gave those two the easy side the first time. See how the path is curving around here? It looks like this might lead right to the beach. Look! There’s sand on it now.” She pointed ahead to where they could see light shining on the path, and white sand lay across the dirt.

“Oh, thank goodness,” Marcus sighed. “I’m so done.”

As they exited the trees, they saw that Leopold and Jarel had already loaded the water casks back into the boat and had pushed it back to the water.

"Come on, guys!" Leopold called, one hand on the boat. He waved at them with the other. "High tide made it a lot easier to move the boat, but we need to get around the island and fill these casks so we can get back to the ship before dark."

Marcus realized that they hadn't brought any food with them, nor had they been able to look around for anything to eat while on the island. This had definitely been a long, difficult day already. If they weren't going to get fresh water out of it, this detour would definitely not have been worth the danger they'd encountered.

Finally, they were all seated in the boat, and Jarel was rowing them away from the beach and making his way around the island.

Marcus's stomach rumbled. The others looked at him and laughed. "One good thing to come out of all this," he said. "I'm actually looking forward to eating some fish when we get back on the ship tonight!"

Jarel rolled his eyes. "At last, we get to eat one meal where Marcus isn't whining about the food." Leopold laughed again.

Boehlkea patted him on the back. "You do have to admit, Marcus, you complain about the fish quite a lot."

"Well, I'm sorry," he said. "It's just boring eating the same thing every day. I've never been that much of a fan of fish, anyway."

Leopold snorted. "That doesn't even make sense, Marcus. The fish here in Lysomnus aren't even like the fish back on Earth. It's much more like chicken."

"Well, maybe I don't like chicken, either."

Jarel spoke over his shoulder as he pulled back on the oars. "You sound like a spoiled child who is used to getting anything he wants."

Marcus clamped his lips together and stared at the island as they passed by. Tears stung his eyes, but he refused to wipe at them and let the others see how much Jarel's comment had hurt. It made it all the worse because the other boy was right.

Marcus *had* been a bit spoiled in his life before Lysomnus, even with the challenges he'd faced in his life. He knew that his parents, who were tough on him as they tried to make him work through the challenges of his disability, gave him things because they wanted to make him happy. He had grown up with parents who, while they worked hard for it, made good money and were willing to spend it on him to make sure he had the best of everything.

Now, he was living in a world where benefits like that didn't exist. What was available was whatever happened to be at hand, and everyone worked for what they got. Anything people needed that they couldn't make or grow themselves, they had to trade for. Many things would never be available to him in Lysomnus, and he would have to adapt to that. He was struggling with that adaptation with much more difficulty than he would have expected.

"Marcus," Boehlkea startled him out of his thoughts. "We're here. Are you just going to stay in the boat?"

"He is pouting," Jarel said. "Just leave him there while we get the water."

"I'm not," Marcus said. "I know I have some things to work on. I'm not perfect, but I *am* trying."

Jarel looked at him, startled. "Okay," he replied, "Sorry about what I said." Then he extended his hand, taking Marcus's in a firm grip, and helped him out of the boat.

The beach on this end was just a narrow strip of sand, curving sharply in a crescent that led into the small section of jungle below the rocks. Boehlkea led them through since she had been this way before. While there wasn't a path here, the trees grew much farther apart, and there weren't nearly as many vines, making it easier to walk.

"This is the easy part," Leopold said as he stepped out of the trees behind Jarel, each of them carrying two casks. Boehlkea carried one, and Marcus walked behind them. He would keep them safe if the cats made a reappearance while they retrieved the water.

When they reached the pool, Leopold and Jarel bent to fill the casks while Marcus and Boehlkea kept a lookout. With only two of them, it was hard to watch all directions at once, particularly since they knew how hard the cats were to see against the white stone that surrounded them.

Marcus had just turned to look down toward the jungle again when he heard a loud yowl above him, followed by a splash. Jarel and Leopold both shouted.

When Marcus whirled around, he saw something small and white sinking into the pool near the turmoil of the waterfall. Boehlkea dove into the water, visible in its clear depths as she darted across the pool.

"What is she doing?" Leopold yelled. "I think it's one of those murder beasts! She's going to get herself killed!"

"It's far too small to be one of the beasts," Jarel said. "And how could one of them fall from up there? "He looked up at the top of the waterfall and inhaled sharply. "Uh-oh," he said. Marcus and Leopold looked up, startled to see several large creatures looking down at them.

Boehlkea broke the surface of the water at their feet, holding up a soaked white bundle.

"Marcus! You must help!" she cried.

Marcus dropped his cane and reached out, taking the cold, sopping-wet clump of fur. As it dangled limply in his hands, he saw that it *was* one of the cats, except this one was clearly an infant. It was tiny, and no fangs were visible in its mouth, which hung open lifelessly.

Without thinking, Marcus pulled the baby to his chest, bowed his head, and reached into it mentally with his power. He could sense water inside its lungs and pain in its head from the fall. He pulled gently, and water poured out of its mouth. The pain in its head slowly eased. Finally, the tiny creature took a breath and mewled.

Leopold called out wordlessly and pointed. One of the adults was working its way down the path, eyes locked onto the infant in Marcus's arms. The beast's mouth was open, and Marcus could see the fangs resting against the roof of its mouth. He turned toward the path, moving carefully across the white sand. While keeping his eyes locked on the adult, he carefully lowered the baby in his arms to the path. It waited, eyes shifting from him to the baby.

Once on the ground, the infant mewled again and stood, moving shakily on wobbly legs toward the large cat on the path. Marcus backed up. The beast walked slowly forward, lowered its head to take the baby in its mouth, and turned and ran up the path. When Marcus looked at the summit where the cats had all been looking down at them, it was empty. He blew out a shaky breath.

"Damn, Marcus, did you just make peace with murder beasts?" Jarel marveled. "That was impressive. Maybe you really can save the world." He shook his head and squatted back down to continue filling the last cask of water.

Boehlkea walked out of the water onto the sand. "That might be the understatement of all time," she said, shaking her head. "Thank you, my brother." She wrapped damp arms around Marcus. He didn't mind. He was pretty sure he was in shock.

Leopold was just sitting on one of the casks, head in his hands.

"Are you all right, Leopold?" Marcus asked as Boehlkea released him.

"I don't even know, man. How much more dangerous can this trip get?"

Jarel put an arm around Leopold and pulled him close, kissing him lightly. "Don't even ask. I've learned that when you ask how much worse things can get, life just keeps *getting* worse. So don't even tempt fate." Then he patted Leopold on the back. "Now comes the fun part. We get to lug these back to the boat! At least we probably don't have to worry about being attacked by those creatures on the way back, thanks to Marcus."

"You know, I could probably help you guys move them back to the boat," Marcus offered.

"*No,*" Boehlkea said. "Even if it doesn't drain your power, it affects you, Marcus. And I know you are dead tired and in a lot of pain after today. We're doing this the regular way and getting you back to the ship to eat and rest."

"Okay, okay," Marcus said, holding his hands up defensively.

"Have fun lugging heavy casks of water through the jungle."

As much work as it was, it didn't seem to take that long to make it back to the boat. Jarel said he was more worried about getting them all back on board the ship before sunset; once the casks were loaded back into the rowboat and they were all seated, the sun was sitting firmly on the horizon, sending orange and red rays across the glassy surface of the Diluvium.

Jarel rowed strongly away from the island once Leopold had pushed them off the beach and jumped in. The stocky blond boy looked despairingly at his sodden boots as he settled into his seat.

"Never did get a chance to see if there was something to make a replacement for my footwear," he said. "I can just feel the blisters on my ankles."

Boehlkea snorted. "After everything we encountered back there," she said, waving her long fingers back at the island slowly dwindling away behind them, "I'd think a few blisters were a small price to pay. I'm surprised Jarel can even row this boat after he nearly died today."

"I feel remarkably well," Jarel said after a strong pull on the oars. "There is definitely some restorative boost in addition to the healing Marcus performs."

"Thank you again, man," Leopold said to Marcus. "I don't want to imagine how it would feel if I had lost Jarel back there."

"I'm just glad I got to him in time. And that you came to save *me* in time. I wasn't exactly in the best position myself when you came along. That island is an extremely dangerous place. I wonder if anyone has ever been there before. It certainly isn't marked on the map as a place to avoid."

They fell silent as they approached the ship in the waning light of the setting sun. Jarel rowed the boat alongside the ship, and Leopold grabbed one of the ropes to hold the boat steady. He told Marcus to start up the ladder. By now, Marcus was tired and hungry enough to be light-headed and hoped he wouldn't fall from the ladder as he climbed. Boehlkea ascended directly behind him, reassuring him the whole way up.

Once they had made it over the side, Marcus sighed with relief. As he and Boehlkea leaned over and waited for Leopold and Jarel to tie onto the boat so it could be lifted aboard, he realized that the two boys would not be able to pull the weight of the boat with the added full casks of water, even with Boehlkea's help. Before anyone could say anything or they could begin climbing the ladder, Marcus closed his eyes and lifted the boat with his power.

He heard startled exclamations from Leopold and Jarel as they felt the boat rising beneath them and Boehlkea yelling at him for using his power again. Marcus didn't care. He wasn't going to allow his friends to struggle and do all the hard work when he could help them so easily. It wasn't fair for him to sit by and let everyone exhaust themselves when he *knew* he could do this and still have the strength to do what he needed; he could feel his power within himself, and it was stronger than ever. If it was taking some kind of toll on him, then it was worth it to help his friends. His chest grew warm, and then hotter, until the sensation spread throughout his entire body.

He had just lowered the boat to the deck when everything went black.

CHAPTER EIGHTEEN

RECOVERY

Marcus

Marcus could hear the voices first. They were blurred, disjointed, and he couldn't make sense of what they were saying. It was little more than muffled background noise. Then the rushing feeling of coming back to consciousness, like waking from a dream.

He opened his eyes. The stars spread above like a blanket of lights, each shining in its own space, not bright enough to blind him. He heard a gusty sigh.

"Finally!" The voice was Boehlkea's, and quavery with relief. The stars were blocked out as she bent over him, her blue eyes luminous, her scales glowing in the darkness. "How do you feel?"

Marcus thought for a minute, taking account of his body. "I hurt. And I'm hungry."

Leopold laughed from somewhere nearby. "So, back to normal, then?" his friend's voice sounded shaky as he uttered the words.

Jarel stepped into view, not much more than a dark outline in the starlight. "It seems that using your abilities under such extreme physical circumstances as you experienced today was too much for you, as Boehlkea warned. I would advise resting for the remainder of the journey. Hopefully, that will be enough to restore you, or we're all in trouble."

"Ugh," Marcus groaned. "It's not the power that got weak; it's just my body." He rolled to his side and sat up slowly. Boehlkea knelt and grabbed his shoulders, supporting him from behind. "I think once I eat and get some sleep, I'll be fine."

"If it is your body that was not up to the task tonight, then it is your body we must depend on to save us all when we reach that island. It will be for the best if you stay in your bed until we get there." Jarel said firmly.

"Hey, who put you in charge? "Marcus cried out angrily.

"We all talked about it while you were *blacked out*," Leopold broke in. "You've been gone a long time, Marcus. It's not like you just passed out for a few minutes; you were, like, dead to the world for at least an hour. We were starting to wonder if you were going to wake up or not."

"Oh." Marcus wasn't sure what to say to that. He let Leopold and Boehlkea help him to his knees, and Leopold helped him to his feet.

"I'm going to get you to bed, and Boehlkea is going to make you something to eat," Leopold told him. "Jarel's going to get the sails ready, although it's hard to say if we'll be making much headway tonight. Not much of a breeze, even."

It took much more time and effort than Marcus expected to reach his room. He was exhausted, even after the time he'd spent lying on the deck, which he suspected hadn't been all that restful. He hoped Boehlkea wouldn't take too long to bring his food. By the time he made it to his bed, all he wanted to do was curl up under the covers and sleep. Instead, he remained sitting and waited for food.

When Boehlkea appeared, she had a bowl of the fish stew she'd made the day before.

"Lucky for you, Marcus, I had some of this left so I could just reheat it for you," she said, handing him the bowl and spoon. He took them eagerly and sucked in a mouthful, chewing and savoring the flavor. He marveled that he'd ever complained about the food. It was delicious!

All too soon, the bowl was empty, his spoon scraping the last dregs from the bottom. He licked the utensil clean and handed the bowl and spoon back to Boehlkea.

"Thank you, sister," he said. "That was wonderful."

Boehlkea's eyes widened, and she smiled with pleasure. "You're welcome, brother," she said. "Now get some sleep!" She left the room.

Leopold patted Marcus' leg where it was buried under the covers. "Time to rest, buddy. Think you made her happy, calling her sister outright like that. I'm glad you have family here." He looked down and swallowed. "You're lucky to have her."

"I know," Marcus said. "I'm glad you found Jarel, though. At least you have someone who cares about you and can help you with the grief of losing your family."

Leopold smiled. "Yes, he has really made a difference in my life already. I am lucky."

Marcus removed the prosthesis and slid it over to Leopold. "Can you put this on the table? I can't sleep with it on."

Leopold did, looking down at Marcus, who could barely keep his eyes open. He pulled the covers up over his friend's shoulder. "Sleep well, bro. See you tomorrow." Marcus was asleep before Leopold closed the door.

The next day, the swaying of the ship woke Marcus. The wind must have picked up, he thought. As he rolled slowly onto his back, he had to put up his hand to block the sun that shone through the slit in the wall of his room. The sun must be fairly high in the sky to be shining in so brightly! He wondered how late he had slept. He turned and pulled himself to a sitting position, reaching for his cane and getting to his feet. His entire body hurt, but his back was throbbing even more than usual. Clearly, the previous day's exertions had been very hard on him.

He put his prosthesis on and went out into the hallway. After using the bathroom at the end of the hall, he returned to the stairway and looked at it grimly. He knew it was going to be difficult to get up to the deck. Stairs were difficult for him on his best days; feeling like he did today, he wasn't sure he could make it.

A shadow at the top of the stairs descended quickly, resolving from the gloom to reveal Boehlkea's glowing skin.

"Marcus!" she scolded. "What are you doing out here? Did we not make it clear that you are to remain in bed?"

"Well, I did have to use the facilities," he said, waving his prosthetic hand in the direction of the bathroom.

"Of course," she said. "But it looked like you were thinking of coming upstairs. Now get back to bed!" She pointed firmly into his room. Marcus sighed and walked back to his bed. This was going to be a boring few days if he had to just lie here in bed and do nothing. He didn't even have any books or anything to keep himself occupied.

"You're going to come in and visit me, right?" he called out to Boehlkea.

"Of course I will," she answered. "But I just came down to see if you were awake, so now I have to go and get you something to eat. I'll let the others know you're up, and maybe they'll stop down to keep you company throughout the day as well." He heard her running lightly back up the stairs.

Blowing out a frustrated breath, Marcus sat down on the bed, swung his legs carefully onto the soft surface, and bent his knees. He made himself as comfortable as possible with the pillows behind him, then pulled the map out to look at it again.

He traced his fingers along the sea, marveling at the distance they'd already traveled. It blew his mind to think that four teenagers were sailing a ship across the great Diluvium alone. He thought of Janke and Maril, whom he'd barely gotten to know. It was awful that they'd both been swept overboard during the storm that had whipped up so suddenly. Marcus wondered how long they had battled to keep the ship safe and moving through the winds and waves before they'd lost their lives. He felt terrible for Jarel. Without Janke and Maril, Marcus was sure that all of them would have been lost in that storm. Instead, Jarel had lost the only parents he had known.

As he looked at the map, he noticed again the stacked diamond symbol at the edge. Two diamonds, with a line running through them from top to bottom. He rubbed his fingers gently over the marking. What could it mean?

It was too bad he hadn't been able to find a book that showed a complete map of Lysomnus. After traveling across much of it on foot and flying over a lot of it with the Stondefel, he had a pretty good idea of what the landmass looked like—at least a large portion of it. He didn't know much about what lay west of Thicce Colpat or south of Grasian, which he'd never seen, but only heard about. Come to think of it, if Lysomnus was a planet, did the Diluvium wrap around it from the west coast, where Fisc was located, to the east coast, where the human bruwe had been? Considering it only took a few hours to fly across most of the landmass on the back of a Stondefel, and a few days to sail the Diluvium, clearly Lysomnus was a fairly small planet. He wondered if the double diamond shape was some indicator of the other coast being over the edge of the map.

A knock at the door roused him from his musings.

"Marcus? I have your lunch," Leopold peeked his head around the door. "Oh good, you're decent."

Marcus snorted derisively. "Like I'm just going to sit around in here in the nude? You guys are just going to walk in and out of here checking on me all the time anyway," he scoffed.

"You got that right," Leopold grinned as he pushed the door open with his shoulder and entered the room, holding a tray in his hands. "Got some goodies here for you. Fish, fish, and more fish. Boehlkea said the last of the root vegetables are rotten, so we're stuck with just fish now. Since we didn't get the chance to find anything else on that island yesterday."

"Oh, well," Marcus said nonchalantly. He didn't want to complain after the way Jarel had chastised him about being spoiled. "At least we have food at all."

"Yeah," Leopold agreed. "And Boehlkea tried several ways of cooking it. So there's a little variety. She said she's going to try to find some sea-type plants that we could possibly eat, but she's not sure if it's possible this far out since the water is so deep. If there's a reef or something, maybe..." Leopold sounded doubtful. "Who knows if what she finds is even something we could eat. Could be toxic, for all we know."

"Let's just give her the chance to even look," Marcus said, swallowing a mouthful of fish. "We'll worry about edibility if she finds anything. The Muirnati had many edible sea plants—I know, I ate several kinds while I was visiting them. I think she knows far more about the sea than any of us, even if we are farther out than she or any other Muirnati have ever gone.

"Where's Jarel?" he asked.

"He's on deck. He was watching the sails all night, dozing off and on since there was no wind. Then I took a shift starting early this morning when I got up while he slept, and now he's back up there. Wind picked up about mid-morning, and we're making good time now. Hopefully, we're just a few days away, as long as the wind keeps steady and we don't have any more storms."

Marcus shuddered. "Don't even say that," he said. "Look what happened last time. I can't even imagine losing any of you to another storm like that."

"Well, I don't think you'd lose Boehlkea," Leopold winked at him. She waited the last storm out in the Diluvium. "Maybe if one of us got washed overboard, she'd see us and save us."

"That's not funny," Marcus glowered at Leopold. "It didn't work out so well for Janke and Maril, did it?"

That sobered Leopold quickly. "Yeah," he said, looking down at his hands. "I guess you're right. I really liked them, too. They were nice people. I know they really cared about Jarel. I think he's just been trying to avoid thinking about what happened to them." Leopold put his hand over his eyes.

"Hey," Marcus said. putting his left hand on Leopold's arm. "I get it, believe me. We've all suffered so much loss, it's hard to keep seeing it. You want to be there for Jarel, but you just went through it yourself."

"Yeah, that's definitely it. I just hope... I don't want to lose anyone else, Marcus."

"I'm going to do my best to make sure that doesn't happen."

Leopold pointed at the tray in Marcus's lap. "Okay, enough seriousness for now. Eat that fish before it gets cold."

Behind them, Boehlkea breezed in the door, still dripping from a swim in the sea.

"I found some plants! There's an underwater shelf not far from here—good thing I saw it because it's shallow enough to damage the ship—and it had a whole array of plant life growing on it!" She grinned excitedly at the boys.

"Do you think any of it is edible?" Leopold asked nervously.

"Pretty sure," Boehlkea said. "They're not much different than most of the varieties we harvest in the deeper waters around Fisc. I know Marcus had some when he was staying with us in Fisc. There was probably some in the food the Arigani brought out to us before we left, too." She looked at Marcus, eyes pleading with him to help her convince Leopold of her ability to find food that was safe.

"Leopold, just try it. Boehlkea is not going to poison us. I've eaten sea plants before, and we need the food before we get scurvy or something."

"Okay," Leopold sighed. "Let's give it a try."

"Great!" She brightened. "I'll cook some of them up tonight for our evening meal. I think you're in for a treat."

At dinner that night, both Leopold and Jarel exclaimed over the flavor of the sea plants Boehlkea had added to their dishes. Marcus smiled as he met her eyes; they were both pleased.

"I think this one is my favorite," Leopold said, holding up a bulbous purple sea fruit on his fork. "It's sweet and yet not too sweet and tastes so good with the fish. Just amazing," he added, pushing the whole thing in his mouth, cheeks bulging.

"Gross," Jarel remarked. He ate neatly, each type of plant or fish separated on his plate, nothing touching anything else. "Sometimes I wonder what it is I am attracted to about you."

"My incredible sense of humor," Leopold answered loftily after swallowing. Marcus and Boehlkea both laughed. Leopold held out a hand. "See?"

Jarel rolled his eyes. "Of course, I'm sure that's it."

"Thanks for letting me out of bed to join everyone at the dinner table, by the way," Marcus said.

Boehlkea smiled. "I think you need to get up and move about at least once a day, besides bathroom breaks. Leopold told us that during your—recuperation?—after your accident, it was important for you to move, even though it was painful."

"Yes, my doctors kept harping on me about that after every surgery. I didn't want to do it, but Leopold here was worse about pushing me than even my parents were," Marcus grimaced. "He was always pressuring me to get up and try to walk."

"I'm nothing if not persistent," Leopold chortled.

"Sometimes to the point of annoyance," Boehlkea remarked as she popped a final piece of fish in her mouth.

"If everyone is done eating, I will clean up here," Jarel said, rising with his plate. "You can both get Marcus back to his bed."

"Already?" Marcus sighed in disappointment.

"Yes, you need to rest as much as possible," Boehlkea said. "While moving is important, you must not tax yourself again. You gave us all such a scare after your collapse when you used your power on that island." She nodded at Leopold, and they both helped Marcus to his feet.

"I'm not an invalid," Marcus muttered irritably, pulling his arms from their hands. He grabbed his cane from its resting place against the table and made his way to the stairs. Pulling himself up with the handrail, he ignored them both as he wished he could stomp a bit to express his annoyance at their coddling. He knew that would hurt him more than it would affect them. He was even more annoyed when he realized halfway up the stairs that he needed to stop and rest. Determined not to let his friends see how exhausted he was, he pushed through and made it the rest of the way to the deck.

Once he had made it, he noticed the bright glare of white light on the water and looked up, seeing the brilliance of the moon directly above the ship. It seemed to loom overhead, grossly large compared to when he'd glimpsed it while traveling with Cornus, Leopold, and Sadie shortly after first arriving on Lysomnus.

Marcus sucked in a cold breath through his teeth. He hoped they were getting close to their destination; the moon was obviously dropping out of orbit much faster than he had originally anticipated. How much longer could it stay in the lower orbit before it was pulled into this planet's gravity?

He noticed the shattered pieces of the celestial body were no longer trailing behind it anymore. He wondered if they had already been sucked into the atmosphere and burned up. Some should have been large enough to strike the surface; he hoped none of them had hit anywhere that would have hurt any of the people of Lysomnus.

Leopold and Boehlkea came up beside him.

"Kind of terrifying, isn't it?" Leopold said quietly. "I sure hope you can do what you think you can because if you can't, I don't think anyone is going to make it."

"We must have faith in my brother, Leopold," Boehlkea said, looking past Marcus at his best friend. "His power is strong, and we know that a small cube of the Halfriez was enough to help him, even when he was only beginning to manifest his power. I believe he will be able to perform this miracle."

"I only hope we can get there in time," Marcus peeled his eyes away from the spectacle above them and continued along the deck. "It won't matter what I can do if we're too late."

Jarel spoke up behind them. "I think we are only a day's trip away. By this time tomorrow, I believe you'll be proving whether you can do it or not."

Marcus took a deep breath and looked back to where Jarel stood, the sharp planes of his face highlighted in the moon's glow. "You just get me there, and I'll do what I have to."

Once he was lying in bed and the others had left, Marcus found himself unable to relax. His stomach was in knots. For all their plans and all his confident words, now that they were close, doubt filled his mind, and worry chilled him to the bone.

What if he failed? This wasn't like any other situation he had ever faced before in his life. It wasn't like learning how to walk again or use a prosthetic arm. Those things had been hard, but the failures, while difficult, had only helped him. He had to try over and over again until he succeeded. The efforts made him stronger.

Even here in Lysomnus, the challenges had been formidable, but ultimately, he'd been able to overcome them. Learning to understand and control his power was a process. Facing his own shortcomings and accepting them, understanding himself, and learning to change and become a better person was hard. No one wanted to admit they were selfish, but he had been. Then he had faced the worst situation he'd ever been in and had killed an actual villain, even though he hadn't tried to. He'd rescued Davidia, his sister, and ultimately saved the people of Lysomnus. If he had failed, the oppression of many people would have continued. He himself might have remained a prisoner and been forced to use his power for terrible things.

Now, though, the situation was different. If he failed this time, this world would be destroyed. Every living thing on this planet would die. He knew he was afraid to die, but he was willing to do so if it saved Lysomnus. What terrified him the most was the idea of failing.

Marcus finally understood the desperation of his friends and their requests for him to rest. He had been overconfident in his ability to simply do what he'd set out to do when they arrived at the source of the Halfriez, but his collapse after the exhaustion he'd experienced on the island of the beasts had proven that, while he might mentally have full confidence in his power, his physical body was very fallible. From what he'd seen of Nun the Wiser, it didn't really have anything to do with being disabled, either. Her body had been severely diminished, her right arm nearly as unusable as his own, the flesh eaten away by decades of using her power. His mind, his power, was only as strong as his body. If he wasn't physically able to do what he needed to do, then his power alone wouldn't be enough.

Marcus sighed and rolled onto his side. He'd never felt less like sleeping, and now he knew he needed all the sleep he could get. He reached into the pocket of his shorts and pulled out the Halfriez cube, staring at the tiny flame flickering within.

Well, it had helped put him to sleep once before when he'd been desperate to return to Lysomnus and find his father. Maybe he could use it to fall asleep on this restless night. His eyes shifted to the gleaming silver links of the Stikke on his left wrist. At least he knew there was no risk of accidentally going back to Earth anymore.

Marcus rolled onto his back and closed his eyes, trying to remember just how he'd done this the first time. He brought the Halfriez, pinched between two fingers, to his forehead and slowly slid it across his skin. He concentrated on sleeping. As before, nothing happened immediately, but he tried to be patient. When he reached his left temple, he felt a small beat, as if a tiny heart had settled beneath his skin. He stopped moving his hand and felt himself begin to drift away. The last thing he felt was his own hand slowly slipping back to the bed beside him. He didn't feel the Halfriez tumble away from his relaxing fingers.

CHAPTER NINETEEN

THE CRYSTAL ISLAND

Marcus

The room was bright when he opened his eyes, and the first thing he felt as he started to move around was the hard chill of the Halfriez against the skin of his hand. He grasped it quickly and returned it to his pocket, wanting to ensure he didn't lose the precious talisman.

He decided to stay in bed and just pulled himself up to prop against the pillows in a sitting position. Hopefully one of the others would remember to bring him some food soon—his stomach was growling. He wasn't sure what time of day it was, but he felt like he'd been sleeping a very long time.

Before too much time had passed, he heard footsteps on the stairs. A knock on the door and a pause caused Marcus to call out.

"Come in, hurry up! I'm starving to death!"

Leopold looked around the door as it swung open. "Phew! You need a bath! Smells horrible in here."

"Thanks a lot," Marcus said. "What do you expect when the only time I'm out of bed is when we eat supper?"

"I'm just giving you a hard time. Although you *are* a little ripe, buddy. Boehlkea is bringing you a bucket of water and some soap. You can wash yourself, though. I am *not* giving you a sponge bath.

Our friendship only goes so far."

"As if I'd let you," Marcus snorted. "What'd you bring me?" He nodded at the tray as he swung his legs out of the bed and reached for his prosthesis.

"Surprise, it's fish! Ha, ha, and also some more sea fruit and veggies. So that should make it tastier."

"Gimme," Marcus gestured for the tray. "I'm starving here."

Leopold laughed. "Guess anything starts to look good when your stomach starts rumbling. You slept half the day through again, by the way. You really must have overworked your bod the other day."

"I guess," Marcus said. "It always has taken me more time to recover when I've really pushed things, and I think since we got to Lysomnus it's really just been one long push. Every time we've had a break to sleep, I think I've slept a long time."

"True, true. Now that I think about it, that is the case. Even when we first got to Thicce Colpat, you slept, like, a whole extra day," Leopold mused.

"Yeah," Marcus mumbled through a mouthful of sea vegetables.

"Gee, bro, that color of drool really goes well with your skin," Leopold laughed. "It's the perfect color of mucus."

Marcus wiped his chin unselfconsciously on his arm. He was too hungry to care.

Boehlkea breezed into the room, a steaming bucket clutched in one hand, clothing draped over her other arm. She stopped short. "Oh, Marcus. This bath can't come a moment too soon! It *stinks* in here. And your face!" She giggled. "You have green slime smeared all over your chin!"

"Ugh, take this," Marcus said, handing the nearly empty tray to Leopold. "Just leave me that stuff and get out!" He indicated the steaming water and clothing Boehlkea carried.

The pretty Muirnati girl deposited the items on Marcus's bedside table and, giggling, dashed out. Leopold followed, laughter echoing in the hall as he closed the door behind him.

Marcus groaned. He sniffed his armpit. Ugh, he *did* smell bad. He looked into the bucket and saw a washrag floating in the water. There was a small, shell-shaped soap sitting on top of the clothes Boehlkea had left beside the bucket.

Marcus slowly took his clothes off, holding them away from himself as if just now realizing how dirty they were. He'd been wearing them since the morning they'd stopped at the island. They were ragged, stained, and smelled strongly of body odor as well. Why hadn't anyone said anything? Well, he supposed they'd all been too worried about his health to concern themselves about his dirty clothes.

He washed himself thoroughly, then dried off with the towel. He donned the shorts and sleeveless shirt Boehlkea had brought him. She'd seized all his clothes once it started to get really warm and said she was going to "fix" them for the weather.

Feeling very refreshed after the meal and the bath, Marcus was about to lay back down on top of his bedcover when he realized he had left the Halfriez in his dirty shorts, which were now lying in the corner. He flipped his cane over and used the curved handle to lift up the shorts, pulling the Halfriez from the pocket when it was within reach. Then he started to drop the shorts back on the floor. Catching himself, he realized he was being a slob. While he understood the others were willing to help by bringing him food and bathwater, he shouldn't expect them to pick his dirty clothes up off the floor. He hooked the shirt too, and set both of them on the bed, and carefully carried the bucket of dirty water to the bathroom.

He was just returning to his room when Leopold came pounding down the stairs.

"Marcus! You've got to come see this!"

Marcus did his best to climb the stairs quickly behind his friend, curious to see what could possibly be so urgent. It must be important if Leopold wanted him to climb to the deck, rather than get back into bed.

As they reached the deck, Marcus looked around, but didn't see anything unusual. Jarel and Boehlkea were both standing on the bow, staring intently at something. Leopold headed in that direction, waving impatiently at Marcus to follow him.

"Okay, okay, I'm coming," Marcus said, waving his cane to remind Leopold that he could only go so fast.

"Sorry, Marcus," Leopold replied, slowing his pace to match his friend's. He stubbed his toe on the deck as he tried to both walk slowly and hurry, and Marcus laughed.

"We'll get there, Leopold. Just be patient. Am I going to miss it?"

"No, you're right, it's not going anywhere. It's just—wow, you're really going to be—just hurry up!"

Marcus marveled at Leopold's excitement. He hadn't seen his friend this excited in quite a while.

When Marcus arrived at the railing his eyes were riveted to the sight in the distance.

Rising from the water ahead were luminous shafts of crystal of varying heights, each enclosing a single flickering flame. Some ended just above the water; others soared far above the waves that lapped at their glassine edges.

"That's it," Marcus whispered, staring at the object of his search. As he stared at the beautiful display, he reached out with his mind and felt a pulling sensation, as if the Halfriez was calling him. "It needs me," he said.

"What?' Boehlkea asked, turning her head to look at him. "It *needs* you? You can feel it? Like in your head?"

"Yes," Marcus said. "It's calling to me. I reached out, and now that I've made contact with it, it wants me to come to it."

"Uh, that's just weird, dude," Leopold said, shaking Marcus's shoulder carefully. "Snap out of it."

"Huh?" Marcus looked around, feeling dazed.

"This sounds like just another problem," Jarel said, shaking his head as he walked down the stairs to the lower deck.

Boehlkea grabbed Marcus's face, turning it until he was looking at her. "Are you all right, Marcus? Because you did not sound okay for a minute there."

"I think so." For a moment, all Marcus had been aware of was the call of the Halfriez, pulling at his mind. He didn't want to mention that he could still feel it pulling deep inside his head. "I'm fine, don't worry."

"Man, I hope you are, because that was really freaky. And we don't need any more freaky right now," Leopold said.

"Can you get me something to sit on? Since we're getting close, I don't want to just lie in bed all day. I can still rest if I sit up here. I'd rather watch during this last part of the trip, now that we're within view of the island."

"Sure," Leopold said, eyeing Marcus warily. "Just don't start up with that "it wants me" stuff again."

"I will sit here with you," Boehlkea said. "I think you need some company to keep your mind off the end of this journey." She followed Leopold, returning behind him with a box from the hold. She sat on the box when Leopold brought Marcus's deck chair up.

"Thought we had stowed this thing for good," he said, panting as he set it up for Marcus to sit down.

"Thanks," Marcus said. Leopold nodded.

"I'm going back down with Jarel while you two chat and watch that... thing."

They waited quietly while they heard him clump back down the stairs.

Marcus was increasingly distracted by the pull inside his head. He wondered if it would get worse as they approached the island. Then he looked away from it as he felt Boehlkea lay a hand on his arm.

"Marcus," she said, "I wonder if this is a good time for us to talk a little bit about our experiences with our father? I know that your life with him on Earth was very different than mine was here in Lysomnus."

Marcus smiled. "That sounds like the understatement of the century. Like, you grew up knowing that he came from another world, and that he had another life and family, and I didn't even know that this place or you existed until just a short time ago."

Boehlkea's blue eyes grew serious. "I know that was one thing that greatly disturbed my mother. She knew our father her whole life. They fell in love when they were very young—not long after he started coming to Lysomnus. Just as she believed he was ready to settle down and start a family with her, he told her he had married a woman on Earth and that woman was having his baby there. She was devastated."

"I can't imagine how that felt," Marcus said, concentrating on Boehlkea's face. He could still feel the Halfriez island pulling on him, despite his concentration on their conversation. "I know if my mom had known that he had a family somewhere else, she would have felt the same way. I don't even know if she would have stayed with him. Your mom made a difficult choice."

"I think it was something she thought very hard about," Boehlkea said. "I know that many Muirnati had already questioned her decision to join with a human, especially considering the way that the other humans already treated us. But they knew the Talents were and always had been different. I think she felt his betrayal deeply after overlooking that difference."

"Do you think it had something to do with the fact that she was having his child?" Marcus looked at her consideringly.

"Hm. I hadn't thought of that before. Other than telling me how hurt she was about his other family, she never had an unkind word to say about our father. She always said what a wonderful father he was to me, and he definitely always showed me love and treated me wonderfully as I was growing up. I only wished I saw more of him—he only came to see us once in a while."

"I told myself he was a good father," Marcus said. "I loved him. I know my mother and I both overlooked a lot of imperfections in him; he honestly didn't spend a lot of time with us. I guess we don't want to think of our parents as having faults, but I definitely learned that he had many. He saved my life—and Leopold's and Sadie's—when we tried to go home, though. And he didn't try to come back with us so I could save him. He said he would be endangering Lysomnus if he did."

Tears filled Boehlkea's eyes. "He sacrificed himself for us all at the end, in a way. And I didn't get to see him again, after what he said to me in that house. I wanted to talk to him. I don't know how to feel about what he called me. Sometimes I wonder if he really loved me."

Marcus sighed. "I know, and I feel awful. I'm the one who sent him back to Earth. I feel so guilty. I didn't know about the disease that was killing everyone there, but I'm still responsible for his death. I sent him back out of anger, and I took him away from you—even though I didn't mean to. How can you forgive me for that?"

Boehlkea smiled, sending the tears in her eyes trickling down her face. "Exactly for the reason you said—because you didn't mean to do it. If you had meant to send him back to die, or meant to stop me from seeing him, I could blame you. But none of what happened was your fault, Marcus. We all make mistakes and have to live with regret. You have to figure out how to live with that, forgive yourself, and move on with your life." She leaned over and wrapped her arms around him. He lifted his own arms and pulled her against himself tightly.

"I love you, brother, and there is nothing for me to forgive."

She let go and sat down on her box, looking back at the island, which was visibly closer. As Marcus looked, he felt the draw of it increase inside his brain.

A sudden vibration from his hip grabbed his attention, and he slapped his hand over it. Boehlkea noticed the movement and looked down.

"What is it?" she asked.

Marcus pulled the Halfriez cube out of his pocket. It was vibrating between his fingers, the flame inside dancing crazily. Boehlkea reached out with one finger and touched its smooth surface, feeling the trembling stone.

"Oooh! Why is it doing that?"

"I have no idea," Marcus said. "It just started. It must have something to do with the proximity of the source island, I guess?" He could also feel the increase in the pressure in his head. It wasn't painful or unpleasant; in fact, it felt natural, like he was supposed to follow the pull. He didn't mention that to Boehlkea, though.

Leopold came back up the stairs behind them.

"Jarel says he's pretty sure we'll reach the island right after sunset, which will be fairly close to moonrise, so you will probably be able to do… do your thing not too long after we get there," Leopold said, looking at Marcus. He swallowed nervously. "I really hope this goes okay. I gotta admit, I'm scared out of my mind."

"I feel the same way," Boehlkea said, reaching out and taking Marcus's hand. "I do not want to lose my brother so soon after I have found him. Of course I want to save our world, but I am scared of what could happen to you, Marcus."

Marcus realized his own fear was completely gone. His body felt strong despite the pain, and he could feel the power within him. He was ready to do what he needed to do, and was confident that he would succeed. He wondered why he felt so sure of himself now when he had been so afraid just hours before. Perhaps it was just the anticipation; now that the time was nearly here, he was ready. The call in his head amplified again and became so strong he stood up and grabbed the railing to stop himself from jumping overboard and swimming to the crystal island as it loomed closer.

As the others tried talking to him, Marcus didn't even realize he was just standing at the railing, staring. Leopold and Boehlkea shouted in his ears, shook him, and Leopold finally tapped him lightly on the lower back in a desperate attempt to break his connection with the island. The pain broke through, and he turned to Leopold, gripping his back, anger clouding his hazel eyes.

"Why did you do that?" he asked, with a look of betrayal.

"Because you were like, lost to the world, man. We've been yelling at you and you acted like we weren't even here. I didn't know what else to do to get through to you."

"Really?" Marcus was surprised but still found it a struggle not to look back at the Halfriez island. He could almost feel ethereal fingers sliding around his face, trying to turn his eyes back to those crystalline towers, the flicker of the flames drawing him back...

Whack! Boehlkea slapped him across the face. "You've got to stay with us, Marcus! I don't know what's going on with you, but how are you going to move the moon back to where it belongs in the sky if you're staring at those crystals?"

"I'm sorry!" Marcus shouted. "I can't control it. It's so hard, I can feel it calling me. It's like I *belong* there..." He waved the hand holding the vibrating Halfriez cube toward the island, not daring to look up. He knew as soon as he did, he would be staring at the island again. The *call* of it was tearing him apart.

As the sun finally sank behind the island, the prismatic effect of the crystals set the ocean on fire. The waves themselves carried the vibrant reds and subtle oranges in the foam that seethed overtop each curl as it rippled across the surface of the Diluvium.

Everyone found themselves mesmerized by the beauty of the view. Even Jarel, standing beneath the mast, could see the colorful beams of light that were refracted by the prisms the Halfriez had become. He stared in wonder as the sinking sun sent shifting colors across the sea all around them.

Marcus sighed as the sun finally dropped too low to affect the island, and the sea gradually returned to the dark blue it had been before. He felt the pull within him dragging him forward with an almost physical force, but the effect was pleasant, as if he was being carried home.

As the ship approached the island, Boehlkea stayed by Marcus's side while Leopold left to help Jarel guide them into position near the crystalline structure. The boys returned to the bow to drop the anchor.

"This is as close as we're going to get," Jarel said, eyeing the Halfriez warily. "We'll have to lower the rowboat to get you over to that thing."

"Yes," Marcus said. "Let's do that."

“Now?” Leopold asked. “I thought we’d wait until the moon had risen.”

“I think I should be there, ready to start as soon as the moon is where I need it to be,” Marcus replied, eyes still glued to the island.

“Perhaps one of us should go with you, to be sure you are safe and can keep your mind on this task,” Boehlkea said, putting one hand on Marcus’s shoulder.

He looked down at her, blinking slowly, as if just remembering she was there.

“No. I will need to be there by myself. I don’t know what will happen, how the amplification of my power will affect anyone nearby. It’s too dangerous,” he said.

“Let’s go lower the boat, then,” Jarel said, taking Leopold by the hand and leading him off the deck. Boehlkea followed, looking back at Marcus apprehensively.

Marcus stood at the railing, watching the flames inside each crystal flicker. He cocked his head to one side, a small smile playing about his lips as if he were listening to a voice whisper. When he heard the others calling, he nodded and made his way down to the lower deck and the waiting boat below.

Only Jarel was seated in the boat. When Leopold moved to assist Marcus down the rope ladder, Marcus waved his friend off without a word. He merely shook his head and tossed his cane to the deck, easing himself over the railing. His descent was almost careless, as if he had no worry of falling, despite his pain and the difficulty of using his prosthesis well on the unsteady rope.

Once they saw he was safely seated on the boat, Boehlkea and Leopold called down.

“Good luck, Marcus!”

“Be safe!”

“We love you!”

Marcus didn’t look up at them. Jarel did, shrugging helplessly, and then started rowing in the direction of the island.

CHAPTER TWENTY

THE ULTIMATE CHOICE

Marcus

As they reached the island, Marcus felt as if his body were vibrating as strongly as the Halfriez cube inside his pocket. Jarel looked at him without a change of expression, so he didn't think it was a physical manifestation. An anticipation greater than anything he'd ever experienced filled his mind, and he stretched out his arm for the lowest crystal platform before it even came into reach.

"Just wait, Marcus," Jarel said. "Let me get a little closer, or you'll fall right into the water."

Marcus looked irritably at Jarel's black eyes, which gazed over Marcus's shoulder. "You could hurry up."

Jarel took his hand off the oar as the boat bumped against the crystal of the island and waved. "There you go, your highness."

Marcus looked to see the first Halfriez platform right next to the boat. Jarel kept the boat steady as Marcus set his hand on the crystal. He stiffened, as if he were being electrocuted. He closed his eyes in response to the sensation.

Jarel

When Marcus opened his eyes, Jarel was startled to see they were glowing with a bright white light, Marcus climbed easily onto the Halfriez and stood tall, as if he'd never been injured or in pain. He turned and walked up the levels of crystal, which rose like stairs made just for the length of his stride. In the middle of the island, he swung around and sat down, arms resting at his sides as if he sat in a chair. His eyes shone in the twilight.

"Mighty waters, it's a throne," Jarel whispered, and began rowing back to the ship as fast as he could.

The others were waiting for him as he tied off the boat and climbed the ladder.

"What happened?" Boehlkea and Leopold cried out in unison, seeing the frightened look on his face.

"I—I don't know if I can describe it," Jarel said. "It was just unreal."

"Please try," begged Boehlkea. Leopold grabbed Jarel's hand and squeezed, nodding desperately.

Jarel tried his best to explain what had happened when Marcus touched the crystal surface of the island. With a shiver, he pulled Leopold close to his side and held him as he talked. He had difficulty describing the way Marcus's eyes had glowed from within after his initial contact with the Halfriez. The way the other boy had simply marched up the steps, and found the seat in the middle of the structure that seemed to be made to fit his body perfectly.

"He sat down on it like it was a throne, like he was a king," Jarel whispered. "Staring out at the sea like some kind of-of sorcerer. I don't know. It...it changed him, maybe? I hope not. For all our sakes, I hope Marcus is still in there."

All they could do was make their way to the bow of the ship and wait, hoping that Marcus would still do what they'd come all this way for him to do.

It felt like it took forever for the moon to rise. They were anchored on the side of the island and could not see Marcus where he sat on the crystalline throne. They all wondered if he was even aware of the rising moon, much less prepared to save Lysomnus as he had promised.

The three of them watched for hours, wondering if Marcus was watching the celestial body ascend. He had to see it; the crystal structures of the Halfriez island were illuminated with white light as the immense, broken moon shone down on them, lighting up the entire Diluvium around the island.

"Jeez, come on, Marcus!" Leopold muttered. "What is he waiting for?"

"Maybe he is waiting until it is higher in the sky?" Boehlkea wondered.

"Maybe he's not even in there anymore and he's just going to let us all die," Jarel said, turning and stomping down the stairs to the lower deck, arms folded angrily across his chest.

Marcus

Marcus was not waiting. He was lost in a dream of flickering flames, of crystalline beauty, of power building in his mind. The Halfriez around him had amplified his power a hundred-fold, then a thousand-fold, and then an exponential amount he couldn't comprehend anymore. As the power built within him, he had realized he had to ignore the world around him and he must now focus on *control,* or he would simply die.

At first that pull had simply been a pleasurable sense of coming home, but once he had touched the island, he had lost his sense of self. Every bit of his identity had been wiped away by the immensity of the power within him. The staggering explosion overwhelmed his mind. Marcus could have destroyed the planet without even realizing it; with a careless thought he could have reached back through the portal dimension and obliterated the Earth.

He battled for control over the vastness of the energy. It swelled and he felt the stars as if they were contained within him. The universe was within his grasp. If Marcus spread out his hands, he could clap them together and galaxies would cease to exist. A question loomed in his mind. Marcus felt the offering as the intensity of the Halfriez joined with the strength of his own power. He could become a god.

"No," he groaned, and he heard his voice echo across the void. "I don't want this. I only want to save my friends."

Immediately the surge began to lessen, his expanded view of the universe disappearing as the energy pulled back inside him. He could still feel the immensity of the power, but he was able to regain control of it.

Blinking his eyes, he felt tears sting with the burning that usually came when he hadn't blinked his eyes for a long time. Marcus stared around himself, seeing the crystal glowing with bright white light. As he looked up, he saw the massive, cracked surface of the moon directly above him.

His friends must be frantic, wondering why he hadn't done anything as the moon rose high in the sky while Marcus sat on the island. He imagined their fear and disappointment, watching the looming moon with no action from him.

Marcus stood up, staring up at the shattered moon. It was the closest he'd ever seen it, a glaring eye daring him to defy it, ready to drop to the surface of Lysomnus and destroy everything and everyone he loved.

He closed his eyes and gathered the power surging within his mind, and heat surged instantly within his body. The boundlessness of the energy still terrified him, even though it had released him from the promise of godhood. It *had* to be enough now, with the offer of such power!

With a scream, he opened his glowing eyes and raised his arms, pointing directly at the moon, *pushing* with every ounce of energy he felt inside. A brilliant beam of force shot straight into the sky, through the atmosphere of the planet. Marcus felt through his left hand that he could meld and control the energy, and as he moved his hands apart, both the flesh and the metal, the beam widened.

He felt with his mind and found the moon within the force of the power stream and enveloped the celestial body within it. The pull of the energy brought the two broken pieces back together, forming them back into the glowing globe the moon had been before it had been shattered.

Marcus *pushed* the sphere away from the planet, feeling the change in the gravitational pull each body had on the other. He didn't know how, but just as he had known he could control the entire universe, he knew when the moon was in the right place to return to its correct orbit. With a groan, he released the power. The glowing beam disappeared instantly.

Marcus slumped on the crystal throne, feeling more drained than he had since his collapse on the deck of the ship. His head hurt abominably. The pain in his back was worse than ever. As he looked down, he noticed that the flames in the crystals around him had been reduced to small yellow flickers, barely visible. He wanted to cry out, afraid he had destroyed the valuable island, but he didn't even have the energy for that. All he could do was lie with his head on the crystal behind him and wait for someone to come; he didn't feel like he would ever move again on his own.

Maybe they wouldn't come, he thought after a while. He couldn't remember anything after reaching the crystal island, other than the ongoing battle in his head to remain human. But he knew he'd been pretty rude to Jarel before that, since he'd been feeling the constant pull of the island and couldn't wait to get here. Now he couldn't even remember what that pull had felt like.

After a while, he heard a sound. Gentle splashing from around the side of the island, getting louder. Before long, the boat came into view, with Jarel, Leopold, and Boehlkea all on board. Jarel brought the boat to a stop, and Leopold reached cautiously for the lowest Halfriez platform, tapping it quickly with his fingers and pulling them away before returning his hand and pulling the boat closer.

"It won't hurt you," Marcus tried to say.

"Marcus, we can barely hear you," Boehlkea said, concern plain on her face as she carefully stepped out of the boat and began to make her way up the steps to him. "Are you okay?"

"Mm-hmm," he replied, unable to raise his head. "Jus' tired."

Leopold looked at Jarel, then climbed out of the boat. "I'd better go help bring him down." Jarel nodded.

Together, Boehlkea and Leopold had to carry Marcus down to the boat. He was unable to move enough to help them even by holding his head up. They ended up sitting him in the bottom of the boat, his back braced against Leopold for support.

"I've got you, buddy. See, we knew this was going to be too much for you."

"But you did it!" Boehlkea exclaimed, holding Marcus's hand tightly with both of her own, stroking the skin with her thumbs. "The moon is back where it belongs, and it even looks like it did before. How did you do that?"

"Kind of hard to explain," Marcus mumbled.

"Jeez, Boehlkea, give the guy a minute," Leopold said. "He just moved a whole moon. I think he needs some time to recover."

"Oh, right, sorry," she said. "I'll stop asking you questions. You need to sleep and eat."

"I'm just glad his eyes aren't glowing anymore," Jarel said as he rowed them toward the ship. "That was creepy."

"I'm sure it had something to do with the Halfriez boosting his power," Boehlkea said. "He certainly looks fine now, other than plain exhaustion."

When they reached the ship, it turned out to be quite an ordeal to get Marcus on board. He was simply dead weight, since he was unable to help physically by even holding on to anyone. His power seemed to be completely unusable; when he felt for it, other than a distant swirl deep within his mind, he was unable to access it.

Finally, Jarel rigged a harness around Marcus's upper torso and shoulders, and he and Leopold climbed up to the deck, pulling Marcus up that way. Boehlkea climbed the ladder next to Marcus as he ascended, reaching out to keep him from bumping against the side of the ship.

Marcus was safe in his bed before they even retrieved the boat. He was asleep before they left his room.

When Marcus woke up, he found a tray with still-steaming fish stew on the bedside table. Despite a body full of intense aches and pains, he sat up and then began wolfing down the food, sucking in air as the hot stew burned his mouth. While sleeping had refreshed him somewhat, he could still feel fatigue creeping around the edges of his consciousness. Marcus was sure that after he ate, it wouldn't take long for him to go back to sleep.

Just as he burrowed back into the covers, Boehlkea knocked lightly and poked her head around the door.

"Marcus, I know you're still tired, but you need to come up on deck. There's something odd we think you should see."

Groaning, Marcus threw the covers back and sat up.

"Are you sure I need to see it? You guys can't handle it without me?"

"I—I think this may be important, Marcus." Boehlkea looked frightened, which got Marcus on his feet. She handed him his cane and his prosthesis, and he followed her slowly up the stairs.

When he made it up to the deck, he saw Leopold and Jarel up on the bow deck. Boehlkea led him up to where the boys were standing. Marcus saw they were still anchored near Halfriez island.

"Why are we still here?" he asked.

"No wind," Jarel answered shortly.

"But look, Marcus," Leopold pointed, past the island.

Marcus followed his friend's finger to see another ship on the horizon. He felt a jolt of fear.

"What the—"

"That's what we said," Jarel remarked grimly. "No one in Lysomnus knew how to build a ship. So who is that?"

"And are they coming toward us?" Boehlkea wondered.

Marcus adjusted his gaze to the Halfriez columns, noticing that some of the flames had grown just a fraction, changing in color toward the original orange they had been when he'd first seen them. Most were still very small and still the same faded yellow. He wondered if the island would recover. He hoped they wouldn't be left unprepared in a dangerous situation if the other ship was hostile.

"Well, maybe they're friendly, just out fishing or checking out the ocean, or something," Marcus said, trying to be positive.

Jarel eyed him. "Or maybe they saw the light show you put on and are coming to find you." Marcus swallowed and looked away. He felt again for his power, hoping he could get the ship moving without waiting for the fickle wind. Again it stayed out of his reach, as if it was lost deep inside.

"Well, if the wind comes up, we can just sail out of here and stay ahead of them, right, Jarel?" Leopold looked hopefully at his boyfriend.

"Maybe. If the wind comes up."

The four of them stood at the railing, watching the other ship as the sun moved across the sky, and waited desperately for the wind to pick up.

CHAPTER TWENTY-ONE

A STRANGER APPEARS

Marcus

Several hours later, Marcus felt the first puffs of a breeze begin to blow against his face. Despite his fatigue, he'd insisted on staying up top with his friends in his deck chair, not wanting to get caught unaware if the other ship were to approach them.

As they had watched and waited for the wind, it appeared as if the other vessel was getting closer.

"I think they're having the same problem," Jarel said. "No wind. They're almost as dead in the water as we are. I wish I knew how they were still moving at all. Maybe there are still some air currents where they are."

As he felt the breeze begin to pick up, Jarel dashed down and began to unfurl the sails, preparing to get underway.

"Hopefully this wind becomes a strong one!" Leopold shouted as he and Boehlkea cranked up the anchor. Boehlkea slammed the lock in place and then turned to Marcus, her blue eyes dancing.

"We're going home, Marcus!"

Marcus smiled. "Thank goodness. I'll be glad to get back and see Sadie again."

"I feel the same way about Melacar. I miss him and my mother so much. I can't wait to see them."

Leopold had run to the back of the ship to control the rudder while Jarel manipulated the sails. Now he shouted to get their attention, and everyone looked as he pointed off the back of the ship. Everyone hurried to join him.

"Man, they must have caught the same wind we did," Jarel said, seeing the ship growing larger behind them. "I wish I knew how they were moving faster than we are. It makes no sense." He shook his head.

"Why are they chasing us, that's what I want to know!" exclaimed Boehlkea.

"I still think Jarel's right, that someone saw the light from what Marcus did and came to see what it was," Leopold said.

"But that ship already passed the Halfriez island!" Marcus said.

"Well, if they saw our ship sail away from it, they surely guessed we had something to do with it. They saw the island was empty as they passed by." Jarel's eyes were grim as they stared back at the ship that was quickly catching up to them. "Oh, wait, I can see how they're doing it now," he said.

"What?" asked Leopold. "How are they going so fast?" He stared harder over the railing as if to see for himself.

"There are oars coming out of the sides of that ship," Jarel said. "They must have people in the hold, people who are rowing even when the sails are useless." He turned and looked at the other three. "That means they have a substantial number of people on board. We are going to find ourselves outnumbered."

A jolt of fear ran through Marcus's body. That ship had to be coming for him, and he was sure they would be willing to hurt his friends to get to him. He knew the others would never give him up without a fight. Desperately, he felt for his power again. Again, there was nothing except the sense that it was there, but he couldn't reach it or do anything with it.

"Don't let yourselves get hurt for me," he pleaded. "That's the last thing I want."

"We're not going to let anything happen to you, Marcus,"

Boehlkea said. "You don't get to tell us to let someone take you or hurt you while we stand by and let it happen."

"Yeah," Leopold said. "I think you know us better than that."

"Even *I'm* not going to let that happen," Jarel said with a scoff.

Marcus sighed. They were not taking this seriously enough. He remembered how terrifying it had been facing Nun the Wiser and Eris, with the entire group of empowered humans behind them. This situation was even more of an unknown.

It was a matter of less than an hour before the other ship caught up to theirs. At first, all they could see was one figure standing by the railing. Marcus could make out a human man of large stature, standing with his arms crossed, staring at them. As the ship began to draw alongside theirs, ropes flew through the air, with three-pronged metal claws on the end that hooked on to their railings and pulled both ships together.

The people who had thrown the ropes slithered into view. They were tall, with thick green scales covering their upper bodies. Muscular arms ended in stubby, three fingered hands with short, opposable thumbs that manipulated the ropes. They were legless, but their lower bodies coiled below them in solidly muscled tails. The scales smoothed out and their muscles rippled under the skin as they moved. Their heads were flat, with dark yellow eyes that protruded above, and they had thick, curved jaws lined with sharp teeth.

The human held his hand up in the air. His curly red hair was pulled behind his neck in a club. Green eyes stared at them from a ruddy face. Thick lips sneered back from his large teeth.

"Hello, the ship!" He yelled in a deep voice, as if they were not standing three feet away.

"Can we help you?" Marcus asked.

"Why yes, you can. We saw quite a light show from our land last night, and thought we would investigate. When we sailed out, we saw your ship near Crystalline Island. Then you ran away. Why did you do that?" The man smiled as if trying to be friendly, but Marcus noticed that his smile never reached his cold eyes.

"Sorry," Marcus said. "We've never seen another ship like ours, nor heard of another land besides Lysomnus. Naturally we were afraid and decided to return home."

"Lysomnus? What is this place you speak of? We know only of Dremheim and thought you might be from a distant part of our land." The man chuckled.

"Dremheim? What is Dremheim?" Marcus was confused. He looked at Boehlkea and Jarel, but they looked as lost as he felt.

"What are your names?" the man asked.

"Why should we tell you?" Marcus asked.

"It seems courteous. My name is Barzil T—just Barzil will do, for now."

Marcus and the others looked at each other.

"Come on, come on. Share your names, now that I have shared mine."

The green people to either side of Barzil began to hiss in agitation.

"Fine. I'm Marcus, and these are Jarel, Leopold, and Boehlkea." Marcus indicated the others.

"And you are all from this world?" Barzil indicated the three boys, ignoring Boehlkea.

"I think we are done answering your questions," Jarel said, pulling Leopold away from the railing. "Marcus, Boehlkea, get back."

Barzil waved a hand and several of the green creatures sprang over the connected railings, their powerful tails whipping behind them. As they landed, they slid rapidly across the deck of Marcus's ship, stopping their progress by coiling their heavy tails beneath them and springing back toward the rail. They quickly seized each of the teens by their arms and held them firmly.

"Now," Barzil laughed, climbing over the joined railings, "now we shall get some answers." He pulled a long knife from a sheath on his leg. Marcus struggled to find his power again. Nothing.

He approached Leopold first. "That other boy wanted to protect you," he said, putting a finger under the blond boy's chin and tipping his face up. "And you might resemble the bloodline... What is your name?" He gripped Leopold's jaw between his thick fingers and began to squeeze.

"Leopold!" the boy cried out.

"Your *full* name," growled Barzil, squeezing harder. Marcus could see Leopold struggling against the man's grip until he finally gave into the pain.

"Larson!" he said, the word sounding mushy with Barzil's hand still squeezing his mouth. Tears pooled on his eyelids. Jarel was struggling against the green creature holding him in place. Marcus could see scratches weeping blood on the dark skin of Jarel's arms.

"Pah!" Barzil scoffed, releasing Leopold's face. "Weak! You could never be the one."

He walked over to Jarel, who spit at his feet.

"Ah," Barzil crooned. "This one has spirit. Perhaps he is the one I seek." He traced the tip of his knife blade along Jarel's jaw.

"You already know my name. There is nothing more to tell," Jarel sneered at the red-haired man.

Barzil slapped Jarel hard enough to start his nose bleeding. Leopold cried out, but Jarel only glared at the big man.

"What is your name?" Barzil asked angrily.

"Jarel."

"Your full name!"

"Jarel."

Barzil hit him again, this time with a closed fist. "Tell me your name, boy."

"Jarel."

Suddenly a thoughtful look crossed Barzil's face. He turned and walked over to Leopold, grabbing him by the hair. "Tell me your name, or I'll put this one's eye out." He held his knife by Leopold's eye, pressing against the skin until blood welled up. Leopold yelped in pain and fear.

Jarel hung his head, blood dripping from his nose. "I promise you, I have no other name."

"What a waste of time!" Barzil shoved Leopold away, nearly

knocking over the creature holding the boy in place. He strode over to Marcus. Boehlkea burst into tears.

"I'll not play around with you, boy. You're the only one left who could have done what I saw last night. What's your name?"

Marcus glared at him, hazel eyes blazing with anger.

"I know you don't want to tell me, and you think you'll just stand there and try to resist. But I'll not hurt *you* to get you to tell me. No, next I go for the fishy little girl." He wagged his knife at Boehlkea. "Think I'll start with that cute nose of hers." He bent down to growl directly into Marcus's ear. "Now tell me your name."

"Marcus Talent," Marcus whispered, tears of rage standing in his eyes.

"What's that? Couldn't rightly hear you, boy. Speak up!" Barzil stood up straight, sliding his knife back into its sheath and held a hand mockingly behind his ear.

"Marcus Talent," Marcus said, raising his voice.

"Ah, there it is! Just who I was looking for! I knew you had to be here after that light show I saw last night. Got some 'talent,' don't you, my boy. Back to the ship, men, and head home. Don't bother with these three, we don't need 'em." He jerked his head back toward the ship, and the scaled creatures released Jarel, Leopold, and Boehlkea, grabbed their hooked ropes, and leapt back onto their ship. Immediately, the two ships began to drift apart.

"Marcus Talent, I've got special plans for you," Barzil said with a grin, wrapping Marcus in a bearhug and lifting him up so his feet left the deck of the ship. Marcus groaned in agony, swinging his cane and trying to hit his assailant. Jarel and Leopold both took a step toward him as Boehlkea cried out her brother's name.

In the time it took to inhale, Barzil and Marcus disappeared.

EPILOGUE
THE SACRIFICE

Steam rose from the caldera as the morning rays of the sun struck the damp volcanic rock. Talons clicked as Anneberg paced back and forth. His thoughts were troubled.

His eyes turned with grief to the place where his ward, Awar, had slept. Older Stondefel mentored their younger brothers, teaching them the ways of the Stondefel and their responsibilities to the rest of Lysomnus.

The sudden flap of leathery wings and a shadow overhead caught Anneberg's attention, and he looked up to see Aldinoch descending to land near him in his caldera.

"Hello, brother," Aldinoch rumbled, folding his wings neatly to his back. "The look on your face is a reflection of the feelings in my own heart. The Stondefel have suffered a most grievous loss, and losing my ward, Apep, is overwhelming me. I do not know how to cope with this pain."

Anneberg sighed, his massive shoulders collapsing as his grief finally overwhelmed him. He covered his face with taloned hands and finally wept. Molten tears slid down his face and dropped to hiss on the stone below. "So many of our young brothers were lost, the hope of our future gone." he said when the storm of his grief had passed. "The loss of my own ward, Awar, was so painful for me. He risked himself to save Lysomnus and paid with his life. As long as our Stondefel lives may be, we must have another generation to take our place."

"I have been pondering this conundrum myself," Aldinoch grunted. "It has been a long time since we increased our population. We added several young brothers many years ago, and we thought things were going to be fine as we grew old. Now I feel it is imperative to at least gather to discuss a renewal, no matter how difficult it may be."

Anneberg's fiery red eyes met Aldinoch's. "You are correct, my brother. It is beyond time to call the Council together. I will visit our brothers to the east if you head west. Should we request an evening gathering?"

Aldinoch nodded. "Agreed. I will see you then."

Anneberg waited until the other Stondefel had vaulted into the sky before taking off himself. He thought it was best to begin at the farthest end of the volcanic range, and work his way back along the Beornan Rokk. He and the others should arrive at the Council Flat near the time of the meeting.

At the far end of the long volcanic chain, Anneberg circled down to the shadowed depths of the last caldera. Anneberg hovered above the wide opening and requested entry, waiting respectfully until an ancient voice responded.

"Please enter, Anneberg. You know you are always welcome here, my son."

The Stondefel facing Anneberg from the shadows was colossal. He was twice again as large as Anneberg. Deep crevices ravaged his body and face. "What is the purpose for your visit, Anneberg?" The older Stondefel asked.

"Adromelech," Anneberg said solemnly with a bow. "It is an honor to be in your presence."

The older Stondefel waved a long-taloned hand at him. "Your deference is not necessary, Anneberg. I am just old, and that makes me no more special than any other Stondefel. What brings you here to my home?"

"Aldinoch and I have discussed the recent decimation of our younger generation. We feel it necessary to call a meeting of the council and discuss the possibility of their replacement."

Adromelech sighed. "We have mourned the loss of the young ones for long enough. I, too, have been pondering the necessity of creating the next generation before it is too late."

"Aldinoch and I are gathering all the brothers together for a meeting this evening." Anneberg said. "I came here first, to your home on the eastern end of the Beornan Rokk and plan to work my way toward the Council Flat."

Adromelech stepped forward and laid a heavy, long-taloned hand on Anneberg's shoulder.

"Skip the next two, brother. I will stop and talk to both of them. They will listen to me when they might not want to hear you."

Anneberg bowed his head in gratitude. Then he launched himself into the air and made his way down the mountain range.

The older Stondefel Anneberg spoke with agreed it was imperative the Council must meet to discuss the situation. Anneberg shared their grief as several of them had lost a young brother to Nun the Wiser and were mourning a loss, just as he was. Some of the younger Stondefel were only a little older than those who had been lost. While they felt the pain of losing their brothers, they were less aware of the dire need for replacements but were interested and willing to come and learn more.

Finally, Anneberg came to Armaros's empty caldera. He needed to rest as he waited for Armaros, who was out on patrol. He settled to the surface of the caldera to work through the ache that talking to each Stondefel had worsened in his heart. The day had reminded him over and over of Awar and the young Stondefel's eagerness and affection. Each conversation had felt as painful as a fresh wound, and he was sure it felt the same to them. His mind was full of images of Awar from the early days as a small Stondefel who could barely fly, to the brave young Stondefel who had spied for them—an act which had cost him his life.

Even while he suffered the pain, the weariness of the day's exertions caught up to him and Anneberg was soon dozing in the warmth of the waning sun.

The scrape of talons on stone woke him from his doze.

"Anneberg!" exclaimed Armaros. Dust swirled around them as Armaros settled and closed his wings. "What brings you to my home?"

Anneberg once again went through the process of explaining his intentions. Armaros, another young Stondefel who had never had a younger brother to mentor, understood the need to increase their population, but was unsure about what was required.

"Come to the council meeting, my brother," Anneberg urged. "More will be explained there."

"Before we go, let us enjoy a meal together," Armaros said. "I have been on patrol for hours, and I'm sure you are hungry after flying and discussing this with others all day."

Anneberg agreed, stomach rumbling at the mention of food. He waited hungrily as Armaros opened a vein of magma in the floor of his caldera. They caught the red liquid in steaming handfuls as it bubbled up, drinking eagerly. After their appetites were sated, they took off, flying straight to the Council Flat. When he saw the angle of the sun, Anneberg was startled to see how late it had become. He must have slept longer than he had realized.

"Anneberg! Armaros!" Agatho cried out as they approached. "There you are!" He dropped his voice to a conversational level as they landed. "You are the last."

"We can begin then," Anneberg said somberly.

"Indeed," replied Agatho, gesturing to the others, who arranged themselves in a somewhat disorderly circle.

"We have gathered to discuss a serious matter," Anneberg began, "the reproduction of our species. We have lost our entire younger generation. There is no one to replace us when we grow old and rejoin the mountains."

Another Stondefel spoke up, smaller than he.

"Some of us are still young, Anneberg. It is a lot to ask of us to make such a sacrifice."

"Consider, young Andhaka," said a much older Stondefel, Anzu, "that you would not be here if someone had not made the sacrifice for you."

"However," said Armaros, "can we afford to lose the years of wisdom when someone makes that sacrifice?"

"You are young," Anzu replied. "You have not yet experienced the pleasure of mentoring a younger Stondefel brother. It is quite gratifying. This is the most important way our knowledge and experience is passed down and shared from one generation to the next. The process itself imparts that knowledge and memories to our new brothers. Did you think you simply learned everything you know at the hands of your mentor?"

Andhaka bowed his head.

"The process itself is frightening to think about."

"Perhaps that is our fault," said Aldinoch. "We should teach more about it while we are mentoring."

"I believe we do not think about discussing it because it doesn't happen often," Anneberg said.

"I know I am not ready, and I do remember how it is done," said Andhaka. "I feel as though I have just begun to live." Armaros nodded in agreement.

"We would never ask it of you or expect you to volunteer at your age," Agatho reassured them.

"Enough debate," said Adromelech, his ancient voice stern despite its croak. "I had already been thinking of this need, and had decided to convene the council and volunteer before Anneberg came to me. No more discussion is necessary. I have lived a good long long life and I am tired."

"I, too, have been thinking about this," said Anzu. "No one else needs to concern themselves with the question of making such a sacrifice. As one of the oldest Stondefel, I feel it is my duty to be a part of the next generation. We possess the knowledge necessary to pass on." He and Adromelech nodded to each other.

The other Stondefel looked at each other. While saddened, they had expected this. It was usually the way, the oldest and wisest among them volunteering to create new Stondefel. The younger ones who had denigrated the sacrifice out of fear bowed their heads out of shame.

"No, young brothers," Anneberg said, laying a hand on Armaros' and Andhaka's shoulders. "Do not be ashamed. Anzu and Adromelech do this willingly, wishing to impart a lifetime of wisdom and knowledge to the next generation. No one would expect either of you to offer yourselves up for such a thing—you are not ready." Even as he said the words, Anneberg felt a terrible sorrow inside—Adromelech had taken him in to be his ward long ago.

Anzu and Adromelech moved ponderously to the center of the circle. A deep and resonant hum throbbed throughout the throng of Stondefel. The ground vibrated beneath their feet. A low sob of pain escaped Anzu's lips, echoed a moment later by a groan from Adromelech.

The elderly Stondefel bent forward at the torso, wrapping their arms around the first two of their six legs. Tipping over simultaneously with a ground-shaking crash, each segmented section curled underneath until it met the front talons, which grasped the top of the rear legs firmly just as the rear talons grasped the top of the rear legs. The spike-tipped tail swung forward over the entire folded body and pierced the folded back of the bent torso. Lastly, the wings opened and wrapped around the entire body.

The rocky substance of each elder Stondefel's body shook and slowly merged together into one great, creased boulder. Humming with their heads bowed, the rest of the Stondefel surrounded them, lovingly laying their hands on their oldest and largest brothers anywhere they could reach.

Large cracks spread rapidly as each stone body melded together, then many smaller cracks spread even further as the enormous stone quaked. When Andhaka cried out in fear and Armaros withdrew in shock, Anneberg and Agatho brought them gently back into the circle and placed their hands onto the dividing stone. Comforting smiles met red eyes filled with pain,

Every Stondefel carefully moved taloned hands over the pile of stone that was all that remained of their oldest brothers. Their humming deepened, a low rumble that matched the vibrations of the rock beneath them in the Council Flat. Soon cracks began to form in the smooth stone beneath their hands, forming individual sections that separated from the whole. With a sound like a sigh, each original Stondefel separated into four new rough pieces of misshapen stone.

With gentle caresses, the Stondefel helped each section form into smaller versions of themselves until eight small Stondefel stood inside their circle where Anzu and Adromelech had been only moments before.

"I am Andras," said the first in a coarse, high-pitched voice.

"I am Amaymon."

"I am Agares."

"I am Akves."

"I am Allu."

"I am Aliel."

"I am Alchino."

The last said "I am Abraxas," and the older Stondefel rumbled in welcome.

"Welcome, young brothers," Anneberg said, in a voice hoarse with emotion. In his mind's eye, he remembered a day in the past where he stood and welcomed a young Awar in this same way.

"Who will volunteer to take in and guide these young brothers and love them like their own?" Agatho asked. He stood with one hand on Amaymon's shoulder, leaving no doubt he intended to take in this particular young Stondefel.

Anneberg hesitated as each young demon was chosen by an older brother. His heart still felt torn raw from losing Awar, he was unsure of his ability to commit to a new younger brother. Anneberg looked up, and Abraxas met his gaze with ancient eyes. The young demon reminded him of Adromelech, who had been his own mentor and had loved him like a son. Anneberg could do no less for a young Stondefel created by the sacrifice of his old beloved brother.

Anneberg held out one taloned hand.

"Come, Abraxas. Let us go home."

THE TALENT CONTINUUM, BOOK TWO:

THE CRYSTAL ISLAND

ACKNOWLEDGMENTS

As before, I must remind everyone that no writer writes alone. The support of family and friends is critical to the process of creating stories and bringing them to life. I wrote the first draft of *The Crystal Island* in 2021, knowing that *The Talent Continuum* was going to be a complete series. My kids were my first beta readers, along with my youngest sister, and their enthusiasm after reading *A Discovery of Talents* made it easier to keep going. Everyone wanted to know more about Marcus and his friends, and they all had a favorite character by then.

I had the benefit of working with some amazing and talented writers by the time I started editing *The Crystal Island*, since I was invited to work on a short story, comics and poetry project with several women and nonbinary people with the overturning of *Roe v. Wade* in June of 2022. *The Dark Side of Purity* was the outcome of that collaboration, with works by Ai Jang, Lindz McLeod, Damon Barret Roe, and Zebib Abraham. It is also where I met my cover artist, Dany Rivera. I learned so much by collaborating with other writers, and by writing short stories.

I consider Lindz McCleod to be a writing mentor, since she is a distinguished published writer herself, has achieved a PhD, and we spent nearly a year communicating while she edited *A Discovery of Talents*. I learned an incredible amount from her about writing.

I've done some cross-editing with other writers as well (A.M. Weald comes to mind) with short stories, and that again has taught me so much. A.M. is an incredible writer, and if you haven't read her books yet, you're missing out.

Elyse (my Brave Little Friend) I owe so much to you for bringing me into an amazing writing group and your constant support of my work. You're an incredibly talented writer and I wish the best for you.

Vivian (Mom) I know you waited for years for this book, and I hope it is everything you wanted it to be. Your support and love have meant so much to me, particularly at a time when so many other people chose to turn their backs and walk away.

And lastly, to you, dear Readers, for taking an interest in my books and these characters. Thank you for supporting disability, neurodivergent, and LGBTQIA+ representation. I couldn't do this without you.

PHOENIX

ABOUT THE AUTHOR

Phoenix McDonald was born in Richmond, Virginia, and spent most of his childhood moving around the country with his parents before settling in Wisconsin. Decades later, he moved to Portland, Oregon to be near his grandson and found himself to be at last at home.

A lifelong fan of speculative fiction, Phoenix writes fantasy novels, and horror and sci-fi short stories.

Learn more at therealphoenixrises.com.

OTHER WORKS BY THE AUTHOR

"The Talent Continuum, Book One: A Discovery of Talents" (2024)

"Sight and Sound" and "Smuggler's Blues" in A Cold Christmas and the Darkest of Winters anthology pub by Cinnabar Moth

"Karma" in Bomemilk II anthology pub by Gutslut Press

Creative Nonfiction "The High Wire" in Yuzu Press November 2021 Edition

"In the Dark Places" in Toilet Zone 3 anthology pub by Hellbound Books 2022

Poem "Childhood Demons" in Raven Review's winter 2022 issue

"The Last Glass" short story in Featured Creators section of Full House Literary's April 2022 edition

"Skeleton in the Closet" in 206 word stories flash fiction anthology pub by Bag of Bones

"Life Support" in Hell Hath Only Fury anthology pub by S.H Cooper and Oli A. White

"Legacy" in The Future's So Bright anthology pub by Water Dragon Publishing October 2022

"The Earth is Not Your Home" in Expat V (EXPVT) anthology pub by Expat Press Jan 2023

"The House of Cups" in The Dark Side of Purity anthology pub by Band of Bards May 2023

"Childhood Sweethearts" in No One Should Kiss a Frog anthology pub by MacKenzie Publishing June 2023

"Message in a Bottle" in Colp-Desert/Dessert anthology pub by Gypsum Sound Tales August 2023

"Dory's Sacrifice" in From the Yonder Volume IV pub by War Monkey Publications Fall 2023

"Raising Hell in Blockbuster" in Captured pub by Inky Bones Press August 2024

www.ingramcontent.com/pod-product-compliance
Lightning Source LLC
Chambersburg PA
CBHW081138300726
48982CB00006B/996